FLIGHT TO MONS

Alexander Fullerton

timewarner
paperbacks

A *Time Warner* Paperback

First published in Great Britain in 2003
by Little, Brown
This edition published in 2004
by Time Warner Paperbacks

A CIP catalogue record for this book
is available from the British Library.

ISBN 0 7515 3498 6

Typeset by Palimpsest Book Production Limited, Polmont, Stirlingshire
Printed and bound in Great Britain by
Clays Ltd, St Ives plc

Time Warner Paperbacks
An imprint of
Time Warner Books UK
Brettenham House
Lancaster Place
London WC2E 7EN

www.TimeWarnerBooks.co.uk

FLIGHT TO MONS

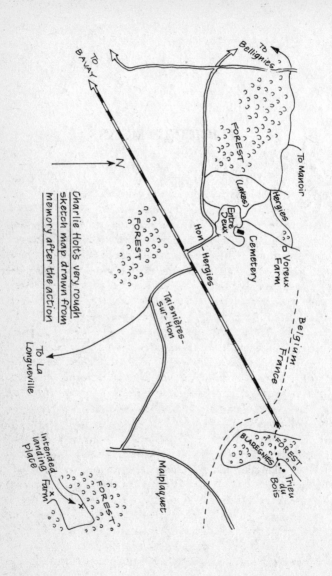

Charlie Holt's very rough sketch map drawn from memory after the action

TO BAVAY

N

TO Bellignies

To Manoir

FOREST

(Lakes)

Hergies

Entre Deux

Voreux Farm

Hon — Hergies

Cemetery

FOREST

Belgium
France

Taisnières-sur-Hon

To La Longueville

FOREST

Trieu du Bois

BLAREGNIES

Malplaquet

FOREST

Intended landing place

Farm

1

Cold – despite the heavy flying-suit and the fact he'd only been off the ground about twenty minutes. But – December, for heaven's sake – with the sun barely up, and only high enough over the Dover Strait to spread a smeary, pinkish glow on the close-packed roofs of Eastbourne, most of which was abaft the beam to port now, and flush the frosted slopes of Beachy Head, beyond and around which the sea's glitter was visible only through gaps between drifting banks of mist. A thousand feet was too high, he decided: if there was a U-boat down there – not that there would be within at least five miles, on account of shallows: the Head Edge to start with and then shallow patches as well as a whole litter of wrecks – but except for *those* hazards the bugger would be as safe as houses.

So try 750 feet. Charlie Holt gently tilting the great gas-bag downwards . . .

Thinking of houses – he'd taken off from Polegate heading northwest, into the wind, and circling left-handed over Folkington and Willingdon he'd looked for Amanda's place, which was in open country on the Jevington side of Eastbourne, but failed to spot it. Lingering darkness and ground mist would have contributed to this, of course, but also the fact one had a few other things to do – like keeping this ship in the air and pointing the right way.

Hell of a situation, though. Simultaneously thrilling and alarming.

Mind on the job now, Charlie. Easing the ship down: 900 feet, 850. A quarter-turn on the elevator handwheel had tilted the ship's tailfins – the flaps on the fins' trailing edges – enough to put down-angle on her. Very sensitive to their controls, these SS airships. Until his transfer to Polegate from Pulham in Norfolk only a few days ago, he'd been flying a Coastal – bigger in all respects and clumsier, with two engines, one at each end of the car, and a crew of five. He'd flown SSs – Submarine Scouts – before that, of course, and mostly here, at Polegate, but he'd forgotten how handy they were. Crew of two: himself and his observer/wireless operator, namely PP O'Connor in the front cockpit there. Charlie didn't know what the 'PP' stood for, and since his maintenance crew, including the coxswain PO Harmsworth, quirkily called the poor fellow 'Wee-Wee' – which one could hardly do oneself – PP O'Connor he'd doubtless remain. He had a Lewis machine-gun in that forward cockpit as well as the wireless set; it was used mainly for exploding mines.

Sun wasn't going to last long, wasn't going to be in any hurry to disperse that mist. All the sun had to climb into was cloud, inky blackness above a horizontal band of blinding orange fire. Blinding, so don't look at it, idiot . . . The sea was what you were supposed to look at – spotting U-boats and floating mines being the *raison d'être* for the Royal Navy's 200-odd airships that were based around Britain's coasts. The country had been brought close to the point of starvation in recent times, a lot closer than most of its population realised. This was 1917, the worst year yet in terms of losses of ships and cargoes; there'd been about 600 sinkings up to the end of '15, more than a thousand in '16, and in this one year – which wasn't over yet – 2,500. Airships were a very effective counter to the submarine threat, though, especially now that the convoy system was being rigorously enforced; it was a fact of which the Royal Naval Air Service could reasonably be proud, that not one ship had as yet been lost when escorted by a blimp or blimps as well as surface ships.

Seven-fifty feet. Still more than somewhat murky down

there. Not solidly, but a confusion of drifting banks and patches; in the short term the sun *wasn't* going to be much help. So make it 500 feet now. Might mean valving slightly – letting a little gas out. Engine thundering away meanwhile: it was a 6-cylinder, 100-horsepower Green, with a 'tractor' propeller – meaning it pulled, as distinct from a 'pusher'. And since this was head-in-air stuff, open cockpits, that thunderous buffeting slipstream of pre-iced air didn't make it any warmer; and these 'oversea patrols' often lasted eight hours, sometimes ten.

SS-45 at 700 feet and descending steadily, with Beachy Head well astern now. Back on the field at Polegate several other airships would have lifted off, be heading for their own designated patrol areas. In theory – and in better conditions than these – sunrise might be as good a time as any for catching a U-boat on the surface. If it had been up during the dark hours to charge its batteries – as submarines had to do – and hadn't quite finished charging, it might be tempted, especially in poor visibility, to stay up another half-hour or so. Bastard would hear you, for sure – when you were down this low he'd have to be stone deaf not to – but with his own engines pounding, usually driving him along at low speed while also pumping ampères into the box, you could hope to be reasonably close by the time he woke up to the danger and pulled the plug.

One had a very wide field of view, of course, far more than any escorting destroyer or trawler could ever have; when you were over a convoy you'd spot a U-boat breaking surface, or the white feather of his periscope, on the convoy's far side where an escort didn't have a hope of seeing it, or out ahead, where it might be waiting on the convoy's route. Then if you were in a position to steer over it and drop a bomb – well, glory be, but the odds were about a hundred to one you wouldn't. Your best endeavour would be to direct an escorting destroyer to the target, signalling either by wireless or by Aldis lamp. While simply being there, having the Hun see you and take avoiding action – such as going deep – rather than getting his torpedoes into some

3

helpless merchantman, was an end in itself; in fact the primary objective. Getting ships and cargoes into port. Food, munitions, fuel. And lives – especially those in troop transports to and from the French ports. One had been told that as long as the soldiers saw a blimp over them, they'd go below and get some sleep; otherwise they'd huddle on the transports' decks, as near as they could get to lifeboats.

Five hundred feet. Levelling her now. With much of the sea's surface at least in sight, though befogged to a variable degree. Course still southeast, at this stage. You steered with your feet on a rudder-bar, using the eye-level magnetic compass, and while continually searching for U-boats had also to keep an eye on the altimeter, the airspeed indicator, the statascope – rise-and-fall indicator – fuel gauges, gas-pressure gauge and engine controls. Left hand on engine controls – primarily the throttle, of course, operated by lever-action on a Bowden wire – and right hand on the elevator-wheel. And whichever hand you could spare for the lines controlling the gas and air valves on the envelope. There were 60,000 cubic feet of hydrogen gas in the envelope up there: hydrogen of course being inflammable, or when mixed with air, explosive.

Charlie had tried to explain some of the technicalities to Amanda yesterday – whether or not she'd had the slightest interest in any of it, and in point of fact it had been fairly obvious she hadn't. He'd given her lunch in the Queens Hotel in Eastbourne, and after that, at least partly as an evasion of what was actually in his mind and he was hoping might be in hers too, although he hadn't the nerve to put it to the test quite this soon – see the hope go up in smoke *quite* yet – he'd suggested, 'How about giving my new ship the once-over?' The proposal came in natural-enough sequence to exchanges in which she'd mentioned how frequently airships from the Polegate field passed over her cottage, causing her to think of *him* and wonder what he might be up to, and where, and he'd told her something about the different types of ship that were in use now – the Coastals he'd been flying from Pulham, these SSs and the

4

newish SSZs, of which Polegate now had six; and from that he'd offered her the guided tour.

Yesterday being Sunday, flying and patrolling were in progress as usual, of course, but he and SS-45 had happened to be enjoying a day off, his first since he'd arrived here in mid-week, first chance he'd had to go in search of her – or rather of *them*, as he'd thought of it: Amanda and her husband Don Bishop, a doctor, captain in the Royal Army Medical Corps. Charlie had banged with the knocker on their cottage door, shouted, 'Mandy? Don? You at home, you in there?' To be honest – if one had taken time off to assess one's feelings and be straight about them – calling to either or both of them, but in truth having a hell of a lot more interest in Mandy than in Don. And just moments later sent almost staggering by her precipitate and highly vocal emergence, her arms tight around his neck, voice sobbing and moaning in his ear – up on her toes to manage that – 'Charlie, Don's dead! He was killed, he's *dead*! Oh, Charlie, Charlie *darling*!'

Mind on the job, Charlie, old darling . . .

Checking the time and figuring distance-run: the upshot being that in another four or five minutes he'd be bringing the old blimp round to port. Would be ten miles southeast of the Head then, his orders requiring him to come round to NE at about that point and make for Dungeness while maintaining roughly that distance offshore, passing – oh, Bexhill, Hastings, Rye – then in the vicinity of Dungeness picking up a five-ship convoy on its way out of the Dover Straits. The convoy would have a surface escort of some kind and at least one airship over it – as likely as not a Coastal from Capel-le-Ferne, near Folkestone. It might or might not tag along for a while, but either way Charlie would be reversing course and shepherding the convoy back this way, round Beachy Head and on westward to the Solent or thereabouts.

Turning now. Using about ten degrees of helm. Fully daylight – in a half-hearted sort of way, with mist patches still thick here and there. Wind coming up a bit though, should soon clear them. The black overhead had softened to shades of grey with a pool of mirror-brightness behind it in the east-to-southeast sector. Cold-looking greenish sea. The wind wasn't much as yet – 15 knots, maybe – but having it on the quarter now you'd be carrying a few degrees of rudder to offset it.

Bumping just a little as he eased the helm and adjusted the elevator-wheel to hold her at 500 feet. Ships of some kind were visible a few miles out to starboard; he lifted the binoculars one-handed, using the eyepieces to push up his goggles. Destroyers, from the direction of Boulogne.

This was the moment at which PP O'Connor began to scream. Banshee fashion – the only way he could be even faintly heard, of course – mouth agape, eyes crazy in that wild look back over his narrow shoulder, more like a crazed Dervish than an Irishman, and emitting what was effectively no more than a kitten's squeak over the big engine's pounding roar. Charlie had seen it anyway, didn't need the wild gesticulations, PP struggling to clear the Lewis gun while simultaneously jabbing frantically down ahead of them and to port – not far off, at that, as near as dammit where you'd have wanted it, *prayed* to have it! Charlie had dropped the glasses, had SS-45 dropping too, tipping her rounded, silvery, bamboo-strengthened nose down and valving – to get her down even faster – while also kicking on port rudder, less an alteration of course than a matter of converging with the target. Hardly believing in it but there it was, no fantasy or figment: U-boat on the surface in a welter of white foam, must have surfaced only seconds ago, Hun skipper then hearing the Green's racket, taking one appalled glance skyward, leaping back into his open hatch and pulling the plug. SS-45 descending fast – in *just* the right place at *precisely* the right moment – the submarine's vents pluming spray and her forepart already sliding under, whitened grey-green flood engulfing her conning-tower now too; this airship at 150 feet and still dropping, slanting down, Charlie with a hand on the bomb-release gear. Two bombs, each of 110 lb, slung from the bottom of the car right below his cockpit seat. Released and – gone. U-boat gone too – under, in that swirl. No problem then in checking this ship's descent, as the loss of the bombs' weight jarred her upwards, from, oh, 100 feet, maybe less, and he was working to get her bow up now.

Bombs like black eggs, finned, wobbling in the air to start with; with his head over the car's side, seeing them start down as it were right under his nose he saw the wobble clearly in that slow-seeming release, then followed them mostly in imagination until they smacked into the sea on the leading edge of the now extending and narrowing area of disturbance. The bombs had delayed fuses on them, wouldn't explode on hitting the sea's surface, but shattered it now – three seconds later – like twin hammer-blows smashing glass from underneath, upward gouts of, oh, quivering sea in mounds, a huge air bubble, and then—

Oil. A black island of it in the froth, subsiding then as it spread. SS-45 lifting nicely, PP O'Connor already tapping the news out on his wireless, which having a transmission (and reception) range of about 80 miles would be delighting not only Polegate but the Capel airship station and those destroyers at a few miles' distance on the beam, and one might guess the RNAS Portsmouth Command headquarters at Warsash on Southampton Water, with *U-boat destroyed by bombs from HMAS SS-45 in position Beachy Head – distance and bearing* . . . Charlie had scribbled the figures on a signal-card, half-risen and reached over to thump PP on the shoulder, push it at him; then with the ship steady and in trim, passing 300 feet and back on course, lifted his Aldis lamp – there was one in each cockpit, wired from the same 12-volt accumulator – sighted on the leader of the two destroyers and began to call, flashing the letter 'A' over and over until the bugger'd wake up and flash acknowledge-ment. Charlie muttering, *Come on, come on!*, using his right elbow on the wheel to take the angle off her as she soared up through 400 feet, wanting the destroyers in on the act so they could get themselves over this way to search for any wreckage that might float up.

At Polegate they'd have realised he had no bombs remaining, but the signal of congratulation had concluded with *Continue patrol as ordered*. Point being that the prospects of SS-45 finding yet another target for bombs she didn't have were so remote they didn't have to be considered; besides which, no U-boat skipper could know she didn't have any, so her deterrent effect wasn't impaired at all. In any case you were looking for mines as well as for submarines. Charlie had her at 2,000 feet now, steering SSE across the convoy's van, convoy consisting of five small steamers in two columns with an escort of two trawlers; their air escort, a Coastal, had turned back eastward signalling by light: *Heard you got one, SS-45. Bravo. This little lot's all yours now*. It hadn't been close enough or at an angle for Charlie to read the number on its bulbous, trilobe envelope – could have been any one of dozens of former squadron mates, but as he hadn't bothered to identify himself, probably was not, was more likely a newcomer.

Pumping fuel. Had to be done about every half-hour, pumped to one of the two overhead tanks from which the engine was gravity-fed. He was coming down to 1,000 feet now. Still tingling with that sense of triumph. At about half-throttle, letting the convoy come to *him* – convoy making about 12 knots, judging by their wakes and bow-waves, while the trawlers looked to be making about 15, allowing them to zigzag around a bit, mainly on the convoy's wings. Tossing around too: from up here the sea looked flat enough, but it wouldn't be for the suckers who were down there in ships as small as that. He knew just how it would be for them, had served for about a year in a minesweeper, when he'd first gone to sea in '14 as a sub-lieutenant RNR – Royal Naval Reserve – through having graduated from *Worcester*, one of the two most notable of training ships/colleges for officer-entry to the Merchant Navy. He'd told Amanda yesterday, on their way from the main entrance and guardhouse to the sheds, 'All sorts of backgrounds, us lot. As you'll have noticed from those you met last year, I dare say. Pukka RN turned RNAS, RNVR, direct-entry to the RNAS – from public schools or universities, don't you know – and a few like me. I'm a bit of a rarity, truth to tell. Seen any of those chaps, have you, since I left?'

'No. You were my only contact, really. And Don of course had mostly Army and medical friends.'

'Not even Tommy Caterham?'

'Oh, Tommy. Yes. Not *seen*, actually, but he wrote to me after Don was killed. He'd read a piece they did about him in the *Gazette* – the Eastbourne one, you know?'

Tommy had been one of her beaux – or would-be beaux. As he, Charlie, had been, years and years ago, pre-war in Ross-on-Wye, before Don Bishop had been heard of. Tommy Caterham was RNAS too, a seaplane pilot in the squadron based at Newhaven.

Charlie switched the subject back to where it had been: 'I should have said, quite a few of us started life as pongoes, too. My CO at Polegate for instance is a lieutenant-colonel in the Royal Engineers, now disguised as an RNVR commander.'

'Pongoes, you said?'

'Sorry.' He'd glanced round at her, guiding her into 'A' shed. 'Army, naval slang for. Is said to derive from the name of some primitive tribe with exceptionally foul habits. Not therefore a term one would employ in the hearing of old Peeling, for instance. The CO, that is.' Or in the hearing of an Army widow either, he supposed. But she wasn't 'an Army widow', for God's sake. This was *Mandy* – even if they *were* being a little self-conscious with each other, at this stage and in the circumstances. He went on, 'But you know the Royal Flying Corps started up in 1912, and in '14 the Admiralty took over its naval operations, including airships. Had only four or five, then – but personnel came over too, of course. That's our origins, anyway. And here, if I may introduce her to you, is HM Airship SS-45.'

'It's vast!'

'Looks big in her stable, doesn't she? But that newer-looking job – there, see? – an SSZ actually – is slightly larger – 70,000 cubic feet of gas, compared to this one's 60,000. Hence a third cockpit in that one's car – with that much extra lift she can carry an engineer as well as pilot and wireless operator. You realise the cars are aircraft fuselages? Wingless and tail-less, that's all. This is an Armstrong – Armstrong-Whitworth – and those are Maurice Farmans. But the blimp I was flying at Pulham, known as a Coastal, has a crew of five, a much longer car. Pilot sits there like Captain Bligh telling all and sundry what to do, whereas in this tiddler one does every darn thing oneself.'

She was pointing: 'What's that great tube for?'

'Air scoop. Behind the prop, see, where it scoops in the slipstream – when one opens the right valves it does, valves we call crabpots – to drive air under pressure into . . .' He'd paused. 'Don't want to blind you with science and technicalities, Mandy.'

'But why air? I thought that – envelope, you call it – was full of gas?'

'It is, but it has two sort of balloons inside it, called ballonets, one each end more or less, and when one lets gas out, as one has to do, to lose height quickly, for instance—'

'You *are* losing me, rather.'

'Well, forcing air into the ballonets increases the pressure, makes up for the loss of gas. Otherwise the envelope might just collapse.'

'I'll take your word for it. Charlie, did you *want* to come here from – er – Pulham?'

He'd looked at her, thinking of saying, '*Now* I'm glad I did', and managed not to. Her smile was slightly tremulous as she glanced away, and he remembered that she always had been – well, quickish on the uptake. And sensitive now, of course, perhaps dangerously so – which was a good reason to proceed with some degree of caution. He covered with, 'Didn't mind one way or t'other, really. It was fine, up there, but, you know, change as good as a rest. Fact is it's rather a sad story, how it came about, *why* I'm here. Pilot of this ship was a man called Rupert Hoskins, friend of mine from our training days as it happens, and he broke his back. The ship's mended, as you see, but he's in hospital in Portsmouth and – well, God knows how long—'

'How did it happen?'

'Heard of Wormwood Scrubs?'

'The prison?'

'We also build airships there. Big common, bags of room, and quite a large establishment, one of our main constructional bases. They'd sent old Rupert up there to nursemaid an Italian – we're selling them several SS ships, and he was demonstrating this one, acting as observer so the Wop – a commander – could try his hand as pilot. But coming in to land he somehow lost control – turned her across the wind, most likely – crashed through a fence, Rupert's thrown out and does his back in, but the Wop's trapped in the car and carried up – head down, apparently, must've been swinging by his legs – to about seven and a half thousand feet, and eventually ballooned down – quite gently, must've been – in Walthamstow, wherever that may be. Only broke his arm, after all that, although they say he was fairly gibbering with fright.'

She'd laughed. 'So would I have been.'

She really is a *very* pretty girl, he thought. As well as – oh, *wow* . . .

She was suppressing her amusement now, saying quickly how sorry she was, for the friend with the broken back, then giving way and adding, 'But I see the Italian as a *little* man, with pommaded hair and a droopy moustache. Hanging upside-down . . .' Laughing again: more relaxed, more *herself* than she'd been all day.

He'd told her, 'They rebuilt the ship – here, at Polegate. Same envelope, that wasn't damaged, but the car's new, and the engine of course, and all this steel-wire rigging. Only they were short of a pilot here, Pulham decided they could spare me – a swap, actually, they were getting another chap from here to train in Coastals . . .'

11

'And here you are. But what an *awful* shame, for that poor boy. Is he about your age?'

'Twenty-three, I think. I'm twenty-four – as you may remember. You're twenty-two, aren't you. Birthday is – don't tell me . . . July?'

'September. And yours is in June. Same month as Mabel's. She's three years older than you, isn't she? Still working on the farm, is she?'

'Yes. Yes, she is.' Mabel was his sister. 'But what a memory for birthdays! Tell me, did you ever ride pillion on a motor-bike?'

'No.' Small frown. 'I'll stick to the side-car, if you don't mind. Did you get it where you've been, in Norfolk?'

'I have the use of it, that's all. It's old Rupert's. A Douglas – as you may have noticed.' She'd looked vague, and he'd reminded her, 'Rupert with the broken back. The *bike* is a Douglas.'

'Ah . . .'

'Thought the side-car might be a bit rattly, that's all. But maybe a cinema in Eastbourne one evening? Chaplin, I noticed, at the Tivoli.'

'*Would* be fun, some time. And thank you for showing me your' – she was looking up at the blimp – 'your SS-45.' Turning back to him: 'Home now, Charlie?'

From ten miles south of Beachy Head, course due west for Selsey Bill: distance about fifty miles, then say another ten to see them right into Spithead. It was overcast and cold, wind still from the northwest but gustier than it had been, visibility reasonably good now, except that with the surface as ruffled as it was you wouldn't see any periscope feather. You might if the 'scope was left up all the time a U-boat was running in to launch its torpedoes, but they never did that, always dipped it every few seconds or half-minute, say, so it was never there long enough to catch your eye as a contin-uing white track. In present conditions, even then it most likely wouldn't. Whereas in a real calm—

Forget it. December 3rd today. Might be a long time, a

12

lot of long, cold patrols, before you got *that* sort of a calm again.

She'd told him that Don had been actively working to get himself posted to France, agitating for it over a period of months, had been advised by his CO to pipe down, get on with the job he had, which was important enough and in which he was performing very well. He should think himself very lucky *not* to be over there in the 'Sausage Machine' – live men fed in at one end, corpses piling out like sausages at the other. The colonel had reminded him – in Amanda's presence – 'You're a *doctor*, Bishop, not sausage-meat!'

Charlie had nodded. 'But he got there.'

'Nothing *I* could say made the slightest difference . . . Oh yes, he *got* there. Wangled it finally through an uncle who has influence in high places and to whom I shall never speak as long as I live.'

'But *why* did he . . .'

'All he'd say was he had to get into the thick of it, out of what he called this cushy job which an older man could do. Incidentally, I'm working in much the same area now. Liaison between RAMC and hospitals all around the Eastbourne area. Troop trains come in full of wounded and they have to be allocated and transported to wherever beds and wards are available. Walking wounded come in carriages with seats, stretcher cases in luggage vans. Then of course there have to be records of who's gone where, and contact with relatives, relatives' visits, and so forth.'

'How long have you been doing this?'

'Since Don went off to France. His CO fixed it – knowing they needed people, and how lost I was feeling – or at least his wife did. I believe *she*—'

'I'd have thought you'd go home now, though, lick your wounds there. Your parents, surely, must be terribly concerned.'

'They didn't want me to marry Don in the first place. I don't know why, not really, except with the war and – well, fear of exactly what's happened now seemed to be Mummy's line. Oh, and that he was close on ten years older than me. But what's *that*? And what she'd have had against me marrying a doctor – you'd have thought they'd have seen it as – well, *security*, for God's sake. Security – isn't that a laugh? Anyway, I don't want to go home, Charlie. What's at bloody *Ross* now, for God's sake, except drooly false sympathy on the surface and "I told you so"s, and—'

She'd checked, shaking her head. Charlie had parked the Douglas at the back of the cottage, in a yard containing a stack of logs and a coal-bunker. She'd asked him as he gave her a hand out of the side-car, 'Do *you* understand him doing what he did, Charlie? I mean *why*?'

'Conscience perhaps – what you might call white-feather conscience? If he thought he was conspicuous in his cushy job – either his own feeling, or someone had made some such comment? With hundreds and thousands of wounded flocking in, might have felt he ought to be a front-line doctor, taking the chances *they'd* all taken?' Amanda was groping in her bag for the door-key, not looking at him. He'd finished rather awkwardly, 'At least, I mean, if he'd been a single man—'

'But he wasn't. As I see it that's rather the point. Or is that self-centred of *me*?' She had the door open. 'I'll light a fire. And upstairs there's an oil-heater.'

You could smell the oil. There'd be oil-lamps too, he guessed. Low ceiling, and that typically farmhouse odour. But why start talking about 'upstairs', unless . . . Shaking his head, answering her question – did he think her resentment of what had happened was selfish – with, 'No, I certainly do not.' Face to face, at close range – *very* close range, at lower levels actually in contact – 'Frankly, how *anyone* – well, it baffles me – how Don could have—'

'Baffles.' A smile. Heart-shaped face, wheat-coloured hair, blue eyes on the slant; her hands had moved to rest lightly on the sleeves of his reefer jacket, above the lieutenant's stripes and the RNAS symbol of a golden bird. 'The word to me isn't "baffles", Charlie – it's more like "mortifies".'

'Yes. I can understand that. Mandy, I'm so *sorry*, I—'

'Do better than that though – *can't* we.'

'Better than—'

'Memory failing, Charlie? Long ago and far away?' Moving against him. 'You've never stopped wanting me, Charlie. *Have* you?'

'Well . . .'

Since you mention it . . .

He didn't say that. Only had it flash through his mind, sort of clowningly. Didn't have to *say* a bloody thing.

2

He was back over Polegate a little after three pm. He'd been recalled, didn't need permission to land, could see the ground-handling party already out there in mid-field and brought her in low, bow-down and into the wind, cutting power during the approach until the blimp was almost stopped, no more than stemming the wind and with the skids only five or six feet above the ground. He recognised the burly figure of Bob Bayley, flight lieutenant-commander and currently acting as Peeling's second-in-command, presiding over that team of about twenty men; might have been more than that, but another SS had just landed and was being walked into 'A' shed by *her* attendants. With this lot, despite Bayley's supervisory presence, the man doing the real work was PO Harmsworth, SS-45's coxswain. In fact they were all making an easy job of it, had hardly needed to bother with the guys – the mooring lines dangling from the envelope's bow and stern and from both ends of the car – and now they had only to reach up and grab hold of the skids, then the rail that surrounded the car's base, and haul down. Charlie had pushed the throttle shut, could hear the wind then and the creaks and groans of the car's suspension, and men's voices – men who were having really to hold her now: a blimp on the ground in any wind was a lot more to handle than she'd ever be in the air.

Those were cheers that he was hearing now, and a bellow from Harmsworth of 'We got her, sir!'

Meaning he could switch off. As he did now. He and PP O'Connor would remain in their cockpits until the ground crew had walked her in, though. Accidents could and sometimes did occur. For one thing they were going to have to turn her across the wind before reaching the shed, and a freak gust might hit her while they were preoccupied with their cheering. They'd have passed their own lines through the eyes in the ends of the ship's guys, but once the wind really had the bit between its teeth and meant business, trying to hang on could be fatal – had killed men on occasion, jerking them off their feet and flinging them – to quote Kipling – to roost with the startled crows.

Going smoothly, anyway. At walking pace towards the end of the shed, under Harmsworth's eagle eyes, and into the partial shelter of the wind-screens now – like cricket sight-screens only much bigger and patchy grey-brown instead of white. Entering – still on the turn and under tight control – then within a few minutes safe inside, could all relax. Harmsworth calling to him, standing back abreast the car, 'You done us proud, sir!'

Charlie pointed at PP O'Connor's rather small, round head: 'Guess who spotted the bugger first!'

'Wee-wee' stood up and bowed. There was a storm of applause, in which Charlie joined. He'd give Amanda a call pretty soon. Then get on the old Douglas, buzz round and maybe take her into Eastbourne. Then back to the cottage. Or the other way about, and of course back to the cottage later, if that was still on the cards, on *her* agenda as well as on his. Which – well, it *would* be. This definitely was a good day. Not a bad moment, either – easing cramped muscles and exercising half-frozen extremities, longing for a cigarette but even enjoying that longing, through knowing the rapture of it didn't have to be postponed for more than minutes. You didn't smoke when airborne or in the shed. Other luxuries to come shortly were hot water, food and drink. Lunch had been bully-beef sandwiches in the airship with coffee from a vacuum flask, and that had been some

17

while ago. A cigarette was the absolute priority, though, in say two or three minutes' time. Then de-freeze the bones in a hot bath, *then* call her.

On the ground, he told Harmsworth and the engineer – AM, Air Mechanic – 'Like a bird all the way, not a hiccup. You look after her well.'

They'd be carrying out all manner of routines on the engine, once it had cooled. Checking everything else as well – control wires and lines, valves, the car and its wire suspension, valves in the envelope and the envelope itself. He told Harmsworth, 'I'll see you later', and O'Connor, 'Well done. You were quick on it, I must say.'

A grin and a shrug. 'Happened I had me eye on the spot when the Fritz come up, sir. You was gettin' the measure o' them destroyers, as I recall.'

'That's true.' It was, too – if O'Connor hadn't been on the ball and the U-boat had gone under again lightning-fast they might *not* have seen it. He looked back at the coxswain and jerked a thumb in the direction of PP. 'He went off like a steam whistle. *Howled*. Should've heard him!'

Bob Bayley met him as he left the shed. Heavyweight, balding, wearing a submarine sweater under his reefer jacket. He stopped and stared at Charlie angrily.

'No fish?'

'Regrettably not. Had to get her up again fairly smartly to spot the convoy I was meeting.' After dropping bombs or using the Lewis to explode a mine, it was more or less *de rigeur* to scoop up a bucketful of stunned fish for the mess. Canvas bucket, slung under the car, its long line coiled inside. The truth of it was that Charlie had been too wild with delight at having sunk the U-boat to have given thought to fish suppers. He acknowledged this to Bayley. 'Sorry.'

'First thing crossed my mind when I saw your signal.'

'Well, it *would* be.'

Now Bayley grasped his hand, was shaking it. 'Seriously, though – bloody marvellous, Charlie. Absolutely capital. The

Old Man's tickled pink, of course. He wants to see you, incidentally.'

'I'll unfreeze and get out of this suit first.'

'Right. Oh, here . . .'

Cigarette. *The* cigarette. He had a match for it, too. Backs to the wind, hands cupped around it. Charlie inhaling smoke and narrowing his eyes in ecstasy as it trickled out.

Bayley said, 'Shouldn't make the skipper wait too long, he's got a visitor he wants you to meet.'

And who might that be, he wondered, in his cabin, divesting himself of the flying-suit. The old man wanting to show him off as the hero of the hour, he supposed. Impress some mayor or town councillor, newspaper editor or other local nabob. Wrapping a towel round himself and shambling down the central passage to the washplace, where on his way in he'd turned on a hot tap. The hut was warm enough, thanks to there being a coal-burning stove at each end, and the iron bath wasn't more than a quarter full. Thinking – letting the cold tap gush into it: really did gush, in contrast to the hot one's trickle – about the heating arrangements in Amanda's cottage, the strong smell of the oil-heater in the bedroom and the fact that by the time they'd come downstairs the living-room fire had burnt itself out.

Nothing else had. Not for either of them. She was a revelation. Wild-cat, crazy . . .

Telephone her *before* reporting to old Peeling, he thought. He'd promised to call as soon as he could, i.e. when he was on the ground and at least partially unfrozen, and she'd be waiting for the call. In any case he *wanted* to: to hear her voice, and reassure her. In what way reassure her, though? Short of saying, 'I love you.' That was the line one had to be careful not to cross; had not crossed last night, and must not, mustn't even approach or seem to hint at, even allow to show in one's expression. He'd be reassuring her of his friendship and concern for her – genuine concern, compassion and, all right, physical desire, admiration, need to *be* with. Just not that other word. 'Can't wait to be with you' might cover it. Would be the truth, too. Recognising this as he lathered himself with Wright's Coal Tar soap made him pause and think again how very, *very* careful he'd need to be. Especially after a drink or two, or when/if one began to feel more than usually emotional or excited.

Excited *now*, damn it!

Out of the bath though, towelling himself. Ruminating on the fact that a year ago, when he'd been stationed here at Polegate and seeing quite a lot of her and Don, even if he'd thought he might have stood a sporting chance with her he wouldn't have done anything about it. Another man's wife; one's own former girlfriend, sure, but out of bounds, absolutely. He'd known her when he'd been about seventeen and she was extremely attractive even then; in fact they'd attracted each other and had definitely misbehaved a little. *More* than a little. At Ross-on-Wye, and thereabouts. Then he hadn't seen her for a few years and Don Bishop had somehow come up on the inside track and gone the whole hog, married her – which Charlie would not have done, hadn't at that stage (or at this one, either) any thought or intention of marrying anyone at all. They'd got together again down here through her and Don having met an RNAS acquaintance of his, and she'd asked him did he by any chance know a man by name of Charlie Holt: she'd heard that he'd become a naval airman from her parents, who'd have got it either from his father or his sister Mabel. Anyway, they'd met up, and there it was, Don and Mandy were (or had seemed to be) a happily married couple and now his good friends – no question of either Charlie or Amanda doing anything to disrupt that or even – certainly as far as *he'd* been concerned – allowing such a thing to cross their minds.

He called her from the wardroom, getting through to the office she worked from, of which she'd given him the number, and asking for Mrs Bishop. Holding on then, alternating gulps of draft beer with bites of corned-dog and pickle sandwich.

Mandy's voice then, somehow taking him by surprise . . .

'Amanda Bishop speaking.'

The surprise element was the thrill her voice gave him.

'*Hello*, Amanda Bishop!'

'Charlie.' Her voice dropping instantly to a lower key and volume. 'Oh, Charlie. At *last* . . .'

'Sorry. Couldn't have called any earlier, though.'

'I know. Kept telling myself you'd still be in mid-air somewhere. Found myself scanning the azure skies.'

'Azure?'

'Well – occasionally. As a matter of fact they look fairly azure to me *now*, figuratively speaking. How are you, Charlie?'

'Looking forward to seeing you this evening.'

'Only just' – mimicry of a flat (or guarded) tone – 'looking forward?'

'Breathlessly. Can't wait. Rock hard. That better?'

'*Slight* improvement. Actually, deuce of a lot.'

He began, 'I'm not alone though, now—', a sub-lieutenant having just pushed in, pilot of the ship that had landed before he had, and Mandy cut in with, 'Nor am I. But I was thinking – as well as about *that* – might make us omelettes. Got lots of eggs, and—'

'I thought I'd take you out. Place used to do rather good fish suppers?'

'Weber's Cabin?'

'It's still going, then. Capital. I'll—'

'There's Sattery's, too. But let's eat at the cottage – please?' She dropped her voice still lower, almost to a whisper. 'I can't talk much either, let's just agree on that?' A sigh. 'Now I'm thinking about what you said just then. Charlie, you really do—' She checked.

He put in, 'I do what?'

'Never mind. Later. What time, though?'

'You said you get back at six or six-thirty, so – seven?'

'Six twenty-nine?'

21

'All right. I'll bring a bottle. Got something to celebrate. I mean apart from – you know . . . You all right, Mandy?'

She whispered, 'Better than I've felt in weeks.' A quick amendment then: 'No, not *weeks* . . .'

'Days?'

'Want the truth, Charlie?' He waited, and she whispered, 'Ever. *Ever*. Hear me?'

He still had that in his mind when he told the leading writer in the CO's outer office, 'Flight Lieutenant Holt. I was told Commander Peeling wanted to see me.'

'Aye, sir—'

Peeling's voice called from behind the flimsy partition, 'Come on in, Holt!' Then as he went through, 'Taken your time, haven't you?'

'Had to clean up, sir. Sorry. Would've shaved too, only didn't want to keep you waiting.' Apologetically touching his rather wide, blue-black jaw, and looking at the CO's visitor – a major of the Royal Marines, who was treating him, Charlie, to a close inspection out of sharp, deepset eyes, one each side of a Roman nose that wasn't quite straight. A boxer or rugger player, probably; or he might have come off a horse face-down on hard ground at some stage. Not all that big, but fit, hard-looking. Getting up to shake hands he was perhaps an inch shorter than Charlie – who was five-eleven – but they'd weigh in fairly equally. He'd be – early thirties. The CO was introducing him: 'Major McLachlan, Royal Marine Light Infantry.'

'How do you do, sir.'

A nod. 'Congratulations are in order, eh?'

'Well, by God they are – yes, Holt!' The CO had half-risen, leaning forward across the desk to shake his hand. Long, donkey face, the upper lip a vacant space which before they'd switched him into naval uniform would no doubt have been filled by a bristling military moustache. Intoning, '*Splendid* piece of work! Our first from this station, what's more! Must have been damn quick on it, eh?'

Charlie told him, 'Observer spotted it before I did and screamed blue murder. Airman by name of O'Connor. Then it was sheer luck, we couldn't have been better placed.'

'I'll look forward to seeing your report of it. O'Connor, eh? But now sit down. Smoke?'

'Thank you, sir.' Peeling pushed a cigarette box towards him, told Charlie as he sat down and lit up, 'Major McLachlan's from NID.'

Naval Intelligence Division. He told Charlie, 'One of the offshoots of that division, you might say. And coming down to brass tacks, we need someone to fly an airship on a rather special mission, and Commander Peeling's suggested you might fit the bill. What d'you say, Holt?'

Exhaling smoke, Charlie glanced at Peeling, back at the Marine. 'May I know a bit more about it?'

McLachlan nodded. 'Sensible reaction. And yes, you may. Not in any detail at this stage, mind you, but – the *general* picture, certainly.'

'Why I'm suggesting you for it, Holt –' this was Peeling, chipping in – 'is that you're about as experienced and competent a pilot as we've got, and since you've only been here a few days you haven't had time to put down any roots, as it were. It also happens that we have a Lieutenant Higham rejoining in a few days' time – from a delivery trip to Italy – so he could take over SS-45.'

'I'd be getting another ship for this job, then?'

'Brand new – an SSP. Brand new and with certain modifications which in fact aren't complete yet. You'd have to go up to the Scrubs in a day or two, when she's ready for trials, and –' a glance at McLachlan – 'there's considerable urgency about it, I gather.' The major nodded. Peeling said, 'Better tell him what you can about it. But you'd be bringing the ship down here, Holt. When she's ready and you're satisfied with her. Conduct certain exercises and – whatever else may be required. Major, I'm sorry . . .'

Another, perhaps slightly curter nod. McLachlan not one to suffer clowns gladly, Charlie noted. Asking now, 'Know much about the SSPs, Holt?'

'I know they only built six and then discontinued them. Been a few accidents, haven't there – two very recently, in fact. SSP-2 and 4, I think. And SSP-3 came to grief near Faversham, earlier on. Flying into or out of Kingsnorth, I imagine. Leaves only numbers 1, 5 and 6 still in commission. But if this one's brand new . . .'

'It is. Or *she* is. We're talking about SSP-7. Would that run of bad luck with the earlier ones discourage you?'

'Don't see why it should, sir. As far as I've heard, the accidents weren't connected in any obvious way. They're powered with hundred-horsepower Greens now, same engine that I have on SS-45, no complaints there. The "P" stands for "pusher", of course – which I must say I prefer.'

'So far so good, then. And now – exercising your memory a bit further – what can you tell me about SS-40?'

A blink. Two blinks. Getting close to the end of his cigarette. He nodded. 'Did hear about that. Last summer – here, Polegate – she was put through her paces for the benefit of some delegation from the War Office?' He saw the major nod, and added, 'Envelope painted with black dope for night flights across the lines in France.' He looked at Peeling: 'Envelope eighty-five thousand cubic feet, sir, wasn't it?'

'I believe it was, but I wasn't here then, so—'

'Anyway' – McLachlan impatient, drumming fingers – 'that gives you at least some inkling?'

'Am I right in thinking they did a trial run or two in France, it didn't work too well and the Army called it a day?'

McLachlan confirmed, 'As a reconnaissance vehicle – correct, wasn't much use. Could only be used on dark nights, obviously – moonless or with solid cloud cover – and in those conditions they were as blind as the Huns on the ground, looking up. But as the demonstration here proved, at about five thousand feet with her black envelope she was invisible from the ground even to searchlights.' A pause, eye to eye, Charlie waiting for further revelations. The major told him, 'The big difference is that this is one specific operation, and its purpose is not reconnaissance.' He added, 'Although in the interests of

24

security we'll let it be assumed that it's simply a repeat of the SS-40 experiment.'

'And when it's done – that's to say if it comes off and I and SSP-7 survive it – that'd be the end of it?'

'Here and now we're concerned only with the one job, yes. Which I may say is potentially of very considerable— could be *extremely* rewarding.' The sharp nod again. '*Vitally* so. It would be difficult to over-stress how vital, Holt. So now' – he glanced at Peeling, checked the time as he turned gimlet eyes back on Charlie – 'decision, please?'

'One other question, sir.' This one was for Peeling. 'If I take it on – when it's done, do I come back here?'

'Would that be your preference?'

'Would indeed, sir.'

'Then I don't see why you shouldn't. Sink a few more U-boats for us, eh?'

'I only wondered – if you're giving SS-45 to this new chap . . .'

'Doesn't have to be permanent. Wouldn't do to leave her sitting in the shed unused, that's all. Then again, we might take SSP-7 on our strength here, and you might prefer to stay with her. Why, though?'

'Roots were here before, sir.'

'*Were* they, indeed?' Half-smile, and a glance at the major. Teeth showing, eyebrows raised, as if awaiting further information. A shrug: 'Any case – top-hole, you'll take it on, eh?'

Charlie nodded, looking at McLachlan. 'I'd like to, sir.'

He asked Amanda, late in the evening, 'Don't you think you *should* go and see your parents?'

'*They'd* say I should. But having really got going in this job, in fact taken on rather more responsibility now than I was given in the first place—'

'Not spare them a long weekend, even?'

'Wouldn't be worth it. All that way . . .'

This was in her bed. They'd come up to it not long after he'd arrived at six-thirty precisely and had two drinks each of the Plymouth gin, which he'd bought from the wardroom messman. Gin and lime for her, gin and water for him: the water came from the farm's own well and was ice-cold. The cottage was warm, though: she'd had time to get a fire going before he arrived, and had the heater on upstairs as well. Amanda at that stage in a tweed skirt and a shirt that must have been Don's; it hung way down outside the skirt and there'd have been room in it for two of her. He hadn't commented on it because he hadn't wanted to mention Don, risk sending her back into that slough of despondence and self-questioning. She'd asked him, holding up her glass, 'What are we celebrating, Charlie?', and he'd told her, 'First and foremost, I'm celebrating *you*.'

'But something apart from us, you said?'

'Yes, well – I don't want to go on about it, but the fact is this morning I bombed and sank a U-boat.'

'Charlie, you *didn't*!'

'Actually did. It was surfacing right under me, all I had to do was ease her down a bit and let the bombs go. Double whumph, then bubbles and oil where it had gone down. Huge amount of oil.'

'And – Germans?'

'No. Split a submarine open when it's submerged – which it was, by the time the bombs went off—'

'How many Germans would there have been in it?'

'Thirty or so, probably. I'd sooner think of the ships it would have torpedoed by now – *British* sailors.'

'And perhaps Americans and—'

'Not in these waters. French, certainly. No – there's a Yank battle-squadron with the Grand Fleet up at Scapa now, and some destroyers I heard at Harwich. Troop ships bringing their chaps over use the Mersey and the Clyde, mostly – escorted in by RNAS Coastals, incidentally.'

'Here's to them. And to you, Charlie.'

'One more now. So drink that up.'

'I'll be sozzled!'

'One thing I kick myself for is that I was so bucked by our having sunk the thing that I forgot to pick up any fish. One carries a bucket on a long line purely for that purpose

– after any whumphs there are always stunned ones floating, easy to scoop up. I'd have brought you a couple. Sorry. Next time, I swear.' He'd poured new drinks, put hers in her hand and raised his: 'To us.'

'Us.' An arm up round his neck and her face turned up to be kissed, lips parted and flavoured with gin. '*Love* you, Charlie . . .'

Kissing her, instead of answering that. Keeping in mind how bloody dangerous . . . Reaching to put his glass down, still kissing and then pulling up the baggy shirt: could have got in there with her, almost . . . Murmuring mouth to mouth, 'Let's go up?'

And quite a bit later, with her slumbering, rather deliciously wrapped around him, he was thinking again about McLachlan and his secret operation. He was going to have to break it to her that he'd be away for a while. For only a few days, initially. McLachlan, walking with him to the mess, and a lot more affable after Charlie had signed on, so to speak, had insisted, 'Not a day longer than it absolutely *has* to take. Suppose you get yourself up to the Scrubs on Thursday, check the ship out for whatever still needs doing, and if necessary raise a bit of Cain, uh? Can't put up with any dawdling. Once she's flyable you'll need a couple of days of – well, flying, I suppose – minor adjustments, would you expect?'

'Par for the course would be at least that long. And there'll be a crew to organise: observer-w/t operator – wireless-telegraphy, that is – and engineer.'

'I'm less than sure about that, Holt. If I were you, I'd concentrate entirely on the ship.' He stopped walking; it was as cold as charity on the field, but at least one could talk without risk of being overheard. 'I'd better tell you this. You'll have one – well, passenger, who'll need to be taught the essentials – to act as observer, or whatever you'd want from him, to justify his existence so to speak. And that's all – you and this man whom you'll train.'

'Train – in two or three days?'

'He won't need to know all that much. Since he has to go with you though, he may as well make himself useful. As

27

your CO mentioned, there'll be some practices to carry out – when you get back down here, that is – and he'll have to pick up as much as you can instil in him during that time.'

'And you're saying I'm not to have an engineer?'

'I'm told that's not so very unusual. Would you agree?'

'Up to a point. When one takes up a makey-learn pilot, for instance, space and lift usually don't permit, so as instructor one uses the engineer's cockpit. Mind you, that would only be on short flights. In the normal course of things—'

'This won't be any "normal course of things", though. Far from it. And as a matter of fact it *will* be quite a short flight. Well – there and back again, of course. No, you'll have your makey-learn *observer*, and you'll need to be your own engineer. Can do?'

'I have done, on occasion, out of plain necessity.'

'So I've been given to understand. May as well tell you – confidentially – the reason for this weight-saving is to allow for passengers whom you'll be bringing out.'

'From behind the lines?'

A nod. 'I'm assuming you'll keep all of this to yourself. You'll realise why when we start going into detail. Meanwhile, for a rough time-schedule, let's say between three and six days at the Scrubs – I'll be joining you there on Friday, by the way – then another few days here. How are you on night landings?'

'Well, I've done some . . .'

Not in enemy territory, he hadn't. Obviously with no ground crew either. And without the least notion of how the weather might be. In mid-winter, at that, getting towards Christmas. No help from the ground, certain major hazards added to the normal ones, and – hell, *anything*, a bloody hurricane, could be!

Amanda stirred against him, murmured sleepily, 'Charlie. Charlie to the rescue.'

'Rescue?'

'Of me, silly . . .'

This was when, after she'd woken enough to be making

sense, he'd tried to persuade her to visit her parents at Ross-on-Wye, telling her that she ought to do so if not for her own sake, for theirs. He remembered them – rather vaguely. At least could visualise her father, who'd been a solicitor but was probably retired now. Crusty, dried-up little man. Complete contrast to his own father, who was a big man and an auctioneer as well as a farmer.

Fairly thorough-going bastard, too.

Anyway, Amanda wasn't having any. She added to what she'd said already, 'They'd only go on and on trying to persuade me to go and live up there – which frankly I wouldn't dream of. Heavens, Charlie, would *you* like it if I did?'

'Just visit them is what I thought. Fact is, though, *I'm* going to be away for a bit, and—'

'Where and how soon, how long?'

'Thursday, I have to go up to another airship station, take over a new ship. That involves flying trials and so on, possibly four or five days. Say a week, to be safe. Then I'll be bringing the ship down here for another few days, another sequence of trials. See you then, obviously – please – but then I have to take her off on another trip. It's all too boringly technical to explain, as well as confidential.'

'How long away the second time?'

'Honestly can't say. Too many unpredictables. A week – fortnight?'

'I just keep fingers and toes crossed and hold my breath, then?'

'But if you did go up to Ross—'

'No. Another thing is I couldn't ask for leave this soon. This is a *paid* job, you realise. I couldn't, even if I wanted to – which as I've said half a dozen times I don't . . . Charlie?'

'Huh?'

'After these trips you're going on, will you be stationed here again?'

'Yup. I made that a condition when I was asked if I'd take it on.'

'Ah. *Ah.* That's all right then!'

3

The girl cycling into a rear courtyard of the Château de Bellignies, her bike's wheels with their near-smooth tyres bumping off gravel on to uneven flagstones, was young, slim, quite tall, with an emerald scarf tied over her dark hair and a hip-length coat that might have been some tramp's cast-off. She must have *found* it somewhere, the lieutenant thought: it was not only extremely scruffy, but much too big for her. She was wearing it open and pushed back like the flies of an old tent. Otto Ketteler smiling as he came out of the stone porch to meet her, taking further inventory of her turn-out for this coming interview: long, oatmeal-coloured skirt hiked up clear of the bike's chain, high-necked fawn blouse and over it a green-and-brown-striped waistcoat.

She was dismounting. He stopped where he was, flicked away the stub of a cigarette, called, 'Good day, Fraulein Martens.'

'Hello, Otto.'

'Please.' A finger to his lips. He was brown-haired, blue-eyed, about twenty-six, topped her by an inch or two despite those long legs of hers. He murmured warningly, 'Mam'selle or Fraulein Martens, and Leutnant Ketteler.'

'Got it.' Walls had ears, and all that. Plenty of ears around anyway, troops all over the place. They'd stopped her at the guardhouse and telephoned the duty officer – which was how Ketteler had known to meet her at this entrance.

The château was a rest-and-recuperation centre, when it wasn't required for Staff and Army Commanders' conferences. Before that, it had been used as a Red Cross hospital and she'd worked in it. She unhitched the now ankle-length skirt and pulled the old coat straight, brushing it down as she stopped in front of him, casting an eye over his well-pressed uniform, highly polished riding boots and the walking stick. He'd been shot in that left hip about six months ago. She began, 'This person who wants to question me—'

'Hauptmann Gustav Koch.'

'He's secret police, you said?'

'Hardly secret. A soldier too, not a policeman. But yes, effectively, you might call him that. And I do beg you—'

'Checking I'm not some kind of spy, is that the purpose of all this?'

'Or perhaps verifying that you *are*. You may find that amusing, Hilde, but I should take it seriously, if I were you.'

'Seriously – *you* surely don't suspect—'

'As it happens, I do not, but it's what *he* thinks that matters. He's waiting for you. I'll take you in, introduce you, and if he allows it I'll stay. His French isn't all it might be, peculiarly enough.'

'I'd like it if you were able to remain.'

She'd pulled the scarf off. Deep green in colour, it went with everything else that she had on – even though it was silk and distinctly a cut above the rest. Not only silk, but from Brussels, and expensive: he'd given it to her, quite recently. Shrugging the coat off now as she followed him inside. 'Might leave this here, d'you think?'

'By all means.' In the hallway, looking at the rat-catcher's garment down his nose. 'Anywhere you like. Outside might be better.'

'It was my mother's, and before that I don't know whose. Someone bigger than either her or me – *possibly* my father, but—'

'I hope your mother's well?'

'My mother – *well*?'

'I'm sorry. The question was – an expression of sympathy, I suppose. No, I'm sorry.'

'She's certainly far from being *well*. And our doctor's old and doddery himself – in any case comes only once in a blue moon, which in some ways is just as well . . .'

'I'm sorry, Hilde. But – come along now. The *hauptmann*'s in the blue salon, which is now his office. And it wouldn't help to keep him waiting. Do please bear in mind that this is no mere formality – he has very clear responsibilities, and there *are* certain things in your recent past which frankly—'

'Could be misleading.'

'Could.' A nod. 'As you say.'

'Have you discussed me with him?'

'Oh, to some extent . . .'

'And?'

'My impression was that he thought I might be prejudiced in your favour – for some unknown reason.' No smile, though, only a jerk of the head. 'Come on.'

She followed him out of the vestibule and along a corridor – formerly servants' quarters, this part – around a corner, then another, via a swing door into a wider passage and eventually to the double doors of the blue salon – which the Princess had always referred to as the small morning room and had used, Hilde remembered, as her own office, leaving the library for the sole use of her brother, Prince Réginald.

The lieutenant halted, threw a glance round at her, and pushed one of the doors open. 'Herr Hauptmann . . .'

A rasp of German from inside told him – them – to come in. Hilde spoke no German, only French, a smattering of Flemish and about a dozen words of English. When she'd told Prince Réginald's messenger this the other day – well, three weeks ago – he had commented, 'What a pity. To be in such a position and to all intents and purposes deaf to what's going on all around you.' He'd been annoyed that she'd refused to give him the information which, despite her lack of German, she *had* acquired.

She hoped to God that man had got back all right.

'Fraulein Martens?'

Surprised tone, as if he'd expected her to look different – older, or younger, whatever. He was a stocky, pale-faced man of about thirty, she guessed. No smile, and no greeting other than that; only, after Ketteler had confirmed the obvious – and who the hell else would she have been, Koch having summoned her to this interview? – pointing at a small, gilt chair and telling her in brutally accented French to sit down. He was occupying one of the Princess du Croy's Louis Quinze chairs, behind a desk of the same period; Hilde was able to categorise both pieces because the Princess had appreciated her interest in such things and had talked to her about them. The Princess had been sentenced to fifteen years' hard labour, which she was now serving in the Siegburg prison. She was in fact lucky not to have been put against a post and shot as her friend Nurse Edith Cavell had been. Her brother Réginald had got away to Holland in the nick of time.

Ketteler had offered to interpret, and Koch had told him with a look of surprise that he thought he'd manage all right. Then changed his mind: 'On the other hand – wait, your presence *might* be helpful. Yes, stay, please.' Gesturing towards the back of the room, where he'd be out of Hilde's sight. She'd guessed at the substance of that exchange in German, but there was more now which she didn't follow. Ketteler's French did happen to be excellent; slightly accented, naturally, but nothing like as crude-sounding as Koch's.

As most Germans', in fact.

'You are Hilde Martens. Belgian, born in Antwerp, 1898. You live with your mother at Taisnières-sur-Hon, are employed now in some domestic capacity at the Manoir Hergies, but formerly worked at this château.'

She nodded. 'Yes.'

'Is your father still alive?'

'I don't know.'

'Don't *know?*'

'He went off when I was still a little girl.'

'Went off where?'

'I've no idea.' She shrugged. 'Just ran out on us.'

'Was this before the war?'

'I did say, m'sieur – when I was a little girl.'

A scowl, but then accepting it, continuing, 'Well . . . You and your mother are Belgians, but she prefers to live in France?'

'It's where our house is. The house bequeathed to us by my aunt.'

'Some domestic capacity', he'd called it, in his slow and ugly French. Hilde was Madame de Semeillions' housekeeper at the manor, but if he didn't want to know it, the hell with him. The hell with him anyway, she thought. Otto Ketteler's presence in the room was doing a great deal for her confidence; she was surprised that Koch had allowed him to remain. The language problem, of course, which was ridiculous – one would have thought that any secret policeman worth his salt—

He'd made a note; now looked up from it, frowning.

'In 1915 you were a – a *probationer*, as it was termed, at the Berkendael Medical Institute in Brussels?'

She nodded.

'The term *probationer* meaning a student nurse – enrolled by the spy and traitress Nurse Cavell?'

'Madame Cavell was *directrice* of the Institute. Speaking as one who knew her well, monsieur, I can assure you that she was never a spy – or traitress, either. She was a deeply religious, dedicated—'

'Your view of her is very much distorted, but also immaterial. She and her accomplices received a fair trial, and before that she had made a full confession, pleading guilty to all charges. This is recorded fact and not open to contradiction. Please confine yourself from now on to brief and direct answers to my questions!'

She blinked, waited. Behind her, Otto Ketteler cleared his throat, reminding her of his warning to her to take this business seriously.

All right, so with these creatures there was no fairness, no justice. But if one knew the truth and didn't stand up for it, wasn't one guilty of supporting and perpetuating lies? Edith Cavell herself had always been at pains to inculcate that principle – the absolute supremacy of truth – in her pupils, and had exemplified it in her own life.

'Very well.' Koch looked down at his paperwork.

What was 'very well', she asked herself? The fact she'd pusillanimously let his last statements go unchallenged? Not mentioning, for instance, that the confessions they'd got out of Madame and others could only have been obtained by trickery? Or that a charge of treason brought by Germans against an Englishwoman in Belgium could make no sense to anyone but a German?

At the time of that judicial murder – 1915 – she, Hilde, had just turned seventeen. And on that crucial night – October 11th – she hadn't gone to bed at all. From five to six am on the 12th she and the English nurse – Sister Elizabeth Wilkins, who in the Institute had been Madame's right hand – and a few others, nurses and probationers, had stood huddled against the rain outside the grim portals of the St Gilles prison to witness the removal of Madame to her place of execution – the national shooting ground, *Tir National*, on the Place des Carabiniers, four miles away.

Hilde could see it now, often did revisit the scene in memory: not the *Tir National*, the prison – grim, castellated, in all its implications hideous. Sister Wilkins had rung the bell and begged a guard to allow them a visit to Madame Cavell, and the guard had fetched the prison's Belgian governor, M. Maron, who of course worked under the orders of a German commandant. He'd told them that if they waited they might catch a glimpse of her when the motorcade came out. She'd be in the leading car, he expected. She was being very brave, extremely self-composed; the warders who'd had contact with her were as deeply impressed as they were sorrowful. He, Maron, entirely understood these young ladies' feelings, and offered his most profound sympathy. To his enormous regret and chagrin he was unable to intervene in any way, not even to allow them a few moments in which to exchange farewells with the poor dear lady. Having said this he'd gone back inside and they'd waited that full hour until the big gates were swung open and a limousine emerged with Miss Cavell in the back, stiffly upright in her blue nurse's cloak. Nurse Wilkins had moved to the kerb, the others crowding in around her; she and Hilde saw the white oval of Madame's face as she turned her head and saw them. For a second, perhaps two – a snapshot, no more, then the big car had swept on, followed closely by a second in which was the architect Philippe Baucq, who was to die with her.

Koch had asked Hilde – sneeringly – 'Is it *not* a very strange coincidence, fraulein?'

'I think perhaps I haven't quite understood . . .'

'You worked for that woman – at 149 Rue de la Culture in Brussels. Then you turn up here at the Château de Bellignies, former residence of the Prince and Princess du Croy, one might say the hub of the organisation in which your *directrice* played the leading role!'

'Monsieur, if I may say this – because it's the only way I *can* answer – I very much doubt the existence of any such organisation, or that the Princess was concerned with anything beyond running the château as a Red Cross infirmary. I'm here now only because you sent for me. I work at the Manoir Hergies, where Madame de Semeillions has been so kind as to provide me with employment – that's to say, to re-engage me – enabling me to support myself and my mother, who – I realise this may not interest you, but it is relevant to my situation – is old and sick, incapable of supporting herself. She and I live at Taisnières because it is our home, has been since – oh, 1903; a house which as I say was left to my mother by my aunt – my father's sister. As I mentioned, my father deserted us, and she, my Aunt Béatrice, was so ashamed of his behaviour that she invited us to live with her. I was then four or five years old. You see some coincidence in *that*, m'sieur?'

'In your position, fraulein, a sarcastic tone of voice is highly inappropriate!'

More throat-clearing from Ketteler.

'I beg your pardon. I am only trying to understand and to make myself understood. The coincidence, or what you see as one – may I explain this, please? – is the fact I was living here, in the house at Taisnières-sur-Hon, since I was – yes, just five – and that when I was twelve I began as a nursery maid at the Manoir Hergies. I worked well, I suppose; anyway Madame de Semeillions was kind to me even then, exceptionally kind, and after I had expressed an interest in becoming a nurse she brought me here to the Princess du Croy. This was early in 1914, before your army had over-run us, and the Princess had offered this château to our government as a hospital. In which I may say German wounded as well as French and British were cared for. I was taken on as a – a drudge, you might say, an emptier and washer-out of bedpans and so forth . . . Are you able to follow what I'm telling you, m'sieur?'

'Mostly. But in fact if you were to speak more slowly . . .'

'Perhaps the lieutenant would interpret?'

Ketteler, invited to come forward, spoke to Koch in German. What Ketteler had said, he told Hilde afterwards, was, 'If you like, I'll give you a written summary of all that. Most of what she's telling you I know already, I've questioned her myself on her background.' Koch had agreed: it would be useful, he'd said, in case there was anything important that he'd missed, and since he'd need to have a record of the interview in any case, for his files. Not that this would by any means complete his enquiries. But – yes: and a brief summary now, please.

He listened to it, then asked Hilde, 'How did it happen that you moved to this so-called "Institute" in Brussels?'

'I worked here, as I was saying, as no more than a nurses' drudge. But I stuck to it, did what I was told, and the Princess most kindly asked me if I'd like to go into proper training to become a nurse.' She was speeding it up again, not giving a damn that he'd be getting only about one word in ten.

Telling him, 'It happened that the Princess knew and thought highly of the *directrice* of l'Ecole Belge d'Infirmières Diplomeés – known also as the Berkendael. But whether she'd accept me or not, she warned me, would be up to Madame entirely – whether or not she found me suitable. If she took me on I'd spend several years as a probationer, would have my board and lodging but be paid very, very little, would eventually however end up with a diploma and a satisfying, worthwhile career ahead of me. That's what I wanted – I was out not only to become a nurse but to better myself. For instance, I was reading all the time – I'd always liked to read, and Madame de Semeillions was so gracious as to advise me and lend me books from her library.' Slowing a bit now, wanting him to hear this bit. 'The career prospects went up in smoke, of course, when your people saw fit to close down the Institute – with my training far from complete. It reopened, as you may know, at another address, but the people were all different, and in any case, without Madame . . .' A shake of the dark head. 'I came back here – what else? – to look after my mother, and to support us both – as I have mentioned – I found employment at the Manoir again.'

He'd caught that bit. Commented, with a glance at Ketteler, 'The Manoir has connections with this château, I understand.'

'Yes.' Ketteler told him in German, 'It provides overflow accommodation when major conferences are being held here. It's a substantial house and conveniently close. It was there – as I told you – that I met Fraulein Martens. Four or five months ago, the first time, when I was turfed out of here for several days. Then again more recently when we were honoured with a visit from General von Ludendorff and – others. I assisted, in fact, in the staff work for that conference – being now aide to Major von Bodenschatz, as you know – but I still had to move out, giving up my room here to a more senior officer.'

'All right. Fraulein Martens.' He checked himself, changing his mind. 'Leutnant Ketteler – to save time, and for the sake of clear understanding, interpret this to her, please. Sentence by sentence, now . . . The matter of the Cavell woman, and of the Princess du Croy. We know for a fact, and both of them admitted, that English and French survivors of the battles of Mons and Charleroi – both significant German victories – were first hidden and treated here, were then moved in small groups to 149 Rue de la Culture in Brussels – and to other addresses, all as arranged by Cavell – from where as guides became available they were taken by night to the Dutch border and smuggled across. The Princess du Croy and Cavell were the organisers and perpetrators of these criminal activities. Cavell *personally* led groups in the dead of night through the town to places where she had arranged for guides to be waiting. She *admitted* this. Is Fraulein Martens expecting me to believe that although she worked in both places she knew nothing of such activities?'

Ketteler interpreted the question, then gestured to her to answer it. Hilde nodded. 'Precisely so, m'sieur. I knew nothing of any such activities.'

'You expect me to believe this?' he repeated.

'The police and military in Brussels accepted it. We were all questioned a dozen times. None of us believed there could have been any such activities. And as you must know, anyone they thought they could bring a charge against was sent for trial. Speaking of which, m'sieur, am I on trial here now?'

'You may well be, before much longer.' A nod to Ketteler, and a dismissive gesture. 'Very well, lieutenant . . .'

In the rear courtyard again, Ketteler said stiffly, 'You were at some points dangerously defiant, Hilde.'

'Since I've done nothing either to be ashamed of, or even that infringes *your* rules, I don't see why I shouldn't be. But thank you for your help in there.'

Walking out of the yard, pushing her bike, Ketteler limping beside her. He was escorting her to a side gate, to which he had a key. Tall, wrought-iron, less than a quarter the width of the main entrance which she'd come in by and which was directly *en face* of the château. Those were double gates, a carriage entrance, and the guardhouse was a timber hut just inside them; this smaller gate was close to an apex in the surrounding twelve-foot wall, up the hill from the larger one. Ketteler, glancing back at the château's single, conical tower – visible over trees that were fast losing the last of their leaves now – shook his head. 'I did very little. But I *will* try to persuade him that it's simply your defensive manner, that you're not as hostile towards us as you sound.'

'Are you sure I'm not?'

'There you go, you see.'

'I find *you* pleasant enough. You put yourself out to be, and you succeed. Because you find me attractive, of course. Though why you bother, where you think it'll get you – there's one place I can assure you absolutely it will *not*—'

'I enjoy your company, that's all. No – not *all*. I do find you attractive. Any man would. Even your little outbursts – in an odd sort of way. I suppose what I'm saying is I admire your spirit. And between ourselves we can talk honestly – intimately – speak the truth to each other as either of us sees it, uh? One truth though, incidentally, which you should beware of, is that many – including that man in there – react badly to hostility. I'd hate to see you in real trouble with the likes of that one, Hilde.'

'But since I've done nothing – absolutely *nothing*—'

'His sort are a power unto themselves, you see. You might say it's what *they* decide you've done, or might do . . . Tell me this now – let's test your logic. You claim your Nurse Cavell did nothing wrong?'

'I tell you she was a saint!'

'As you've said before, but—'

'Certain things she confessed to, and she wouldn't have if it wasn't true. She always, *always* spoke the truth. I'm sure she'd have refused to speak at all if they hadn't convinced her that all the others had confessed, involving her. The

40

same trickery would have been applied to them. Those who were allowed to go free may be the ones who were persuaded or bribed to start the ball rolling, enabling that trickery to start. Eight acquittals, five death sentences, the rest to prison – but three of the death sentences reduced to prison with hard labour after the world reacted as strongly as it did to the barbarism of those sentences, especially that on Madame Cavell, whom they arranged to kill so quickly it's obvious they'd determined from the start to have her blood. The worldwide outcry, though – we heard it was your Kaiser who'd intervened on behalf of the other three, scared that what they'd done might bring America in against you although of course they're involved now anyway, uh? But that theory about the trickery – it isn't just mine, I should tell you, we all – we who were left free – discussed it endlessly.'

'You maintain, then, that Nurse Cavell did nothing criminal – only perhaps out of the kindness of her heart helped a few hundred British and French soldiers to escape?'

'If she did that, even. Well, yes, she did, she admitted it. But then, she would never have refused to help – oh, a lame dog, let alone a lame soldier or – why, *anyone* in need or in danger.'

'So you see her as an innocent, every action justified?'

'*Yes!*'

'But they shot her.'

'*Your* people did, Otto!'

He'd unlocked the padlock on the gate, was relocking it behind them. Glancing round at her with an eyebrow cocked: 'In your own case, however, you think you can defy an investigator such as Hauptmann Koch *without* putting yourself in danger?'

'If you want me to allow that under German rule there's no justice, truth or humanity . . .'

'Couldn't accept that, no. I'm arguing only that in the interests of your own safety you should be a little careful.'

'Not accept it although you know as well as I that if I were to shout it aloud in public – what I just said – I'd be arrested and shot?'

41

'That temper of yours, Hilde . . .'

'Listen.' They'd crossed the lane, were pausing now with a view across meadowland backed by a dark mass of forest – the Forêt de Mormal, its northern fringes – and to the left, downhill, a corner of the village's grey stone. She'd stopped with the bike between them and the disreputable old coat dangling from her shoulder, interrupting him with, 'As an example of your German justice and humanity, Otto – this is me testing *you* now – what took place at Louvain in August of '14?'

'Louvain. Yes. But an army advancing rapidly, finding itself shot at by civilians—'

'Justifies murder? Well, before Louvain – Andenne. You burnt Andenne to the ground and shot more than a hundred of the townsfolk as reprisal for – what, some of us had resisted your invasion of our country, it's criminal to resist, so take so-called hostages and murder them? The same at – oh, Tamines, and Dinant – Dinant sur Meuse, where they took people out of the church, from mass, slaughtered six hundred in the town square, women one side and men the other, two firing-squads in the centre? And you know what a German officer declared during the destruction by fire of Louvain and the slaughter of its inhabitants? That it was being done in order to teach people *respect for Germany*?'

He winced. Leaning on his stick, gazing across the park-like meadow to where on level ground below *Haute Borne* a company of troops was being drilled, a *feldwebel*'s bawled orders rising like screams for help. Hilde looking up at darkening cloud, thinking it must soon rain, and that she'd better get along in any case. She shook her head. 'All right – I should keep my mouth shut. What you'd call being careful. But in any case, I apologise. It's because you're so different from the kind who did those things or ordered them that I can talk to you. It's unfair of me, I'm sorry . . . Will Koch leave me alone now, d'you think?'

'I don't know. With his sort, frankly—'

'But he'd have no *reason*!'

'Wouldn't stop him looking for one. The new broom, eh?'

'You mean anything he could do to make a splash . . .'

'To show how thorough he is.'

'Show who?'

'All of us. Me, Major von Bodenschatz, the *kommandantur* in Bavay . . .'

'Thank heavens *you're* here, anyway. And as you said – which I hope is still the case – likely to be here until late February or early March when you launch your great assault?'

'Did I say that?'

'Why, yes.'

'Then – forget it, please?'

'All right. But why – well, never mind, in any case . . .'

He'd looked startled – still did. Forcing a smile though, shaking his head. Must have forgotten he'd told her those things; or hadn't expected her to remember them. And was still anxious, wondering what *else* he'd said? Or *remembering* what else? That, probably: what she'd said had reminded him, triggered memory or half-memory of an evening after a luncheon banquet here at Bellignies and a sea of cognac when *he'd* forgotten to be 'careful'. A would-be erasive wave of the hand now: 'Fact is, I know nothing of any "great assaults", and with this damn hip showing little sign of mending, I might be left here – oh, till the cows come home!'

'As long as *any* of you are here, Otto, as far as I'm concerned you personally are welcome. Please believe me, in recalling those dreadful incidents I was not attacking you. I swear it. I won't speak of them again either, it *was* unfair.' She turned away, preparing to mount. Having barely noticed that sudden panic and the clumsy cover-up. At least, having done her best not to let him *see* her noticing it. So he could forget it again, or decide it didn't matter, that she obviously hadn't made anything much of his drunken bombast. She flipped a hand to him: 'Bye, Otto . . .'

4

Charlie, at Wormwood Scrubs, gazed up at SSP-7's sleek
black belly, his eye then following wires and lines from
the car to her rudder, elevators and valves. They'd moved
her only this morning from the construction shed into this
ordinary one, having telephoned Polegate last evening
asking when they could expect someone up here to take
her off their hands.

This was Wednesday. McLachlan's proposal had been that
Charlie should get here on Thursday and that he'd join him
on Friday. McLachlan was now expected some time
tomorrow, but probably not before Charlie had taken the
new ship up on her maiden flight, first thing in the morning;
there was some conference the major had to attend in
London before he could get away. Not that his presence
struck Charlie as in any way essential at this stage: in fact,
if he'd elected to stay away until the initial trials were
finished, that would have been fine. Except of course for
the satisfaction of one's natural curiosity about the mission.
Charlie wasn't being asked, though, only told. When the
call had come last night – via old Peeling's office – he'd
been 'ashore' with Amanda; he'd taken her to see a Chaplin
film at the Tivoli in Eastbourne and afterwards to a fish
supper at Sattery's Imperial Restaurant, before returning to
her cottage for what both he and she had regarded as the
main event. He'd only been given the news on his return
to base a little after midnight, when they'd stopped him at

the guardhouse with a message from the duty officer. He could hardly have gone thundering back to wake her up there and then – in any case should have been back on the station *before* midnight – instead had telephoned her at her office soon after eight-thirty this morning, and she hadn't liked it much.

Anyway – SSP-7 was a fine-looking ship, and the prospect of taking her to France on some clandestine mission was really quite exciting, despite a qualm or two when recalling McLachlan's hints of a night landing with no ground party to receive one, and obviously no certainty of the weather – wind, in particular. The problems in this were actually quite daunting; McLachlan might be aware of them, might not. Might just not give a damn, for that matter, might simply be relying on Charlie to cope with them.

The black dope did give her a certain style, he thought. An air of mystery: shiny-smooth and black as night, with an allegedly 'silenced' 100-HP watercooled Green engine, also sparkling new. The twin fuel tanks' aluminium gleamed through the fabric cradles in which they were slung on the envelope's black flanks, one each side; the fuel pipes providing gravity-feed to the engine were shining copper, their assembly as a whole wishbone-shaped – a branch from each tank and a stop-cock above the engine. The car, a modified version of those being built now for the new North Sea-class ships, was a lot more roomy than the Maurice Farman he'd had on SS-45. Three cockpits: his own in the middle, and each of the others – he guessed, judging it by eye – having room for two reasonably-sized men to sit side-by-side.

At a pinch . . .

McLachlan's prescription, no doubt. McLachlan had referred to bringing *people*, not *a person*, out.

Two, say. As long as they didn't turn out to be heavy-weights; and with only one other man on board, no air mechanic, and an envelope holding 85,000 cubic feet of gas. As long as one didn't have to valve too much, since losing gas meant losing lift – what was technically called 'static' lift.

Hallet, the pale, thin-faced engineer lieutenant who'd supervised her construction, pointed out, 'No Lewis in her yet. We've given you an extra forty pounds of ballast to compensate for it.'

Charlie nodded, had already noted the festooning of sand-ballast bags. Sand-ballast only: at this time of year you didn't want water-ballast, with the icing problem. He said, 'They'll give me a Lewis at Polegate, I dare say.'

'Looks good though, don't you think?'

He agreed, '*Looks* fine.' Thinking, *Handsome is as handsome does . . .* Pointing, then: 'That lacing in the suspension's a bit fancy, isn't it?'

'Necessitated we thought by the shape of the car. Could have stuck to the standard rig, but . . .'

'The second fin's on account of the car's length too, I suppose.' To balance the whole ship against the transverse effect of wind on the car's extra-large sides. The main stabilising fin was right aft on the black bag's stern, with the rudder hinged to it, and this extra one was immediately for'ard of it. Charlie asked the engineer, 'What about the engine modifications – going to be much quieter, is she?'

'Should be.' Shake of the head. 'No. *Is*. The requirement's that she shouldn't be audible on the ground when she's at four thousand or higher. You'll check that out, won't you? It'll lose you a couple of knots, of course – can't have your cake and eat it. Would you like my chief artificer to go up with you in the morning?'

'Why, yes – if he's agreeable.'

'He likes to see his babies up on their first jaunts. And as you haven't brought either an observer *or* an AM . . .'

'You could lend me another body for the initial trim – yes, please. As it happens there's a leatherneck major arriving tomorrow forenoon, supposed to produce some spare hand who'll act as observer but knows sweet FA about any of this stuff. I was thinking, might be better to teach him some rudimentary engine care and put him in the after cockpit. Think your artificer'd take *that* on – I mean, give him the necessary tuition?'

'Show him how to use the starting handle and change a plug, you mean?'

'Or spot a petrol leak. And start-up on an air-bottle – in case he drops the handle overboard. That sort of thing.' He shrugged. 'If the leatherneck approves, of course.'

'I'll ask him. Artificer's name is Berriman. If he demurs, *I*'ll take it on. Although I'd have thought you'd do better to have an AM with you, and train him in whatever other functions are expected of him.'

'Well, that's likely to be fairly – what's the word? – esoteric.' Charlie paused, thinking that it surely would be; the passenger had to be some kind of cloak-and-dagger merchant who'd know what to do when you landed him behind the lines. He added, 'Besides, McLachlan – that's the leatherneck – may have some special reason to put his man in the fore cockpit. Up to now I haven't been taken into his confidence to any great extent.'

To be fit for an early start, he turned in soon after dinner in the wardroom and a few drinks with men he'd known on other stations. Whichever naval air station you landed up on, you invariably ran into friends and acquaintances from times past, and he'd spent about six weeks here at the Scrubs two and a half years ago, doing his ballooning course. The station had been new and quite small then – just one shed, and this accommodation block only half-built.

Would have been with Amanda now, he thought, pulling his window shut against an icy north wind. A farewell supper in the cottage had been the intention for this Wednesday evening. On the 'phone this morning he'd told her soothingly, 'Have to put it off a week, that's all. Make it a *reunion* supper. Soon as I'm back I'll call you – or if it's late I'll just buzz round.'

'You say a week, but starting a day early mightn't you be back before the weekend, now?'

'I'd hardly think so.'

'But *might* be?'

'If everything went swimmingly, no snags at all – which

would not be anything like the norm, unfortunately. Although it's a fact no one's dragging their feet on this one, so – not *totally* impossible, I admit.'

'Fingers crossed, then.'

There was a Gotha raid on London during the night, but Charlie neither heard nor saw any of it, only learnt of it over breakfast from some who'd been woken by the *crumps* and gone outside to see the show – flashes of AA guns and a few exploding bombs, at one stage a bomber screaming down in flames, others caught in searchlight beams, and so forth, all the usual air-raid stuff. None the less valid for that – truth was that the guns which had so deterred the Zeppelins that in the last year or so they had left London alone, restricting their attentions to industrial targets and other population centres, had brought down quite a number of Gotha bombers in recent months.

Charlie had in fact woken for no apparent reason in the early hours, guessed now that it might have been distant percussions rattling the window, although all he'd been aware of was waking with Amanda in his mind again, the concept of her waiting for him to respond emotionally – the question then being wasn't he pretty well bound to, eventually? He *was* fond of her, *liked* her, had done so for years – and sexually was much more than 'fond': was crazy for; was indeed having consciously to *work* at retaining emotional control; was not, God damn it, as cold a fish as that control made him seem even to himself.

'Any word of damage done?'

Talking about the night's air-raid still. Hallet, the engineer, saying no, not that he knew of. No one else had heard anything either. Hallet said, 'Perhaps when your leatherneck shows up he'll tell us the score.'

'May indeed.'

Questions then about this leatherneck – what was *he* for? Charlie shrugged. 'The ship I'm here to collect. Army want another shot at – you know, the recce stunt they tried last year and gave up on? Well, this chap's organising it.'

'Gave up because they could only use her on pitch-dark

nights, pongo observers unable to distinguish between their arses and their elbows.'

'Maybe they've been taking lessons. Trying again now, anyway.'

Eight forty-five. He was in SSP-7's central cockpit, with Chief Artificer Berriman in the after one and a w/t operator by name of Crookshank for'ard. This was an afterthought: Hallet had been going to lend him an air mechanic, primarily as ballast, but they'd dug this spare observer out from somewhere or other and it was just as well to have him along to put the wireless through its paces. In case of mishap you might need to communicate with the station – if you force-landed in another county for instance, and needed to let people know where you were and in what condition. A first ascent was always a little speculative.

Any ascent could be. Charlie recalled Amanda's amusement when he'd told her about the Italian commander who'd been whisked up to seven thousand feet hanging by his heels. And whether or not it was justified, SSPs had acquired a certain reputation, on top of which this one had had modifications of its own – larger envelope and specially designed car, to kick off with – which were as yet unproved.

He looked down at the crowd of men below him on the shed's floor, and raised a gauntleted hand to Hallet. 'Ready when you are.'

Ready to be 'walked out' of the shed. An SSZ had been taken out ahead of them, should be in the air by this time. SSP-7's skids were now about six feet off the ground, the ship's buoyancy had been tested and the trim adjusted by shifting a few bags of sand; overall, she was just a little on the light side. Which was what one aimed for. The ballonets inside the envelope had been pumped up by a portable air compressor – so-called 'portable', at any rate moveable, on wheels and trundled clear in recent minutes by three or four burly airmen, along with the fabric tube by which it had been connected to the scoop – aluminium air scoop, abaft and just above the four-bladed pusher prop.

Moving out: airmen each side of the car like pall-bearers, others ahead and astern, handling the steel-wire guys. Charlie in his seat, bulky in the heavy flying-suit, doing some more last-minute eye-tracing of lines to valves, rudder and elevators. Behind him Hallet's chief artificer, Berriman, had fitted the starting handle to the engine and was waiting – standing, leaning on his cockpit's edge and singing rather loudly – if 'singing' was the word for it – 'Hello, Hello, Who's Your Lady Friend?'. A bit much, Charlie thought, at this time of day. Steadily out into the near-freezing air now. Wind about force 2, north by east. The fore guy handlers had been joined by others now, sent by the station's second-in-command, a diminutive RNVR lieutenant-commander who was out there in the open, short legs spread and arms akimbo. Charlie had met him in the wardroom last evening.

They were turning her into the wind, Berriman stopping to the crank handle, looking round at Charlie, who nodded and called, 'Start up!' He could feel the 'lift' – the upward pull against the hands and men's weight restraining her – and that was as it should be. The big engine coughed, grumbled into life. Crank handle disengaged, and the trim was about right. He raised both gauntleted hands – all the signal they needed to let go and stand clear, although out of habit he also shouted – inaudibly, thanks to engine noise as he dropped his left hand to the throttle and eased it open – the ritual command: 'Hands off!'

Lifting, in a smooth build-up of power and with the elevators tilting to bring her nose up by a degree or two. Field, sheds and upturned faces receding. A hundred feet on the altimeter: hundred and fifty. Starboard helm – right boot pushed forward to turn her well clear of the station's tall wireless mast; although she'd clear it now in any case, it was something to stay away from. On this initial flight one would be testing the ship's steering as well as lift, elevator and valve controls – essentially, that she was capable of flight, i.e. manoeuvrability in three dimensions.

Five hundred feet, and under helm. The prison with its exercise yard back on the quarter now – about due south

– and that great cemetery – Kensal Green – northeast. SSP-7's rounded black prow swinging smoothly, under less helm, to put that as well as the Grand Union Canal and the main line from Paddington away to port. Further afield, Kilburn, Brondesbury and Willesden – an open green patch there – now well abaft the beam. And passing just about under her now, slightly off to starboard, North Kensington – that sprawling mass of rooftops. Holding her at this height and on this course now – to ensure she'd fly straight and level when she was asked to. The compass was about right: he'd check it more accurately on a later outing, flying on a pre-arranged triangular route with allowance for wind direction and strength; or maybe a jaunt to some other station and back again – down-river to Kingsnorth, for instance.

The elevators, operated by the elevator wheel, seemed well adjusted. No reason they shouldn't be, but until you'd tried them out you didn't know. Extraordinary defects did sometimes show up on maiden flights. He'd left the field well astern by this time, and by way of a destination thought of the polo field at Hurlingham – down there ahead some-where. In the ballooning course, all take-offs had been from that field. But turn somewhere short of it: take her up to say 2,000 feet *en route*, then go about in a really sharp turn – to ensure the rudder and its controls could take some strain when it had to; also to see how tight a turning-circle she could manage – and fly back over the same route. He'd have been up about half an hour or forty, forty-five minutes by that time, which for a first flip was about right and would leave long enough for engineers and riggers to make all their checks by, say, early afternoon, when he'd take her up again, perhaps with McLachlan's stooge on board. Better to have some sort of plan in mind, in any case, rather than just doodle around; it was also advantageous, or might be, to have in mind a fairly large, flat, empty space – such as the Hurlingham field – where if things did go awry you could put her down.

Meanwhile, though – *up* . . .

After crabpot open: some air into that ballonet, driving

gas for'ard at the same time as using the elevator to tilt her black snout up, for a steeper climb. Appreciating meanwhile one great advantage of the pusher prop – that you weren't in its slipstream as you were when the engine was in front of you. Much more comfortable than it had been in SS-45 in the past few days' oversea patrolling. Crookshank, the w/t operator, Charlie noticed, was leaning forward, slightly crouched, in that for'ard cockpit: trying the wireless out, probably. He'd have paid out its aerial to hang vertically below them – it had a lead weight on its end – soon after they'd left the ground. Berriman – Charlie twisted around to look back at him – was obviously quite happy – whistling, by the look of him, and now nodding, raising a thumb, his lips still compressed in some inaudible rendition. No engine problems, anyway. At this rate, touch wood, *might* get back to Polegate by the weekend. Needing a few days there, of course; and from as little as McLachlan had divulged, mostly practising night landings. Which would *not* delight Amanda. Or suit oneself either, from that angle. Sneak away to the cottage some forenoons or afternoons, maybe – if she could do the same. At weekends, for sure. Not that one was likely to be there more than one weekend . . . But *unassisted* night landings, for God's sake. Landings and take-offs too, presumably. And how the hell was one going to manage *that . . .* ? Close to 2,000 now – shaking his head in keeping with that thought – and an eighth of a turn on the elevator wheel, to take the angle off her. Thinking that behind enemy lines you obviously couldn't either land or take off in daylight – couldn't even *fly* in daylight, no matter how black the bag was painted: bloody Huns'd be on you within minutes.

And come to that, having got down in darkness, wouldn't be able to spend much time on the ground, either. Great black monster stuck out in the middle of some field . . .

Two thousand feet, and levelled. With the whole of London and its surrounding hills on display down there: Richmond, Twickenham, Hampstead – oh, and Crystal Palace. Not to mention Old Father Thames. But having been up for – twenty-one minutes – hard a-port now. Looking back at the artificer again – he'd been making some adjustment to the engine, was dumping himself back in his seat just as Charlie looked round. He wagged his head and again raised a thumb. Charlie moving one hand in a circling motion, conveying his intention of going about and heading back. Berriman nodded, gave him the other thumb as well.

So – round we go.

Feeling rather good about this trial flight. Wires dragging the rudder hard round to port, and the ship already turning – instantly and positively responsive. On a turn, however tight, a blimp didn't heel as a winged aircraft did. Just swung around. Smooth and level – achieved by Charlie's left foot pushing at the rudder-bar. It *was* a small, tight turn . . .

So tight that the lacings on the starboard-side suspension of the car went. Steel-wire rope snapping in a series of jolts and whipcrack explosions mostly drowned by the engine's noise, so that twanging *cracks* were all you heard – but those wires gone, the whole damn lacing on that side. The car and the three inside it – *as yet*, still in it – toppling, then coming up hard in the grip of as much wire lacing as was still attached to the port-side suspension. Charlie in full awareness that steel-wire rope parting under strain was lethal, *bloody* dangerous, like scythes whipping, slicing; could decapitate or cut a man in half – cut an airship's *car* in half, let alone the soft underbelly of its envelope, certainly mince up other lines, controls. The car had flung itself over to starboard anyway: Charlie clinging, bracing himself back inside it, boots still on the rudder-bar but knees, elbows and shoulders spread against the cockpit's sides to jam himself in, gloved hands as and when they could be spared clamping to its rim. The port-side suspension seemed to be holding – this far, but don't bloody count on it, Charlie boy – and both the others still there, thank Christ, not hurtling earthward, but – hell, no reason to think you've seen the worst yet, nothing *like*. For instance, if one of those wires had slashed through either of the overhead fuel lines to bring a stream of petrol down on a hot engine, flames then reaching in a swift flare-up to those 85,000 cubic feet of gas . . .

Hadn't, anyway. And four or five seconds having passed since the wires had carried away, they'd only be trailing now. Until the *other* lot went. Then the whole caboosh would be hurtling earthward. From 2,000 feet. He was holding her level, he *thought* – not the car but the ship, no way of levelling the car – but had recognised that he had no control of the starboard elevator. Considerably reduced control overall, therefore, and thoughts returning momentarily to the polo field; but having already turned her – had now taken the helm off – he'd have had to have turned her back, then located it, and maybe on that turn carry-away the portside suspension, too. With the full weight of the car and three men on it now, it was a miracle it was still holding; an essential was to avoid imposing any *further* strains.

Engine still fine, anyway – by the sound of it – and he still had the throttle in easy reach. Throttling down a little, slightly to ease *all* strains. And he had her on course, had 'met' the swing with starboard rudder. Physically not easy, but it had been accomplished. You weren't upside-down like that Wop had been, but you were definitely on your ear. Gently now, using the wheel on the remaining elevator control. *Very* gently. And valving: hoping to God the lines to the valves hadn't also carried away. As – merciful God – they had not. Yet. One action at a time, though, apart from steering, which – again, thank God – was footwork. But needing one hand for holding on, while envying Berriman and Crookshank for being able to devote two hands to that single purpose. Needing one hand and – as much of the time as possible – both elbows – forearms – to exert pressure on the cockpit's sides. Would have expanded his whole body to fill it more tightly, like one of those toads that blew themselves up, if he could have. It actually *wasn't* easy, and inside his Sidcot suit he was soaking wet. Did have her on course – the compass, set in gymbals, was OK – but not *quite* on course now: bring her back to starboard just a little. That uncontrollable elevator was putting the black bulk of her slightly on the tilt, despite the extra fin's stabilising influence, thus affecting her steering as well as – *now* – the process of getting her down from about 1,900 feet to something like 100, say.

Valving was one way to do it. On that same principle of sparing the port elevator and its control wire any non-essential strain. She was slightly nose-down anyway: altimeter reading just under 1,800 feet. Air into the ballonets therefore, by opening the crabpot valves, admitting slipstream via the scoop. In descent, with external air pressure increasing and the gas contracting as a result of its squeezing effect on the envelope, by expanding the ballonets you kept the envelope full so that it retained its shape. And since it was the lightness of the gas that provided lift, its contraction (and the ballonets' expansion) made her heavier, allowing the descent to continue, in fact increasing the *rate* of descent. He felt more or less in control now: muscles complaining, but procedures proving effective, reinforcing confidence. Still very much aware that the port-side suspension might carry away at any moment, which would mean curtains – goodbye, Amanda darling. Fifteen hundred feet: needing to speed up the descent, get a little more bow-down angle on her. *Very* cautiously with that elevator now: increasing the angle by just a degree. Thirteen hundred, and valving again. Wanting to come in to the Scrubs field low, without any sudden, steep descent creating further strains and ending as it might in really *crashing* down, smashing up the car as well as throwing out its occupants, with possible breakage of skids and struts, not to mention bones and skulls. One thousand feet. He hoped Crookshank might have been in touch with base by wireless, alerting them to the situation so they'd have chaps ready out there on the field. Eight hundred feet, valving. Seven-fifty. Lucky to have such a light wind, for sure. He could see the sheds now. Home, sweet home. *Am* getting back to you, Mandy, but won't be with you this weekend, that's for sure. Not even if I manage to put her down with skids, struts and car intact – of which there's no certainty at all.

Five hundred feet, valving again. Nose down another degree or so? Nose directly into wind, compass needle on north-by-east. Fractionally throttling down. Two large groups of men down there ahead in mid-field, and a smaller group between them. Three hundred. The crowd on the ground now shifting, being marshalled on to either side of the ship's anticipated line of approach and final descent, where he'd put her – touch wood – into their waiting hands. The handling-guys dangling from her bow and stern and from the car would be what they'd go for – steel-wire ropes fitted with 'eyes' through which the handling teams would as often as not loop their own rope lines: in any sort of wind that was the way to do it, but in present conditions Charlie was hoping to make it easy for them, as well as for himself . . . Hundred feet. Eighty. Throttling down, and more valving, SSP-7's black snout right into wind; she was slowing as engine revs reduced. Couldn't reduce by too much too soon or you'd lose control. Fifty feet. Thirty. Shifting sea of white faces and dark-blue caps and uniforms down there, teams of them closing in on either bow. Twenty feet. Fifteen. Going to be all right, believe it or not – already damn near *there*! Ten feet: levelling her with the port elevator alone and cutting power still further – throttling down to nothing – they had the guys in hand, could hold her bow into the wind and pull her down. Hands reaching up to grab hold of the car's lower – starboard – skid, and the engine stopped, switched off, Charlie hearing the wind and – for the second time in two days – cheering.

5

The car had landed on its starboard skid, and the ground team on that side had been quick to move in and lend support, preventing it from toppling and the struts from buckling, simultaneously helping Charlie and the other two to extricate themselves. Wire-rope guys were meanwhile in hand for'ard and aft, SSP-7 being held bow to wind and fairly motionless, her black bulk heaving as if panting from strenuous exertion. Crookshank *had* been in touch by wireless: the station's doctor and stretcher bearers had been standing by – looked disappointed at finding they weren't needed after all – and the field had been closed to other airship movements during this period of emergency. An indication of this was the negative flag – small black crosses on a white background – flying at the yardarm over the signals and w/t hut, warning any incoming pilot to stay clear. Both field and sky were empty now, anyway, except for this beached whale of an airship and the crowd surrounding her. Berriman growling at Charlie, 'Owe you our lives, sir. You was right about them fancy lacings, was you *not*, by jingo!'

They had a couple of dozen airmen lifting the car's starboard skid so a trolley could be pushed under to support it while they were walking the ship in. Engineer Lieutenant Hallet meanwhile, who'd been among the back-slappers, had moved round to the port side to inspect however much of the suspension was still intact. Pointing: 'Deuced lucky. Look at *that*. Really deuced lucky, Holt!'

'Need a new rigging plan now, anyway. Will they get on with it right away?'

'Certainly they will. As per handbook and Admiralty instructions – any essential variation to be approved by you as well as by me. All right?'

'Rig as on the SSZ cars, wouldn't you think?'

'Well – I don't see why not. *Yes* . . .'

'Haven't built any here though, have you?'

'We're supposed to be assembling two very shortly. One reason for wanting *this* job off the premises double-quick, as it happens. So we do have the rigging plan, fortunately.' He'd given Charlie a cigarette; they were watching the lads walking SSP-7 back to her shed. 'Nasty experience you had there, Holt. And to the extent that approval of the modifications was left to *me*—'

A sharp voice cut in from behind them. 'Am I right in deducing that the fitting-out of SSP-7 has been largely *experimental*?'

McLachlan. In greatcoat, capped and booted. Buttons and major's crowns on the coat's epaulettes agleam like gold, deepset grey eyes sharply critical. A bird-of-prey look, Charlie thought – and perhaps equivalently lethal at that – if he had reason to be, or thought he had. Hallet had turned sharply, frowning at the interruption, but now saluted. Charlie, doing the same, introduced them: 'Engineer Lieutenant Hallet – Major McLachlan.' Twenty yards away the station's half-pint-sized first lieutenant was heading back towards the station offices; presumably he'd brought the major over. He was a fitness fanatic: in the wardroom last night had talked of nothing but the station's desperate need of a squash and/or fives court and his own efforts to raise funds for it. Charlie said, answering that rather superciliously-put question about SSP-7's fitting-out, 'To some extent, has to be, since the Admiralty called for modifications – in particular to the car, which meant modifying its suspension, too.'

'Which is how I'm told you came to grief – or *nearly*.'

'Nearly.' Charlie nodded. A few snowflakes were swirling

on the wind. He said, 'It'll set us back at least one day, unfortunately. Although as far as we'd gone, everything seemed to be on the top line. I'll need to repeat this morning's flight tomorrow, anyway. I'd hoped to go up again this afternoon, taking up your makey-learn observer if you had him here – the passenger you want me to carry as observer?'

'Well.' A glance at Hallet, then away at the black stern-end of SSP-7 disappearing into the shed. A nod, then. 'We'll talk about that, Holt. Matter of fact we've a great deal to talk about.'

'But on that subject—'

Hallet cut in, 'If you'd excuse me, sir.'

'Certainly.' Touching his cap in acknowledgement of the engineer's salute, Hallet setting off towards the shed, and Charlie trying again: 'Subject of the passenger – you suggested he might work his passage as observer. But if I'm not to carry a mechanic, I've been thinking it'd make better sense to put him in the after cockpit and teach him some rudimentary engine maintenance. In fact – frankly, sir, it's either that or take up an AM anyway. If I might explain –' starting towards the shed, in Hallet's tracks, to give the major an eyeful of SSP-7 in all her glory and explain a few fundamentals – 'when one takes off, for instance, they walk her out of the shed – as you saw her being walked in just now – and when the trim's right, car's at about shoulder height, well, you've got to start the engine, obviously, and that's done from the rear cockpit with a crank handle. Couldn't even start, you see, without someone in that cockpit.'

Could, actually. Hadn't thought of this before, but you could have ship and car slightly lower and have the prop swung from outside by someone on the ground. Or on a step ladder, say. Anyway, McLachlan had accepted it: a flap of the arms signifying that. A raised eyebrow, then: 'What else would he have to do? In flight, is the engine controlled from that position?'

'No. By me. Throttle's in the midships cockpit – mine – with all the other controls. But what else – well, another way of starting up – if he'd lost the crank handle, for instance

– is by a compressed-air bottle. One of the engineers'd show him, it's quite straightforward. Or changing spark-plugs, or fixing a leak on a pipe – fuel pipe or water – well, we carry sticky tape, simple enough. AMs have been known to use chewing-gum. But I'd say an hour or two under instruction by our chief artificer – a WO by name of Berriman—'

'Didn't you say – at Polegate – that on occasion you'd acted as your own engineer?'

'Different type of airship. When I started in '15 – well, until well into '16, too – the cars were the fuselages of BE.2c aeroplanes. Wings and tails removed, otherwise just that. Prop's in front, of course, so you sat in its slipstream – as one does in all the SSs, as it happens, with various other types of car. But when you had engine trouble in those ships, needed to clean or change plugs, or – oh, replace the magneto, that was a frequent job – you'd take her up to about three thousand, stop the engine and then what we call "balloon" – just drift, no engine power, hang there in the sky – let the engine cool down if necessary, then get out and—'

'Get *out*?'

'Climb out on to the skid, sidle up beside the engine and do whatever needed doing, then hang on with one hand and use the other to swing the prop to start her up again.'

'Are you pulling my leg, Holt?'

'No, sir. I've had to do it dozens of times. We had Renault seventy-horse engines at that time and they tended to over-heat and conk out. In fact, when they began to run a bit rough we'd do it – change the plugs, or clean them – *before* any conking out. The first really good engines they gave us were Rolls seventy-fives, purpose-built for airship use; but the Green's more reliable still.' He added, 'Two great things about this "pusher" system, incidentally, is you can do whatever's necessary from the after cockpit – *without* getting out – and you're not in the slipstream.' They were entering the shed. 'Here she is. Crikey, they aren't wasting any time . . .'

Ladders on wheeled trolleys were being positioned on

both sides of the 30-foot-high envelope, and at car-level the wrecked suspension was already being cut away with hack-saws. Charlie pointing: 'Tailfins – with the rudder hinged on the back end of this after one. That's another modifi-cation – second fin to balance wind-effect on the larger car, especially broadside-on. Those horizontal things – one's out of line, its control-wire was cut when the suspension broke away – those are the elevators, and I control them from my cockpit.' Holding his two hands out flat, horizontal, tilting them up and down. 'Primarily to put up- or down-angle on the ship – tilt her, as hydroplanes do on a submarine. The similarity to submarining is really quite close. For instance, sub going deep, she's sinking into increasing water pres-sure, which squeezes the hull, compresses it, she displaces less and so gets heavier. So in order not to carry on deeper and deeper they have to pump out water-ballast from internal tanks. Principle of Archimedes? Well, as we climb in an airship we're rising into *less* dense air, the gas in the envelope expands and increases what we call the "lift" – really the same thing, only in another dimension.'

'So how d'you check that?'

'Well, we can valve-out gas – to a limited extent, one doesn't want to lose more than one has to – and eventually it can't expand any more in any case because the envelope won't let it. That's our ceiling – also known as "pressure height". Gas is let out through automatic release-valves. Makes us rather safer than a submarine – if they didn't or couldn't lighten themselves on the way down they'd go deeper and deeper until the pressure crushed them. Same as if we went on up we'd burst – and the release-valves ensure we don't.'

'The "envelope" as you call it is pretty strong, I imagine?'

'Oh, yes. Can be holed – if you crash into a tree or fence, or that sort of thing. My wires parting this morning could have slashed it to ribbons if they'd been long enough to reach it. Envelopes are made by Vickers, up at Barrow – subsidiary company called the Ioco Rubber and Waterproofing Company.' He nodded. 'Cornered the market, I gather. No flies on Vickers. But yes, the material's two thicknesses of rubberised fabric with rubber between them and on the inside surface, and then aluminium "dope" on the outside as weatherproofing.' Pointing again: 'That object there, called the scoop . . .'

The major seemed to be taking it all in – and it might help if he had some understanding of the problems, what could be done and what couldn't. Eventually they'd be talking about night landings and take-offs without ground party assistance, and he'd certainly have to be made to comprehend *those* near-impossibilities. Best, Charlie thought, to wait for him to open the batting on all that, then give it to him between the eyes: *No, sir – sorry, not a hope* . . .

A revelatory exchange of conversation then with Hallet, the engineer lieutenant. They'd been about to leave the shed, McLachlan having absorbed about as much airship lore as Charlie thought he could use – for the time being, anyway – and the engineer had intercepted them, asking, 'Know all about it now, sir, do you?'

McLachlan turned a sharply suspicious eye on him, then evidently decided it had been a pleasantry, not a jibe. He said, 'A lot more than I did before. Although references to the Principle of Archimedes – whatever the deuce that might be—'

'Simply that a body immersed or partially immersed in water experiences an upthrust equal to the weight of water which it displaces. Which does have parallels in the operation of airships as well as *water* ships.' Pointing up at the ship's black belly. 'Amount of lift, for instance, depends on the weight of air displaced minus the weight of gas displacing it.'

'Ah.' Fingering his moustache. 'I suppose that's what Holt was trying to convey to me.'

'Well – best not let us baffle you with science, sir.'

'Water off the dog's back, absolutely. Start baffled, *finish* baffled – what? How long d'you reckon these repairs are going to take?'

'Riggers'll be at it the rest of the day and if necessary all night. I'd expect to have her ready for you by 0900.' Looking at Charlie: 'All right?'

'Let's make that take-off time, if you're sure of it.'

'Fact is, sir –' Hallet to Lachlan – 'as I was telling Holt, we're as keen to get him on his way as he is to be on it. But he mentioned that you have some mystery man who may fly as observer, alternatively might want instruction on engine maintenance, start-ups and so on?'

'Yes.' Sharp nod. 'I do. Can you lay that on?'

'Is he on the base yet?'

'Yes, again. Will you be doing the instructing?'

A nod. 'I've got to be here – supervisory capacity, most of the time fairly idle, so if you'd care to send him along . . .'

'After lunch? Say 1400?'

Hallet checked the time and nodded. 'Perfect. An hour, say, or two hours at most.'

'Be in the wardroom at lunchtime, will you?'

'Well, yes.'

'We can walk back here together after lunch, then.'

'And the – er – pupil . . . ?'

'Me.' Tapping his own chest. 'Didn't tell you this before, Holt, because until last night it wasn't certain, needed clearance at a higher level.'

Staring at him. '*You*'ll be flying with me – sir?'

'Any objection?'

'None at all. Far from it. Hadn't expected it, that's all. You're – er – happy to be taking an air mechanic's place?'

'As you explained it, I have to. Don't I?'

'Well – as a partial solution to what may be a weight and lift problem . . .'

'Settled, then – I'm your mechanic. Useless one, I'm afraid, I'm a duffer when it comes to things mechanical. There'll be room for my bicycle in the observer's cockpit, I imagine?'

'Bicycle.' Hallet showed mild interest. McLachlan added to Charlie, 'Only on the outward trip, won't have to bring it back.' He nodded to the engineer. 'See you later, Hallet.

Now, Holt, my turn to lecture *you*. Very much for your ears only – all right?'

'Understood, sir.'

'Well – on that score, mind telling me what are the so-called "roots" you have in Polegate?'

At their first meeting in the CO's office, Charlie remembered, when he'd asked whether he'd be returning to routine oversea patrolling duties at the Polegate station on completion of this job, old Peeling had said something about putting down roots – effectively (though unknown to Peeling, of course) a reference to Amanda. Charlie glancing at McLachlan as they emerged from the shed into a minor blizzard – or, say, light snow-shower: not a lot of it, but travelling more or less horizontally on the wind it was fairly blinding, certainly would be when one was airborne. At present the flakes were melting as they hit the ground, but you couldn't count on that continuing, and once it really set in – well, it wouldn't help much. Certainly wouldn't have added much to the joys of spring an hour ago. He said, squinting into it, 'One thing, before I answer that, sir – you're going to need a flying-suit, like this one. Called a Sidcot. Darned cold up there, you'll find. I'll make out a chit and get the CO to authorise it.'

'I'd be grateful. Thank you.'

'I'll have it sent along to your cabin. The "roots", though – the answer is I don't talk shop to her, don't intend to, and if I did I doubt she'd listen.'

'Very well. You'd be amazed, though, how much does leak out through idle chat. Wife or lady friend swears she won't say a word, then decides that telling a "best friend" or two couldn't do any harm – she'd tell *them* in the strictest confidence, don't you know.' Pausing, the snow swirling around them; out in the centre dark-blue figures were moving at the double to form a handling party for a Coastal that was coming in, its familiar, less-than-beautiful bulbous shape greyish through the curtain of snow. McLachlan added, 'Only way to be safe is not let 'em know anything in the first place. What's this?'

'Snatch-block. For hauling-down and mooring purposes.' He toed it with his boot: an iron block – or pulley – set in concrete flush with the muddy grass. 'In anything like a strong wind, a ship coming in can drop what's called a trail-rope – long hemp cable, much longer than the guys – and the ground party grab hold of it to pull her down, or run ahead of her and use it to hold her bow into the wind. With a direct pull, though, they can be jerked off their feet, flung into the air even – it's happened, men have been killed that way. So, snatch-block like this – see, it opens – shove the bight of the trail-rope in and kick it shut. Then it's not a direct or vertical pull, you can put a whole team on it, tug-of-war style.'

'More than one, is there?'

'Probably a dozen – here and there. Thing is, when a ship's coming in and it's really blowing, if you let her bow go off the wind – hell, the wind takes charge, *anything* can happen.' He changed the subject: 'One thing, sir – the question of security. Chaps were asking me at breakfast what this was all in aid of, and I said – as I remember you suggested – that it's a re-run of last year's experiment with SS-40 – night reconnaissance over the lines.'

'Good. The obvious thing, isn't it? We'll stick to that. But tell me now. Are you reasonably conversant with the current situation on the Western Front?'

'Only from what the papers tell one – and odd gossip, here and there. There's been – oh, third battle of Ypres, hasn't there, since July, and culminating now at Passchendaele – all at a standstill again now, pretty damned horrible, casualty figures quite unbelievable.'

'You can believe them, Holt. And look here – no good beating about the bush, I'm going to speak plainly and frankly, entirely between you and me and the gatepost, eh?'

'Right.'

'The third battle of Ypres should have been terminated long before Passchendaele. Rhymes with "Holy Grail", incidentally, and that's how a certain eminent commander seems to have regarded it. *Enormous* cost in lives and bloody

65

misery, quite unspeakable. And Passchendaele itself – or rather the sea of mud on which the village of Passchendaele used to stand – well, if Haig knows what's made it worthwhile, he's about the only one who does.'

Charlie shaking his head. The snow was mostly melting off his leather flying-suit but it was clinging to McLachlan's coat and cap. The major insisting, 'This isn't defeatist or subversive talk, Holt, it's calling a spade a spade in order to give you a realistic picture of the current state of affairs. Highly relevant to what you and I'll be setting out to do, you see. Tell me, though – Passchendaele apart, what else?'

'The Cambrai offensive. Only – what, a fortnight ago? We heard they were ringing church bells in London. Great breakthrough, one was told, then it got scuppered somehow? Tanks involved in large numbers, weren't they?'

'Was to have been a tank *raid*. Haig's Third Army under General Byng. A raid, no more, no attempt to seize and hold territory. Wouldn't have lasted more than eight or ten hours. Then the concept changed, it got bigger, finally involved III and IV Corps, four hundred tanks and a thousand guns. No preliminary bombardment, tanks in sections of three carrying damn great fascines – timber bundles – to drop into trenches so they could cross them – each tank section thus able to cross three lines of trenches, flattening the wire and blasting strongpoints in between and behind 'em. Infantry following up of course. Kick-off 0620 November twentieth – yes, just over a fortnight ago – and thanks to the absence of any preliminary bombardment, for the first time in living memory the Huns had no warning. And it *worked*. Smashed through the Hindenburg Line on a six-mile front – everywhere except at one point, a place called Flesquières.'

'Flesquières . . .'

'Mean something to you?'

'Man I knew was killed there.'

'I'm sorry. Anyway, it failed there because the divisional commander in that section's a blithering idiot, and by the second day it was failing everywhere else because – incredibly

66

– we had no reserves at all. Imagine it – troops including tank crews exhausted, out of fuel and ammo, and no backup, no support at all – they'd punched a hole right through the Hun lines and there was no way they could take advantage of it. Huns got their wits together and began reoccupying points they'd been driven out of, and on the thirtieth counter-attacked in tremendous strength and a hurricane of gas and smoke-shell. So, back to the start-line, after – well, you're right, on the twentieth the church bells had been deafening.'

Charlie nodded. No comment of his would have contributed anything. That Coastal was down now, being walked towards the sheds by the dark-clad teams around it; the snow had whitened its flanks and tail and was beginning to settle on the field now, he realised.

McLachlan said, 'And that's where we are now. Having lost practically every yard we'd won at such horrific cost. I have maps with me, I'll show you – the stalemated lines we'll be flying over. But now – strategic *probabilities*, Holt. How General von Ludendorff will be seeing his prospects and future moves. Any guesses?'

'He must know it can't be long before the Yanks get into it in strength. So I'd *guess* . . .'

'You'd guess right – Yanks have to be the key to it. Especially since the French are virtually played out – half a dozen mutinies in the last six or eight months – and we're stretched thin, covering a lot of what was their ground as well as our own. To be fair to Haig, that was probably the bee in his bonnet in going on and on at Passchendaele – keeping the Hun busy, take pressure off the Frogs. So we and the Canadians advance seven miles at the cost of 265,000 men and the Frogs call that Britain fighting to the last Frenchman. Eh?' He went on, 'Contrast that to the fact that with the collapse of the Russian and Roumanian fronts Ludendorff has a huge windfall of reinforcements available to him now. Forty divisions, no less. What he must be seeing through that monocle of his is that he's got at least a chance of knocking us out before the Americans get into it with their huge resources and fresh, keen armies – and if he *doesn't*, he'll lose the war. It means he's got to move pretty fast – really not waste any time at all – otherwise be pipped at the post. Question is, *where* will he attack, and how soon?' A sideways glance, gloved forefinger wiping snow from one eye: 'Be quite something to know that, wouldn't it?'

Charlie nodded. '*Wouldn't* it. I suppose military intelligence—'

'We're about to be joined.' Movement of the head, indicating the station's first lieutenant, that under-sized games-addict, approaching from the direction of the administration block in company with a much taller man whom Charlie recognised as the CO, whom he'd met briefly – 'making his number' as it was called – when he'd arrived yesterday. McLachlan had stopped, gaining a few more seconds' privacy. 'Continue with this later. In a nutshell, though, Ludendorff must know that this next spring Germany either wins or loses. He's got to move fast and strike hard. And now hear *this*, Holt – around the middle of last month, in a château close to the Franco-Belgian border, vicinity of Mons, he presided over a conference of all his army and divisional commanders and their staffs. Purely military assembly – no Kaiser, no Crown Prince, no Hindenburg either. Just soldiers. Wouldn't have minded being a fly on *that* wall, eh?'

Charlie qualified, '*German*-speaking fly.'

'There was one – who apparently shot his mouth off afterwards. And we – you and I – are going to bring out the person to whom he shot it off.' That sharp nod again, gleam of the hawkish eyes. 'Put *that* in your pipe and smoke it!'

6

So the outcome of the war itself might hang on the success of this operation, Charlie realised. It was a staggering and also frightening thought. With so much at stake, McLachlan or whoever gave him his orders was going to press on with it come hell or high water, accept *any* degree of risk.

But – holy smoke – if one made a job of it, managed to bring back intelligence of that quality and significance . . .

In any case, he'd had it darned easy this far. A small amount of hazard now and then – like this morning's snarl-up, for instance – but on the whole it was all a bit of a lark. Discomfort of sorts from time to time – like getting half-frozen on those long oversea patrols, and bumped around in bad weather, quite often hungry – but not in even the tiniest or remotest way comparable to the horrors that millions of one's countrymen were enduring – or had endured – as touched on briefly this morning with McLachlan. Think of *those* fellows. Think of the score to date. Grand total – well, God knew, one heard and read all sorts of figures, but on the Somme one remembered hearing – at the start of it – 60,000 casualties in one day. Men blown apart, torn apart, drowned in liquid mud or sniped while stuck in mud. Mules and horses as well as men simply disappearing under mud. In the last few months – 3rd Ypres and Passchendaele – as McLachlan had said, more than a quarter of a million men.

Don Bishop's former CO had given Amanda that figure,

and told her, 'Could well be revised upwards.' Comfort for her, that Don might be only one of that great mass of dead? Oh, but he hadn't been – the Cambrai offensive had been a comparatively small, short-lived thing. In which he – Don Bishop – needn't have taken part. But think of it – having for whatever reason actually *wangled* his way into it, to have caught his packet almost immediately – automatically, inevitably. As one had read not long ago in some newspaper, that a subaltern drafted to the Front now – or whenever that was, a few months ago maybe – had a life expectation on average of three weeks. Not that Bishop had been a subaltern, or even a combatant, strictly speaking.

Charlie immobile as a stuck pig, lost in thought and imagery of that hell on earth, halfway through divesting himself of his Sidcot suit prior to getting cleaned up and shifted into uniform and then over to the wardroom mess for a beer or two before lunch, a chat and a few laughs. Well – even in the trenches there'd be laughs, they wouldn't begrudge one *that*. He was in motion again now, thoughts returning to their starting point – hell or high water, *any* risk . . .

Except those that could be foreseen and either avoided or reduced. In other words, make sure that McLachlan acquired some understanding of what could be done and what could not. From that angle it mightn't be a bad thing at all that he was coming along – as distinct from issuing instructions, wishing one the best of luck and later dutifully attending the memorial service.

Come on now, Charlie, you aren't dead yet . . .

Checking the time: 1140. Wrapped in a towel, then, shuffling along to the washplace, thinking that McLachlan, having spent half an hour socialising with the CO, would probably be unpacking and stowing whatever gear he'd brought with him. Brice, the first lieutenant, had said he'd arrange for the issue of a Sidcot on temporary loan, so that was taken care of. Half an hour or so to kill, therefore.

Ring Amanda?

* * *

In the wardroom bar, McLachlan was telling Hallet and some others, 'A house in Mayfire was hit and burnt to the ground, I heard, but otherwise they fell in open spaces. Hardly worth the buggers' while, you'd think – especially as ack-ack brought three of 'em down.'

'Did you see any of it, sir?'

'No. I was in dreamland, thankfully. Ah, Holt. They say I can sign chits for drinks, so what'll you have?'

'Thank you, sir. A beer, please.' The steward had heard and was drawing one. Charlie nodding to a fellow pilot, flight lieutenant by name of Graham whom he'd last seen about ten days ago at Pulham. He asked him, 'That your Coastal I saw bumbling in this morning, Joe?'

'In the snow-shower.' A nod. 'Why aren't you at Polegate?'

'Getting a new ship – right off the stocks. SSP-7.'

'Another SSP? Thought they'd called a halt on those. Reckon she'll stay up, do you?'

'Never know. Always hope, isn't there.'

'Congratulations, though. U-boat, we heard?'

'Sheer blooming luck. Honest. Surfaced right under me. And if my observer hadn't been damn quick on it—'

'Never mind all that, you *got* it, and you'll be in for a gong, eh? But guess who was asking after you, this last Sunday evening?'

'First Sea Lord?' The steward had brought him his beer. 'Thanks.' He shook his head. 'No. I give up.'

'Molly, no less!'

'Molly. Well. Great heavens . . .'

'When I was a lad –' Hallet, sipping gin and water – 'ladies' names were not bruited about in the mess.'

'So who's bruiting?'

'More to the point, who's Molly?'

'Really.' Graham looked appalled. 'Anyone who has to ask *that* . . .'

Charlie told McLachlan, 'Barmaid at the Royal in Great Yarmouth. Cheers, sir.'

'So you have roots in Great Yarmouth too, Holt?'

He fingered beer froth off his lip. 'Charming girl, but not quite in the same category, sir.'

'Ah.' Flicker of an eyebrow. 'Polegate's serious then, is it?'

'Well.' He shrugged, evaded with, 'Actually more Eastbourne than Polegate.'

The Marine smiled. 'All right, Holt. Tell me, though – any brothers or sisters?'

'One sister. Older than me. Helping my father out on his farm – in Herefordshire, that is.'

'Big farm?'

'For that part of the country, yes, it is. He started small, then bought out neighbours, one after another.'

'So that's what *you*'ll do, eventually.'

'No, I don't think so. You married, sir?'

'Oh Lord, yes. Lord, yes.' A casual glance around: conversation was general, they were on their own. 'But listen – have you given any thought to what I was telling you out there?'

'Certainly have. It's tremendous, isn't it. If we can pull it off, why—'

'As tremendous an issue as one could imagine. Potentially gigantic. And we *will* pull it off – don't let yourself doubt that for a moment. Talk later, eh? I got the monkey-suit, by the way. Meet for a good long talk at – five-thirty, say?'

'Could we make that six o'clock, sir?'

Because Amanda hadn't been in her office when he'd called. She'd likely be out most of the day, some male colleague had informed him; between five-thirty and six might be his best chance of catching her. Would he like to leave a message?

No, he wouldn't – hadn't. He wanted to hear her voice, was all, wanted her to know he was thinking of her, and as she had no telephone at the cottage he could only get her in working hours. Anyway, McLachlan agreed readily enough – six o'clock. That little man – Brice – had offered him the use of an office adjacent to his own in the administration block, where they could talk without interference or others' flapping ears.

* * *

He got through to her at five-forty.

'Charlie. How lovely. I was told someone had called and wouldn't leave his name, *hoped* it might be you. We've been having one of our mad days here. Where are you?'

'Hop and a skip away, that's all. Mandy – *terrific* to hear your voice. All I wanted, really.'

'Absence making the heart . . .'

'*Doesn't* it, though!'

'I'm glad. You wouldn't believe how glad. Going well, is it? The weekend . . .'

'Afraid not. Wish it could be, but . . .'

'When would you guess? Tuesday? Wednesday?'

'Really can't tell. Won't be hanging around, I promise you. Had a slight setback today, unfortunately, that's what's scuppered any hope of getting back for the weekend, but—'

'What kind of setback, Charlie?'

'Oh – a technicality. Barring any repetitions, *might* be with you Tuesday. Can't call you during the weekend at all, of course, but—'

'Sunday I'm lunching with the Sneems. Don's chief, as was. They have a very nice house near Seaford.'

'Man who got you the job – or his wife did. Well, good. How'll you get there?'

'He'll either come for me, or send a car, or fix a lift – some other guest. They're very kind. She, especially. I think *he* just does what he's told. Anyway . . .'

'Yes. Won't keep you. I'll call tomorrow – as long as I'm on the ground at some time during the day. Look after yourself, Mandy. And if we *can* make it back by Tuesday—'

'*We?*'

'Well – I'm not flying solo, you know. But Monday, even – not totally impossible. I'll have a better notion of it when I call tomorrow. Any snow down there yet?'

'No. Although it's cold enough. You've got some, have you . . . Charlie, I'm *so* happy that you miss me, and—'

'Show you how *much* I've missed you – Tuesday for sure, best not tempt fate saying Monday.'

*　　*　　*

73

McLachlan told him at six, 'I am now a fully qualified amateur grease-monkey, you'll be glad to hear.'

'Got the rudiments of it, have you, sir?'

'The beginnings, anyway. Astounded at the complexity of *your* job, I might say – all those lines to the valves.'

'Two lines to each valve, one to open it and one to shut it, does make for a bit of confusion sometimes. Mind you, having them in different colours helps quite a lot.'

'In the dark?'

'Well, no – but having acquired a certain familiarity with them, as one does soon enough . . . Any case, *you* won't—'

'Damn right, I won't. As well to have some idea of what goes on, though. One thing – I was about to ask, and something else cropped up – what's the rip-cord for?'

'Ripping-panel on top of the envelope. Yank on that cord, you open it – the envelope – right up. Lets out all the gas, whole thing collapses. Emergency use when on or close to the ground and in serious trouble – huge gusty wind, for instance. Once you've ripped there's nothing you can do except pack the whole thing on to a tender – or a train, whatever – and get it to wherever it can be sewn up again.' He added, 'Goes without saying, in France, no ripping. Long walk home, eh?'

'Be somewhat alarming to pull it in error at a few thousand feet, say.'

'Couldn't happen. Absolutely couldn't.' He took a bit of a plunge: 'Changing the subject, one thing I've been meaning to put to you, sir – you do realise that when the ship's airborne it's her pilot who's in command?'

'My dear fellow – I wouldn't try to tell you how to fly the blessed thing!'

'No. Right. Only thought I should mention it.'

'I command the operation, you command the vehicle. Clear enough. In any case –' jerking the door open, taking a look outside then pulling it shut again – 'for the time being I'm a trainee, aren't I.' He came back to the desk. 'But here and now I want to tell you what it's about, where we're going and why. Smoke?'

'Thank you, sir.' McLachlan had one going already, and while Charlie lit up he began unfolding a map of France, spreading it on the bare-topped desk. Northern France, Charlie saw: top-left corner, Calais; bottom right, Charleroi and Mauberge; centre, Lille; upper right, Brussels. The major's forefinger poked at Mons.

'See here – Franco-Belgian border. The scale of this is one centimetre to two kilometres. And here' – bottom, left of centre – 'Arras. To the west of which – forty kilometres roughly – a small town called Frévent, and five kilometres further west the village or hamlet of Boubers-sur-Canche. That's where we'll be flying *from*.'

'From there to Mons?'

'Not quite. That locality, but – here's Mons, and our target is – *here*.'

Charlie peered at the name of a town on the French side of the border.

'Bavay.'

'Near there. We'll switch to a larger scale in a minute. This is to give you the overall view – straight-line route from Boubers to this district being – as near as dammit – hundred and twelve kilometres.'

'Seventy miles. Take us – well, depending on the wind and conditions generally – hour and a half, two hours.'

'I thought you could make about fifty knots?'

'With no headwind – fifty land-miles per hour, let's say as maximum. But they've "silenced" the engine, which has to involve some loss of power, and on top of that if we want to be as quiet as possible we won't be bashing along at anything like full throttle. Got to find our way, too – if there's cloud – ten to one there will be – and we have to come down fairly low to spot landmarks, I'd throttle back as much as the wind permitted. *Everything* depends on the wind – also factors such as cloud and moon, of course. Wouldn't be realistic to count on more than thirty knots.'

'Call it two hours, then.'

'With luck and favourable conditions might do better, but—'

'Take off as soon as it's dark – say five pm GMT – get there and land about seven. Take off then by – say five am – land back at Boubers seven ack-emma. On that basis or something like it I'd have as much as ten hours on the ground.'

'On your bicycle.'

'As you say. But as a rough idea of the timing, let's work on that?'

He nodded. 'This pencilled line is the front, I take it?'

'Yes. So we'll cross it just to the south of Arras, then pass south of Valenciennes. Small alteration to port there to leave Bavay to starboard?'

'Perhaps. What navigational aids along our route, I wonder.' Looking closely at the map, he wasn't seeing any, except towns and villages which might or might not be (a) visible, (b) identifiable. Especially as you'd need to stay up out of sight and sound range. 'No rivers of any size . . .'

'No big ones that I know of. Except – well, at Arras, this one – the Scarpe – but you won't need it, will you, you'll see Arras itself, I'd imagine? Perhaps La Sensée here – at right-angles across your course. Then south of Valenciennes, this one, the Rhonelle. Never heard of it. But rivers show up in moonlight, right? We might ask for advice on that – on landmarks including rivers – from the RFC. They have a Handley-Page squadron based not far from Boubers-sur-Canche. Handley-Pages are the largest bomber aircraft we've got – correct?'

'Largest anyone's got.'

'I know of this particular squadron because one proposal – made in London a couple of days ago – is for a diversionary bombing raid on the railway marshalling yards at Namur. See – here. Major rail junction for war supplies from Germany – the Ruhr, especially. All right, fifty miles east of *our* area of operations, but on precisely the same line of approach. Huns in and around Bavay and Bellignies would have been hearing aircraft overhead for some time before we'd be there; hearing us they'd have no reason to think we were actually paying them a visit. A straggler passing over like the others did. And Namur's an entirely believable target, sort of thing those fellows are doing now in any case. The overlords are looking into it, anyway, and I'm rather inclined to push it – what do you say?'

'I'd say it's a thumping good idea. However much quieter they've made her, our approach won't be anything like noiseless. And when we're getting her right down to land – well, crikey . . . No, I'd say that's a top-hole scheme, sir.'

'Good. But tell me – how vulnerable are we to air attack, I mean by Gerry fighters?'

'If they find us, we don't stand a chance.'

'So how come you patrol fairly safely over the Channel day in, day out?'

'Out of Hun fighters' range, sir. Other side of the Dover Strait's a different matter. They've airfields anywhere on the wrong side of Niewpoort – at Zeebrugge – so off North Foreland, for instance – well, we lost a Coastal off Dover, back in April. Brandenburg fighter seaplanes are the chief menace – or they *were* – over those waters, anyway.'

'But you do have a Lewis gun?'

'It's main use is for exploding or puncturing floating mines. Otherwise, it's not as much use as you might think – especially not against small, fast, highly manoeuvrable and better-armed attackers. Not sure we *will* carry one, anyway – with the weight and lift problem – and no one in the for'ard cockpit anyway, just your bicycle.'

'Your view is we shouldn't take one, then?'

'On the whole – for those practical reasons, and the fact the gun and a couple of belts of .303 weigh forty pounds, which we'd save. Huns do put night fighters up, I gather, but only when they know there's something on. Our best chance is simply not to be heard or spotted.'

'But if a raid on Namur *is* laid on . . .' McLachlan rubbing his jaw, hawk's eyes blinking. 'We don't have to decide until we're about ready to leave Polegate, anyway.' Charlie let that go, with a private reservation that when that time came it would be a decision solely for SSP-7's skipper to make.

Leatherneck rattling on with 'But as we can't yet put a date on either Polegate or France – I'm thinking of the moon now: it's currently waning, and today's the sixth – so suppose we're at Polegate by Tuesday, practise night landings and/or take-offs the rest of the week – wouldn't want longer than that, would you? Cross over to France on the Saturday – fifteenth, right?'

'Coming up to the moonless period.'

'Advantages and disadvantages, I suppose . . .'

'Given the choice, I'd go for a moonless night. Navigationally a bit tricky, maybe, but – what I was saying before, if we have to come down to see under low cloud – well, the darker the better, if towns or villages show lights and I can tell one from another – which is a big "if", certainly, but with careful preparation – a track-chart, you might call it, and weather conditions allowing me to keep a fairly accurate DR – dead-reckoning position, that is.' He wagged his head. 'Sorry – thinking aloud – but what that comes down to is having a good notion of our speed over the ground, so as to stick to a schedule I'd work out in advance. And – yes, listen to this, sir – you're right, this moon *is* on its last legs, and if we could get over to France a bit sooner, be there with everything on the top line for a moonless night *and* weather conditions reasonably favourable . . . See, we don't need three, four days at Polegate, anyway – two, say. And if we got there Monday rather than Tuesday, then over to France on Thursday – today week?'

'Barring further accidents or defects, of course.'

'Oh, certainly.' Crossing fingers. 'But that way we'd be giving ourselves some possible choice of weather conditions. If necessary waiting a day or two; alternatively, if it looks good, just bat straight off!'

Drawing hard on the last inch of his cigarette. It was a Players, and he'd enjoyed it; all he had were Woodbines. He'd been economising lately: suppers in Eastbourne didn't come all that cheap, and he had no resources beyond his pay, which his father, although he could well have afforded to, declined 'as a matter of principle' to supplement. *Given you better schooling than I had, boy, and now you're earning a damn sight more than I did at your age* . . . All right, that's the way the old swine saw it – who gave a damn. Charlie stubbed the Players out in the brass base of a four-inch shell. McLachlan was unfolding another map, the large-scale one no doubt, Mons and that frontier area. Charlie asked him, 'Can you say exactly where you'd want me to put her down?'

'Not exactly, no. Roughly – yes, of course. Within certain limits, the choice must be yours, mustn't it.' Hands spread, smoothing the map out, then using a propelling pencil's tip as pointer. 'See that village?'

Charlie got it in focus. 'Bellignies?'

'That's the place. Actually, *Bellignies*.' Correcting Charlie's French pronunciation. 'See Hergies – and Hon-Hergies?'

'Hergies. Oh, yes.'

'The Hon is a river. Little one – I doubt you'd see it from the air – not without a moon, anyway. But here, now – Taisnières-sur-Hon. That's very much of interest to us. I gather you don't have much French?'

'None at all, sir. Except for "*bonjaw*", "*common tally voo*" and "*parly voo Ongly*".'

'Luckily I have a little more than that. In fact I speak it adequately – and I get by reasonably well in German. It's why I'm in this job. Partly. And this' – forefinger circling over those villages – 'is the area to which we must have access. That's to say *I* must, on my bike. You've got landing problems to sort out, all of which is very much your business. All I can say is, the closer we can be to *this* place – Taisnières-sur-Hon – the better, from my point of view.'

'Scale of this map . . .'

'One centimetre to two hundred and fifty metres. Call it yards if you like, we don't have to be that pernickety.'

'Very large areas of forest . . .'

'Forêt de Mormal. Most of it's to the south of Bavay here, but, as you can see, large enough patches all over. Around Bellignies, between that and Hon-Hergies here – a straggle of it around Taisnières, but not enough to be of much use

'– and this much bigger area here . . . See this long straggle of a village?'

Charlie read its name. Malplaquet. 'Something familiar about that. A battle? Duke of Marlborough?'

'Bloodiest battle of the eighteenth century. 1709. As you say, Marlborough – in alliance with Eugene, Prince of Savoy – fighting the French, naturally. French under Louis the Fourteenth. Huge mass of cavalry, Marlborough had, but – well, neither side taking any prisoners, simply carnage.' He shrugged. 'We've done better since, of course.'

'The Somme.'

'Quite. Here, though, to get at the enemy that great horde of cavalry had first to fight its way through these miles of forest.' His hand encircled the whole area. 'Forêt de Mormal.'

'At a glance, *this* spot mightn't be too bad.' In the forest southeast of Malplaquet, what looked like a very large clearing open to the south. At least, *partially* open to the south. You'd be surrounded by forest except for that gap, which on the scale of 250 metres to a centimetre looked to be about 300 yards wide. Might handle that all right, he thought. And inside, you'd have open ground measuring about a thousand yards east to west, five or six hundred north to south. Pointing at it: 'If we could come in from the south, and set her down in here. In through this gap then ideally around to starboard – wind permitting. Easier saying it than doing it, of course: and for all we know it might be blowing half a gale. But given reasonably good conditions – trail-rope with a grapnel on it maybe. Entrance that wide, then practically all-round screening . . . Wind direction anything from say nor'-nor'west to northeast – I mean I could adjust the exact line of approach, d'you see?'

'I'll mark it for you.' Small pencil cross in the middle. 'Wouldn't be bad for me at all – the distance from there to Taisnières. Ideal, in fact. But have a long, close look, take your time over it, see what alternatives . . . Might have more than one in mind, allowing for different wind directions – for a westerly, for instance?'

'There's a building here . . .'

'Farmstead. "Farm of the wood of the Abbess", that says. Could be just that – a working farm – or a ruin, or stuffed with Huns. RFC might tell us – 207 Squadron might know about it already, alternatively might take a gander at it for us.' He made a note, checking the map reference and adding, 'That's the Handley-Page bomber-squadron based at Ligescourt, about fifteen miles west of our field at Boubers-sur-Canche. Enough geography for the time being, I'll give you some background now. You'll have heard of Nurse Edith Cavell, I suppose?'

7

Friday, December 7th. This flight was to be a rerun of yesterday's. Simply to fly, manoeuvre around – climb, descend, turn left and right, steer a straight course over a few miles, turn and fly back again. And make sure she could turn under full rudder without falling apart. He was sure she *would* be all right, having revisited her last night with McLachlan and Hallet after dinner in the mess, checked out the new rigging plan and seen the work in progress. Now he and McLachlan had met for breakfast in the wardroom at eight, both of them in flying gear and the major as keen as mustard, only asking whether one ever got airsick. Charlie had told him yes, in rough weather, high winds, with the ship being banged around, it had been known; but there was no wind this morning, only clear sky and a hard frost that would affect the ship's lift. He'd explained, 'When the gas is much warmer than the air around it, you get what's called "false lift". Can be a help, if you want to whizz up fast. Need to watch it, though.' Jerking a thumb: 'Sun's getting up now anyway, warm the place up a bit.'

He'd clammed up after that; breakfast was never a conversational meal on airship stations, no more than it was in wardrooms afloat, for that matter. In any case, what was in both their minds couldn't be discussed in public. In Charlie's, for instance, recollection of the major's breaking off a long discourse last evening to point again

82

at the village of Bellignies, telling him, 'Should've mentioned – the château here is where Ludendorff held that planning conference. Belongs to a noble French family by name du Croy – the Princess Marie du Croy being a friend and associate of Edith Cavell, hand-in-glove with her, as in fact she confessed at her trial, in aiding the escape of British and French soldiers via Brussels and over the border into Holland. Which is where our courier came from, incidentally, although you don't need to know all that – he came to London to alert us to the existence of this girl and the intelligence she'd swap for being brought out, you see.'

'Sorry – you've rather lost me, sir. Girl, you say . . .'

The hawk's eye, and a twist of the lips. 'Not scared of girls, are you, Holt?'

'Not as a rule.'

'Glad to hear it. Anyway – listen. After the battles of Mons and Charleroi – 1914, remember? – the Forêt de Mormal was thick with British and French survivors, wounded and otherwise, in hiding and being hunted by the Germans. The Princess du Croy had turned her château into a Red Cross hospital, these chaps were filtering in or being brought along by local country people, she was taking them in, nursing and sheltering them, and as they became fit transferring them to Brussels – to Edith Cavell, who sent them on their way to the Dutch border. That's where *she* came into it, and where the chaps she helped came *from*. The girl I'm now telling you about was a trainee nurse – probationer – under Edith C, and after the bust-up – arrests, trial, and Edith's murder by firing-squad – she returned to Taisnières, which is where she and her mother had lived, I think pretty well all the girl's life. The Princess du Croy had been instrumental in getting her taken on for training by her friend Edith, you see. The girl's name is Hilde. Hilde Martens. It seems she has a German friend – a *leutnant* – who's based at the château and was present in some capacity at that conference, and he spilt the beans to her. No doubt in some unguarded moment, eh?'

Charlie had nodded. 'And it's this girl we're hoping to bring out. But you said *two* people?'

'Yes. She and her mother – who's in some way crippled. The girl won't say a word unless we bring them both out, that's her price. Mum's English-born, apparently, might be in danger if it became known to the Huns – especially in view of Hilde's Cavell connection, I suppose. Huns don't like us much, you know. Prime example is the 1915 death sentence for Edith Cavell, but only fifteen years' hard labour for Princess du Croy. Well – I say *only*, but it can't be any picnic, can it, especially for a woman with that sort of background. Whose younger brother, incidentally – Prince Réginald – is running the intelligence-gleaning service which passed us the tip about Hilde Martens. He'd sent a courier in to the Bellignies district, very much his own – that's to say Réginald's – home ground, to nose around for any whispers of what might have transpired at Ludendorff's conference. Oh, yes, there's a manor house a couple of miles from the château, and he – the courier, also Prince Réginald, I think – knows the woman who owns it and lives there. The Prince would know her, of course – he and she must have been close neighbours, until he skipped and his sister was arrested. But the manor's used by the Huns as overflow accommodation when the château's chock-a-block with generals and suchlike. Woman's name begins with "S" – I've a note of it elsewhere. I'll be mugging all this up, of course, before we set off. And the girl, Hilde – oh, this is it, she works for Madame S, and – wait a minute – correction. I've got it straight now – Hilde told Madame S that her young *leutnant* had shot his mouth off – trying to impress her, no doubt – and Madame S got a message out to Prince Reggie. *That's* how it all started. You're pretty well in the picture now. Rather more than you need to be, actually – *I'll* be coping with what you might call the social scene.'

'On your bike.'

'As you say. For getting to the girl and her mum at Taisnières, anyway. Getting her and a crippled old woman back to wherever you'll have parked the ship is something else, obviously. Farm-cart, perhaps. Or whatever I can find or the girl can offer. Thing is, it's been decided that we should simply blow in and get them. No word in advance to her or to Madame S, or even to Prince Réginald in Holland, as there's reason to doubt the strength of their security. And certainly, by not giving them any reason to think we're doing a damn thing – well, security's one hundred percent, one side of it we *don't* have to worry about, eh?'

'No advance contact at all?'

'None. It was quite hotly debated, but that's the decision. The alternative would have been to inform Prince Réginald, who might then have sent his courier back in, but—'

'No question of getting help from locals, then. That's *my* interest – as a possible solution to the problems of putting her down unaided. But, all right . . .'

'You're thinking of a reception party. Handlers, or . . .'

'Something of that sort. Doubtful value, I admit, but—'

'With security vitally important, you see – you'd need to give them the exact place, date and time – and as you say, doubtful value – some bunch of rustics with little or no idea idea of what's wanted.'

'I suppose.' He'd shrugged. 'Anyway, we'll manage somehow.'

'Of *course* we will.' The nod of certainty again. As if he knew even the first thing about landing an airship in the dark without any handling party. What it came down to was that he was determined it *should* be achievable – Charlie could blooming well *make* it so.

They were chatting again now, after that properly silent breakfast, on their way across the frozen field to the airship sheds. McLachlan grousing that the leather helmet he'd been supplied with was too tight, Charlie assuring him that it would stretch, that new ones always felt tight to start with.

'Why are these called Sidcot suits?'

'Because they were invented by a man called Sidney Cotton. Australian, RNAS.'

'Well. We live and learn.' McLachlan pointed: 'Your ship's handlers, I suppose?'

A couple of dozen of them, in coats or oilskins and rubber boots, converging towards SSP-7's shed. Combatting the cold by swinging their arms about, beating gloved hands together, collective breath rising like steam above them. But the sun *was* poking up, there behind the sheds and windbreaks and the Silicol gas plant that was identical to the one at Polegate.

'You think less than an hour, this flight?'

'Yes. Then they'll check her over before we go up again – *way* up – this afternoon. As we would have yesterday.'

'Back on the ground about ten, then. But I'll have to leave you to it this afternoon. Various points to be gone into in London – arrangements for Boubers-sur-Canche, and what we want from the RFC. Best set in motion right away, and discussed face-to-face rather than on the telephone. Take a *real* mechanic up with you this afternoon, eh?'

'I'll arrange it now with Hallet.'

'And I'll be with you again tomorrow, having set all that in motion.'

'But detail of the Handley-Page diversionary attack to be left for us to discuss with them when we get there?'

'Has to be – we won't have a date or timing until then, will we. In outline, though – as I've noted it – we're suggesting they pass within a few miles of Bavay *en route* to and from Namur. And either pass over us at Boubers before we take off, or make a dog-leg around the north side of Valenciennes – that's if they want to take off later than we do. So we can fly at whatever height suits *us.*'

'And the Boubers arrangements, as discussed last night.'

'Mechanics and riggers, tools, engine spares, tentage, fuel, gas – what else, specifically?'

'Check it over before you push off, shall we?' Charlie had been having a few ideas, during the night and early morning, and some of them he'd already discussed with Hallet. There was a tremendous amount of planning and preparation, he'd begun to realise. At first sight – well, just hop aboard, buzz over to France, pick a dark night (or a moonlit one) for a quick flip across the lines; but it wasn't like that at all. Most of the planning came into McLachlan's brief, but Charlie as pilot needed at least to be consulted in a lot of that. That was Hallet now, he saw, emerging from the shed through the crowd of airmen who'd just reached it; spotting them, he raised a hand in greeting and turned back in. Time – eight-fifty. When they joined him inside, under the loom of what he'd said some of his team were calling 'the black beauty', he asked McLachlan, 'Fit for the plumber's role, Major?'

McLachlan shaking his head, growling, 'Plumber of extremely limited ability, you'll have realised.'

'I'm sure you'll have no problems, anyway.' Meaning that he was confident the ship was sound now, and telling Charlie then, 'I've put out a query about yellow dope. For the voicepipe, Berriman's proposing plywood – if you don't mind the "pipe" being rectangular?'

'Preferably of small cross-section – couple of inches, say?'

'A voicepipe's an excellent notion.' McLachlan hadn't heard of it until now; it was one of the things Charlie had talked to Hallet about last night, when he'd revisited the shed before turning in, studied the rigging plan and seen the work already half-completed. He'd hesitated over the voicepipe idea, torn between the likely benefits of being able to communicate with his passenger and the possibility of said passenger not being able to resist the temptation to pass orders through it. By and large though it would be best to have it: the passenger could call for help or advice if he needed any. Which he certainly might. Cocking an eyebrow now: 'But *yellow* dope?'

'Beech trees. As mentioned in that soldier's notes. Cheyney?' He glanced around, saw that only Hallet was in earshot, and was talking to a PO rigger now. Cheyney was the name of a former lieutenant of the 2nd Dragoon Guards who'd been cut off from his unit during the retreat from Mons and had gone into hiding in the forest, gathering around him a group of about forty soldiers and preparing for guerilla action of some kind – to fight their way out, whatever. But when the Germans had begun hunting them with dogs he'd turned his party in to the mayor of Bavay, who'd placed them in Red Cross care and then formally notified the local *kommandantur*, and they'd had the luck to end up as POWs instead of being shot out of hand, which apparently had been closer to the norm. Cheyney himself had later escaped and made it back to England, and his file had been turned up by McLachlan's people, who'd then had him brought back from Flanders – a lieutenant-colonel now – and questioned him about the forest and that area generally, and any local personalities he'd met or known of who might be of assistance. He'd met the now absent – imprisoned – Princess du Croy, for instance, and Madame 'S' – a name which McLachlan found in his notes at that point and which turned out to be de Semeillions; and one detail of Cheyney's account of it all had been that 90 per cent of the Forêt de Mormal was beech, the rest of it oak.

Charlie continuing to McLachlan, 'See, if we were delayed, still on the ground in daylight – please God we won't be – but anyway, beeches are about the only trees still with some leaves on this time of year, aren't they? Yellow or russet. I thought streaks or splashes of that on her topsides – *if* any's obtainable. As camouflage to fox any overflying Huns, of course. Remote possibility, maybe—'

'I'd certainly hope so.' McLachlan still looking startled. 'Sitting out a whole day – if we were stuck there in daylight at all we'd have to stay put until dark, wouldn't we?' Shake of the head. 'Your province, rather, but—'

Hallet, rejoining them, nodded towards the car. 'Ready when you are.'

The same observer/wireless operator, Charlie saw. He called to him, 'Taking your life in your hands *again*, Crookshank?'

McLachlan managed the start-up procedure well enough, and the flight went well – over the same course as yesterday's, and making the same one-eighty-degree turn without any snapping of wires. A new defect did show up – the control lines to the rudder had had to be rerigged and weren't in balance, so that steering a straight course meant seemingly carrying a few degrees of helm. It could be rectified easily enough before the afternoon flight, in any case. Back on the ground Charlie asked Hallet, 'Make a start on the voice-pipe, too?'

'This evening, more like. They'll be knocking it up in the chippy's shop meanwhile.' McLachlan hadn't shut off the petrol cock above the engine. He'd climbed out, leaving it open – Charlie could see it from where he was standing, the T-top of it in line with the pipe instead of at right angles to it. The chief artificer – Berriman – was up there now, shutting it and for good measure the two higher ones as well, where fuel lines ran from each tank to their junction above the lower one. Nobody said anything, and McLachlan didn't see it or realise there was anything he should have done and hadn't. Charlie told Hallet, 'I need to see your chippy, too. But listen – Major McLachlan can't be with us this afternoon. Borrow one of your AMs, can I?'

'Of course.' Looking across the shed, and pointing: 'Just the man for you.' He called, 'Stavely – here a minute.'

Boiler-suited, coming from a stripped-down engine on a test-bed. Shortish, squarish, heavy-jawed; small, suspicious eyes moving from the engineer lieutenant to Charlie and McLachlan and then back again. Like a young bull's, those eyes: a young bull wondering which one of these three to charge. Nodding to the engineer then: 'Sir?'

'Chief Artificer mentioned that you were chocker, not having got off the ground much lately.'

'Fact, I've not, sir.'

'Your lucky day, then. SSP-7 this afternoon with Flight Lieutenant Holt, height trial, take-off at two.'

'Aye – thank ye, sir.' Less a smile than a look of cautious satisfaction. Speculative glance at McLachlan, as if wondering what might be wrong with him.

Charlie said, 'Glad to have you along, Stavely,' and

surprised him with a handshake. 'We'll see if we can find her ceiling. OK?'

See McLachlan on his way, he thought, then visit the ship-wrights, *then* put a call through to Amanda. He and the major having changed out of their flying gear met in the office they'd used yesterday and settled down to review the arrangements to be made – requested, or proposed – at the Admiralty this afternoon. Admiralty or wherever: McLachlan had said next to nothing about that end of it. Charlie querying for a start though, 'Ground crew at Boubers – don't think we put that on the list, but will it be laid on anyway?'

'Will be, yes. Army'll provide it. When we sent SS-40 over, they gave us a subaltern and forty men. That was an entirely military ventue, of course – so, yes, I'll make sure it *is* laid on. But give me your view on this proposed diversionary bombing raid, Holt. I told them we liked the idea, and it found favour at that meeting – a few days ago, this was – but since you and I talked about it I've been wondering, rather. You said Hun fighters have blimps pretty well on toast, right? Lewis guns not much use as a defence – etcetera. Well – if we send Handley-Pages over, buggers'll put night fighters up in droves, won't they?'

'Might, I suppose. But the RFC have been raiding quite deeply into Hun territory of late, one's heard – and getting away with it, supposedly. You might raise that, perhaps – how the RFC see it, pros and cons?'

'Yes. I will. The concept when we discussed it in London was that after they'd passed over our target area – the Bavay district – the sound of one more aero engine might not excite as much interest as it would if the night had been quiet up to then. And when the sound faded – which would be because we'd landed – they might assume we'd passed over as the others had.'

Charlie agreed. 'That's the aspect I like. If there's low cloud so we have to come down low to see what's where, "silenced" engine or not, they'll hear us.' He shrugged. 'In fact they'll be deafened . . . Tell you what, sir. Suggest the bombers take a different route home after they've hit Namur. For instance –' checking on the map – 'south here to Dinant, say, before they turn east?'

'Might not be too keen on that. Especially if there are fighters up. As well as ack-ack and searchlights all alerted by that time.'

'But if the whole purpose is to divert attention—'

'If you were a Handley-Page pilot, would you want to hang on behind the lines any longer than you had to, after dropping your bombs?'

'Dare say not, but—'

'I'll raise it anyway. You have a ruthless streak in you, Holt.'

'But with so much hanging on this operation, sir . . .'

'Yes – I know. Unlikely they'll see it that way, though. Only at the very highest level will anyone have any notion of what's behind this. A recce operation is all that squadron will be told, for instance.' He shrugged. 'But I *will* raise it.'

Charlie was saying – while stuffing his pipe with naval-issue tobacco – 'We *could* do without the Handleys, obviously. Might even be better off on our own, crossing the lines high and unheard, *no* searchlights or ack-ack.'

'Expect to achieve that anyway, don't we? High, inaudible and invisible – isn't that the whole idea?'

'Yes.' He touched the wood of the table. 'Except that the Huns *will* be standing-to, Handleys having stirred 'em up. Chance worth taking anyway – I'd say – for the benefits at the other end.'

'And it's still your preference not to take a Lewis with us – right?'

He nodded, holding a Vesta to the pipe. 'Because we need to save all the weight we can. No gun, no wireless. Take the wireless to Boubers with us maybe, but not on the operation itself. Won't have anyone in the for'ard cockpit to use it or a Lewis anyway. On the way there, one bicycle, on the way back, two females.'

He wondered whether the women might be fat. Possibly not, on wartime rations and Hun occupation. McLachlan was still adding to his notes: in a small, very neat hand, Charlie noticed, total contrast to his own untidy scrawl. Glancing up now, laying down his pencil: 'Anything else?'

The chief shipwright perused the sketch Charlie had made for him.

'Matter what sort of timber we use, sir?'

'No. As long as it's strong and smooth – sandpapered smooth, I suppose – and tapered, so it'll pull out of the trail-rope when I want it to.'

'Oak might be your answer. I got some nice pieces as'd lend 'emselves well enough . . . Two o' these, you say?'

'One as spare, I thought.'

'Two foot long, two-and-a-half-inch diameter the thick end, two-inch the other, thick end flattened with an 'alf-inch 'ole in it. Care to show me how you see it working, sir?'

'Got a bit of line?'

'Well – spunyarn—'

'That'll do.' Looking round for another prop, he saw the ring-shaped handle of a hot glue-pot. Glue was what the workshop smelt of, mostly – that and wood-shavings. 'Are you familiar with scrulex anchors, Chief?'

'I know what they *are*, like.'

'Take this as being the ring on the top of one. Trail-rope's to have an eye – or a bowline, say – in the end of it. The bight of that loop's pushed through into the ring as far as it'll *go* in – like this – and held there by having one of these small spars through it. My finger's the spar now. Follow? Long as the pull's on it and it doesn't break, it's holding fast – eh?'

'But with the weight you might have on it . . .'

'That's why it has to be smooth and tapered, Chief. Incidentally, the hole in the thick end's for securing a long line to it. White Line, I'm thinking of – Italian hemp, three-pound line, say.'

'Twenty-fathom lengths . . .'

'One in number.' Charlie nodded. 'And nothing bigger, because of the weight. Strong enough to wrench the toggle out, and away we go!'

The CPO smiled knowingly. 'Who'd be doing the wrenching, though?'

'The ship would – if I found I couldn't. Turn the line up on some fitting – a round turn on the Lewis mounting, say.'

'Like pulling a tooth . . .'

'Very much like that, Chief!'

'Well.' A nod. 'See what we can do, sir.'

'*Very* much obliged.'

He'd ring Polegate, he thought, for the cordage he was going to need – White Line, a twenty-fathom length of it. Three-pound line meaning that would be the weight of a twenty-fathom hank of it. Might have to get it from the dock-yard at Portsmouth, so Polegate would be the best bet. Talk to Bob Bayley. Ask him to get a couple of scrulex anchors, too – in case Stores were out of them. And an axe, because if the toggle *wouldn't* come out, there'd be nothing for it but to chop away the trail-rope.

Call Amanda, too – before lunch, in case she was out later, as she had been yesterday.

He made a list anyway – axe, scrulexes, grapnel, White Line, blankets, first aid kit. The first three items were (a) heavy, and (b) metallic, so would have to be stowed care-fully prior to swinging the compass – which might be done on the ground at Polegate – and their weight taken into account when roughly calculating the lift. Scrulexes did have to be heavy; they were made of steel, three inches in diameter, were screwed into the ground two feet deep by means of a crowbar through the mooring-ring on top, the ring being screwed down to ground level to provide an extremely solid mooring. A worrying factor meanwhile in regard to weight and lift was that the Belgian girl's mother might be enormous – even on short rations – if she was so disabled that she couldn't move around without assistance. It had been McLachlan's reference to commandeering a farm-cart for that purpose that had put this fear in Charlie's mind; he was trying to convince himself that the old girl might just as likely have some wasting disease, be absolutely skeletal.

Or be like his own mother, who'd been tiny. As well as pretty. And cowed. She'd been dead five years now. How she'd ever brought herself to marry that loud-mouthed bastard . . .

The telephone was in the lobby-entrance to the wardroom bar, and the operator who got the number for him was a female. They had quite a lot of them on some of the naval air stations nowadays, mainly clerical workers, but they seemed usually to be hidden away and were invariably billeted *well* away; when accommodation as distinct from civilian billets was provided for them, it was always as far away across the airfield as it could be.

This one got RNAS Polegate for him first, and the exchange there put him through to Bob Bayley's office, where he left a message with some minion, and after that he had the same girl get Amanda's number for him, mentioning that it was an RAMC depot of some kind – no question of it being a *personal* call – and after a few minutes she told him, 'You're connected, sir.'

'Thank you very much.' There was a Scotsman on the line, and Charlie asked for Mrs Bishop.

'May I enquire who's calling?'

'Is Mrs Bishop not there?'

'She is, but who shall I say is calling?'

'Admiral Sir Cloudsley Shovell, tell her.'

He'd always liked that name. He could hear the Scot mumbling in what might have been disbelieving tones, presumably to Amanda, then her sharp squawk of '*Who?*', before she caught on and must have snatched the 'phone from him – confident enough to open with, 'Charlie?'

He told her, 'Poor chap drowned somewhere off the Scillies two hundred years ago. That's how you knew it couldn't be him, uh? You all right, Mandy?'

'Hundred per cent better than I was a minute ago, despite your crazy—'

'Crazy about your voice – and the picture of you in my mind. But listen – *Monday*. All things being equal, barring accidents or other setbacks, ingrowing toenails or—'

'Talk sense now, Charlie. D'you mean it – Monday, *truly?*'

'As ever is. Can't guess what sort of time, but with any luck I'll be with you that evening.'

'I can't *wait*. Oh, but this is *wonderful* . . . I suppose you can't go the whole hog, make it Sunday?'

'I'd make it tonight, if I could. Make it *now*. Wanted to let you know, anyway – *and* hear your voice. Be at work tomorrow, will you?' Glancing round, seeing Brice, the first lieutenant, obviously waiting to use this 'phone, sucking at an empty pipe and looking testy. Mandy answered that question with 'Saturday mornings I come to work, yes.'

'I'll call then, if I can. Can't be sure of it though, might be flying, and I can't reach you on Sunday, obviously, so *maybe*—'

'Monday. Six-thirty – or earlier, if—'

'Might find me waiting at your door. Howling.'

A whisper, 'Love you, Charlie.'

'Bye . . .'

He hung up, nodded to the little man as he moved away. Wondering whether Amanda would be content with a continuing affair without commitment or talk of love. Or for how long she might. And whether what he felt for her might *not* be love – as well as lust? Although even if it was – what difference? Explain to her that he simply couldn't *afford* to marry? She mightn't believe him, knowing as she must do that his father was fairly rolling in it, thanks to the old swine's questionable auctioneering tactics and having cheated neighbouring farmers right, left and centre in his stealthy acquisitions of surrounding land (this actually she might not know, although her solicitor father most likely did). He'd crowed once, Charlie remembered, 'Get to know on the quiet a bloke's up to his neck in it, and he's got something you want bad – see, you *got* it!' What further philosophical advice might he dispense, Charlie wondered, if his son and heir had been close enough to him in spirit to discuss anything so personal and private as this relationship? Ten to one, something like, 'Don't have to marry 'em all, boy, just because they spread their legs to you! Fact, bloody good reason not to!' Something on those lines. Couldn't be sure of the son *and heir* assumption, either: if he could fix it legally so his beloved Mabel could take over the land, *wouldn't* he?

8

Lust was mutual anyway. Had been in those earlier times, too. Maybe those 'love you Charlies' were the way she justified it to herself. After all, why *should* she love Charlie? Remembering her in Sattery's Imperial Restaurant in Eastbourne this last Tuesday evening, though – Sattery's advertising slogan printed across the top of the menu card being *The House for Quality and Civility. We roast and grind our own Coffee on the Premises. Bedrooms by the Day or Night –* Amanda running a fingertip over this and murmuring, 'Day or night, Charlie! Imagine! If we couldn't wait between the soup and fish?'

Having been married, he supposed, might account for some of it. Then Don insisting on getting himself sent over – as by her own account she'd seen it, walking out on her. Then only a few weeks later, the even greater shock – loss, deprivation, loneliness. And recrimination. Which might actually be directed at herself, in the sense that Don's determination to get to the Front could somehow reflect on her . . . Bishop had been a somewhat withdrawn, silent fellow; might have disappointed her as a lover?

Would *that* send one to the trenches?

Might. If one was excessively conscious of it. Or if she'd *made* him conscious of it.

Charlie had lunched and was now back in his flying gear, heading for the shed and the two pm take-off. The earlier clear sky hadn't lasted, but there were still gaps here and there in grey, fast-moving cloud. Wind on the ground about force 4. It was coolish, all right, but he didn't think cold enough for snow. Odd, to have had that one flurry, day before yesterday, and no more since then, giving one no indication at all of any general trend, leading to how it might be in a week or ten days' time – which weatherwise was all that really mattered: in fact, mattered fairly desperately.

Figures in one's head then linking to it – mental arithmetic, such as weight of car, rigging, engine and fuel, one and a half tons – according to Hallet, so it would be accurate enough – and deduct that from the gross static lift of 85,000 cubic feet of hydrogen gas which would be something under three tons. All right, not quite that much: the 85,000 cubic feet wasn't all gas, it included the ballonets. In mitigation of which one had to bear in mind that despite a much larger than usual envelope, ballonet size had remained the same and was thus proportionately smaller. Roughly, therefore, by rule of thumb and at this stage splitting no hairs, disposable lift say 1.4 tons. From which subtract the weight of two bodies, his and McLachlan's – averaging 160 pounds, say, but call it 350 pounds to include heavy suits and boots – and of course the scrulexes and other bits and pieces – so 500 pounds, say, roughly a quarter of a ton. You were looking at a net disposable lift of about 1.15 tons.

That would be on the way over. On the return trip – touch wood – you'd have the weight of two extra people: 300 pounds? (Hoping to God that mama on her own didn't weigh that much.) But subtract then the weight of the stuff you'd leave behind in the Forêt de Mormal: one bike, one axe, two scrulexes, any unused rations and maybe cordage – trail-rope even, which was a heavy item. You'd have a fair margin of lift then, he thought. But not all *that* much. So no unnecessary valving of gas. If possible, none at all – keep it all where it belonged, inside the envelope. That was a tall order, of course. The problem being to get her down into that clearing – or into *a* clearing, or at least into the close lee of woodland, reasonably swiftly; the obvious way if you excluded valving being to nose down rather steeply under a lot of engine power, shattering the night's peace and alerting every Hun for miles around.

That was probably what he'd have to do, he thought. Those lift and weight figures weren't bad at all, but one had to allow for (a) mama being huge, and (b) weather conditions being bloody awful.

He took her up to 1,000 feet while checking the steering, the rudder wires that had been out of balance. A tightish figure-eight above the field was enough to ensure they'd put that right.

Now for the climb. Trimming her bow-up first by letting air via the scoop and the after crabpot valve into the after ballonet – with the effect of expanding that ballonet or air-bag, driving gas into the fore-part of the envelope, achieving initially a few degrees of bow-up angle, adding 'dynamic lift' to her overall lightness and natural tendency to climb. That was 'static lift': putting up-angle on her, the ship as a whole becoming virtually a hydroplane – the submarine analogy again – or an enormously bigger version of one of her own elevators. Her angle to the horizontal was increasing rapidly: to 30 degrees, 35. Charlie and the other two in their cockpit seats virtually on their backs – 40 degrees, almost. Rate of climb with the throttle fairly wide open – 750 feet per minute. Coming up to 780, 800 – which was fast enough, as she nosed up into thinner air, gas consequently expanding. Height 5,000. He valved out some air. In cloud now: from the ground it had looked like a thinnish layer but it was thick enough when you were in it, a grey flow of wet and cold allowing no sight of sky above, none of the ground either. Holding a few degrees of port rudder on her so as to keep circling more or less above the field; later he'd make up for drift by flying up-wind until he found it. Height 6,000. Watching every-thing at once: altimeter, statascope, inclinometer, compass, gas-pressure gauge (manometer), airspeed indicator and rev counter; and the lines to all the valves, so forth.

A glance back at Stavely the AM as they lifted upward out of cloud on which pale sunlight gleamed, thin as a result of being filtered through other, higher cloud – 7,000 feet. Stavely's bullish eyes blinking behind his goggles: no thumbs-up sign, not even a nod – not a demonstrative sort of character, not one for the conventional but usually meaningless gestures. A Yorkshireman, of course. Head turning away as he looked back into the roar and thrust of engine power, watching points that were *his* to watch. Charlie valving air from the after ballonet again now, to trim her towards an even keel. Checking the inclinometer while using the elevators as well in the levelling process, also easing the throttle somewhat. SSP-7 passing 8,000 feet – in cloud again – but one could dispense with the powered lift, let her more or less float on up – more slowly, and in a minute or two or three she'd be slowing further – towards her ceiling. Eight five hundred feet, still ascending at several hundred per minute, at about one-third throttle and on an even keel fore and aft now. He shut that crabpot valve.

Crookshank, the observer, was leaning forward, only the top of his head in sight, probably in wireless communication with the field; sound trials were scheduled for Sunday, but Hallet had undertaken to keep a listening-watch during this flight and note the time at which they passed out of his range of hearing. By his reckoning that should have been at about 5,000 – as it had been, apparently, in the case of SS-40, that earlier experiment. Or it may have been 4,000. SSP-7 now at 8,850 – thirteen minutes after starting up from the 1,000 level. Stavely with his head cocked sideways, listening to the engine's slow-speed pounding. Hardly rising, now – 8,950, and – 9,000. *Any advances on 9,000?* Well, there *was* – 9,100 . . .

But – automatic gas valves lifting. Hearing it, and checking the manometer. All making perfect sense: in present conditions she was at her ceiling, as near as dammit. Atmospheric conditions took a hand in it, of course. This was a lot higher than one needed, anyway. Except maybe to evade Hun fighters. Here and now, why waste more gas, when you didn't have to? Shrugging agreement with himself, and the elevator-control wheel the other way now to put some dive on her. Almost at once – within seconds – those top valves snapped shut and the shrill hiss of escaping hydrogen cut off. Hold on to your hats, boys, down we go . . . Air into the for'ard ballonet, and within a few seconds feeling the start of the growing bow-down angle. Pushing himself back in his seat as the angle steepened, taking rudder off because that made it simpler as well as avoiding having to impose unnecessary strains through a corkscrewing descent. The other two would be jamming themselves back too; by now, they would. Nose-down angle of 20 degrees – 25. Charlie's left hand inching the throttle open to make the most of the dynamic dive-effect – thinking again now of how it might be achieved in France, combining dynamic downward thrust with increased weight resulting from intake of air via the scoop. An impromptu exercise, in fact, in getting down fast while *not* valving out any gas. Thirty-degree bow-down angle: Crookshank's head and shoulders and forward-braced arms in view, as compared to only the back of his head a minute ago, and – quick glance back and up – meeting AM Stavely's somewhat bovine, goggled gaze. Needle sliding around to 40 degrees bow-down, height 8,200 – 8,000 – 7,750 – 7,500.

This was a very fast descent. Hold her as she is now, he thought – 42 degrees. She'd take 50 without rupturing herself, he guessed, but this was acrobatic enough, was definitely more 'dive' than 'descent', would be putting a lot of strain on just about all of her. In France one wouldn't be starting from 9,000 but when (or if) one was over the forest – and knew it – one would certainly want to get her down, out of sight and sound, as fast as possible. From 6,000, say – or 5,000, if engine-noise trials confirmed that at that height she wasn't audible. Might in fact have to commit oneself to a dive like this *without* knowing precisely where one was. At 6,000 now and fairly rushing earthward, through the lower, broken conglomeration of grey cloud. In France, he thought, might make it a swift drop from 5,000 to about

1,000 and hold on at that height for long enough to get some sort of fix – heaven knew exactly how, from *what*, but by that time (touch wood) all would have been revealed – in consultation with navigators from that Handley squadron, for instance. Having (please God as well as please RFC) established one's position, one would take her on down as quietly as ship and weather conditions would permit.

Heart in mouth, he thought. Checking all his dials and the ship's behaviour now, but still imagining *that* descent. Descent into forest in the dark and very likely a much stronger wind than one had here and now. Weather would be the key to it, would make it all manageable or *un*manageable. Five thousand: all right, ease up a little. Keeping the crabpots shut but adjusting the amount of angle that was being held on her by the elevators – turning the elevator wheel back towards him with his right hand, and throttling back with his left. Four seven-fifty. Out of the cloud now but in thicker air, gas in the envelope contracting – compressed – ship becoming heavier therefore and still dropping steadily but less steeply. Actually still *some* cloud around, wisps and whorls of it here and there, but in between that scattering, views of green fields and greenish woods, greys and browns of villages and roads, and plough reddish-brown, even pink. Four thousand feet – no interruptions to the views now, looking for landmarks, to pick up his bearings and set a course for home.

There, for instance—

Spray – and a stink of petrol – from behind and overhead. Lightning-quick glance round and back: goggles already wet from floating moisture in the cloud immediately bathed in gasoline and resultant bands of colour. Stavely on his feet, clinging one-handed to suspension wire and climbing up, up on the seat of his cockpit, with the wind at Christ only knew how many pounds per square inch blasting at him. He pointed – at the cock on the fuel line, which – or in the vicinity of which – was where the spray was spurting from. Charlie turning back to his own job, pushing the throttle shut, engine spluttering and dying – Stavely would have cut off the fuel supply by now, more or less simultaneously – at least, would have if that cock was functioning – and valving out air from the for'ard ballonet to get her bow up, level her at – all right, 3,200. Thanking his stars that the rush of ice-cold air would now be cooling that stopped engine, over which at least some of that stuff must have been spraying. Noise and wind-effect considerably reduced now, although if Stavely hadn't had one hand clamped like a lobster's claw to the overhead suspension, as like as not he'd have gone flying like a leaf. Some *leaf*, Charlie thought – about as solid and competent as they came, his shortish legs straddling his cockpit's seat, that hand/arm locked on the humming steel-wire rope, other hand with a box-spanner in it working at a junction in the fuel line – half-inch copper pipe – a few inches below the cock. Which was why there had to be a joint there in the first place – insertion of brass tap assembly in copper piping – in which the screw-fitting had inexplicably worked loose.

Height 3,000, SSP-7 descending in a slow and dignified manner on an even keel; with no power on her, just ballooning. All wind noise now, wind howling in suspension wires and rigging generally. Charlie met Crookshank's slighty wide-eyed, open-mouthed stare as he looked back and up at the AM, then again at Charlie, who pointed in the direction of the w/t equipment and mimed Morse dotting and dashing – to let them know on the base what was – to coin a phrase – holding them up, up here. Crookshank got the message, which in present circumstances he'd have heard all right if Charlie had screamed it over the wind's howl; since normally you couldn't, he hadn't bothered, was accustomed to communicating by sign-language. Screaming could engender fear, in any case, and he didn't know Crookshank all that well. Although he'd taken that last shenanigan calmly enough.

One knew Stavely well enough now, though: watching him again (after checking height just under 3,000, rate of descent about a hundred a minute), seeing that he'd separated the pipe from the lower part of the brass tap assembly,

103

and transferred the spanner into the hand he was holding on with. Now pushing the loosened brass screw-ring up so he could bind the top end of the copper tube with sticky tape – one of the items an airborne AM always had close to hand. One-handed, it still wasn't easy: having in ages past done similar things oneself, one knew it. He was leaving the loose end of tape hanging now, dragging from a trouser pocket a seaman's knife on a lanyard and opening its blade with his teeth. That in itself was something of an accomplishment. Now cutting the tape – the reel of it somehow palmed and the knife still open but hanging by its lanyard. Smoothing the wrapping of tape with his thumb, then jerking the pipe back into its former vertical position below the cock. That had been easy enough; the hard bit was forcing the screw-ring down on to it, positioning it then getting the spanner back out of the other hand and working with it – as a hammer to start with, tapping the ring down over the pipe's padded end, before the screwing process. Charlie brought his gauntleted hands up to applaud all this, but the AM didn't look his way, hadn't finished, producing the reel of tape again and binding the outside of the join with about a yard of it. Then – this had taken about another three minutes, and the ship was at 2,350 feet – he reopened the cock and at last found time to look down at Charlie, who signalled by miming action with a crank handle: OK, start her up.

Valving out gas then – as the big engine spluttered into life – having hung around up here long enough and being concerned to get her down before that joint came apart again. Pretty sure anyway that in present conditions and the open field to land in he *could* have got her down without valving.

Hallet told him, 'We couldn't hear you at five thousand feet. Admittedly there were other sources of noise which perhaps you wouldn't get over the trenches in the middle of the night. If that's, as I imagine, when your recce flights or bicycle rides are to take place?'

Charlie shrugged. 'Only ack-ack and the racket of Hun fighters.'

'Oh, surely. Why we had to silence the engine for you, I'm sure. Seriously, Holt, what I'm saying is that going by first indications—'

'You *have* as good as silenced it. That's capital.'

They were watching the dismantling by AMs of the fuel lines from SSP-7's twin petrol tanks to their junction under her belly and their continuance in a single pipe from that junction via the cock to the engine. The whole assembly was being replaced, in case of other weaknesses in it. On Hallet's insistence; this further incident had plainly embarrassed him. And might well have, Charlie thought. It wasn't the main issue in *his* thinking, though – there were several, one or two of which he was deliberately postponing, could only deal with later; here and now the immediate concern was that having McLachlan in that rear cockpit wasn't going to be any damn use to anyone. As he himself should have foreseen, of course, and saw now very clearly. A mischance like this afternoon's could occur at any time – as could any of a couple of dozen other emergency situations – and neither McLachlan nor any other untrained man would come anywhere near to handling it as calmly and efficiently as Stavely had. You could say that such a man was worth his weight in gold, and you'd be right – but not actually surprised, because that was what he was there *for*, had been selected and trained for, not only in terms of technical ability but in other qualities as well.

Conclusion: he, Charlie, was not going to take SSP-7 on this outing without having an AM like Stavely in that after cockpit. Preferably Stavely himself – whom he'd congratulated quietly and sincerely, but as yet said nothing to beyond that. Feeling bound to speak to McLachlan about it first. Speak to Hallet about it too, of course, when it came to borrowing Stavely. A further consequence of all this, though, was that McLachlan would have to occupy the observer's cockpit – as the original intention had been, so he could hardly object to this. In fact he'd be relieved – he'd freely admitted that he had no mechanical interest or ability.

There'd be no wireless or ancilliary w/t equipment in the for'ard cockpit – no accumulator either, which was a weighty item on its own – and no Lewis gun, so he'd have damn-all to do, except, if he wanted, to simply observe. There'd be no slight or disparagement in putting this to him, either – practical necessity was all; his skills and daring would be called for only when you got him there. He was more than welcome to that end of it.

By the same token, however, spacious cockpit cleared of all its usual clutter, he'd have to share it – well, with his bike, that was one thing, and the blankets and stuff of course, but on the way back with the girl and her mother. Who'd be wrapped *in* the blankets, and who'd better *not* be enormous. Although if she was – well, too bad. You'd trim the ship to balance the extra weight for'ard, anyway. And rely heavily on dynamic lift, as well as most likely needing every single one of those 85,000 cubic feet of the static kind. From that angle, this afternoon's flight had been more than worthwhile. She'd gone half as high again as she'd ever need to in France, had got up there fast enough and down again even faster, and without valving any gas at all. *Should* therefore be able to cope with an extra body. All right – and say again – weather conditions could make it all a hell of a lot more difficult, could make valving unavoidable. That would be the worst of all – if by enforced valving you reduced static lift to the extent that with so much extra load you'd have problems getting off the ground.

No option, anyway. One extra body – one *more* – and the for'ard cockpit to be crammed to capacity. Which McLachlan might not find all that comfortable, although this specially-built car's cockpits were much roomier than in the ordinary run of SS cars – Maurice Farmans or Armstrongs especially, but even the new SSZs. Which one might see as having been remarkably prescient of the Admiralty – or of McLachlan's colleagues, whoever they were – in having insisted on those modifications.

The major might have mum on his lap, or beside him and the girl on his lap. Depending on – well, dimensions.

And the major's preference, maybe. Something for him to decide on, anyway. A much bigger issue in Charlie's mind meanwhile was the idea he'd had earlier of timing the bombers' flight to Namur so as to have them passing over Bavay/Bellignies at exactly the same time as SSP-7 was landing there. If that could be arranged it would make landing under power a lot less dangerous, although there'd be other, associated risks to guard against. Collision, for instance, or merely getting in each other's way. Pehaps one flight of Handleys batting over – at whatever height they flew at on such missions – then SSP-7 making her dive from cloud-level to about a thousand feet, then a second flight of Handleys, their noise as it were containing SSP-7's and fading eastward as she herself sank down into that forest clearing.

Hallet, who'd been up on one of the ladders, checking progress, rejoined Charlie now.

'We'll be fitting your voicepipe by and by.' Pointing: 'Prefabricated bits and pieces of it there, d'you see.'

He'd forgotten the voicepipe. His turn to be embarrassed. 'Look, as it happens – I should have mentioned – there could be a change in that. I have to discuss it with McLachlan, but—'

'Discuss what?'

He thought, *Why* wait to discuss it? No matter what, I'm not taking him up in the AM's cockpit. Staring at the engineer, accepting that there wasn't time to pussyfoot around.

'No. I'll just tell him what we're doing. Thing is – slight change of plan – can you fit it instead between my cockpit and the observer's?'

'We *could*, but . . .'

'I've come to my senses, is what this amounts to. If what happened this afternoon had happened when he'd been there instead of Stavely – Christ, I'd have had to leave her ballooning, climb over the top and fix it myself. That or anything else like it. In some circumstances it could be *bloody* awkward – having to do two jobs at once and in two different

107

places, even. What it comes down to is, I *must* have a pukka AM with me.'

'I agree, you should. Thought so all the time. I suppose you want Stavely.'

'Well – if you could spare him—'

Glumly: 'One of my best hands.'

'Only thing is, from where this started, him hankering to get off the ground . . .'

'True.' Hallet shrugged. 'And all right, if he wants to volunteer—'

'I'd be extremely grateful. You're right, he'd have to volunteer – understand it could be slightly hazardous. For the time being, though, keep it under your hat, don't mention it to him yet?'

'Until you've cleared it with McLachlan.'

'Exactly.'

'I'd ask a favour in return from you and him, then.'

Charlie nodded. 'What kind of favour?'

'Expected back tonight, is he?'

'Hoped he would be. To be here for the speed trial tomorrow.'

'Speed trial tomorrow, engine-noise trials Sunday. Well – as I was telling you – the check we ran this afternoon gave what seemed to be satisfactory results. Should have been too – we don't foul up on *everything*, believe it or not. You'll want more detailed answers, obviously, different heights and speeds, although in point of fact there'd be no improvement we could make, she's as quiet as she'll ever be – uh?'

'Dispense with further sound trials, are you saying?'

'I'm suggesting you might run them at Polegate – or on the way down there, even. Fact is, we really do need this shed-space – as I did mention.'

'For the SSZs.'

'Exactly. First one's about ready – certainly will be by Sunday.'

'You want us to clear out on Sunday, then?'

'If you could. If your leatherneck accomplice—'

'He'll like it. Sooner the better is how he'll react to that. Only thing is – depending on successful trials tomorrow . . .'

'Of *course*.'

'Full engine service thereafter? Full-power trials, after all . . .'

'Agreed. So—'

'But also – sorry, this is something new.' Pointing at SSP-7's bow. 'An Eta patch *there*. On the underside and as far for'ard as will allow me a straight haul between it and the car.' A hand on the plumber's elbow, taking him in that direction, also out of earshot of others. 'For a purpose I needn't go into – but a D-ring in it, nothing else. It's simply to reeve a long line through – D-ring as fairlead, line returning to the car.'

'From the ground, you mean.'

'In action – yes. But also, some large cleats on the side of the car – starboard side, I think – set in a triangle, say, three of them about three feet apart, where the line'll be carried and turned up. Abreast my cockpit and in reach from it, and with room for – oh, say a hundred and twenty feet of two-inch line. Follow?'

'Easier if you *would* explain its purpose.'

'All right. Call it a head-rope. Or backspring, effectively. Suppose I'm taking off with no ground crew and a strong wind.' He might have added, but didn't, 'with trees all round'. 'See – taking off at moderate revs – enough to cope with the wind, no more – while the head-rope's holding her bow into the wind – uh?'

'You'd reckon to get her up to the length of this head-rope?'

'*Right*. Then cast off and open the throttle.'

'So you're expecting to be on the ground in a somewhat confined space – at a guess I'd say woodland.'

'Well . . .'

'You'd hope to have her at treetop height before you let go, wouldn't you? Have the *car* at treetop height, that is. Yes.' He was looking up at her forepart. 'About *there*, say. Just abaft the strengthening.' Meaning the radial pattern of bamboo slats encircling her fat, black snout. 'Or as close to that as does allow for a straight haul.'

Clear of the curvature of her forepart there, he meant.

McLachlan asked him that night, 'What's an Eta patch when it's at home?'

Charlie had just come from the shed, where he'd been to check on the progress of that job and the refitting of the fuel-supply line – which had been completed. He explained to the major now, 'What everything's fixed to, on the envelope. You've seen dozens of 'em, taken them for granted. It's a flap of fabric that's sewn and stuck on, holding a thing called a D-ring – steel, D-shaped, flat side against the envelope. Called Eta because it was first used on an airship of that name in 1913, thereabouts. Before that, everything – rigging and anything else – was secured to a net that enclosed the envelope. Anyway, your day went well you say, sir?'

'It's all in hand, yes. Sit over there, shall we . . .'

They were in the wardroom, its only other occupants at this rather late hour a foursome playing bridge. McLachlan, who'd only just got back from London – and had ordered whisky and sodas – told Charlie quietly, 'We're to call on the CO of 207 Squadron at Ligescourt as soon as we get over there. He'll have had orders from his Wing by then – to cooperate with us over the attack on Namur, and so forth. And his maproom will be available to us. Ground crew at Boubers-sur-Canche, that's arranged—'

'Scotch and soda, sir.'

'Ah. Capital.' He sighed the steward's chit. 'Thank you.' Raising his glass to Charlie, then: 'Here's to it, Holt. How was *your* day?'

9

Hilde was on her way home to Taisnières, not because it was Saturday, which was a working day as far as she was concerned, but because the doctor, old Fressin, was coming out from Bavay to see her mother, and Elise de Semeillions had told her, 'Of course you must be there, Hilde. And look – such a long way to come back, why not stay with her then, take the day off?'

'Madame's very kind – as always . . .'

'Such nonsense.' Elise was in her early thirties – tall, red-haired and blue-eyed, with a strong, well-boned face and the lithe figure of a horsewoman. Which she was. The Manoir had a biggish stableyard, although most of its boxes were now unoccupied; resident at this time were only two hunters and three ponies, one of which was used mainly in the trap. Elise telling Hilde, 'Madame is very much aware of how hard you work to keep this old place up to scratch, that's the simple truth of it.' An arm around Hilde's shoulders for a moment, squeezing her. 'Couldn't do without you, Hilde. You know that and so do we.' The 'we' meaning herself and the two girls, currently boarders at the convent at le Quesnoy but coming home soon for holidays. Perhaps also including her husband, Jean-Claud de Semeillions, a colonel of *chasseurs* but in some POW camp in Germany the past three years.

The Manoir Hergies was a kilometre and a half north-west of Hergies itself. Hilde was cycling through the village now – turning right into the main street, then after 200 metres left on to the road for Hon-Hergies. Fields on both sides, stream- and river-fed lakes ahead and to the right, low stone bridges here and there, a few old men and boys crouched over home-made rods. There was no ice on the lakes as yet, although the air felt cold enough for it. She swung to the left, now two rights, on to a road which at this point was raised on an embankment above fields which were not infrequently flooded. Could have found her way blindfold if she'd had to; the old bike might even have made it on its own. Over a bridge – river on her left then and an almost perfectly circular lake off to her right. Leaving the embankment road, curving left, free-wheeling, a long, wide curve that brought her into Hon-Hergies.

Left here, on to a wider road bisecting the village. Half a kilometre of small shops and houses – with not much in any of them, some boarded-up. There were some market stalls in the church square though, and a scattering of women round them. Two little girls playing with an iron hoop, and a donkey-cart laden with rolls of carpet. Hilde pedalling on, saluting people she knew – women, children and oldies mostly. She knew every one of them, was practically on her own doorstep by this time. At the next corner, left . . .

Motorcar approaching from the right, though – from the direction of Bavay. She waited, with one foot on the ground. It was a tarred road and the car was coming quite fast – German car, Germans in it, those high-peaked caps. Waiting for it to pass, as always she took care not to show interest in its occupants – being averse to their taking reciprocal interest in *her*, which experience had taught her could happen.

Ketteler had seen her though, and was telling the driver to stop, pull in. There was another officer in the back, and the soldier-driver, who'd passed the intersection but was braking, stopping about twenty metres from it – in the direction in which she'd be going. She didn't *think* the other man was the policeman, Koch, but couldn't see him now;

since he was one person she definitely did *not* want to meet again, she'd guessed it might be. Ketteler had got out, was stooping at that rear window, talking to the man inside and throwing quick glances in her direction. Hilde moving forward slowly. Not much wanting this encounter, even with Ketteler. She needed to cross to the other side in any case, and a passing cartload of manure was giving her reason not to be too quick about it. Then it was out of the way, trailing its stink behind it, and Ketteler was coming around the back of the car – a Renault, camouflage-painted in the German Army style – and it was starting away, leaving him. So the other one couldn't have been Koch, she guessed: he wouldn't have wanted to leave Ketteler here with her, and Ketteler probably wouldn't have been so undiplomatic as to have suggested it. Or even maybe to have recognised her. She was walking up that right-hand side now, pushing the bike, and the car was already fifty metres away; Ketteler leaning on his stick, waiting for her.

Smiling. 'Going anywhere special, Hilde?'

'Home. Doctor's coming to see my mother – may be there already, I can't stop.' Shaking her dark head. 'What'll *you* do now? Walk back to Bellignies?'

'Is there an emergency with your mother?'

'No. Routine visit, more or less, but—'

'That's good. I'm glad. No, I'm not walking back, the car'll be coming back this way, picking me up here – or hereabouts. I could walk some of the way with you – may I?'

'You *could*, but as I say, the doctor may be there already, and I do need to see him, so . . .'

'I'd slow you down.'

'Well, you *would*.'

'Wearing that smart coat again, I see.'

'It keeps me warm. That's what it's for. Real December weather coming at last, uh?'

'Indeed. But Hilde – allow me one minute. I have – had – a purpose in waylaying you. Something I have to warn you about. Spare me literally one minute?'

She shrugged acquiesence. There was a wide grass verge at this point and a stone bridge over the river, both banks of which were lined with willows. She'd crossed it further back, just before the village; to the right from here it curved southward and then east, describing more or less a semi-circle around the west and south of Taisnières. Ketteler pointing with his stick: 'Pretty, isn't it? Isn't that a truly peaceful scene?' Seeing her impatience, and nodding. 'All right. Sorry. In a few words, anyway, Hauptmann Koch—'

'I thought that might have been him in the car with you.'

'No – and this is the point. He's gone to Brussels. A *working* weekend, Hilde, to consult files and he was hoping individuals who were involved in the Cavell investigation. This is aimed at you, of course – and you rather gave him the idea, I'm afraid, by mentioning that you and the other probationers had been interrogated.'

She swallowed. Not looking at him, facing down-river, as he was. A shake of the head. 'Why he should bother, God knows. Anyway, nothing I can do about it – and he'll get nothing out of it, there's nothing *there* – that could involve *me*, I mean.'

'I thought you should be forewarned, that's all.'

'After more than two years, though – and the fact one wasn't detained, or as far as I know even accused of anything . . . Is it because you and I see each other occasionally that he's persecuting me?'

'I shouldn't think so. Although with his suspicions of you he wouldn't approve of our friendship. No, he wasn't even aware I knew you, until he mentioned your name. But he's the sort who wouldn't be able to sleep if he thought anyone might be getting away with anything. He'd also *love* to come up with something where others have drawn blank. While as grounds for all this there's the fact you spend most of your time in a house which is used as accommodation for officers attending high-level conferences at the château. That's his *raison d'etre* – security around the château. It would justify his sticking his nose into the background of anyone who ever passes even within a kilometre of the place, you see; and as you *were* associated with both Nurse Cavell and the Princess du Croy—'

'As a pupil in one case and an employee in the other. Now as a housekeeper, who in her spare time tends a sick mother. Couldn't you convince him of these simple truths for me?'

'I *have* assured him of all that. But—'

'He thinks you're biased in my favour.'

'Yes. Actually, very much so.'

'That you're blinded by passion? Does he think we're secret lovers?'

'Oh.' Glancing away again. 'He may do.' Shake of the head. 'You want to be on your way.'

'*Must* be. You've had a lot more than your one minute. But thanks for the warning, Otto. Will you – what's the phrase – keep me informed?'

'But listen – another half-minute . . . Hilde, since the fellow *is* in Brussels, might we see each other? A walk in the forest, perhaps, a picnic? I could get the use of that Renault – find *some* excuse . . .'

'Mightn't that be dangerous? From what you've just been saying, if word got back to him—'

'I don't see how it could. And I do want to discuss all of this with you – at greater length please than sixty, ninety seconds. Please?'

'When?'

'Tomorrow? We have our parade in the morning, but after that—'

'Sundays I always spend with *Maman*. She'd be upset if I didn't – if she realised, that is. Some days she barely wakes – well, as I've told you, but—'

'*This* afternoon, then?'

She thought about it. 'Wouldn't want you coming to the house. We might meet somewhere else, though. If you really think it's safe. I'd come by bike, and—'

'Where?' He flushed with excitement. 'What time?'

'Bois de la Basse Lanière?' She waved a hand eastward. 'Vicinity of the lake in the middle there? Say – two o'clock?'

'Make it earlier – could you?'

'Half-past one, then. As long as the doctor's been and gone, which – yes, surely by one he will have – and it's not far, so . . .'

'One-thirty. Hilde, that's marvellous!'

'But listen – you want to talk, fine. Just don't imagine—'

'Don't say it. Even *think* it.' Laughing, and flushed with excitement. *He* was thinking it, all right.

Why, she asked herself, had she agreed to meet him?

Because I quite like him, he has charm and his attentions flatter me, and I'm lonely as well as – rather nervous now. Scared of Koch and what he might dig up, needing to keep Otto on my side, at least get warning from him of what Koch's up to. Like this today; and then please God reassurance when Koch comes back from Brussels empty-handed. Yes, that *please*.

But just stay friends with him – nothing more than that.

Explain that taking a German for a lover gets any woman into disrepute with her own people. Windows smashed, filth through the letterbox, shopkeepers refusing service, jeering in the streets. Well, he knows that's how it is. Didn't have to ask me why I didn't want him collecting me in that car this afternoon, did he?

If the going got rough, he mightn't be all that much use anyway, Koch being a rank senior to him, and with a policeman's special powers. Otto would be looking after number one in any case. Unless he's stupid – which he's not.

Sensitive, more than stupid. A bit of a ninny, even.

At the corner she turned to wave to him where he was standing and looking after her, back there at the bridge. He waved back. Both of us, she thought, with this afternoon's meeting in mind. Might be uncertainties in his, as there were in hers. Thinking about it, she guessed that given the least encouragement he'd go for it: go mindless first, then – well, maybe start thinking afterwards. Or before, even. Two ways that cat might jump: one, getting what he wanted – and had tried quite hard to get that evening when he'd been fairly staggering and fed her that stuff about General Erich von Ludendorff's offensive, the great German attack that was coming in the early spring, using huge reinforcements that were now being transferred from what had been the Russian front – overwhelming superiority in numbers therefore, attacking on an eighty-mile front extending through Ypres, Armentières, Vimy, Arras, St Quentin and La Fère . . . Or – two – *not* being drunk this time – might even now be having cautionary thoughts, wary of Koch and sensitive to the fact he *had* told her all that stuff which he most certainly should not have, and which if Koch brought things to a head might one way or another come out in the wash.

Koch, please God, *would* draw blank in Brussels. Even if his fellow secret policeman – *Leutnant* Bergen – was still there, at his headquarters in Rue Berlaimont. And as long as the French police spy, Quien, hadn't been induced to blab.

Pedalling southeastward now. Taisnières a kilometre ahead. Dr Fressin would expect to be paid this time. For three visits now. The old goat had several other geriatric patients in the village, would be cycling back to Bavay with his pockets stuffed with money, including most of the fortnight's wages which Elise de Semeillions had paid Hilde this morning. Having a fair notion of where a lot of it might be going. She, Mme de Semeillions, had personally helped look after Hilde's mother when Hilde had been working at the Berkendael, had visited the old woman regularly and acted as banker for her – well, for Hilde. Ensuring that there was always food of some sort in the larder and coal for the stove, she'd almost certainly paid a bill or two without mentioning it when the money wasn't coming in all that fast. She'd paid old Fressin too, *must* have done. Despite assuring Hilde both at that time and since that the pittances she'd sent from Brussels in grubby, re-used envelopes truly had covered everything.

A quite extraordinarily kind person. Young enough and full of life but a *grande dame,* indeed. On the money side she'd have known through her friendship with the Princess du Croy, who'd been in close cahoots with *Directrice* Edith Cavell, that the Berkendael probationers were paid practically nothing. In fact she, Hilde, had had freelance earnings on the side which Elise de Semeillions couldn't have known about, might indeed therefore have wondered how Hilde could have spared even the small amounts she did send. She wouldn't have known about the extra income because on that subject Madame Cavell wouldn't have breathed a word to *anyone.* Probationers' pay for their first year had amounted to the grand total of 180 francs, for the second year 240 francs, while for a third year, if Hilde had had one, she'd have been paid 300. One had had one's board and lodging, of course, but there were still certain unavoidable expenses – even such small items as needles and cotton, pencils, shoe repairs, postage stamps. Let alone such wild extravagance as a cup of coffee at *Chez Jules,* a café right next door to the Berkendael in Rue de la Culture and therefore often very tempting. The 180 francs first year's salary, Madame had told them once, was the equivalent in *her* country of £9; she'd added, 'which for a raw trainee—', but then checked herself and admitted sadly, 'No. It's not very much . . .'

She *was* a saint though, that one.

The road ahead jigged slightly to the left and then ran ruler-straight through the village, but before one got that far there was a fork to the right – narrower road, again on an embankment, with the river only about a hundred metres from it. This road curved around the back of the village, and the river curved similarly but further out; the embankment ended before the houses started. Well, it was slightly uphill, this part – and a fact that only once in living memory had the lower houses been flooded. Aimée Martens' cottage was the fourth house along on the right-hand side. Narrow-fronted, it seemed to crouch under the weight of its heavy old slate roof, looked as if any strong blast of wind might send it all sliding into the street, across a pavement so narrow that two people couldn't have walked on it side by side. People walked in the road anyway, there was practically no wheeled traffic: carts and cars tended to go by way of the main street, which was a straighter, wider road.

Hilde, dismounting at a narrow slot of a passage which led down the side of the cottage to its back door, saw that Fressin *was* here. At any rate his bicycle was.

He was in the kitchen with her mother, the old woman on a plum-coloured and threadbare *chaise longue* (which Elise de Semeillions had found for her) and Fressin on a hard chair at the table. A big man, once tall and and broad-shouldered, now stooped and scawny, long limbs asprawl; whereas *Maman* was minute – had always been small, but in recent years had shrunk still further, a good deal of her weight now being in one grotesquely swollen leg. Some disease or infection for which the doctor had no name or explanation but which had set in several years ago. Other than that, she was skin and bone – hands like claws, wrists like sticks. Head turning slowly – probably only because she'd seen the doctor look this way – to blink at Hilde as she came in and pulled the door shut behind her, shedding the old coat and smiling at her mother, crouching to kiss her. The swollen leg was up on the *chaise*, laid out like a great sausage, the other foot on the board floor in a felt slipper, and that raised knee tenting a skirt which Hilde had made for her out of a horse-blanket.

'All right, *Maman*? Not too bad?' A glance round and a nod to Fressin then, who hadn't moved or spoken. 'Doctor. It's been quite a while.' A gesture, then: 'But as you can see . . . Uh?'

'There's really very little I can do. I've examined her, and – well, I can detect no *great* disimprovement from the last time, I'd say.' He shrugged, and added, 'Natural – er – progression.' A nod, and a lowered tone of voice: 'Progressive weakness.' He had a mouth like a squeezed lemon and a few dozen long grey hairs trained across an otherwise bald dome. Watery blue eyes surveying Hilde now. 'You appear to be in good health, mam'selle.'

'I am, thank you. But my mother –' she murmured this – 'really *has* deteriorated, in the last few months. I was hoping you might – well, if there were some tonic or other that—'

'Does she sleep down here?'

'No. Manages to drag herself upstairs – with a little help. Why?'

'With the winter upon us now, you see . . .'

'Her room being directly above this one gets all the benefit of the stove and chimney-flu. With that and several blankets—'

'Does she also drag herself out to the *cabernet d'aisance*?'

'Not often, nowadays.' The outside lavatory, he was referring to. 'Chamberpots, it has to be.'

'You're at home with her here in the evenings, I assume?'

'Nights, yes. Except on rare occasions when I have to work. Even then I usually manage to escape for long enough to – see to her, as may be necessary.'

Aimée Martens croaked, 'You're a good girl Hilde.' She'd said it in English. Adding as they both stared at her in surprise, 'Always done your best for me, I know. I loves you for it, girl.'

The brown eyes closed. Lips slightly parted, spittle bubbling. Thin, pale grey moustache on the ridged upper lip. She was sleeping now, out to the world.

Hilde said quickly, recovering, 'That was English, wasn't it? It's *years* since she spoke any. She learnt it – some – when my father had a job in London – before I was born, that was. But – heavens . . .'

'Quite extraordinary.' Fressin was bolt upright, gazing fixedly at his patient. '*Astonishing*!' Shaking his head – small movements like a twitch – as if having thought about it he didn't believe it could have happened. 'The brain, when by all the signs you'd swear it was – somnolent, as it were – extinguished, even – yet for that moment . . . Do you realise the comment was entirely relevant to what you were then telling me?'

'You understand English, Doctor?'

'A very little. When it's—'

'What did she say, exactly?'

He told her. Adding, 'I understand it when it's spoken slowly and clearly, and simple words – as that *was*, I may say – in contrast to the slurring way she articulates in French.'

'So what can we do for her?'

'*Do* for her.' Almost a sneering tone. Off the chair then, stooping over his patient and gently raising one of her eyelids. Shake of the head then as he straightened; hands to the small of his back as if it pained him. Murmuring, 'Closer to coma than to sleep. She's not hearing me now. What to *do* for her, you ask. I'd say the most important thing is to keep her fed and warm. That really is my best advice. In her fragile condition, if she were to contract influenza – which at her age in any case—'

'Is there no kind of tonic you could prescribe? At the Berkendael, I remember—'

'I could prescribe a tonic, yes. But as you know, medicines are in short supply, and anything of that sort would be expensive.' Glancing around at the wretchedness of the furnishings. 'And not necessarily effective. Perhaps if she could be persuaded to eat a little more. *Bouillons*, for instance – and in the mornings perhaps *bouillie d'avoine.* Easy to take, you see, as well as nourishing. Does she manage to feed herself at all?'

He'd been telling her, in effect, that if her mother could be nursed through the winter, to see perhaps one more spring: 'Don't set your sights any higher than that, mam'selle . . .'

For which advice she'd been obliged to pay him. But thinking of it now – what price a dash across Belgium to the Dutch border, hidden in the back of a lorry or ambulance or whatever else they might come up with? Then at the border itself – what, pick-a-back, or on a stretcher? One had heard that for those who *had* got away to Holland – fit young men, for God's sake, soldiers on the run and youngsters wanting to join up – even for them it had been a marathon. At the frontier itself, for instance, a river to ford and wire to negotiate in pitch darkness, virtually under the feet of patrolling guards and – at this time of year, for sure – freezing cold.

So *how*, for God's sake?

Cycling northeastward out of Taisnières, with a kilometre to cover before the right fork that would take her down to Riez de l'Erelle at the southern end of Malplaquet; telling herself that what she'd asked for was simply unattainable. She herself hadn't realised until now how utterly impossible . . . So even if that man – the messenger who'd come from Prince Réginald and whom Elise de Semeillions had called 'Michel' – even if he *had* managed to get back into Holland, she, Hilde, wasn't likely to hear any more from that quarter. Elise had tried several times to reassure her, telling her that Michel was as cunning as a fox, had got himself in and out several times in recent years, and so forth. It was actually *no* reassurance: even if he did make it back, another doubt was whether her offer to them would be taken seriously in any case, whether they'd believe she did possess the information she'd told him she had. They – Michel's bosses – being the British. And then again, whether the fact she'd put a price on it – her own and her mother's removal to safety – might actually be held against her. They might conclude: *That's what she's really after – all she wants!*

That, plus the fact that even if they were prepared to try to meet her terms, there simply wasn't any way they could. Since obviously she wouldn't move without her mother – which she'd made plain to Michel – and the fact *Maman* was old and crippled.

Forking to the right here. Basse Capellerie off to the right, Haute Capellerie on the left, with more flood-barrier on that side. Otto Ketteler would be taking the lower, straighter road, she guessed, driving himself down from Bellignies and through Bavay. Nursing his fond/lascivious hopes or expectations, obviously. Which faced her with a different problem altogether, an entirely personal one on which she hadn't yet come to any absolutely firm decision. Except that the best answer might be to play for time. Reverting to the big one, therefore, the one that truly and *fundamentally* mattered: if they decided to take a chance on her and on her information being as one might say kosher – Elise de Semeillions *had* assured Michel that she'd known Hilde pretty well all her life and that she was absolutely to be relied on – if they concluded that the information she was offering might even win the war for them, or at least save them from losing it . . .

Well, *what?*

Thoughts swam, collided, ricochetted . . .

Weaving through a herd of cows – six or seven of them, tended by a boy with a stick – she saw one thing they *might* do: send Michel back to persuade her to cough it up *without* conditions. Or maybe offer to bring *her* out, while pointing out the physical impossibility of bringing out *Maman* as well.

If they took that line – well, what? Let it go, just *tell* them, be done with it?

Maybe. In fact – what else?

Passing through Riez de l'Erelle. Outlying patches of forest off to the left and a few buildings, farm buildings mainly, along the road on both sides. Stopping now at the main road which ran north through Malplaquet, up to her left. Cyclists passing: all women, all with baskets on their bikes. Most of them would be on weekend foraging expeditions, visiting farms or street-markets in villages other than their own. She got going again – straight over and into a side street that was a short cut to the untarred forest road, a *route blanche*. From there – a left turn on to it, 200 metres ahead – she'd have about two kilometres to cover. She was hungry, hoped Otto would bring a really decent picnic.

10

Course due west, height 2,000 feet, making good (he reckoned) about 38 mph, while carrying a few degrees of starboard rudder to offset a light breeze from NNW. He'd get a more accurate speed check when he overflew the river Arun and set course for the out station at Slindon, vicinity of Arundel – distance between the rivers Ardur (north of Shoreham) and the Arun on this track being ten and a half miles. He'd taken off from Polegate about an hour ago. There was enough of the old moon left to illuminate the rivers as well as the coastal railway and, about a mile and a half to port, the coastline and soft gleam of sea.

This time last evening he'd been with Amanda in her cottage. It hadn't gone quite as he'd anticipated, that reunion.

'Out station', though, actually meant *mooring*-out station – a sheltered location where blimps could be moored when there wasn't shed-space for them on their airfields. The Slindon one was on the edge of woodland; you moored in the lee of the wood, not in it, but it was similar enough to the terrain in which they'd be putting themselves down in France.

Yesterday, Sunday, after an early breakfast at the Scrubs, to Charlie's surprise McLachlan had come up with a new and, Charlie thought, entirely practical idea on the subject of getting themselves down without any handling party on the ground.

'Holt . . .'

He'd had his nose in a cup of coffee and his mind occupied with plans he'd initiated the day before, for the ship's engine-noise trials to be carried out during the flight down to Polegate on a slightly roundabout route. Two runs over the Scrubs first, both at 5,000 feet but the first at half-throttle and the second flat out, then over the air station at Farnborough at 6,000 feet, and again full throttle – shouldn't be detectable at all, since at that height you were likely to be in cloud – and finally at Polegate, where he'd bring her down from 6,000 with pauses at 5,000, 4,000 and 3,000 at varying engine speeds. Ground observers' reports when collated would give him all he needed – what speeds he could or couldn't safely make at those varying heights over Hun-held territory.

Weather conditions permitting, of course. Engine power having to be matched to winds that might be anything from light airs to gale force. In gale force you ordinarily wouldn't fly, but with the importance that was being attached to this operation, maybe you'd have to.

Frightening notion . . .

McLachlan was still staring at him – frowning slightly. Charlie said, 'Sorry, sir. Thinking about—'

'What *I*'ve been thinking about is our landing without any chaps on the ground, the hazards as you've explained them – very major problem you said it was at one stage – and a possible or at any rate partial solution.'

He held the hawkish eyes, and nodded. 'I'm all ears.'

'You'll bring her down to within a few feet of the ground, you hope with the grapnel on your trail-rope snagged in hedges or undergrowth, and – as you tend to reiterate – the wind state permitting—'

Charlie cut in, 'Wind *is* a vital factor, sir. Sorry if I harp on it rather, but the truth is we have to count on a good measure of plain good luck. I've got to get her down, pretty well static and close enough to the ground for Stavely to jump out and secure her to whatever's handy and strong enough and in the right place, and/or knock in a scrulex for either the new head-rope or—'

125

'Why not Stavely out on one side and me on the other?'

'Well – if you were willing to do that . . .'

'Of course I am. From what you say it'll be a bloody difficult, perhaps even *impossible* otherwise.'

'And two pairs of hands'd be better than one. It'd help enormously. Certainly would. But at the same time create its own new problem. One man's weight removed suddenly at that stage of things presents *a* problem, but double that, and –' he shook his head – 'Christ. Even in the best of weather conditions . . .'

'As you said, though, two pairs of hands . . .'

'Yes. It's swings and roundabouts. Putting it plainly, the danger is that as you jump, she might suddenly shoot up a hunded feet or more!'

'Couldn't you take her in trimmed heavy so that the loss of our weight returns you to the status quo?'

'No. Because we have to be what you might call vertically manoeuvrable. At six thousand feet, no less, to cross the lines – avoiding searchlights and AA fire. Our best defence against Hun fighters, too – we can climb faster than they can, get out of their reach. That's how Zeppelins get away with it over London nine times out of ten: by the time a fighter can struggle up to that height the Hun's higher still – and gone. Anyway, *our* problem . . .'

Gazing at McLachlan, thinking about that sudden loss of weight, equably sudden upward lurch. Lose control at that stage, you could shoot up a *thousand* feet. He and Stavely wouldn't have a hope in hell – they'd be launched into space themselves. And to hold her in control through engine power – you couldn't, couldn't go in at full tilt with trees all round you: needed in fact to be virtually at rest.

On the other hand, to have two of them on the ground for the mooring operation might indeed go some way to solving *that* problem.

Only one answer, therefore. Valve – lose gas – the thing one had been swearing one would *not* do.

McLachlan was pointing at him with his egg spoon. 'There's more to this line of thinking anyway. As far as the actual disembarkation is concerned – what about rope ladders? Primarily in my own interests and Stavely's, I suppose, but I dare say making things rather easier for you – wouldn't *need* to be quite so close to the ground. One ladder from my cockpit and one from Stavely's, so that from even ten or twelve feet—'

'Now that's a *damn* good idea!'

Silence. The Marine decapitating his boiled egg and nodding to himself, pleased to have had his brainwave so well received, and Charlie visualising the detail of it. Rope ladders twelve or fifteen feet long, say, rolled up and secured on the outside of the car. For'ard one on the starboard side and the after one to port – to keep them out of each other's way. You'd need a weight at the foot of each ladder so that when released they'd unroll and drop vertically, not fly out in the wind. Well – what better weight could one have than a scrulex secured horizontally to each ladder's bottom rung, to be detached from it by the users as they reached the ground?

Still have to valve out gas, at that last minute. Back to the further problem that would follow, therefore: getting her up off the ground later in the night with the passengers on board and less disposable lift than you'd started out with. He put down his napkin, nodded to the Marine. One was committed to this, had no option but to see it through, *had* therefore to find solutions. 'Capital notion, sir. I'll get through to Polegate, have a word to Bob Bayley. He'll have put a few things in hand already – he can add rope ladders to his list.'

The ladders themselves would be the only extra weight, and only a few pounds at that. They were to be fitted tomorrow, Tuesday – having arrived this afternoon from Chatham dockyard, which happened to be where Bayley had cadged them from. They were too long, he'd said, were having to be cut down to the required length and respliced, with suitable lashings provided for the scrulexes.

With the widening loops of the Arun a mile or two abaft

the beam to port, from the point where the railway bridged it, he brought her round to starboard – to northwest – with about three miles to go. Twelve minutes past eight. The ten and a half miles between the rivers had been covered in sixteen minutes, so the ship's speed over that stretch at about two-thirds throttle had been as near as dammit 40 mph. She was flying closer to the wind now and carrying no helm – at 1,000 feet, beginning a further descent to 500. Wishing he had the ladders now for *this* exercise. He, McLachlan and Stavely had discussed the sort of drill they'd follow, would be trying it out with ladders tomorrow in the vicinity of Polegate in daylight, then at this time again tomorrow evening in the dark. Tonight, they'd simply have to jump – as they had in today's daylight practice – which meant he'd need to have the ship – the car – within a few feet of the ground.

Not wanting any broken necks.

Five hundred feet. Dark stain of woodland away on the bow to port, blurry miasma of light seeping up from around Arundel to starboard. Using his glasses he could make out the castle's bulk and the cathedral spire. At a distance of – mile and a half, say. Admitting air into the for'ard ballonet now, for a bow-down trim to get her down a little faster; with only a mile to go over open countryside and a few small villages, easing her down – in the process making her a little heavier, too.

There'd been no snow here, although yesterday there'd been plenty around Polegate and Eastbourne, and for the first half-hour of this flight the fields and woods below him had still been patched with it. More so earlier in the day: there'd been a bit of a thaw since then, but it was freezing hard again now. There'd also been snow all over Kent, apparently. SSP-7 passing over a village now – Binstead – at 200 feet. Scent of woodsmoke in the icy air. Off to port about half a mile away was Walberton. He had the topography in clear and recent memory, from having made this same trip earlier in daylight and before that studied the maps. As an exercise for France therefore it was a bit of a fudge. Over there, for instance, he'd need to stay well up, out of sight and sound, wouldn't have anything like such easy and positive identification of ground features.

Hundred and fifty feet. Throttling back. He was over the fringes of the wood now and intending to park her on its eastern flank – the lee side, to get shelter from as much wind as there was. A matter of principle rather than necessity. Starboard rudder now, therefore. Swinging, and at one hundred feet taking some of the bow-down angle off her, to let her down gently and smoothly, since conditions permitted that, and leaning to the plywood voicepipe (voice-tunnel might describe it better: it wasn't a hell of a lot of use, wasn't by any means noise-proof) to bawl through it to McLachlan in his for'ard cockpit: 'Mac! Stand by! One minute!' They'd agreed on 'Mac' and 'Holt' as the way to address each other when airborne – short, clear sounds, not easily mistakeable. Stavely would remain Stavely – the same factor applying, and he had no voicepipe; in any case knew what he was doing and what his skipper would be doing. Like throttling back some more now, easing her down with the black wall of trees rising to port and on that bow as he released the trail-rope, which already had a grapnel on it. (Didn't have to have: you could release the trail-rope and slide the grapnel down it when it was wanted.) Fifty feet. Grapnel would have hit the hard ground and bounced, and some of the hemp rope's weight being on the ground would be lightening the ship, more and more so as she descended, laying yet more of it out astern, grapnel then maybe digging itself in anchor-fashion, dragging through turf and undergrowth. Thirty feet. If there'd been more wind than this, being so close to the wood it might have been pouring over the mass of trees in the form of a waterfall, *downward* as the ship sank below treetop level and into the force of it. Different hazards then – the danger of her being rolled over and/or her bow smacked down into damaging impact with the ground – car and/or its suspension damaged, the envelope ripped, even. As had happened to a pilot by name of Monk at Pembroke a year ago – he'd been damn lucky to come out of it alive. Fifteen feet. Mental note to tell McLachlan the Monk story, the major having had no experience of flying in bad weather – yet – and seeming to think that one exaggerated the potential dangers.

The ship was making very little forward progress now, although still having enough engine power to allow effective control by elevators and rudder; opening both crabpots, letting slipstream into the ballonets to weigh her down with air. As yet had *not* valved. Ten feet. Eight. Crabpots shut, left hand back on the throttle. Six feet. Throttle shut, he yelled, 'Go!', and as the engine died they heard that, then felt and heard the skids touch down. Charlie saw them both clambering over, about to let go. Valving: *had* to. Heart in mouth – having felt the lurch, that loss of weight, but the valving had started first and countered it. Gas-release valve *shut* now, and engine stopped. Very well-timed valving, that had been, as well as minimal. By luck rather than by good judgement? He shouted into the darkness, 'Don't bother securing her – except the trail-rope. Waste of time – we've done it, let's go home!' To Amanda – the Amanda crisis, for God's sake. Course of true love never did – etc. Settle it tonight, anyway. Be with her well before midnight, touch wood. If she'll let me in . . . That thought in a single flash while finishing with, 'All right, Mac? Stavely – one scrulex for the trail-rope's all we need, OK?'

Conditions were favourable – so little wind, and enough moon to see by. It had been an exercise on the face of it for McLachlan – his first night-time excursion – but actually, as neither of the others would realise, for Charlie himself, in that he'd got her down with that minimum of valving, mainly through having left it to the last few seconds. Now had only to let out some air via the ballonets' release valves to lighten her at least to some extent, while also trimming her bow-up. Having prior to that re-embarked the other two, of course. Then as she left the ground he'd release the trail-rope from the scrulex (which Stavely was now planting) by means of the recently devised Charlie Holt Releasing Gear – the timber toggle made by shipwrights at the Scrubs and the 20-fathom hank of 3-pound Italian hemp line to wrench it out with.

Thinking of how it *would* have been, though, if there'd been a lot more wind and you'd had to stay on the ground for any length of time. Take six scrulexes, he thought, not four. Four would have allowed one to anchor a couple of handling guys as well as the trail-rope and the head-rope, but having spares would enable one to shift them if the wind drastically changed direction. One *did* live and learn – or, better way of putting it, things that were really pretty darned obvious did occur to one sooner or later. Not that there was room now for complacency. Just a little too much valving and you wouldn't be able to deflate the ballonets without risk of collapsing the envelope. Which on the ground in France really wouldn't help at all. On the other hand, one could, if necessary, dump a bag or two of sand-ballast – if mum was as heavy as she might be, for instance, or if in adverse weather conditions one had had to valve out more gas than one should have.

He took off from Slindon just before nine, and within minutes was at a thousand feet and steering east, at about the same engine revs as had given her 40 mph but should deliver more than that now, with the wind on her quarter giving her a little help. He'd steer this course for thirty miles, then over the Ouse – which even if the moon was down by that time would surely be visible from this altitude – then alter a few degrees to starboard for the last ten miles to Polegate. Be on the ground by ten, clean up and shift out of flying gear, get to Amanda by eleven.

Get things back on an even keel, please God.

Last night he'd got to the cottage not long after seven, expecting his knock on the door to be welcomed by whoops of joy and shortly after that to be throwing clothes off on their way upstairs – might not even make it *beyond* the stairs, he'd guessed, thinking about it on and off pretty well all day, during SSP-7's engine-noise trials and when he'd put her down on the snow-covered Polegate field at about three in the afternoon. There'd been various things to do then, including a fairly pointless conference with old Peeling the CO, then a far more practical session with Bob Bayley on the subjects of yellow dope, scrulex anchors, Italian White Line and a few other items – an axe was one, a 14-pound hammer another – for which he'd indented. The yellow (or yellow*ish*) dope had come from Howden, up on the Humber to the west of Hull, and one of the biggest RN airship fields, where Bayley said they'd been experimenting with different colours. God only knew what for: yellow for invisibility in some desert, maybe? Actually that might be it: blimps *had* been employed in the Middle East. Howden had sent a drum of the stuff down by rail to Polegate at the request of the CO at Wormwood Scrubs – more likely Engineer Lieutenant Hallet, bless him – and it could be sloshed on that very evening, if Charlie liked.

'That's capital, Bob. Most grateful for all of this. See, I'll be taking her up about mid-forenoon, but – heck, it's quick-drying, isn't it? Mind you, we only want it applied on the top of the envelope – camouflage purposes.'

'Tell the painter what you want. Why not see the job started yourself?'

He'd had to, obviously, had gone up on one of the riggers' long ladders to see it wasn't laid on too heavily – not wanting a bright-yellow blimp to dazzle Hun search-lights and fighters, or dope in such quantity that it might run down her sides. Only a bit of a patchwork or stripey effect to break up the otherwise equally noticeable solid black. *If* she happened to be on the ground in daylight – God forbid – and Hun aircraft passed over with sharp-eyed observers in them. Anyway, the painter assured him it would be dry in a hour or two, let alone tomorrow forenoon. So that was fine, but Stavely was there as well, poking around the engine in a boiler-suit – as a first-class, conscientious AM *would* have, after the day's full-throttle trials – and Charlie had chatted with him for a while. Not that Stavely was much of a chatterer – far from it – but Charlie liked the man and thought he'd done well to steal him from the

Scrubs. In consequence he hadn't got away as early as he'd thought he might.

Needn't in fact have set off even that early. His first sight of the cottage had told him she wasn't there. No lights in its few small windows, no scent of chimney-smoke, and the snow's surface unbroken all around, both in front and at the back where he parked the Douglas in the yard.

So *now* what? He was wearing a greatcoat over his serge uniform, half-boots with thick socks in them, a vest under his shirt, and sheepskin gloves, but it was still very cold. Might become less so by morning – there was a steady dripping from the roof guttering, and not much wind, but – hell, wait maybe half an hour . . .

She might be spending the night with Colonel and Mrs Sneem, he'd thought. Having lunched with them, and Seaford being – oh, a good ten miles by that winding, narrow road, with this snow to make driving hazardous. And she hadn't been expecting him until tomorrow.

He got into the bike's side-car – certainly wasn't warm, but, quoting the Bairnsfather cartoon character Old Bill, *If you knows a better 'ole, go to it*, he settled down and got a pipe going. Telling himself he'd wait twenty minutes or half an hour, then call it a day – back to the mess, and ring her in the morning. But within just minutes he heard the car – Sneem's, a Morris as it happened. Didn't know for sure it was Sneem's then, of course, only sat tight and mentally crossed his fingers. The car was coming very slowly down the slight incline, tyres muffled by the snow, being driven so cautiously that it was almost at a halt before it turned into the yard. Masked headlights a weak yellow, stubby bonnet, body a dark, white-patched cube. Morris Ten, he thought, as the lights such as they were washed over him where he was now prising himself out – pipe jutting, cap somewhat askew. Car door jerking open in the very second that it stopped, and Amanda jumping out, in overcoat, hat, scarf gloves, for some reason pointing at him – '*Charlie?*'

'Who else'd sit here patiently all day and half the night?'

'But you said *Monday!*'

'Managed to improve on that, and no way of getting in touch with you, was there. Only been here a quarter of an hour, to be honest. Might've given up pretty soon. Who's that?'

The car was being reversed with its wheel hard over, to put it in a position to drive out. Reasonable thing to do, Charlie thought, no matter how long its driver had *meant* to stay. Amanda had stopped a few feet short of him and the bike. No hug – not much point, admittedly, in thick coats, headgear, etc., but would she have kept her distance like this if there'd been no third party present?

'Colonel Sneem, Charlie. I did tell you I was having lunch . . .'

'You did indeed.' The car's lights went out, driver's door opened, and she'd turned that way. 'Colonel, this is Flight Lieutenant Holt. Charlie – Colonel Sneem.' A smallish man, no features visible as yet. He'd swung the door shut and was coming around the bonnet, treading carefully through the snow. Amanda inviting him, 'Colonel, you'll come in for a cup of coffee, thaw out a bit before . . .'

Before making new tracks home to Seaford, Charlie thought. Of course he'd have been coming in, in any case – why else would he have got out of the car, or brought it round to the back here? If he'd only been bringing her home he'd have dropped her at the front, *then* turned by backing into this yard. He'd now grunted acceptance of the invitation anyway, and Amanda was leading them round to the front door, remarking as she went that 'thawing out' might not be anything like immediate; with no fire in there all day it was going to be igloo-like. She'd get a fire going though, and the stove *would*, she very much hoped, boil a kettle. She was twittering a bit, Charlie thought. Door open, after some fumbling round the keyhole, and she was in, calling back, 'Charlie, you must be *frozen*!'

'Hadn't been here all that long.' He'd already told her that. 'After you – sir. You were Don's CO, I think?'

'Friend of his, were you?'

'Of them both. Known Amanda for – oh, donkey's years. Mandy, I'll set the fire – the makings all here, I see.'

'Lovely.' She was lighting an oil-lamp – one of several. 'And I'll see to the stove and coffee.'

'What can *I* do, my dear?' Sneem. *My dear*, indeed. Charlie, on his knees at the fireplace crumpling up a news-paper, thought, *Best thing might be to bugger off, old chap . . .* He was short and pasty-faced, with thinnish greying hair shiny with oil. Late forties had been Charlie's estimate, from a single glance in the first glow of lamplight: impression of a triangular face, small, sharp chin, pointed nose and rather large, round eyes. Like something in a cage – you might feed it nuts or bamboo shoots. Amanda had gone through to the kitchen: water gushed into a kettle before she called back to Sneem, 'Nothing, really. I'll just riddle the stove, wake it up a bit. There's still some life in it, thank heavens!'

'You're RNAS – stationed here, the airship station, Holt?'

'At Polegate. Yes.' He had the fire more or less ready to light. 'Been away, off again shortly. Chasing one's tail around the place, just at this stage . . . You run all the hospitals and suchlike over a big area, must be – I mean, Seaford, and—'

'Eastbourne's the hub of it. But I don't exactly run the hospitals. We've had to expand the RAMC establishment and services enormously, of course. Right from the start we had our own training camp at Whitbread Hollow – training recruits in ambulance work and emergency dressings, all that how d'ye do, sending 'em on to divisional training then, d'you see. As it happens, I set all that up, and young Bishop took over the running of it. We were under canvas ourselves to start with – at Cow Gap, know where that is? But with such a spread of military camps all over – as you must have seen for yourself, bird's eye view, eh? – as well as an urgent need of more and more hospital beds for the wounded coming in, then the need for literally thousands of billets – and recruitment of Red Cross volunteers – all now very ably organised by Mrs Bishop – Amanda, I should say . . .'

Yapping on, while Charlie put a match to the paper – the

Eastbourne Chronicle, he'd happened to notice – and it flared up immediately, began to crackle in the kindling. The split logs arranged wigwam-fashion over all that would soon ignite. It was surprising, he thought, that this talkative quack hadn't known of his existence. Amanda keeping her own counsel – for reasons of her own? When she'd just spent half a day with the fellow, you'd guess she might have broken a silence with, 'Oh, must tell you, very old friend of mine just reappeared, flies one of the naval blimps you see bumbling over . . .'

Unless they talked medical shop all the time. Or with Don killed so recently, Sneem or his wife might not have approved?

Or just *he* might not have?

'Know a flight lieutenant by name of Caterham, by any chance?'

Charlie had just stood up from the fire, and Sneem had edged closer to it, unbuttoning his British Warm. They'd both thrown their caps down on a table. Charlie nodded – looking at him in the face now and no more impressed than he'd been at first glance. A nod: 'Certainly. He's based at Newhaven – or was. Flies a Short 184. Amanda knows him too – like she knows me, from way back. Why – I mean how . . .'

'Had him to lunch with us today. My wife's idea. Asked Mrs – Amanda – whether she knew any *young* people whom we might ask – to jolly things up for her, don't you know.'

'And did he?'

'Very much so. Excellent fellow, I thought. He'd known Don quite well, apparently.'

'Yes, he was around a bit when I was here at Polegate, year or so ago.' Turning then, seeing Amanda in the kitchen doorway, looking apprehensive, definitely. He told her, 'Tommy Caterham, we're talking about.'

'Yes. I heard.' A glance at Sneem. 'Coffee won't be long.' Then: 'Oh, you *have* been clever with the fire, Charlie!'

'Don't you want to light the one upstairs, though? While I watch the kettle for you?'

'Well.' Her laugh wasn't entirely natural. 'You really *are* a genius.' For remembering that she had a heater up there, he supposed. He'd known the suggestion with its *possible* implications might have embarrassed her, had thought in the same instant, Why the hell *not*? The general line of his thinking being at this stage, *Easy come, easy go.* Although a counter to that was, *Why cut off your nose to spite your face?* Amanda adding, on her way to the door beyond which were the stairs, 'Only a small oil-heater up there, no fireplace, but it does – contribute.' Voice diminishing as she went up: 'The low ceilings help, of course.'

Charlie went through to the kitchen, saw the kettle on the black iron stove but no steam yet. He was wondering how she'd try to handle this – have him and Sneem leave more or less together? If so, would one comply?

No. Bloody well would *not*. And Sneem had a wife to get home to, wasn't likely to hang around too long. Might say he'd been stuck in the snow somewhere. Although conditions weren't all *that* bad: Mrs Sneem might well smell a rat. She'd know where the smell came from, too. Kettle still not boiling. He went back into the other room, found Sneem standing at the fire holding his coat open to its warmth: he'd put another log on. Charlie said quietly, 'Rotten business – Don Bishop, that's to say.'

'Yes.' An assessing look, as if wondering how much Charlie knew about it – how much he might be in Amanda's confidence, how close they actually might be. As Charlie sensed it, anyway, that was his *real* interest. In other words, *Amanda* was. He'd sighed, shaken his head. 'Need not have gone to France at all. I tried to dissuade him, in fact.'

'So she told me.'

'Then he needn't have gone forward as it seems he did. When that attack went in – the Cambrai show that started off so well – he insisted on going in with the infantry immediately behind the tanks, to set up RAPs.'

'RAPs?'

'Regimental Aid Posts.'

'But *could* he have – insisted?'

'You might call it "volunteered". Anyway, I don't know who'd have stopped him. Might have been on his own, in fact. He was determined to be in the thick of it, that's what it comes down to.'

'Well . . .'

The same obvious question – *why?* It must be on her mind, he guessed, day and night. In fact it *was* – she'd said so, the other evening. But it must virtually *possess* her, and she'd feel a need to explain it to other people – wouldn't she? – as well as to herself?

To exonerate herself?

She was back: clattering down the stairs, still in her outdoor bootees, asking brightly, 'Kettle doing its stuff yet?' Hurrying on through, Charlie telling her, 'Not when last seen, but—'

'It's starting now.' Calling back to them, 'Do sit down. Won't be a jiffy.' Rattling on, 'That was a brilliant idea you had, Charlie, the place is becoming almost habitable. Low ceilings really do help, don't they? Help to get some therms into the pair of you before you stagger back out into the blizzard . . . Hooray, it's actually boiling!'

Sneem murmured – neither of them had moved from the fire's warmth, and Charlie had put yet another log on – 'Can't escape the feeling I should have stopped him going. Damned if I know how I could have, in point of fact, but –' movement of his head towards the kitchen – 'feel so damn *sad* for her, don't you know. Oh, him too, of course, and for his people, naturally, but . . .'

Blathering on. *Awful* little swine . . .

He brought the ship in to the Polegate field after making a sweep to the south, passing quite close over Amanda's place in order to come in on a course of northwest by north – into the wind – dropping to fifty feet, the guardhouse and Coppice Avenue off to starboard, sheds and gas plant fine on the bow. There was still snow lying around – you could bet it would be frozen hard – and the roads, incidentally, more dangerous than they'd been last night. A ground crew of about thirty men was out there, opposite this western end of the sheds, and they'd lit the flares to guide him in. Twenty feet, ten. Throttling back. Easy as pie. Wondering whether she'd have heard him passing over and guessed it might be him. That burly figure commanding the handlers was Bob Bayley. Seemed to spend a lot of his time out here. Handlers splitting into two sections, one each side: edging in now, faces all upturned, airmen in overcoats, caps and leather or rubber boots, some having grabbed the handling guys, others reaching to the skids. So – throttle shut, engine puttering out. Behind him, Stavely would be shutting off, shutting down. Time – nine fifty-two. Get to her by ten-thirty, with any luck. He'd told her last night, 'As long as I can make it by midnight,' and her answer had been, 'If you're quite sure you want to. I can't swear *I'*ll—'

'Earlier than that if possible. Early as I can. Mandy, darling – *please?*'

First time he'd called her darling. Next thing you knew it'd be, *I love you, Mandy darling.*

On the other hand, it might be curtains. The thought of *that* gave him what felt like a constriction of the gut. Ridiculous, even shaming, but . . .

How it took one, that was all. He said goodnight to Stavely, reminding him, 'Ladder drill tomorrow'. Stavely's comment was, 'Blooming trapezes next.' Laughing, he joined McLachlan for the walk across to the accommodation buildings.

'If all goes well tomorrow, sir . . .'

'Wednesday, to France. I'll tell London that, first thing in the morning. Take off Wednesday at first light, eh? Save a few hours, could mean saving a whole day on *that* side. Ground staff should be well on their way by now – waiting for us, even.' A nod: 'I'll check on that.' A hand grasped Charlie's shoulder then. 'We haven't done at all badly, you know. Most of it *your* doing, of course. Golly, Holt, if we do pull it off . . .'

'Medals and promotion?'

'Count on it. *Count* on it!'

He shook his head, reminding himself that one thing *not* to do was count on anything at all. But – back to practicalities – 'Only point of more exercises tomorrow is really for you and Stavely to try out the ladders. But I don't think we need go as far as Slinfold. We could do it – well, Jevington way, for instance, five minutes' flight instead of an hour each way.'

'I've no idea why we went so far in any case.'

'Because in the CO's mind it had to be one of our own mooring-out stations, so that's what went into the orders. In fact, with so little wind we didn't need the shelter.' Another thought struck then: 'Since we're on the ground *you're* now my CO, sir – all right to take all-night leave?'

11

She was in a woolly dressing-gown with striped pyjamas under it – Don's obviously – trailing over her slippers. The fire was blazing, blazed even higher in the draught from the open door. He shut it quickly, turned the iron key and pushed the bolt across, moved towards her – but she'd stepped back, was holding him off, forearms horizontal, keeping twelve inches of space between them.

Hint of a smile on her lips, for all that. They were smiley lips in any case. Actually, irresistible.

'Made it earlier than you thought you might.'

Kissing. Arms dropping to her sides. Not quite there, but heading in the right direction.

'Mandy – I can't *tell* you—'

'I haven't enjoyed the day much, either.'

Looking for a short-cut, he took a chance on her sense of humour and/or forgiveness: 'Heater on upstairs, is it?'

She twisted away. Charlie tossed his flying helmet over to the sofa: leather helmet being better than a naval cap on a freezing night and on the bike. She nodded, with a glance at the door to the stairs: 'As a matter of fact it is. *But* –' pointing at him – 'on that subject, Charlie Holt—'

'Mandy – please, don't start.'

'So who *did* start?'

'All right, I grant you—'

'Grant me, hell. I'd done *nothing* – not a single solitary

thing that I should not have done, you had no damn *business*—'

'I know, but—'

'There's no granting and no "buts", Charlie. And as for talking about my bedroom heater in front of Arthur Sneem . . .'

'That was – ungentlemanly, I admit. I apologise. But you see, I thought—'

'You had no right to think *anything*! Just because we've slept together – God's sake, Charlie, what's the *matter* with you? What am I – some sort of chattel, mustn't know or speak to anyone else? Whatever's the problem it's with you, not me!'

'I'm – prone to jealousy. The sexual kind, anyway. Remember that now, but I'd forgotten – at least, for *years* . . . That's you, you see. I *never* felt so – with anyone else, I mean, I never . . .'

'What are you talking about?'

'Telling you I'm in love with you, I suppose.'

Gazing at him from a few feet away, her slant-eyes narrowed as if wondering whether she could believe that. Shaking her head slightly then. 'Is that supposed to make up for accusing me of – God knows – playing fast and loose, or—'

'I made no such accusation!'

'All *but*, you did. As good as. *Implied*, Charlie. How you looked – at *me*, damn you – and your tone, your attitude to Arthur . . .'

'He *is* after you, in any case.'

'Well – if he is, is that my fault?'

'He's a slimy toad.'

'He's never laid a hand on me, anyway – and if he did –' shake of the head – 'I'd handle it – without your help, or your approval or disapproval. Charlie, look. He brought me home, that's all, he and Dorothy had had me to lunch – oh, and let me tell you *this* – Tommy Caterham picked me up and took me there – they'd asked him if he would. I hadn't seen him since Don was killed, incidentally. He'd

142

sent me a note of condolence which naturally I acknowledged, and then he rang me at work. Rang me this morning too, you might as well know!'

'What for?'

'Why'd you imagine? You with your *vivid* imagination? He'd wanted to bring me back last evening – would have if Dorothy Sneem hadn't said she thought it'd be better if Arthur did. With snow on the roads, and – I don't know, but she was quite insistent. Tommy has a snappy little two-seater thing. They'd arranged it like that, anyway – he'd fetch me and Arthur'd bring me back. On *Dorothy*'s insistence, Charlie!'

'All right.'

'*All right*, is it? You mean you don't actually *object*?'

'Rubbing it in a bit, aren't you?'

'I'm giving you the facts, so you'll see how plain *stupid*, Charlie—'

'May I explain how it seemed to me at the time – how I got off on the wrong foot, so to speak?'

'Why not? I'd be interested. See where I went wrong.' She laughed. 'Actually allowing myself to be given a lift *home*, for instance!' She straightened her face: 'All right. Sorry. Sit down. Want coffee, or—'

'Want *you*, that's all.' Moving to the sofa he tried to bring her with him, but she swerved like someone avoiding a rugger tackle, perched on the arm at its other end, told him, 'Sit.' Pointing to *that* end. 'Dorothy gave me this, incidentally.' A book. He took it from her: Rupert Brooke – *Collected Poems*; and on the flyleaf, *To dear brave Amanda, from her friend Dorothy Sneem*. Amanda took it back out of his hands. 'Go on, then.'

'Yes. Well. First of all, he'd driven into the yard and parked, got out of the car and you *then* asked him if he'd come in – have coffee, so forth. What had he got out for if he hadn't been on his way in anyway? He'd have dropped you right at the door, wouldn't he? So it struck me you'd issued the invitation simply because I was there, to have *me* think it was spur of the moment – in other words, it was an obvious attempt at wool-pulling.'

She lifted her hands. 'Perhaps I sensed the sort of conclusion you might jump to.'

'You were certainly nervous. That's the second thing. Weren't yourself at all. Stood well clear of me – huh?'

'Well, in front of *him* . . .'

'Why be shy about it? He's twice your age – and if he's so concerned for your welfare, wouldn't he be glad for you, having an old flame turn up? But that's something else – when we got in here and exchanged a few remarks it was obvious he'd never heard of me. I'd have thought you'd have mentioned it. Old *friend*, you might have said, at least. To his wife, if not to him. Let not the right hand know what the left hand's up to, is how that struck me. Anyway –' her expression wasn't noticeably understanding or encouraging – 'I was wrong, you were simply – on edge for some *other* reason, right?'

'Tommy called me this morning to ask if I'd go out with him.'

'*Did* he? Is that what's put you on edge?'

'No, and you're being facetious now.'

'Will you go out with him?'

'I don't know. I may.'

'You didn't mention to *him* that I was around either, I suppose.'

'No, I didn't. I suppose – well, perhaps because I've been thinking – rather wrapped up in it, actually – that what we have between us *matters*. I mean, it isn't ordinary or casual, it's important, and very much *our* business. I couldn't chat lightly about you, Charlie, pretend – well, that you *didn't* especially matter. Like – ha-ha, guess who blew in a week ago . . . I don't think how I feel about you is anyone else's business. Even though tonight *is* the first time you've mentioned love – loving *me* . . .'

'Well . . .'

'We were *very* close at one time, weren't we? Might even have been in love. Don't you think we might have been? I've never forgotten a minute of it. May have been just a bit of fun to you, but – Charlie, when you turned up the

other day I thought, God, it's *him*, the one man who *ever*—'
She stopped as abruptly as if she'd bitten her tongue.
Shake of the head, hair swirling. 'I wasn't going to talk
like this if you came here tonight, Charlie. I don't know
why I *am*.'

'Tell you something. Every time I thought about you today
I felt like I'd been kicked in the belly by a horse.'

'Hah.' A knowing movement of the head. 'That's a *sure*
sign.'

'Thought I might have lost you.'

'Let's just finish what we were talking about specifically.
Listen. If Arthur Sneem does have ideas such as you think
he has – that's *his* business. He may have – I dare say *does*
– but don't blame *me*. I haven't encouraged him in any way
at all. Heaven's sake, the very idea's ridiculous!'

'I agree. *Wretched* little—'

'And as for Tommy – if I *were* to see him, go out to dinner
with him or something – damnit, why shouldn't I? Are *you*
renouncing all contact with other women? You and I aren't
married, Charlie!'

'I'd like to be.'

'Oh. Hold on there. Some girls might take that for a
proposal!'

'Statement of fact, more like. But I couldn't afford it.
Even if you'd contemplate it – which for all I know you
wouldn't. And even if after this job I'm on at the moment
I got promoted—'

'Is that likely? Not that as far as I'm concerned it's—'

'Possibility was mentioned, that's all. I can't talk about
it though, shouldn't even have said that much. Anyway –
tonight's the last time I'll see you for a while, as it
happens.'

'Oh. *Oh.* I thought you said – several days here, *then* . . .'

'We've managed to cut a few corners, you see.'

In fact, tomorrow night would be their last before departure, but he felt he was bound to keep the evening free for
further deliberations with McLachlan, map-study and whatever else might have come up by then. Also to make it an

early night, in preparation for take-off at first light, as McLachlan had suggested.

'So you're off tomorrow?'

'Lucky it didn't have to be today. To have had to shove off with all *that* still between us.'

'Might we resolve never again to have anything come between us?'

She'd got up, moved to stand over him, her knees against his, and he pulled her down – half beside him, half on top.

'I'm head over heels in this, Mandy. Don't know how, but – look, for a start, keep Tommy Caterham at a distance?'

'All right.'

'You mean it?'

'I would have anyway. Christ's sake, what d'you think I am?'

'Well – that declaration of independence . . .'

'If he – or anyone else – asked me out to dinner, *keeping distance* doesn't have to mean *exist in isolation*, does it?'

'No. No, of course . . .'

'Who was the last girl you had – much to do with, Charlie?'

'A barmaid in Great Yarmouth.'

'My God. *Really?*'

'What's wrong with barmaids?'

'I dare say nothing.' She shrugged. 'Or nothing *much*. Anyway, I've no business asking – that was the point of the question, wasn't it? Speaking of drink though – I'd get us one, but I've nothing in the house except some cooking sherry.' Eyes on his – about an inch away. Lips, too. 'Ought to have champagne.'

'I'll get us some, first day I'm back.'

'I love you, Charlie.' That took about a minute. Then, coming up for air, 'Did you get a meal this evening? If you came straight here from flying . . .'

'Had a snack earlier on.'

'Don't want to supplement it now?'

'You know what I want now.'

'What *I* want, too.'

'That's good. Absolutely *wonderful*. This whole thing is. *You* are. And the heater's on, you say, so—'

'Shut up about the bloody heater. Charlie, I'll make you a *scrumptious* farewell breakfast.'

Over a second, much more ordinary breakfast in the Polegate wardroom at seven – as distinct from Amanda's kitchen at five – McLachlan asked him how he thought he'd earn his living after they'd won the war. Charlie had told him during some conversation when they'd been at the Scrubs that he wouldn't be doing the obvious thing, taking over his father's farm, but hadn't mentioned what he did have in mind. And the two of them weren't talking any shop because there were other pilots at the table with them. In close proximity and earshot, for instance, were Havers, Swallow, Watson, Scott and Sinclair, all of whom were scheduled to take their SSZs out on oversea patrol in the course of the next hour.

Charlie, crunching toast, glanced round at his fellow flight lieutenants and one flight sub-lieutenant before answering that question. Swallow suggested, 'Go back to the briny, won't you, Holt?'

He admitted, 'Could do.' For some reason the aroma of eggs and bacon here wasn't half as fragrant as it had been at Mandy's. Visual memory accompanying it, of course, of Mandy herself back in Don's pyjamas – dishevelled, gorgeous. He nodded to McLachlan. 'Mercantile Marine. Where I'd just started when, to coin a phrase, the balloon went up.' Toast poised again, but adding first, 'Could do that, I suppose, but I don't think so. Not unless all else fails.'

'So what's "all else"?'

Shrugging, munching – the munching an excuse not to bare his brightest hopes to all these fellow pilots; such hopes being close to home – *this* home – in a way, he was disinclined to encourage competition where it might not exist already. They were amusing themselves now anyway, suggesting alternative careers for him, ranging from lavatory attendant to Chief Rabbi. He told McLachlan later though, on their way to Number 2 shed, 'You asked what I thought I'd do post-war, sir. The answer is, I hope – by hook

147

or by crook – stay in aviation. I reckon it's the future. I mean – speaking generally. So if one was in on the ground floor, so to speak . . .'

'This kind, or aero*planes*?'

'Airships. Not dirigibles – they'll have had their day – but rigids, such as Vickers are experimenting with up at Barrow. And at Cardington in Bedfordshire, one's heard. I'd give a lot to get into that team – or one of 'em.'

'These would be – might one say Zeppelin-type airships?'

'Yes. Germans are way ahead of us, of course. In design and construction, that is. Our one really brilliant designer, man by name of Barnes Wallis, has disappeared into the Army, I heard. Despite which, Vickers have completed one – HM Airship number 9, it's listed as – and one hears they've improved versions in hand. My bet is the commercial future could be terrific. Very large load-carrying capacity – cargo or passengers – over huge distances.'

'Although you're scratching your head over the weight of a blanket or a tin of bully beef!'

'No parallel at all, sir. Nothing *like*—'

'You might explain that to me some time. But – look here. That recent conversation you and I had. If we get these females out – as we *will* – you might find you could just about pick your own next billet. Barrow, for instance.'

'I'd sooner have that than accelerated promotion or a medal!'

'Why not all three?'

'Ah. Well . . .'

They watched while SSP-7 was walked out of the shed and then, when two SSZs which had been berthed behind her had been brought out, walked back in again. Stavely joined them then for scrulex drill – mainly for McLachlan's instruction, but the AM's first sight of a scrulex had been at yesterday's practices at Slindon, and he'd had problems with it last night. Here, with the ground as hard-frozen as it was, it was going to take some doing, Charlie thought. Petty Officer Harmsworth, who'd been his coxswain in SS-45, was the instructor; Charlie hadn't seen him since the sinking of the U-boat a week ago. The day McLachlan had first turned up. Eight days ago: and the dickens of a lot, he thought, had been packed into that space of time. Watching as Harmsworth demonstrated – placing the scrulex point-down in frozen grass and then belting it with the 14-pounder, getting its steel point in by about half an inch, then pushing the hammer's handle through the mooring-ring, wrapping his large hands around it, straining at it with all the strength he had and only managing to knock it over. So – start again, this time hammering it in further to give it a better grip before starting the screwing process. Scarlet in the face and grunting – he got it moving. Corkscrewing inch by inch into ground as hard as concrete.

Stavely then drove his in. Groaning and muttering curses, eyes bulging, but he managed it all right. Harmsworth meanwhile exerting almost as much effort again in getting his *out* of the ground, and offering it to McLachlan. McLachlan glancing thoughtfully at the PO's wide, thick shoulders, then at Stavely's ox-like build, grimacing slightly as he looked at Charlie.

Harmsworth assured him, 'Bit of a knack, sir, all it is.'

'Hm.'

Charlie put in, 'Most likely softer, where we're going. Get it into this, you'd get it into anything.'

'Aye.' Harmsworth again. 'As the actress said to the bishop.'

Stavely, straightening from extracting his, passed McLachlan the hammer. 'No harder 'n tossin' the caber'd be, sir.'

'That *is* a comfort.'

They all laughed. But he managed it, and was applauded. Charlie thinking, *We have the right stuff here*. He thanked Harmsworth, and told the others, 'Dry run in the shed now, using the rope ladders from the car. No need to put scrulexes in, only grab 'em off the ladders and drop 'em where we'd want 'em. Main thing's to get the hang of the ladders. And those lashings – sort of annoying thing could make for

149

hold-ups when just seconds count.' He asked McLachlan, 'D'you have a knife, sir?' The answer was no, he didn't; Charlie undertook to get him one from pusser's stores.

The yellow dope was dry; and the 'dry run' went all right. He'd explained to them that they'd be going in to France with four handling guys – ropes, not wires – and the trail-rope, and the new head-rope which might not be needed until the take-off for return. When they were there and landing in the Mormal forest he'd decide, in line with wind direction and strength and the topography as they found it, which lines should be anchored and at what angles; but here and now – 'Well, at Jevington, edge of the woods there – look here now . . .' He sketched it. 'Trail-rope here. And two of the handling guys – here, and here. Head-rope –' because he wanted to practise a take-off with it – 'here.' He asked McLachlan, 'Stand the thought of doing two scrulexes, one right after the other?'

'The *thought* appals me – but obviously I'll have to.'

'Sooner you than me, sir. But let's say one handling guy each – on the side you disembark, right? But first you set up the trail-rope, Stavely, and you, sir, head-rope?'

He demonstrated the CHRG – Charlie Holt Releasing Gear – and explained how he hoped it would work in action. Stavely's job, that – setting it up. Charlie didn't want to lose the trail-rope, which might be essential to their safe landing back at Boubers – hence the CHRG – whereas the head-rope would have served its purpose and be released – by him, from his cockpit, the end simply cast off to run out through the D-ring on the ship's forepart.

Jevington was in Amanda's direction, and there were some perfectly useable woods even closer to her. Bigger ones beyond, though, to the west of her and to the north of Friston; one particularly suitable spot, he found – researching this in the station's maproom – to the west of Oxen Dean, not far off the woodland track that led from Jevington to Long Brow. It was an area enclosed in woodland, really quite similar to the site near Malplaquet. In shelter from any northerly wind – west wind, either – and surrounded closely enough to warrant the use of the head-rope.

Maybe. If one could manage without it – well, even in France one might. On the other hand, it might save one's bacon. The wind factor – again absolutely crucial. A lot of this was experimental, and France would be a single outing – you might say one throw of the dice. At least, if you didn't get the luck you needed, there'd never be another. Nor would there be if you miscalculated, got your sums wrong – for instance made insufficent allowance for the women's weights. Rechecking for about the fiftieth time, he still reckoned to be going in there with more than a ton of lift in hand. The difference now was that he probably would be valving, so he'd need every pound of that – of the static lift that he'd have left *after* valving. His calculation took account of all known weights, including the two petrol tanks each holding ninety gallons, and all that loose gear – scrulexes, for instance – and cordage. No radio: if he got into trouble he'd be on his own. But you would be anyway – back here or in London they wouldn't know what had gone wrong, that was all. Wouldn't be sending messages back from Hun-occupied territory, in any case; had considered taking a carrier pigeon but decided against it – against adding to the clutter. He'd have an Aldis lamp in his cockpit and an accumulator to power it; the accumulator would serve other needs as well, and the Aldis was for visual communication with the ground, the air station at Boubers-sur-Canche, for instance, or Marquise (on the coast not far from Boulogne) if engine trouble or other failure obliged him to stop there. Marquise was a very small station which had been British-run, had now been handed back to the French but was still available to put down on in emergency.

The daylight outing went well enough. It was a clear day with a cold wind closer to due north than last night's north-westerly. He passed close over Amanda's cottage – this was late forenoon, but there was a wisp of smoke trailing from her chimney – from the kitchen stove, of course. He'd riddled and refuelled it at about five am. The snow had mostly gone from around the cottage, but there were still patches of it in the yard behind. Ice, more than snow, edging the lane as well. He was glad he'd allowed her to believe he was leaving today: it *had* been a scrumptious breakfast, and an emotional farewell, in the aftermath of a night of love and in the knowledge that it might truly be a new beginning, that decisions did seem to have been taken – subject to this, that and the other extraneous factor, but definitely taken, and mutually exciting.

Poetic line – *not* one of Brooke's – kicking around in his head: *westward, look, the land is bright*!

Westward, hell. Southeastward – the direction from which in certain weather states even here in Sussex one could sometimes hear the rumble of the guns – was where one's thoughts had now to be concentrated. He put the ship down on that hillside with the same minimal amount of valving – proving to himself that it hadn't been just fortuitous timing the night before, that having paid this much attention to it he could do it the same way ten times out of ten – at least, in anything like reasonable conditions. The others seemed to have mastered the ladder drill, and each had inserted a scrulex – which were left behind, to be collected by tender from Polegate in the course of the afternoon. Bob Bayley also had a note of where the one at Slindon could be found, and when that out station was next used he'd have someone pick it up.

Back in the shed at Polegate, Charlie told the others, 'I don't think we need bother with another dark-hours exercise. You'll want to do some maintenance on the engine, Stavely, won't you?'

The AM pushed his cap back, nodded. 'Reckoned on doin' it when we was back, sir.'

'I think we might as well call it a day. Gives you the afternoon for that – and to refuel her – and like the three of us she can have an early night.' He asked McLachlan, 'All right with you, sir?'

A shrug. 'You're the skipper . . .'

12

Hilde heard the pony-trap rolling up the manor's curve of driveway, and went to meet her employer, who'd been away for three days and nights visiting an aunt of her husband's, near Lille. She'd made the journey by train, and old Jeannot, groom and general handyman, had taken the trap to pick her up at the station in Bavay.

By the time Hilde had the door open and was out at the top of the stone steps, Jeannot had clambered out of the trap and was offering Madame a hand down.

'Thank you, Jeannot.'

'Such a pleasure to have you back with us, Madame.'

'A pleasure to be back. Hilde, hello!'

'Madame. Did you have an enjoyable stay?'

'Oh – as always.' Meaning, no great pleasure in it, but glad to have it done with again, especially with the children home next week for Christmas holidays. Glancing up then at the sound of aircraft – German fighters, a dozen of them, flying south. Albatrosses, she thought: with luck there might be only *half* a dozen returning later. She asked Hilde, who was accompanying her up the steps, Jeannot grunting and wheezing behind them with the luggage, 'All well here? How's your mother?'

'Much the same, Madame. Doctor said – more or less – that if she lived the winter out – well, that I shouldn't expect—'

'You told me. Sunday, when I was leaving.'

'Of course. It was on Saturday he came out to us.'

'You *will* get her through the winter, Hilde. Also the spring, and please God the summer, too. You'll see. We'll all say prayers for her, and – oh, Lord, what's *this*?'

German army motorvan – dark green. Soldier-driver and another of them in the front. It had swung in from the lane at a fairly reckless speed, scattering gravel and bumping over an edge of lawn as the driver dragged the wheel over. Jeannot, halfway up the steps with the two cases, paused to stare at it disapprovingly as it ground to a halt behind the trap. Elise telling him rather snappily, 'Take those into the hall, then put the trap away. Hercule can go out to grass. Are the others out?'

'Except for Mignonne, Madame. I thought perhaps you'd—'

'I won't have time. Put her out, too.'

'I'd say there's snow coming, Madame, so . . .'

'So bring them in anyway before dark.'

The German driver had got out, was standing with his gloved hands on the van's radiator, gawping at the house. The other one had come around the back of it and was starting up the steps, his head back as he looked from one to the other. He was a sergeant: had a Luger holstered on his hip. Sent here by Koch, Hilde thought, readying herself for the worst. She'd begun to allow herself to think she might not hear from him again; this was Wednesday now, and from what Otto had said the policeman would have been back on Monday, having gone to Brussels only for the weekend. *Working* weekend, consulting files or other secret policemen – Leutnant Bergen, for instance. She hadn't seen Otto since Saturday, but then she often didn't, for a few days at a time. He'd be there again at the château, surely. The thought occurred to her in much the same way that a swimmer finding herself in difficulties would look round for something to hang on to.

Although he'd have no authority. *Koch* had the authority.

She stood clear of the front door, giving Jeannot room to lumber through with the heavy cases, and watched him dump them close to the foot of the staircase, straightening then with his hands massaging the region of his spine. As he turned, a grimace indicative of pain invited sympathy. Old fraud. Who'd take the cases on up from there? Well, *she* would. Or *would have*. Moving out on to the steps again she heard the sergeant confirm what she'd known in any case, telling Madame in crude, Germanic French, 'My orders are to bring Fraulein Martens to the château. Orders of Major von Bodenschatz. If you please, Madame.'

Orders of Hauptmann Koch, Hilde thought. *Technically* perhaps on the authority of von Bodenschatz – the château's commandant. Koch would as likely as not have a rubber stamp with von B's signature on it. Elise de Semeillions got on well with him – the commandant; he was a grey-haired, lined-faced former cavalryman, now asthmatic and unfit for active service. But Koch, as Ketteler had said, was a law unto himself. The sergeant was glaring up at her, Madame gazing disdainfully at *him*; Hilde sensing both intuitively and logically that her situation was now actually dangerous. Otto had pleaded with her to take it seriously, because to start with she hadn't: it had seemed to her to be no more than a new broom sweeping clean, that two years having passed since the Brussels business she *had* to be in the clear. It wasn't like that now – at least she didn't feel it was.

She started down. Madame demanding of the sergeant, 'Tell me what this is about? I can assure you that Mademoiselle Martens can have done nothing illegal – and she works for *me*, is not available for any other—'

'She has to come with us, that's all. Quickly please, mam'selle!'

Hilde saw the driver go to the van's rear doors and open one of them. Pausing close to Madame, she asked the German, 'Are you arresting me? What for?'

'Just get in the vehicle – and quick. Otherwise . . .'

Elise said quietly, 'If they detain you for any length of time, Hilde, I'll visit your mother and see she has all she needs. This evening – if you aren't back by then. I'll also contact Major von Bodenschatz – or try to.' More loudly then – 'Heavens, girl, you can't go without a coat!'

'No. Of course.'

Feeling stupid: everyone else in overcoats – needing them too, in this wind out of the northeast, cutting as a knife. She'd been unprepared, hadn't been anything like ready for this. Turning back up the steps though, calling to the sergeant, 'Just a moment. Have to fetch my coat . . .'

Except for the absence of Otto Ketteler, to start with it could have been a replay of last week's interview. Same *salon*, Koch the same pale, oddly faceless individual. Behind the small eyes there had to be a brain, but with such a lack of expression the face could have been made of dough.

Treat him with respect, though. As advised by Otto, and because this definitely was not good now. That he'd found reason to interrogate her again, and that he'd sent soldiers and a van, as distinct from a request to call in on a certain day and time – the request relayed to her last time by Otto.

'You were hoping to find Leutnant Ketteler waiting for you, fraulein?'

Because before sitting down she'd looked towards the back of the *salon* where last time Otto had placed himself. She nodded. 'Since you feel the need of an interpreter – or *did*.'

'This time I don't. I believe you'll find my French has improved almost miraculously.' Slight smirk. '*He*'d be amazed. But in any case you must have been glad of his – what's it called – moral support?'

'Of course. A person one knows, when one does not know what one's supposed to have done wrong . . .'

'Whom one knows and with whom one goes off on picnics. Quite. I'll tell you, though, I was glad of the opportunity to see the pair of you together.'

The implication being that that was why he'd pretended to need an interpreter. He'd had *her* fooled, all right. Otto, too. She held the deadpan stare. 'So we did picnic – this last Saturday. Something criminal in that?'

'More just interesting than criminal in itself. Planned it long in advance, had you?'

'Hardly. Madame de Semeillions had given me the afternoon off, and on my way home I happened to run into the lieutenant, who—'

'Do you have a physical relationship with him?'

'No, I do not!'

'I should have asked, *did* you have such a relationship. You won't be seeing him again, you see. But tell me, without any of *that*, what satisfaction did either of you get out of your – er – association?'

'As far as *I'm* concerned – if we really have to go into such an entirely personal matter – nothing out of the ordinary. He's young, quite good-looking, can often be amusing—'

'And confided in you? A military secret now and then?'

'No! Nothing of the sort!'

Koch motionless, a seated statue, staring at her. She shook her head – astonishment now tinged with amusement. 'I wouldn't know a military secret if you rubbed my nose in it!'

'I think perhaps you would. And have some way of passing it out to our enemies.'

'But that's simply ridiculous!'

'Leutnant Ketteler is having similar questions put to him elsewhere, I may as well tell you. Who knows, he may even find it a relief to tell us. I'm sure he never *set out* to give away secret information.'

'Certainly never gave *me* any!'

'Is he in love with you?'

'I have no reason to think so. He was attracted to me, sure, but—'

'Did he try to persuade you into an intimate relationship?'

'He was – flirtatious, certainly. But no, not really. The usual course of flirtation, that's all. What I mean is, the suggestion was *there* – as it tends to be, I suppose.'

'In any case, you'd never have consented . . .'

157

'In the interests of being completely truthful, m'sieur, I can't say I would *never* have. One enjoys flirtation, one's human, and – as I said – he's attractive enough, and amusing. If he'd really pressured me . . .'

'You might have yielded?'

'Might. The fact is I didn't. It's plain truth I'm giving you – the fact is I've done nothing wrong, and to the best of my knowledge and belief, nor has he!'

'If you had, though, it would have been a way of cementing the liaison?'

'What d'you mean?'

'Making sure he didn't lose interest – pick on some easier mark, perhaps, so you'd get no nuggets of information – across a pillow or—'

'You've absolutely no grounds for any such—'

'—or in a wood – after some *foie gras* and a bottle of hock, say?'

'M'sieur. The only picnic lunch I have had with Leutnant Ketteler was the one on Saturday – about which you've evidently been informed – and at this time of year the forest is much too cold for the kind of activity you're suggesting. It's untrue, and you know it. *Why* you'd want to fabricate such slander . . .'

'I want a basis – reason – for your close association with the *leutnant*. A reason I can *believe*, fraulein. Because I now know I'm not dealing with some innocent young girl who's carried away by the heady delights of a little harmless flirtation. I *know* it – hear me? Tell me this – the *leutnant* did have some profound anxieties, did he not?'

Frowning: looking surprised again. 'Not that I'm aware of.' A shrug. 'Not saying he hasn't, but – he never mentioned any such thing to me.'

Except that on the picnic, all he'd really wanted had been for her to recall what he'd told her that night when he'd been sozzled. Arising from the fact that just a few days earlier – the last time she'd been *here*, in fact – she'd foolishly, unthinkingly, referred to something he'd said at that time.

And set his nerves on edge, she supposed.

She'd been delving in her memory. Gave up now. 'No. Nothing he's ever said, that I remember.'

Might he have told a colleague – in confidence – and the colleague gone running with it to this creature?

'We'll move on then.' This after gazing at her intently and wordlessly for another ten or fifteen seconds. Reading her mind – or wanting to give the impression of doing so. Eyes down again now: pale, soft-looking fingers turning a page in a file. All that – about oneself? Or about Otto, too? Koch murmured, 'Move *back*, I should have said – to events in Brussels, year before last.'

'I didn't even know of Leutnant Ketteler's existence, then!'

'No. We're leaving him – for the moment. I'll explain – in case you haven't already grasped this . . . My interest in your association with him is that his duties in the château have included assisting in the organisation of high-level planning conferences. In a very junior capacity, of course, but – well, one conference in particular, last month, prior to my own arrival. See – my *raison d'être* is to ensure that we have adequate security at such times. In fact at *all* times, and by "adequate" I mean *total*. Well – in the case of a commissioned officer with a background such as Ketteler's, there should be no such concerns at all – ordinarily would not be. But when it transpires that he has been enjoying a close liaison – amorous or otherwise – such as he has with you, that naturally comes under scrutiny. And if it's then discovered that this person has earlier been under investigation through her association with a notorious *spy*, fraulein . . .'

'If it's Nurse Edith Cavell you're referring to, she was never even *accused* of spying. Consult your own court records, m'sieur!'

'She was not accused of it for the sole reason that no such charge could have been substantiated. But there were good grounds for suspicion. And certain other parties – with whom you were acquainted, incidentally.'

'Such as?'

'Do you deny acquaintance with a man by name of Quien? Georges Gaston Quien?'

'Quien was – still is, I suppose – a Frenchman and a police spy working under the direction of a Leutnant Bergen – I suppose of *your* department. He somehow gained entry to the Berkendael and put his ear to doors, eye to keyholes, also tried to strike up acquaintance with some of the probationers and nurses. He and another Frenchman, name of – oh, Jeannes. Armand Jeannes. And I personally, may I tell you—'

'*Yes?*'

She'd seen it coming, just seconds ago. If Koch had consulted that *swine* . . .

'You were saying, fraulein?'

'I was assaulted by Quien. An attempt at sexual assault. And yet at the interrogations to which I and others were subjected, after Madame had been arrested, that same creature—'

'Quien gave evidence that you had danced naked in a Brussels nightclub – or *boîte* – known as *Boudoir Rose*. You, fraulein, the innocent little probationer under the wing of the *saintly* Cavell woman!'

'I have never in my life danced naked *anywhere*, m'sieur.'

'With very few clothes on, then?'

'I danced in a supposedly oriental costume that I was given. I did it because at the Institute we were paid next to nothing. I *had* to send money so my mother wouldn't starve or freeze, and the only way to earn any – well, it had to be at night, we probationers worked from dawn to dusk – hard work, too—'

'How did you happen to be taken on in that disreputable establishment?'

'I asked at a café in that neighbourhood for a job as a waitress, and the man suggested, "Try the *Boudoir Rose*. Ask for Jacques Berceau." I wouldn't call his place disreputable: I was protected – by him and by other staff. I could have drinks with customers – this was encouraged – but if any of them tried anything he'd be chucked out on his ear. Does any of this relate to security here, m'sieur?'

'Yes, it does. For one thing, wouldn't you agree that a young woman who's prepared to dance in public even *half* undressed could hardly be regarded as *respectable?*'

'The question's irrelevant, since I did *not* dance undressed, or *half*—'

'Does Leutnant Ketteler know of it?'

'As it happens – no.'

'So you don't exactly boast of it.'

She gestured wearily. 'I've told you. It was the only way I could help my mother. I did not dance "half undressed", and I may as well tell you, while we're at it, it was a solo performance and I had no physical contact ever with any customer.'

'How about with –' consulting his notes – 'Jacques Berceau?'

'Not with him or anyone else! Oh – except for Quien's assault on me. On my way back to the Berkendael, just around the corner from the *Boudoir* – he'd been lurking there, waiting for me. Luckily there were some others passing who heard me scream.' There'd been a curfew in force; Quien might have reckoned on her *not* crying out. Koch hadn't thought of the curfew-breaking – in any case hadn't commented – and she finished quickly, 'That tells you what your friend Quien's like. Take *his* word for anything?'

'One does have to accept his statement as it stands in police records, yes – the fact you danced *déshabillée* before an audience of men.'

'To say I was *déshabillée* is a lie. It was an oriental costume, or supposed to be, and – if you want it plainly – no part of my body was exposed. I'd seen Quien oiling his way around at the Berkendael, and there he was with the rest of them, watching me dance – recognised me, of course, invited me to join him for a drink, and made an indecent proposition to me which I emphatically declined.' She added, 'And then, a month or so later—'

'Ambushed you in the street, you say.'

'Yes. And it's the truth.'

'But –' pointing at her triumphantly, as if he thought he *had* her now – 'after he saw you there the first time, and bought you a drink—'

'I left the drink untouched!'

'—did he not report you to your *directrice*?'

Quien had threatened her with that, told her that if she didn't comply – make herself available to him – he'd go straight to *Directrice* Cavell.

Sweaty-faced, leaning close, mean little eyes alternately gazing into hers and trying to see into the top of her costume, cacophany of loud music and men's voices reducing slightly as a singer appeared on stage; Quien hissed, '*Directrice*'d give you the order of the boot, eh?'

'She would. All right – she *will*. Greatly preferable, I may say, to having anything further to do with *you*.' She went directly from Quien to the gallery where Jacques Berceau was sitting with a party of friends. The girl was into her song, but the hell with that. '*Maitre* – excuse me. The pig I've just left – that one, *there*, at table twenty-three, that rat-faced object – trying to blackmail me. If I don't play games with him he'll go to Madame at the Institute – and I'm out on my ear, huh?'

Berceau got up. Mid-thirties, a heavy-weight with only one eye, having lost the other in a fight with knives in his student days; he wore a black patch over that one.

'A customer we can do without, then. Know his name, by any chance?'

'Yes. Quien. Frenchman. Hangs around the Institute, for some reason, that's how he knows I work there.'

'All right. I'll settle *his* hash.' Berceau started down from the gallery, but Quien had been watching, and skedaddled. Berceau watched him go, before coming back to Hilde and the others. 'He won't be let in here again, you can rest assured of that. But listen now – if they do throw you out, you can dance here six nights a week instead of three. Don't know where you'd live, mind you.'

'I'd get a room somewhere. Or go back to Taisnières,

maybe. I don't know. Thanks anyway – I appreciate the offer
– and for getting rid of *him*.'

'Stick to us *real* rough diamonds, *chérie*. Know where you
are, with us.'

That was on a Tuesday. Her nights at the *Boudoir* were
Tuesday, Thursday and Saturday. She'd expected that if
Quien was going to carry out his threat he'd do it right
away. But Edith Cavell spoke to the probationers every
evening in her sitting-room, expanding on religious
matters as well as medical/nursing ones, and neither on
the Wednesday nor the Thursday was there any change in
her famously 'reserved' manner. Haughty, some called it,
but actually it was shy, self-effacing and deeply thoughtful
– less 'reserved' than 'restrained'. Those who knew her
best and worked closest to her – Nurse Wilkins being the
prime example – practically worshipped her. Even the
probationers – those worth a damn . . . They were a very
mixed batch, in terms of social background. Dr Antoine
Depage – the rather overbearing surgeon who'd founded
the Institute and engaged Edith Cavell as *directrice*, his aim
being to provide Belgian doctors with well-trained nurses
as distinct from nuns who tended to be ignorant, and lay-
nurses with no concept of hygiene – had put emphasis on
recruiting educated girls, but Edith had found the
educated daughters of well-off Belgians to be pleasure-
loving and idle, with little or no sense of duty. She had
several of those. Hence, for instance, her ready acceptance
of Hilde, to whom in her report to the Institute's Council
she'd attributed 'a naturally quick intelligence as well as
capacity for hard work and a great desire to better herself'.
And Pauline Randall, daughter of a circus man, who'd
been brought along at the age of thirteen by the chaplain
of the English church in Brussels; and Grace Jemmet, who
as a result of treatment she'd received for an illness of
long duration had become a morphine addict. Edith had
taken Grace's problems on to her own shoulders, treated
her like a daughter.

But neither Pauline nor Grace would have danced half-naked in any nightclub. They were decent, good-hearted girls, but – Hilde thought to herself – nobody would have asked them to dance anywhere, poor things, dressed or undressed. On the Friday evening, she was wickedly entertaining this thought – probably smiling a little to herself – as Madame closed a medical text-book and told them, 'Enough for this evening, then. Hilde – if you'd stay a few moments, please . . .'

Quick interest from the others: their eyes were averted from her then as they curtsied, said their goodnights and trooped out. The door closed quietly behind Pauline, and Madame said quietly, 'Sit down, Hilde.'

'Madame.'

'I am very fond of you, Hilde. You must know that, I'm sure – and that I find your work more than satisfactory. Also, I respect your anxiety for your mother and your determination to do whatever you can for her. It's far from easy, on the very small amount which is all we can afford to pay you, to cope at the same time with one who is to all intents and purposes a dependant. You need not explain any of that to me, I do fully understand – having given it a great deal of thought in the last few days – the *motivation* behind this dancing business.'

So there it was. Next would be, 'First thing in the morning, pack your bag.' She bowed her head. 'I'm very sorry, Madame. That I should have offended *you*, especially.'

'At greater risk is the reputation of this Institute, Hilde. I already have problems enough with – oh, our council, and as you all must know, with Dr Depage – and if a – frankly, a *scandal* of this nature became known to them, those problems might be considerably exacerbated.'

'I realise, Madame, that I'll have to leave. It shames me that my thoughtlessness should have created such embarrassment for you. Shall I leave tomorrow, or—'

'No, Hilde.' Chin up, eyes defiant. Tiny woman, enormous spirit. Little and quiet, but tough. 'You will *not* leave us. I have wracked my conscience over this, and I have no intention of releasing you. First because I believe you have

164

an aptitude for our profession which will stand you – and others, eventually – in good stead. That's one side of it – I won't have your potential wasted. The other is that if I did let you go – with your sense of obligation towards your mother – my guess is that you might be tempted even further into that cabaret-type *milieu*. Might you not?'

She *had* been thinking of taking Berceau up on his offer. At Taisnières there'd have been no work that would pay even half as well. There could be a future beyond the *boites*, too: there were, after all, such things as theatres. She'd nodded, looking down at her folded hands.

'It's possible, Madame.'

'Another side to this, I must admit, is that I was not at all taken with that *odious* person. Who or what is he, do you know?'

'I don't, Madame. But he's here in the Institute quite often. His manner's that of – one might think, a spy. He'd seen me here, then saw me dancing, and—'

A nod. 'He told me that. No – that he'd seen you first in *Chez Jules* – the café. No mention of his ever having been in this building.'

'The worst of it is – this is a delicate matter, Madame, my apologies – the fact is he made approaches to me, threatened that if I did not comply he'd—'

'Inform on you.' The blue eyes were sharp and hard. 'I see.' A small frown then, a glance towards the door, a lowered tone: 'Did you mean – a *police* spy?'

'I don't know. But there's another, a tall man named Jeannes. He was just loitering, looking into doorways that were open – on the third floor, this was, about a month ago. Sister Wilkins asked him what he was doing and he said he was looking for someone who might tell him where the staircase was. She sent him packing – but I saw him another time on the street with Quien.'

'Why do you imagine a a police spy – or spies – should have any interest in this establishment?'

'Why indeed, Madame!'

'I'll warn everyone to look out for them. Now, Hilde – if

the others ask why I kept you behind, it was to congratulate you on the excellence of your work. That is the truth, one of the doctors did recently single you out for praise, and I *am* pleased with you. But from now on, will you stay away from that dancing place?'

She'd nodded. What else? Madame continuing, 'I'll try – *try* – to find some small sums for you to send your mother. Just a little – now and then. Your contributions are not *all* she has to live on, are they?'

'No, Madame. Madame de Semeillions, to whom in fact I send the money—'

'Oh, yes. I know of her through the Princess du Croy. She's still helping, is she? I'm glad. The Princess holds her in great esteem. I suggest you write and tell her that regrettably your future contributions will be smaller and less regular. You might ascribe it to – a change of circumstances you might say?'

'Yes, I'll do that. But also – with your permission – I'll go to the *boite* tomorrow for the last time. I'm owed some money – which I'll send with the letter – but in any case I must tell them – *him* – he's a good man, actually.'

'Very well.' A glance at the watch which she kept pinned to her uniform. 'I'm glad we've had this talk, Hilde.'

'I'm *most* grateful to you, Madame. I can't say how much. For your thoughtfulness and kindness.'

Koch's last question had been, 'So your saintly *directrice* knew about your cavorting, and allowed it to continue!'

'No. She didn't. I expected her to throw me out, but she decided against that for two reasons – one, I was making good progress, and two, she guessed if she did so I'd as likely as not go into that sort of employment full time – since I *had* to earn money, to help my mother.'

'You say she did *not* allow you to go on with it?'

'She did not.'

'You accepted that prohibition?'

'Of course.' She spread her hands. 'Is this really of importance?'

'Oh, certainly. You say you accepted the prohibition – but in point of fact, despite your deep respect and devotion to the woman, you actually carried on as before.'

'I stayed away from the *Boudoir Rose* for a while, but—'

'Let's drop the pretence, fraulein. This is just playing games. Isn't it the truth that you took the dancing job on in the first place at *her* suggestion?'

'*What?*'

'I've surprised you?'

'The very idea's crazy!'

'On the contrary. Knowing that woman as I now do, I see it as entirely rational.'

She'd gone to the *Boudoir Rose* that Saturday, and had danced, as well as explaining to Jacques Berceau that she'd be unable to do so again.

'Did rat on you, did he, that little squirt?'

'Did indeed. Madame, out of the pure kindness of her heart, didn't sack me, but – I'm sorry, I had to promise.'

'I'm sorry too. I wish she *had* sacked you. Anyway – if you change your mind . . .'

Two or three weeks later Madame again asked her to stay behind at the end of an evening *assemblée* – 'to discuss your mother's situation, Hilde' – and when the door was shut behind the others asked her, 'You have not been back to that place, I take it?'

'Only that once, the Saturday after . . .'

'I remember. But Hilde – I'm sorry, my efforts to find other sources of even small amounts of money have met with no success. We're virtually penniless here, is the truth. Did you write to Madame de Semeillions?'

'Yes. Enclosing the last of my earnings.'

'Perhaps *not* the last. I'm going to surprise you now, Hilde. Shock you, perhaps. But – if you wanted to go back there, would they take you on again?'

Surprised her, all right. It was a few heartbeats before she answered. 'They would, Madame. As it happens, that was made plain. But—'

'I am not advancing this proposition simply – or even primarily – to enable you to resume the contributions to your mother's support. Although it would have that effect, which would be a relief, I'm sure. But I am not hiding behind that, Hilde. The fact is, you could render great service to us – to me – in another way entirely. I have been wrestling with the decision whether or not to put this to you. It is a matter of pragmatism versus – respectability, one might call it. *Appearances.* Well – I take that on *my* conscience.' A nod. 'Bewildering you, am I not. Straight to the point then – I would like you to return to your dancing, and the reason – let me just say first that in telling you this it would be no exaggeration to say I am placing lives in your hands – the *reason*, Hilde, is that I and certain friends are facilitating the escape of French and British soldiers – and young French and Belgians of military age who want to join the Allied armies – by accommodating them secretly here in Brussels. Some in this Institute, others – well, elsewhere – and at intervals despatching them in small groups, with guides, to the Dutch frontier and across it into Holland.' She'd closed her eyes for a moment. 'There. It's said. Does it appal you, Hilde?'

'Astonishes and slightly unnerves me, Madame, but—'

'There's danger in it, certainly. But – when there's a cry for help . . . Hilde, in times like these, when terror makes might seem right, it seems to me that there is a higher duty than prudence. Would you agree?'

'Oh, *yes.*'

'Will you help us?'

'I'm honoured that you should allow me to. What should I do?'

'The guides I've mentioned – there are four of them – would be asked to use the *Boudoir Rose* as what you might call their communications centre. A man who is ready to make another trip would call in there and ask to make the acquaintance of the dancer – do they call you by your own name, Hilde?'

'I'm known – ridiculously enough – as Cléo. But they

could certainly do that, and ask me to join them for a drink – as that beastly one did.'

'It wouldn't attract particular attention, then?'

'Not at all.'

'Good. You'll have their names and descriptions – names that would serve as passwords – and whenever there's another party ready, instructions for you to give them – where and when to make the rendezvous. When they've agreed, you confirm it to me.'

'And that's *all*?'

Koch told her, 'The *Boudoir Rose* was stated to be a frequent haunt of persons who disappeared at the time of the Cavell woman's arrest. See where my so-called *crazy* notion comes from? You worked in that *boîte*, worked also for Cavell, *had* worked for these du Croys. That's enough to make me doubt you should be left at large anywhere in the vicinity of this château. Perhaps anywhere at all. Charges may yet be brought against you in connection with those past activities. *My* interest though is security in this area and, immediately, what may have passed between you and Leutnant Ketteler. Which will be clarified very soon. For the time being there- fore –' he paused for a moment, staring at her, then nodded – 'for the time being, continue at the Manoir, and caring for your mother, but confine yourself to those two locations and the direct route between them. On *no* account attempt either to leave this district or to communicate with anyone outside it. Is that clear?'

'Yes, but—'

'That's all.' He picked up a silver bell, property of the Princess du Croy, and shook it. 'Sergeant!'

13

Friday, December 14th: *finally*, departure for Boubers day. Two days late, thanks to a howling gale. So much for counting chickens. Two days confined to barracks, at that – for security reasons, by edict of McLachlan. And having told Amanda that he'd be leaving on Tuesday, when the weather had been all right, he hadn't even called her.

Weather wasn't exactly perfect even this morning; wind was down, but it had been snowing since the early hours and the field had a couple of inches on it. Still snowing now as a crowd of ground handlers – thirty men under PO Harmsworth – walked the ship out into it. Next to be brought out after SSP-7 was airborne would be Charlie's old U-boat killer SS-45; Higham, her new pilot, had been in the shed preparing to set out on yet another oversea patrol – as had his observer, the celebrated PP O'Connor, now allegedly in for the award of a DSM, which would mean that Charlie almost certainly *would* be getting a DSC for that U-boat – or as he'd put it to McLachlan, for being in the right place at the right time. 'Wee-wee' and Higham had both wished Charlie and SSP-7 good luck: despite all efforts it had become common knowledge that the black pusher's was a very unusual mission. All right – there was the black dope, as had been applied to SS-40 a year ago for an experiment in over-the-lines reconnaissance – but on top of that the rope ladders, head-rope, a load of scrulex anchors and no Lewis gun. Charlie had even had the Lewis mountings, one each side of the for'ard cockpit, taken out. Was carrying no radio either; he'd have taken one as far as Boubers, except that it would have had to be fitted into his own cockpit, since neither of the others could have operated it even amateurishly. There were more than enough peculiarities in fact to catch a curious airman's eye – to cap it all, of course, a major of the Royal Marines in the observer's cockpit, and old Peeling, the station CO, coming out into the driving snow to see them off.

And the bicycle. That had attracted interest, too.

Seven forty-five now, and still darkish, the ship's black bulk blacker still against the snow as the handlers turned her in the partial shelter of the wind-breaks, which on their windward sides looked as if they'd been whitewashed. Wind was north-by-west, so on her track of ESE from Beachy Head to Berck-Plage and thence to Doullens (site of an RFC 'lighthouse', i.e. navigational beacon, near Frévent) she'd have it on her port quarter. Wind allegedly force 4, at this stage.

Trim was as good as one would get it. A bit light, and a touch bow-up. He'd be taking off into the wind, as always – the way Harmsworth's team had her pointing now – then doing a one-eighty to put it astern and settle her on course while climbing to about 1,000. Circle over Mandy's first, he thought. As good a way of getting round as any. Especially as Mandy would be up by now, enjoying her tea and toast.

Ready to go, almost. Stavely had started her with the crank handle, and the Green was ticking over while he fussed with his dials and gauges. They'd taken him to a pub on Tuesday night – Charlie's idea, to which McLachlan had agreed somewhat doubtfully – and it had been reasonably successful: the Yorkshireman looking from one of them to the other over his pint of 'Old' in a comparatively unfrequented corner of the bar, murmuring, 'Guessed you'd be tellin' us what we're at on this caper, sir.'

'Better do that when we're over there.' Charlie lifting his pint. 'It *is* a bit of a caper, I'll tell you that much. But with the ears that are flapping here, what you don't know they can't get out of you – right?'

'Wouldn't be writin' home about it, like.'

'Sure you wouldn't. Home's in the West Riding, I think you said?'

From there on, conversation had been about home; largely about Stavely's two brothers who were even further from it than he was, one at sea in a cruiser and the other in the Army in France. Poor bastard. Then McLachlan, faced with a direct question from Stavely, told them that he came from a place called Gullane, on the coast of East Lothian not far from Edinburgh. It was the first time, Charlie had noted, that the Marine had come up with any information about himself, and sure enough he'd switched it then to geese, migratory, the hundreds of thousands that flighted down over this Gullane place, the staggering sight and sound of their arrival at dusk each evening throughout the autumn. Pink-footed geese, McLachlan had told them: came all the way from Spitzbergen, which was a hell of a long flight.

SSP-7 was ready to flight off now though, by the looks of it. On both sides, handlers' faces turned up this way, waiting for it. For *him*. He glanced round at Stavely enquiringly, and the AM nodded, raised both thumbs. And McLachlan looked as if he was well enough settled in – bicycle and all. So – all right. Charlie lifted both hands, bawled, 'Hands off, let go!' Everyone jumping clear and Harmsworth executing a breezy salute as Charlie eased his throttle open – then wider open, as her bow showed signs of falling off the wind, which had to be countered quickly. Twenty feet. Thirty. More rise on the elevators. It wasn't all that much of a wind, but with the snow in it and one's own goggled face into it, it felt like more than it was. The ship's rounded black snout bang on north-by-west, snow streaming, surrounding, plastering, and the ship powering up smack into it. One of the things you had to look out for was any build-up of snow on the tailfins, which could not only upset the trim but even encroach on one's control of the elevators. Give them plenty of exercise, was a partial answer: you could only go by the feel of her, couldn't actually see them. Couldn't see more than the top of McLachlan's head in the front cockpit, either. Leatherneck making himself as small as possible, crouching with his head retracted somewhat tortoise-fashion. Two hundred feet, at about two-thirds throttle. Time – just short of eight. Two-fifty feet: might stay at this height while making a courtesy call on Amanda. Why not, the cottage was on one's route to the Head – almost.

Port rudder, therefore, bring her round.

Visibility began improving from the moment her bow came off the wind. Using only five degrees of helm (a) so as not to risk letting the wind get the upper hand, and (b) to make it a fairly wide turn, to finish up on a track halfway between Folkington and Wannock. By that time she'd have her tail into it; would also be well clear of the airfield, out of the way of SSZs taking off. Three miles, roughly, from this point of completing the one-eighty to Jevington, although he'd be edging her on to south-by-east before that. Wind and snow all astern now, making things more comfort-able, although in watching the familiar land features sliding under, 250 feet below, one's goggles still needed frequent clearing. Light and visibility were improving anyway: the Polegate field in clear sight suddenly on the beam to port with an SS just lifting from it, and beyond that a train pulling out from Polegate railway station: that familiar bird's-eye view as clear as anything one moment and wiped out in the next as it receded into the snow-filled slipstream. Other side – Folkington abeam, but also slipping away fast. The rev-counter showed engine-speed of about thirty knots, but with the wind astern at this point maybe thirty-five. Airspeed indi-cator reading thirty-three. Wannock, that was: and the lines of comparatively recent building in a curve southeastward from there to Willingdon on the London–Eastbourne road. So Willingdon Hill, which topped 200 feet, had to be about – *there*. Mile and a half, no more. Still couldn't make it out. The snow varied – one minute a curtain, then a thinning swirl through which one could suddenly see up to maybe *five* miles. He was steering to pass between Willingdon Hill and Jevington, then, after taking a close, farewell look at the cottage, take her up to 300 feet. Would have made it

500 and stuck to that all the way across to France, but with the vis so unreliable – at moments even slightly confusing – one was inclined to play it a bit safe.

Snow might not last for ever, anyway. Weather forecasts on that had been vague. The *happy* thought was that no gales had been predicted. Heavy gauntlets with silk gloves inside them precluded the crossing of fingers. But there, now – he'd brought her five degrees to starboard and had Willingdon Hill fine on the bow to port. And Jevington – the village of, on the road leading down to Friston – close to starboard. So that was Harewick Bottom. Dozens of bottoms, around here – Harewick's, Crunden's, Chapman's, Duttle's. Duttle's was more or less Amanda's territory – though she was actually closer to Duttle's Brow, as Don Bishop had pointed out to him, in what seemed now an earlier age, almost a previous incarnation.

Would Don object to one's liaison with her, he wondered? Be aware of it, even? One's own nightmarish vision in that thought was of eye-sockets empty in a shattered skull, empty or mud-filled, scarecrow remnants festooning wire in a silence where so recently guns had thundered. Once or twice, looking at Amanda in quieter moments, he'd found that kind of imagery in his mind and wondered whether she had such visions, too. Whether anyone could not have, even *without* recent and intimate association.

Binoculars, now – pushing the goggles up with their eye-pieces. And yes – *there*. Less easy even from this height to pick out from under the covering of snow, but that was it. Narrow lane curving up past it, defined mainly by still surprisingly dark hedging. Tyre-tracks greyish. It was past eight now – eight being the time at which a colleague came to pick her up. Not always the same one, she'd said, they worked on a roster basis. Anyway, she'd have gone, would not be either seeing or hearing this black beauty powering over. The picker-up would have turned at the cottage, though, to go back down into the periphery of Eastbourne, and oddly enough there was only one set of tracks. SSP-7 passing at this moment not quite over the cottage's smoke-leaking chimney, but as near to it as he'd meant to be, Charlie now seeing that those tracks led out of the yard behind – had originated there. Originated in fact at a still darkish – almost bare – motorcar-sized rectangle where it must have been parked all night.

Or since the snow had started, anyway. That had been not long after midnight. Charlie attending to his business now, edging the elevator control-wheel round – trailing edges of the elevators upward – stern down, up-angle on the ship as a whole. Willingdon Hill coming up abeam to port: course from here to Beachy Head therefore SSE, distance say three and a half miles. Thinking of his job, the ship: in the *forefront* of his mind, damn-all else. Give her a bit more throttle. Having wasted – anyway *expended* – maybe ten or twelve minutes on making a wider detour than he need have, deciding to make up for that, cross the coast with revs on her for 40 mph rather than pass out over the sea and *then* crack that much on her. Forty was the speed he'd reckoned on averaging, allowing two and a half hours for the 100-mile flight; Polegate would have given Boubers-sur-Canche – or Doullens – ten-thirty as his ETA.

Over the coast, near the Head, altering from SSE to ESE. That was all clear as crystal in his thinking. What he was trying to keep *out* of it was an obscenity. And – inconceivable. Telling himself he'd had no business to have gone prying, anyway. All right, had *not* been prying – but wouldn't that be how anyone else would see it? Amanda herself, for instance? After he'd been less than truthful about his own movements – so she'd have thought she was in the clear? She'd told him, 'If Caterham asks me out to dinner, why the heck shouldn't I?'

Some dinner . . .

Leaving Beachy Head to starboard, to cross the coast between there and Eastbourne. The snow seemed to be thinning. Over the coastline, with Eastbourne's promenade starting a mile away to port – a couple of miles of it then, fronting white-edged, dark-grey sea. Settling her on ESE and checking the time – eight-eleven. On this course now, with the wind broader on the quarter, making her 40 mph all right, but no more than that at these revs – which were adequate in any case. One was inclined to nurse her, give her an easy time of it so as to have her in top condition for the flights that really mattered – which she'd actually been *built* for. Airspeed indicator actually showing 42 mph. Sixty miles now to the French coast at Berck-Plage, at this rate a ninety-minute transit – you'd be over Frogland by about nine-thirty. Adjusting revs again – just slightly – and thinking again – *inconceivable*! Turning to look back at Stavely, and the ox-like head in its helmet nodding 'OK' to him; one gauntleted hand raised, circular movement indicating their surroundings, satisfaction in the fact the snow had stopped or damn near had. A few flakes whisking by, feathers travelling like bullets. Speed-through-the-air plus pusher-prop sucking the stuff in, of course. Not a tenth of what it had been, anyway. Shifting back again, thinking that Stavely was – in naval parlance – a very good hand, and glad they'd had that off-duty session in the pub. McLachlan had agreed it had been a good idea and beneficial, giving him and the Yorkshireman at least some recognition of each other as human beings, as distinct from tin soldiers marching behind a guard and band – the fact being that small teams working at very close quarters with each other *couldn't* operate like regiments or even platoons, not even if they'd had any inclination to, which if they had they wouldn't have gone in for this kind of life in the first place. Checking the readings on all his instruments now while an image of that almost snowless rectangle slid back into memory like a magic-lantern slide. If the colleague fetching her had come early and gone in for a mug of tea, taken some time over it – having caught her on the hop, jumped the gun by a quarter-hour or twenty minutes, say – which might have made sense, with the snow coming down as thickly as it had been at that stage?

Would have had to have been parked there several hours to have made that much difference. Snow didn't all melt as soon as a car parked on it. That space had been covered by a car all damn night. Smallish rectangle, at that, matching what she'd said Caterham had – 'little sporty job'.

Too 'sporty' to be bloody true?

Scowling. *Very* funny . . .

McLachlan was craning around to look back at him: now pointing downward into his cockpit and touching his ear before ducking down to the 3-ply 'voicepipe'. Charlie obligingly though unenthusiastically did the same, put his right ear to this end of it and heard faintly, 'Doing well, aren't we, Holt? On schedule navigationally?' Pointless question. The voice-conduit wasn't much use anyway, and took up space, a corner of it tending to catch one on the right knee when putting on starboard rudder – right foot drawn back, that knee having to rise. His own doing, of course – idea originating when he'd thought McLachlan would be in the AM's position and communication with him would be essential. Would have been, too.

He yelled into the thing now, 'Fine! No problems!' Not at all happy in giving such reassurance, knowing all too well how suddenly serious trouble *could* arise – engine run a bearing, shitehawk fly into the prop, magneto failure, blocked carburettor jets, choking on dirty fuel, or—

Tyre-tracks in the snow. Knocked the stuffing out of you. Really had you sweating inside the heavy suit. Fish suddenly out of water, gills pumping, was how you felt – and saw yourself.

So forget it. Stick to *this*. Rock-steady, at 300 feet. Hadn't seen a single ship, as yet, although with the snowfall having apparently played itself out, visibility wasn't at all bad. Odd thought then, as by habit and instinct he more or less systematically explored the sea from right ahead to well abaft each beam, that even if he found himself overflying an entire flotilla of surfaced U-boats now there'd be damn-all he could do about it. Except climb, get out of range of their machine-guns. Having no bombs, no Lewis, not even a wireless over which to pass an enemy report. If there were ships in sight – destroyers or armed trawlers especially, of course – you'd use the Aldis, give them a range and bearing, or in other cases have them pass the message on. Nothing down there now, anyway. Empty grey surface ridged and whorled with white. Overhead, uniformly grey sky with no holes in it. He wished he had *not* decided to pass close to Mandy's place on a whim. Even though he honestly could *not* believe in the 'obvious' interpretation of what he'd seen. Although that was how it had been – he'd *seen* it – no question of illusion or imagination. And in plain fact, with Caterham around and telephoning her – he'd called and asked her if she'd come out with him only – what, five days ago – and when Charlie had asked her *would* she go out with him, she'd said, 'I don't know. I may.' So she couldn't exactly have shut him off; the sod *would* have tried again, and obviously had. Dinner at Sattery's or Weber's Cabin or the Queen's Hotel, then back to the cottage. *Everyone* getting taken back to the bloody cottage . . .

Nine o'clock. Closer to France than to England now. Would have expected to have seen *some* seaborne traffic by this stage. Minesweepers, for instance, or troop-carrying steamers to and from Dieppe. How must it feel, God's sake, for those poor wretches (like Stavely's brother) out of the Flanders mud on all-too-brief leave periods at home, to be shipped back like cattle to the purgatory they already knew all about, knew they'd been lucky to have lived through this far, and that it had to be at least ten to one they wouldn't be coming out of for *another* leave. Wouldn't you think some of them might jump overboard? Swim to that group of four – no, five – steam trawlers a couple of cable lengths off to starboard? Most likely French. He put his binoculars on them: they were showing no flags, but the numbering on their bows looked French, somehow. Searching for a figure 7 – French-type, crossed – but there wasn't one that he could see. A figure on the stern of the nearest was waving, and McLachlan rose slightly in his cockpit to wave back. They had women serving as deck-hands in their trawlers now, so one had heard. Brand-new thought then, as he let the glasses down on their lanyard: quite a few of the drivers in Amanda's RAMC-linked organisation were women, mostly driving their own cars. Suppose one of them had taken her home last night and saved herself an even earlier start in the morning – *this* morning – by staying the night? Snow had, after all, been forecast. Could have slept on the sofa, or even shared the bed. *Could* have. Might not seem exactly probable, but there could be other quite unguessable circumstances which would make it more so; and wasn't it a lot less *im*probable than – than how it *seemed*?

Smudges of grey coastline ahead and on the bow to port. Le Touquet and Etaples up that way. Dead ahead – count on it – Berck-Plage. For the past half-hour he'd been steering a few degrees to port of the course of ESE, which had to be his track-made-good, to allow for the now slightly freshened wind which would otherwise have been edging her further south than he wanted. Coping with a very slight increase in wind force, that was all – *not* thinking by how much it might have risen by this evening or tonight, tomorrow, say. No point in such speculation: however it turned out, you'd handle it. Even if that meant staying on the ground, waiting for conditions to improve. Or worsen. The Handley-Page bombers didn't embark on their long-range bombing operations in rough weather, McLachlan had been told in London, so it mightn't be just one's own decision anyway.

On the other hand, there'd be a fragment of old moon still hanging up there tomorrow – if cloud was thin enough or broken enough for it to show through. So if one didn't go tomorrow – which was desirable anyway, London wanted those women brought out as soon as possible – you'd be doing it in pitch darkness. Maybe tomorrow, even. With cloud-cover anything like total, forget about starlight too. Would have the advantage of total invisibility for this ship. Maybe – all that was still a toss-up. Charlie put his glasses up again. Berck-Plage now well defined – grey roofs and a strip of roadway curving around that blunt promontory, and to the south of it the conspicuous declivity of *Baie d' Authie* – the Authie being a river which he'd be crossing where it entered the estuary, and then again about twenty kilometres inland. Berck-Plage was on the beam, and the estuary's narrowing length dead ahead. He pulled his chart-board up on to his lap and pushed the goggles off his eyes to check over the navigational points he'd earlier noted – pencil notes of distances and place-names on the map's edge, all supposedly committed to memory, although memorising French village names when you weren't much of a linguist wasn't all that easy.

Second crossing of the Authie, anyway, would be at Argoules. That was the '20-kilometre inland' point; from there you'd have another forty, passing directly over Dournez – crossing the Authie yet again – then at fairly regular intervals Regnauville, Chériennes, Fontaine and Quoeux – however the hell you'd pronounce that, the answer being that he personally would *not*. And then Boubers-sur-Canche, which he'd come to think of now as 'Boobers' and which one would search for, in passing over, knowing that four kilometres further on, on the same track, one would be over the small town of Frévent, close to which was the Doullens 'lighthouse'. Recognising Frévent by its size in comparison with those other villages – whose names didn't in fact matter except as reference points by which to check progress and ensure that one was still on track, making the right allowance for wind – not that there was all that much of it. If (or when) he found or suspected that he was over Frévent, he'd turn back, look more closely and carefully for Boobers. It was said to be difficult to spot, being small, with only a single camouflage-painted canvas shed. He'd have the river Canche down there for guidance, though: it passed to the north of Boobers but more or less right through Frévent. And finally, if the chaps at the Doullens lighthouse saw this black beauty hovering around, although they were only supposed to start up after sunset, they'd give him a 'Q' on their beacon – 'Q' being the Doullens identification letter. He could even ask for it – if he thought he was lost – by firing a cartridge of the correct colour of the day from the Very pistol which he had on the floor beside him.

(Making two pistols in all, down there. The other was a Webley-Scott .45 which he'd borrowed from Bob Bayley. Bayley had expressed surprise at Charlie's having refused to have a Lewis fitted, had then remarked, 'Sort of jaunt this looks like to me, you surely should have *some* kind of weapon with you,' and had offered him this six-shooter. Asked by Charlie how he'd come by it, he'd said he'd won it in a game of poker-dice.)

Over land, now, with the Authie's estuary and bay diminishing astern. No sign of any snow down there. McLachlan had his head over the side to port, either being airsick or taking special interest in a village called – Charlie checked the map – Conchil-le-Temple. Anyway, leave him to it. Except for that weight of anxiety – and *astonishment* – in the background, you might say it was a case of so far so good – on track, on course, only forty kilometres to go.

He'd lost count of which village was which, having passed over about twice as many as he'd listed, but he found the Boobers place easily enough, having followed the road that passed through it on the way to Frévent, with the Canche at this point close to the north of it, then the triangular field – *and* its cleverly camouflaged 'shed', which actually stood out like a sore thumb, with other huts around it as well as several lines of tents – just to the south. He took the ship over it on a southerly course, descending gradually and throttling back, then did a slow one-eighty, coming down into the wind at a hundred feet – and less – towards a group of about a dozen or fifteen dark-clad RNAS men who'd been moving out into the centre of the field. They'd be airmen, riggers and AMs, although in fact he'd been given no details of the ground team he'd have here. They'd have been assembled in dribs and drabs from air stations all over the country, he supposed. Focusing his glasses on them – all the faces staring back up at him – at SSP-7, anyway – and McLachlan then pointing at a double column of khaki-clad soldiers moving out at the double to join that lot.

Halting. Turning into line, facing the officer or NCO

who'd been doubling out alongside them. A petty officer with the RNAS team was open-mouthed, bawling and gesticulating in that direction – where the pongoes under their officer or NCO, whatever he was, were now forming fours, for God's sake.

But all right, he'd dismissed them, and the PO was taking charge of them as well as his own lot, had them fairly scampering this way and that – no doubt having seen that Charlie wasn't hanging around, was in the course of putting her down, into a wind that was still about force 4. By the time she was down to fifteen feet he had a crew of assorted naval and military handlers on each side, keeping pace with her and closing in, and the ringmaster/PO standing clear, directing them.

Ten feet. Five. Naval airmen had got the handling lines. So – throttling back. Hadn't valved: with this team on the ground to receive him, hadn't needed to, and until one actually set eyes on it one couldn't know for sure that there'd be supplies of gas here. There should be, if McLachlan's overlords in London had been quick enough off the mark, but . . .

She was in good trim, anyway. Settling down like a big black duck. The PO holding up his arms then, forearms crossed, a signal to make fast or shut down, in this case presumably the latter. Maybe where *he* came from, ground handlers told pilots what to do? In any case – Charlie glanced back at Stavely, who was ready for it: he shut the throttle and switched off, allowed the Green to cough itself into a well-earned rest and the handlers to drag her down.

14

Accommodation at Boobers was in bell tents, which the Army contingent had supplied and put up. One at this end of the line and somewhat on its own had been allocated – by Second Lieutenant Tewksbury, Army Service Corps – to McLachlan and Charlie. Stavely was sharing with two other AMs, while Tewksbury had a tent to himself which he explained was also the Orderly Room, and had a field telephone in it which his signalman had wired to a junction-box in the village. Well – hamlet: Boobers was no metropolis. The officers' mess was a Nissen hut containing a kitchen table and hard chairs – and a stove for warmth; another larger hut was the mess hall for other ranks, and cooking took place in a Nissen that was also the AMs' and riggers' workshop.

Facilities, Tewksbury admitted, were limited and somewhat crude. But the place hadn't been in active commission for several months. Before that it had been used for the assembly of observation balloons and the training of regimental officers in their use. That had been shifted elsewhere now – combined with a parachute training school: the two going naturally in parallel, the soldier pointed out, parachutes having only recently been developed and observation balloons being easy meat for Hun scouts.

'Perfectly adequate, anyway.' McLachlan glanced at Charlie for agreement, added, 'Won't be here long in any case.'

Charlie put in, 'What *is* important – what about (a) hydrogen gas, and (b) petrol?'

'Both here, sir.' Tewksbury fingered the flimsy beginnings of a blond moustache. 'Petty Officer Davies has assumed charge of both, as naval stores. There's a dump of each, well separated. The gas in bottles arrived only yesterday – a truckload. I've put sentries on both. Makes us a bit short-handed, but . . .'

'Thank God for huge mercies. I'd better see Davies right away.'

'Most immediate thing, sir –' Tewksbury cut in – 'is a car's coming to take you to Ligescourt – 207 Squadron, RFC. Their CO's expecting you for lunch there.'

'How very kind of him!'

'On the ball, too. We'd better get out of fancy dress, though.'

The Sidcot suits were made of a grey waterproof material and fur-lined; boots sheepskin-lined. They hadn't brought any more gear than they'd thought they absolutely needed, but could hardly travel around looking like creatures from Jupiter or Mars – which one did, in Sidcots. McLachlan had had to bring civvies too – his cyclist's kit, he called it – but they'd still managed with one smallish kitbag each. Plus McLachlan's British Warm and Charlie's and Stavely's great-coats, which they'd sat in in their cockpits.

Tewksbury said, 'I'll leave you then, sir. Be glad to show you as much as there is to show, when—'

Charlie asked him, 'Is the car likely to be be here soon?'

'On its way now – according to their duty officer, and it's only about twenty miles, so . . .'

'Be a good chap. Pass the word to PO Davies that I'd like a word?'

They'd set it up pretty well, he thought. Had noticed, in disembarking in the canvas shed after the ship had been walked in, a compressor and a roll of linen tubing beside it – for inflating the ballonets via the scoop inside the shed. Also riggers' ladders and other gear. They'd have filled a

184

railway truck at least, with that and their smaller gear, and presumably rations, bedding and so forth. Mental note: check supply of engine oil. Although Stavely would probably have done so already. Anyway – all that, and a car already on its way from the Handley-Page squadron, did suggest that time wasn't being wasted.

Mormal forest *tonight*, even?

Could yet be snags, of course. Something to which no one had given thought. Excluding chances of the weather going to pot – because one certainly *had* thought of that, had been thinking of it for the past week, in fact. He buttoned his uniform trousers, sat down to pull on socks and half-boots. He'd decided not to bother bringing collars or tie: a flannel shirt with a submarine sweater over it, reefer over that, was good enough, and would keep one warm. A black pot-bellied iron stove was contributing in that effort very well, meanwhile; there'd be a soldier-batman tending it and bringing them their morning tea and so forth, Tewksbury – 'OC Boobers' – had mentioned.

Which suggested they'd be spending at least one night here. Although how *he*'d know – except that he'd been in contact with 207 Squadron, who for practical purposes might be seen as one's local authority, their co-operation being virtually essential. Charlie asked McLachlan – thinking of items that might have been forgotten – 'Did you bring a pump for your bike's tyres?'

The Marine frowned, thinking about it. A nod, then. 'Yes. There *is* a pump on it.'

'Sure?'

'I think so. Why?'

'What about a puncture-repair kit?'

'Why on *earth* should—'

'Pulling your leg, really. Wondering what we may have overlooked, that's all. Since they seem to have given us all we asked for, *and* by some miracle got it here in time!'

'*Just* in time. We'd have been stuck without the gas, eh?'

He nodded. 'Petrol one could have scrounged, but gas – yes. Well, might have just *managed*, but . . .'

'You thought it all out very well, Holt. And they've imple-
mented it efficiently. All that's in doubt now are weather
prospects, uh?'

PO Davies, a stocky Welshman with a blue jaw and beetling
brows, had introduced Charlie to the rest of the RNAS team
and was giving him a guided tour of the gas and petrol
dumps, and the vehicle supplied from Doullens – property
of the Royal Engineers – for moving that heavy stuff around
– a five-ton Foden steam-wagon with cast-iron wheels and
solid tyres, which Davies said had them all intrigued and
competing for a chance to drive it – when the RFC staff car
arrived from Ligescourt. Davies had got his scratch team
well settled in and organised, Charlie thought. None of them
knew what they were here for, except to tend to the 'black
pusher', which had to be going on some mission behind
the lines – night-time, otherwise why black dope – but to
do what, or when? Tonight, tomorrow night? Or the night
after that – start of the moonless period? In the shed, Stavely
with assistance from other AMs was conducting a maintenance routine on the engine: oil-change – drums of lubri-
cating oil *had* been supplied – and new plugs, filters, so
forth. All he'd told his helpers was that she had to be on
the top line and ready for when she was wanted, which might
be *any* time. In any case he'd wanted to drain the used oil
out while it was still warm. Charlie had told PO Davies, 'In
my absence, what Stavely says around the ship is what goes.
He knows what's wanted.' That was primarily for the ears
of Davies' own leading AM, who looked and sounded like
something of a know-all. He told Stavely quietly and privately
then, 'Could be tonight, but I doubt it. I'd guess tomorrow,
if the weather looks all right. You'll refuel her anyway, won't
you. And I'll tell you all you want to know either this evening
or in the morning. OK?'

A shrug. 'Buggers reckon I'm holdin' out on 'em. *And*
one of 'em saw the bike . . .'

The car from Ligescourt was a drab-coloured Humber
with RFC roundels on it. McLachlan and Tewksbury were

standing by it, and the driver, an RFC corporal, was hurrying back from wherever he'd nipped off to. SSP-7 at this point had been on the ground exactly one hour; time truly was *not* being wasted.

The corporal saluted, introducing himself. 'Corporal Plimsoll, sir!'

Charlie smiled, as both he and McLachlan returned the quiveringly military salute with considerably less expenditure of energy. 'Famous name you bear, Corporal.'

'Have *that*, sir.' A smile that showed missing teeth. He was about five foot four and sounded as if he might have had rusty nails in his larynx. 'No relation 'owever, far as is known, sir.' He'd opened the rear door: McLachlan slid in and moved over to make room for Charlie, who'd reassured the corporal with, 'Sam Plimsoll was only an MP anyway, not a seaman.' Tewksbury was standing back, signalling to his sentry on the gate. Charlie asked, as they turned out on to the road – sentry presenting arms – 'D'you know of any recent weather forecast, Corporal?'

'Only there was snow comin', then there wasn't. Good enough flyin' weather now, sir, wouldn't you say?'

McLachlan said, 'Thought you'd have turned left, Corporal.'

'Could have, sir. But then you'd be in them little lanes windin' all over. This way it's halfway to Frévent, turn off right – road as good as this one – carry on a while then right again and through Abbeville.'

'Twenty miles?'

'Bit more 'n that, sir. What you was asking, though – I did hear they was reckoning on high winds before much longer. Not always right though, are they?'

Slowing. Right turn coming up. McLachlan said, 'Talking about high winds – or in some such connection, Holt – you were going to tell me about a colleague of yours named Monk, who I gather came to grief?'

'Colleague – yes. Never met him, but – yes, certainly did. Gives you an idea what a really strong wind can do if you're unlucky. This was at Pembroke. SS-42 – on oversea patrol.

Flight Lieutenant Monk. He was coming back from a U-boat hunt because of foul weather kicking up very suddenly – put his ship down, or tried to – well, *did* – got hit by a gust that smashed her into the ground and carried away the port-side suspensions. Not unlike my experience the other day, that first flight at the Scrubs. But Monk's car was turned upside-down, threw his observer out and cracked the fuel tanks, and she shot up with petrol showering out – on top of everything else having shed the observer's weight, you see. Monk with no control at all, just hanging on – right up to seven thousand feet.'

The corporal was listening, Charlie saw. Head aslant, ear trained his way. He raised his voice a little. They were driving southwest now, getting through a village where it seemed to be market day. He nodded to McLachlan: 'Here's where he really *might* have started screaming prayers. At that height, the car's *forward* suspension gave way. Car then hanging vertically nose-down from the rear suspension. Imagine it. What he did – somehow or other – was transfer himself to the axle of the under-carriage. Ship still climbing meanwhile – into cloud and up to eight or nine thousand feet – where she hung for several *hours* – believe this or not – before she got sick of it, or maybe gas leaked and she began to come down, accelerating down and then also spinning. How he hung on, no idea, but he did – what's more, he jumped clear just before she hit the ground. Somewhere in Devon – she'd drifted about a hundred miles. He was knocked about, of course, but—'

'Lived to tell the tale?'

'Yes. Nightmares ever after, I'd guess. There've been similar incidents – at the Scrubs, actually – an Italian, went up to about seven thousand hanging by his feet – but Monk's really takes the biscuit. And just imagine – this is the point – with the particular load *we'll* have.' Two females. One elderly and infirm. Charlie shook his head. 'They don't have to worry – only wait a while, maybe. I'm not taking any weather risks. Not even if I was told to.'

'Although with your new techniques . . .'

'Not exactly guaranteed effective, and not aimed at coping with high winds either. Monk had the bad luck to be hit by that squall, wire-ropes snapped under the impact, then he had no control at all. Nothing he could have done – nothing I or anyone else could have done.'

'Might one say he shouldn't have been in that situation?'

'He was over the sea when the blow started – only hope was to get home and try to land. If he'd known there was foul weather imminent he wouldn't have gone out. And as I said, sir, *we* won't. If we have to, we'll wait for decent weather, no matter how long. Incidentally, they rebuilt that ship – SS-42 – renumbered her as 42A, and a year later she went into the sea and drowned both her crew. Not Monk, no . . .'

Ligescourt. Charlie counted the Handley-Pages lined up outside their hangars. Ten of them. No – nine. If it hadn't been lunchtime there'd no doubt have been AMs swarming all over them. They were very large aircraft, twin-engined and painted olive-green: sixty feet long, upper wings at least twenty feet from the ground, and a wing-span (he happened to know) of a hundred feet. Some of them had their outer wings folded back. For what purpose, he wondered. Well – access to the engines, maybe. Yes, that would be it. The engines were mounted between the upper and lower wings, so the upper was like a lid quite close above them. Like enormous kites, though. Out of sight now, the end of a hanger intervening, Corporal Plimsoll turning into an area of Nissens and timber huts; he drew up outside one marked ADJUTANT.

'I was told to bring you 'ere, sirs.'

'Right.' Charlie got out on his side, McLachlan on his, Plimsoll having opened that door for him.

'Thank you, Corporal.'

'Don't mention it, sir. Be taking you back to Boobers later.'

He'd got that pronunciation right, Charlie had noted. Might have been a jockey, he guessed. Turning as an RFC

officer – captain, equivalent to his own naval rank of lieutenant – burst out of the hut, looking relieved at their having
arrived at last. 'Major McLachlan, and Flight Lieutenant –
oh, sorry . . .'

'Holt.'

Shaking hands. This *was* the adjutant. 'Martingale.'
Shaking hands with McLachlan now. 'CO's awaiting you in
the mess, gentlemen. Short-cut through here – I'll lead,
shall I?' Tall, gangling fellow with some missing front teeth
and the ribbon of an MC on his tunic. Nodding to the
corporal: 'Back here four o'clock, Plimsoll, what?'

The officers' mess consisted of two Nissen huts joined
together, and the CO – greying hair, burly, with a DSO as
well as an MC – was a major by name of Cummings. The
mess was crowded and Charlie saw several RNAS uniforms
amongst the khaki: 207 had been a naval squadron origi-
nally, one of them mentioned. Everyone in sight was
drinking half-pints of beer. 'Suit you, Holt?' It was already
in his hand, but it was what he'd have asked for anyway.
There was no flying scheduled for tonight, he heard the
CO tell McLachlan; they'd been out last night, hitting
Zeppelin sheds at Evere outside Brussels. The defences had
been stronger than they'd expected, and – well, not so good
– in fact, bloody awful: one plane downed and one back by
the skin of its pilot's teeth with a dead observer/bomb aimer
and a badly wounded gunner.

'Anyway –' cutting across McLachlan's commiserations –
'since we'll certainly be flying tomorrow night – on *your*
business as well as our own – a night off won't do anyone
any harm. Tomorrow night suit you, will it?'

'Well – yes . . .'

Charlie put in: 'Does the weather look good for it, sir?'

'As a matter of fact, it does. Whereas for several days
thereafter it does not. Lucky, eh?' A nod. 'You have your
priorities right anyway, Holt. But we'll get down to the
nuts and bolts this afternoon. Let's put the nose-bags on
now.'

*   *   *

They assembled in the maproom, half a dozen of them: Charlie and McLachlan, the CO, the squadron's operations and intelligence officer – Captain Reynolds – and the two flight commanders, Rudd and Illingworth, both captains. While they were all milling around, chatting, lighting cigarettes or filling pipes, Charlie took a close look at a very large wall-map on which the Front was marked with ribbons – red for Allied trenches, black for German, and another stretch of blue, crossing that almost at right angles, from Doullens eastward and over the lines south of Arras, continuing just a few degrees north of east to pass south of Valenciennes. From there it wasn't a lot further to Bavay. Cards scotch-taped to the map here and there gave courses and distances. The extent of the blue ribbon gave a first impression of a very long flight, but in fact it would be only – for SSP-7 – about sixty or seventy miles, from Doullens to Bavay; plus as one knew oneself but couldn't have been shown on this scale, a few more miles to the landing place in the forest where the 'farm of the Abbess' was situated. He had the name of that section of forest in his own notes – *Bois de la Haute Lanière* – and he was going to ask them about the farm – ask this chap Reynolds in his capacity as intelligence officer. Probably wouldn't know, in which case you were committed to a gamble on that score, too.

Well – you *were*. The whole thing was a gamble. Great thing was to ignore that, just bat on as if it wasn't.

Reynolds joined him now. 'Find your way, d'you reckon?'

'Might, just about.' Looking at him sideways: 'This *your* artistry?'

'Well, since you mention it . . .'

'Stroke of luck, the coincidence of our course to Bavay and yours on to Namur, eh?'

'I assumed that was the whole basis of it. Although we could have been going anywhere – diverted and dropped you off, so to speak.'

'I suppose so. Enormous help anyway, we're grateful.' Plain fact was that it had been McLachlan's committee in London who'd sown the seed, then his own and/or

191

McLachlan's acceptance and development of the idea at Wormwood Scrubs. Chancy, inventive thinking translated here into reality and – seemingly – making sense. He checked the scale again. 'Sixty miles for us, or slightly more. Your chaps will have – another fifty?'

'With this slight dog-leg to pass north of Charleroi – yes. We'll be attacking Namur from the northwest, d'you see, then legging it for home *south* of Charleroi. By which time you'll be tucked away in your forest.'

'Certainly would hope to be.'

'I won't ask doing what.'

'No. Better not.'

'But I *can* take it as fact – as in the guff we had from London via Wing HQ – that you'll be flying at forty-five mph and you'd be happy at six thousand feet?'

'Absolutely. Except that once we've passed Bavay—'

'We'll be going into that, don't worry. The speed's ideal, I may say. We fly at ninety, which makes calculations particularly simple – in any given period of time we cover twice the distance you do. And the height's all right – we'll fly a bit lower than we usually do, that's all. Cold up there, mind you!'

'Brass monkey stuff. Wrapping 'em up warm's the secret.'

He went back to sit beside McLachlan, conscious of having held things up. The CO was already getting to his feet, beginning immediately with, 'I'm here only as MC or umpire. Start the ball rolling – ball being in *his* court, to start with.' Pointing at Reynolds. 'Then depending on whether or not his ideas match your requirements –' he'd glanced at Charlie – 'well, bound to be *some* problems – we're here to iron 'em out, that's all. All right?' He'd directed that to McLachlan, and the Marine as it were passed it to Charlie, who nodded. McLachlan explained, 'I'm only a passenger.' Cummings said, 'Intriguing. We might be privileged to hear all about it afterwards. Eh? But now –' to his SOO – 'All yours, Reynolds.'

'Thank you, sir.' He had a pointer – the sharp end of what had been a billiard cue – and touched Namur with it.

'Tomorrow night's target – Namur, railway yard and sidings. Our route from here via Doullens, as shown. Courses are detailed here –' one of the appended cards of notes – 'and that's all straightforward, much as you'd expect.' Reynolds was addressing the two flight commanders, who probably hadn't heard of SSP-7 until about forty minutes ago, in their mess. Telling them, 'As you see here, we'll be by-passing Charleroi to the north on our way in, returning south of it. Bomb-load same as last night's, nothing different in any way, crews'll be briefed tomorrow, five pm. What *is* different though, is that these officers, Major McLachlan RMLI and Flight Lieutenant Holt RNAS, flying airship SSP-7, will be in the air and to a certain extent in company with us – at least, on the same track – from Doullens to where Holt will be putting his ship down somewhere in the Forêt de Mormal – the Bavay area, that is.'

'What for?'

'It's a special operation, extremely hush-hush, waste of time asking, Rudolph.' One of the flight commanders: Rudd, Charlie guessed. Reynolds explaining to them, 'The intention is that our engine noise will cover the airship's as she goes down to land. Her noise cuts out while ours is still fading eastward, and the hope is that Huns on the ground will assume it's all part of the same brou-haha – won't occur to them that an airship might have landed. Heck, why should it, not exactly a common occurence, is it?' Looking down at his notes on a clip-board, and adding, 'A basic of my suggested timing is that Major McLachlan wants as many hours of darkness on the ground as he can get, and for obvious reasons the airship's got to be up and out of it well before first light. The earlier they can touch down, there-fore, the better. I'm suggesting they take off – from Boubers-sur-Canche, by the way – at six pm. All such detail's up for discussion, of course, when I've given you this outline. But – take off at six, say, within minutes they're over Doullens and on their way up to – I suggest – six thousand feet, and on course, same as ours –' pointer touching the blue ribbon – 'to cross the lines south of Arras between six-twenty and six-thirty. I should've mentioned, the airship's speed will be forty-five mph.' He paused, and asked Charlie, 'That your maximum, by the way?'

'Not quite. Not far off it. Engine's a hundred-horsepower Green, should give us fifty or fifty-two, but it's been what they call "silenced" – slight loss of power resulting. Forty-five is aimed at leaving me a knot or two in hand, so if we had the wind on her nose, for instance . . .'

'Wind will be from the northwest, about fifteen mph.'

Force 4 – 'Moderate Breeze', as reckoned on the Beaufort scale. Reckoned on the Beaufort in knots though, not mph, so only *just* force 4. Reynolds was continuing, 'Forty-five mph happens to be exactly half our usual cruising speed of ninety. So we can do the sums on our fingers – no long-division, don't you know.' Polite chuckle from the CO. 'What it comes down to is – if we can all accept this timing – the airship takes off at six, climbing to six thousand over Doullens – she climbs faster than we can, incidentally – and this squadron takes off between six-forty and six forty-five, climbing to *five* thousand.'

Charlie had his notebook and pencil out. So did the two flight commanders. Reynolds referred again to his own notes, and continued, 'From Doullens to crossing the lines, twenty miles, will take the airship about half an hour, so she'll be crossing at about six-thirty, and it'll take us less than fifteen minutes. You'll see action astern of you, Holt, around seven pip-emma. Action in the form of searchlights, ack-ack and flaming onions.' Glancing up: 'Ever see one?'

Shake of the head. 'I've led a very sheltered life.'

'Nasty things, anyway. Green fireballs – phosphorous – aimed at setting us on fire.'

'Mind if I raise one point?' The other flight commander – Illingworth. Reynolds nodded, waited for it, and Illingworth said, 'Not vital or anything, but five thousand feet's on the low side, I'd have thought.'

'Well . . .'

Charlie offered, 'What if I went up to six five-hundred?'

'That'd help, certainly.'

Reynolds said, 'I was putting you at six because that's the forecast cloud-level.'

'Right – but I'm not going to see anything on the ground from that height anyway, so . . .'

'You'd see – well, Valenciennes, for instance. Probably Bavay as well. Their blackout's never all that effective. At least, in the last few weeks—'

'Six-five *would* be a lot better.' Rudd, intervening. 'It would allow us to stack between five thousand and six thousand.' He asked Charlie, 'When you say six thousand five hundred, can we be sure you'd be at that height and no lower?'

'If that's what would suit you, yes.'

'Mightn't be tempted to come down out of cloud?'

'Tempted, maybe – but in the circumstances would not.'

'We sometimes have to climb or dive to get out of searchlights, you see. Diving's best because it's quicker, obviously, but we could make our absolute ceiling six thousand anyway.'

'Fine with me.'

Illingworth concurred. Pipe out of mouth for long enough to say, 'That's capital.' Then on a second thought: 'Talking about crossing the lines, though – are you assuming you *won't* be shot at?'

'*Hoping* we won't. My ship's painted with black dope, and with the silenced engine we're inaudible from the ground at five thousand, so – yes, touch wood . . .'

'Huns have some sort of detection apparatus – acoustical – that picks *us* up sure as eggs. Anyway – good luck!'

Reynolds took over again, suggesting to Charlie, 'From six-five you're going to have to come down pretty steeply near Bavay, aren't you – to identify your landing point?'

'Yes. To start *trying* to identify it. I'm hoping for some help from you on that, incidentally. We have one large-scale map, but—'

'I'll see what I can rout out, presently. Point is, we've got to be well clear of you – pass below you and take the lead – south of Bavay, this is, at –' referring to his notes –

'seven-twenty. That's where and when we overtake you. Could be tricky – you needing to get down and our tail-enders perhaps still under you. Having passed Valenciennes – here – where the defences are strong and usually wide awake, we won't pass more closely than we have to, then passing round Bavay, when—'

Charlie interrupted with, 'I'll be turning up to port about there. Only spitting distance from where I'm aiming to put her down.'

A nod: 'And so will we be. Turning to port, that is – turn as shown. Which I imagine will suit you because although by this time we're more or less leaving you to your own devices, you'd like to have the sound of us over the whole of the area you're going down into – huh?'

'Suggestion.' Rudd. Dark, lean-faced, about Charlie's age. 'Why don't I divert away to port with my flight on our own. Rest could hold on, Illy following his nose, and I'd—'

'You haven't looked closely at this, Rudolf. It's a twelve-degree course alteration, put there for reasons already stated: adjustment of course to pass north of Charleroi, but also let's hope deafening the local Huns, to the benefit of our friends here.'

'But what if I – me, solo – make a *sharper* alteration to port at that stage, confuse 'em with an even wider spread of noise off-track, and then rejoin. It'd be the crucial stage for these chaps, wouldn't it – and no skin off my nose. Twenty-degree diversion from your new course for five minutes, say, then back to rejoin over the *next* five minutes.'

Reynolds was thinking about it. The CO murmuring to McLachlan, 'He's got something there, don't you think?' Rudd asking Charlie, 'Suit you, wouldn't it?'

'Certainly would.'

'Here's another dodge, then. I'll fly as number four in my flight, tail-end Charlie, and being last in line I'll be at the lower end of the stack, nearer five thou' than six. And cloud-level being at or near six, you'll have been bumbling along in it blind at least most of the time, but by then you'd be safe as houses coming down to five – and lower. As low as you like – we'll have gone. Be wanting a sight of the ground, won't you – praying for a good, close sight of it, I'd imagine. Well, I'll start my diversion when number one flight leads round on this twelve-degree alteration – meaning I alter by thirty-two degrees – and at the same time I might poop off a Very.' Looking at Reynolds: 'Green maybe, for "go ahead", telling Holt all clear, he can put his ship's nose down and Bob's his uncle.'

'A Very, though . . .'

'What the hell. We're filling the night with our racket, noise drawing away east, east-north-east – what's one Very light telling anyone?'

15

He'd asked Rudd later, talking more or less on their own, 'What are the chances of Hun fighters interfering?' and the flight commander's answer had been, 'They tend to stick their noses in after we've left the lines astern. When ack-ack cuts out, it's a fair bet the buggers are coming up. Rear gunners' eyes go out on stalks – well, everyone's do.' Short laugh. 'Amongst any other symptoms. But you'll still be well ahead at that stage – higher, too. Won't be you they're looking for.'

Casting his mind back to yesterday's confab with the Handley people, partly to stop himself thinking about Amanda and the dream of her from which he'd woken. Not much wanting to drop off again with her in his thoughts and possibly be re-immersed in it. If there was much chance of 'dropping off' anyway, with McLachlan's snorts and snarls coming in bursts from the other side of the tent. Might well have been what had woken him – in a state of relief and happiness, having dreamt that the car-tracks he'd thought he'd seen around her cottage had been part of a more distant dream, thank God, hadn't ever happened and could be forgotten now, everything between himself and her being as splendid as it had been when they'd said goodbye.

Truly awake then, facing the unpleasant truth that *this* had been the dream. That if he'd had a camera with him yesterday he could have photographed the damn tracks.

That at this moment – 6 am now on his watch's luminous dial – that 'little sporty job' – if that was what she'd called Caterham's bloody vehicle – might once again be parked in her yard.

So frustrating that it was actually sickening. Stupid that it should be, but – there it was. Remedy of course being to stick to one's earlier resolve – concentrate solely on what was happening here and now and in the immediate future around SSP-7. Until one got back there, *forget* bloody Eastbourne.

Anyway, having asked about Hun fighters – Fokkers, Pfalzes, Albatrosses – and Rudd having pointed out that SSP-7 wouldn't be their target, he'd added, 'They'll be looking for us after we've hit Namur, all right. Again, not *your* problem – even further removed from it, obviously – but it's the flight home, when the Hun's dander's up, that gets a bit hair-raising sometimes. They know where we've been, and what we are – therefore where home is – and we've no petrol to waste by that time, and no inclination to hang around out there any longer than we have to, so it's a straight-line course – as it was *last* night, d'you see?'

'Yes. So sorry. Only hope and pray this one won't—'

'Some of 'em were down to three thousand and less, on the way back. As I was telling you – diving and side-slipping out of searchlights and so forth. They have mobile searchlights now, you know, mounted on tenders, race along below us. Gets to be a real old rough-and-tumble. In fact if you have any impression that we fly straight and level . . .'

'I'll stay well up out of your way, in any case.'

'You have – what, Lewis guns?'

'No.' It embarrassed him slightly to admit it. 'Carry one Lewis normally, but – not this trip.'

'No guns *at all*?'

'For various reasons, but primarily to save weight, increase what we call "disposable lift". Again, good reasons to do so. One Lewis with its ammo saves us about forty pounds, and I've had the mountings taken out as well. Two mountings, see, shift the gun to either side of the car as needed. But in any case, a single Lewis against those damn things—'

Reynolds, the SOO, had joined them, telling Rudd, 'He's relying on floating in unseen and unheard. Shoot not, and ye shall not be shot at.' He'd shrugged. 'Reasonably good chance, if the sods don't even know you're there. What's this farm you wanted to know about?'

That hadn't yielded anything worthwhile. Charlie hadn't really thought it would. Only by some chance – if a pilot had been shot down in the area and somehow got away or been brought out, for instance. But no such luck. Nor were the maps in Reynold's files anything like as good as those provided by McLachlan's people in London. Here in fact they had more photographs than maps, mostly aerial shots of the squadron's targets, photos taken by day-bombers, DH9s or 4s, on post-attack reconnaissance flights. The day-bombers crossed the lines at 14,000 feet, apparently, and had a much worse time of it than the Handleys – so Rudd had said. Anyway, Charlie had discussed the choice of that clearing in the forest with McLachlan, and they'd decided to chance it. Its advantages were (a) convenience to the village where the women lived, (b) shelter by forest walls from just about any wind direction, and (c) not being over-looked from anywhere except the farm and a couple of hundred yards of minor road. In daylight, the road might be more of a hazard than the farm, in fact – especially if it was used by Hun patrols. But since they'd be in and out of the place in darkness anyway – could not actually contemplate *not* being up and gone by dawn . . .

So why the camouflage with yellow dope?

Contingency planning. *In case of* such a need. As with the 'voicepipe', there'd been no time to hang about: what you'd thought you might need you'd had to decide on and either reject or implement at once. Now, incidentally, there could be absolutely no question of still being there in daylight – if only for the rather frightening reason that by dusk on

Sunday – tomorrow – winds would be rising from about twenty knots to gale-force.

Sunday, Monday, Tuesday, in fact. He'd copied Reynolds' forecast into his notebook, and here in the stove-warmed dark, with the Marine's snoring in the background and a rustle of night air over the tent's canvas, could see it clearly in his mind's eye: *Light NW breeze DEC 15 veering NE and increasing force 5 by noon 16th, probably 7 to 9 by midnight, gales continuing through 17th–18th.*

On the face of it – perhaps – dead lucky. 'Light Breeze' being force 2 – 6 knots say – and force 5 being 'Moderate Breeze' in Beaufort scale terminology – around 20 knots – 20 to 24 mph, say. In ordinary naval usage one worked in knots because chart distances came in sea-miles – 2,000 yards instead of 1,760 – but when working with land maps one had to switch to mph. Mental arithmetic thus becoming a frequent if not constant exercise; and a lot of the time one settled for approximations. Anyway, as 207 Squadron's CO had indicated yesterday at lunchtime, long before the expected increase to force 5 all his Handleys – please God – would be back on the field at Ligescourt. Whereas SSP-7 *ought* to be back in her shed here at Boobers by first light, if not earlier. *Preferably* earlier, and in any case, with daylight in the offing not long after seven, you'd reckon to be up and out of that forest at the latest by six. Straight up to six thousand, he thought, staying in or close to cloud, and with the northerly wind probably freshening by that time, steering about due west to make good west-by-south for Doullens. At full throttle, too – an hour and a quarter's flight maybe, aiming not only to beat the weather but also to stay out of the way of any Hun fighter patrols that might be up there in the dawn.

As long as one could trust that forecast, though. Not have the pattern shifted forward by say twelve hours. Force 5 and rising by midnight tonight instead of noon 16th, for instance.

No reason it should: simply that it *could*.

* * *

He raised some of his night-time thinking with McLachlan over a breakfast of bully beef and fried eggs.

'What about accommodation for the women when we get them here, sir?'

'A tent? *Our* tent, perhaps? Needn't be long on the ground, need we? And you and I'll be busy.' A shrug. 'You will, anyway.'

'They might be exhausted – the mother, especially. And the weather could be closing in, you see. This is the point, really – by the time we've refuelled, etcetera, wind *could* be force 5 or more. We could cope with *that*, but . . .'

'How long did it take us to get here?'

'Two hours and twenty minutes, with a little wind slightly abaft the beam. With a stronger one – perhaps *much* stronger, and for'ard of the beam – I'd allow an extra half-hour. Best part of *three* hours. All right, if your end of it goes smoothly – maybe six hours on the ground, say – where we're going, Malplaquet I'm talking about – might be taking off from there at about two am, say.'

'Possible – and highly desirable, of course – but not to any extent predictable. Absolutely no way of guessing. Could be easy, could be immensely difficult.'

'Just guessing, then, for the sake of planning ahead, let's say take-off about *four* am. On the ground here then by six. The wind isn't supposed to get up until midday, but even with no snags at all we'll need a couple of hours here. Realistically, let's say take-off for Polegate eight-thirty, nine. Suppose we manage that, and the women are willing and able to re-embark – I'd have thought the mother at any rate would want to put her feet up, get warm, rest, have a square meal, hot bath even – don't you think a billet in the village might suit them best?'

'Might suit them, would not suit *us*. What the daughter's carrying in her head – well, you know all that. Could save a million lives. To which end, security remains paramount, Holt. No question of letting either of them out in public. Don't you see – they've vanished from under the Germans' noses but no one can say for certain *we've* got 'em – I mean, that they're well on their way to England. No – they can have our tent. Or use this hut. Yes, that's it – Tewksbury can put a couple of camp beds in here. And a sentry on the door. As you said – couple of hours, that's all.' Pouring himself more coffee from the enamel jug. 'You sound less sure of weather prospects than you did yesterday, though. Any particular reason?'

'Forecasts aren't always accurate, that's all. Looks all right now, and touch wood should see us back here all right, but – well, suppose the force 7 hits us by noon instead of midnight? I don't want to have to land in a gale, even at Polegate. In fact – as I've said – I wouldn't chance it, if that was how it looked. Which would mean—'

'I can see perfectly well what it'd mean. Several days' delay. Anyway, this time tomorrow when we're back here – earlier than this, in fact – we could get an up-to-date forecast from Ligescourt, eh?'

'Oh, certainly.'

'And with any luck at all . . .'

'Yes. I'm not spreading doom, sir, only thinking ahead a bit. A variation from what's forecast *could* even go in our favour.' He checked the time, and pushed his chair back. 'Going to see Stavely about a few things now. Including the gas top-up this afternoon. Will you instruct Tewksbury about turning this hut into a ladies' bedroom, or shall I?'

'I will. Tell me, though – why a gas top-up when you haven't used – valved – any?'

'There's always some leakage. Valves leak, and to a lesser extent so does the envelope. That's why we'll leave it until nearer take-off time.' He stopped on his way to the door, turned back again. 'With your agreement, sir, I think I'd better brief Stavely now on where we're going and what for. And about the Handleys, since we may see some at close quarters?'

McLachlan nodded. 'But he does not have to know the precise nature of the intelligence the girl's bringing. That'll be on the secret list for months yet.'

'No. Right.'

'While you're at it – have him or someone get the bike out for me? Thought I'd go for a spin on it. They say one never forgets how, but . . .'

'Make sure its wheels go round, and—'

'I might ride into Frévent. And best to do that in my civvies – with identity documents ready to hand, naturally. You go ahead, I'll join you.'

'Dress rehearsal . . .'

'Might call it that. I've got to wear a lot of that stuff under my flying-suit, you realise. Holt – another thing to arrange with Tewksbury is rations. Sandwiches, plenty of 'em – not forgetting hungry women. Thermos's to be filled, too.'

You were down to that sort of detail now. Feeding hungry females, and how frightened, compliant or difficult they might be. Like transporting wild animals . . . McLachlan was coming with him anyway; clapping him on the shoulder as they left the hut: 'Amazing to think of 'em going about their daily business, with not an idea in their heads we're coming for 'em, eh?'

'Thinking of that, sir – if may ask – are your plans more or less cut and dried? I mean, when we get there and you pedal off to that village . . .'

'Neither cut nor dried. I find 'em, tell 'em who I am, explain what an airship is and promise 'em it's safe – try to sound as if I'm the sort of chap it's safe to leave home with in the middle of the night – offering mama a piggy-back, perhaps.'

'On the bike?'

'Of course *not*. Shanks's pony, damnit. How easy or difficult depends on them – their attitude. But the girl's *asked* to be brought out, so . . .' Both hands raised, fingers crossed. '*My* problem, Holt.' Striding off towards the tent then, swinging his arms and hugging himself for warmth. Charlie wondering what he'd do if the girl had changed her mind and wouldn't leave. Or if mama turned hysterical . . .

* * *

Stavely got the bike out, inflated its tyres and oiled it. He'd done all his maintenance work on the Green, riggers had checked the envelope and Eta patches and tensions on the festooning of steel-wire rope, petrol tanks were full and a load of the 10-foot hydrogen bottles were being brought up at this moment on the Foden steam-wagon, he reported. Charlie said, 'Well done. And now it's time I let you in on what it's all in aid of. Held out on you long enough. Reason's only that until a chap actually *needs* to know . . .'

'Don't suppose I do, sir, do I?'

'You'd just get on with it as you have been anyway. Yes, I suppose you would. But –' he checked, looking around – 'man's entitled to know what he's risking his neck for. What's more, things could go drastically wrong, you could be left on your own, with no clue what's best to do . . . Come on, let's take a stroll, see 'em bringing up the gas.' He'd been stuffing a pipe which he'd light when they got outside the shed.

Stavely tapping the bike's seat with a spanner. 'He'll want this putting up or down, likely.'

'Leave the spanner, he can fix it as he likes. Come on.'

The Foden was already clanking its way slowly over from the far side of the field, and Tewksbury was outside what he called his orderly room, addressing a corporal and half a dozen soldiers armed with spades. Stavely said, 'Brown-jobs got hundreds o' them steam wagons, bloke was tellin' me.'

'Brown-jobs' meaning soldiers – the Army. Charlie was putting a match to his pipe: his back to the light breeze, palms cupping the lucifer's weak flame. He began, 'Listen now. We're flying into northern France, Stavely, close to the Belgian border, to collect two women and bring 'em out. One of them – *young* woman – has some very important intelligence – military information, that is – which London is very, *very* keen to get, and she's offered to spill the beans as long as we bring her and her mother away to England. Mother's old and infirm, couldn't be got out any other way

205

than this, and the daughter won't leave her behind. Oh, mother's English-born, apparently, which puts her in danger somehow, but being crippled – well, the girl could have been smuggled out easily enough, I gather, but . . .'

'Know we're comin' for 'em, do they?'

'Apparently not.'

A sideways glance, thick eyebrows raised. Charlie explained, 'Security. Huns have sharp ears and spies all over. If we could've risked it we might have arranged for ground handlers to be there waiting for us. Fact is we couldn't – might've ended up with the wrong kind of reception party, eh?'

'Huns.'

'Right.'

'Major fetchin' 'em on his bike, is he?'

'Getting to their village on his bike, yes. From where I hope to put us down – on the edge of a patch of forest – what the practices at Slindon were for, you see – from there to the village is only a couple of miles. From there it's up to him – he might find a farm-cart, or hoof it with the old girl on his back, whatever. That's his business – he knows his way around, talks the lingo, and all that. But listen – we may have problems getting the ship down in that place. Forest area, and no ground help, obviously. Hence rope ladders, all that. And I need to do it without valving – the weight of the women to think of. Getting in there, another problem's our engine noise. From five thousand feet downward, Huns on the ground hearing us, then they're darned near deafened, and a few minutes later our noise cuts out. Huns asking themselves, what's this, then? Well – with luck, an airship won't be the first thing they think of, but anyway we've arranged for a squadron of bombers to be passing over at the same time.'

He explained all that: the height SSP-7 would be at, the Handleys overtaking at lower levels, and the Very light that would give him the 'all clear'. It had all been agreed yesterday at Ligescourt.

'So when we get down and shut off, we *hope* our arrival

will have been covered by that racket continuing eastward. They'll be going on to bomb a target fifty miles further on.'

'Good luck to 'em!'

'We need some luck too, though. Getting down, as I said, may not be easy – taking off may not be, either. That's why no Lewis, no weights we could do without. The mother may weigh half a ton, for all I know.'

'Both of 'em in with the major?'

'Have to be. Unless you'd like to have one with you?'

'Heck, *no*!'

'Ten to one you'd get the old one anyway. But listen – there are problems all the way along. To be straight with you, it's bloody chancy. Thing is, though, the information in that girl's head – as the major was saying half an hour ago – could save a million lives. Could shorten the war – end it, even – or at least make certain the Huns don't break through before the Yanks have got 'emselves sorted out. What we're doing's aimed at getting the lads out of those *bloody* trenches, eh? One of the million saved could be your brother – Tim, right?'

A grin. 'Tim'll be there at finish. Bet your boots.' A wag of the wide head: 'Don't need to bet, flaming *will* be!'

Charlie had stopped. His pipe had gone out, from so much talking. He and Stavely both watching the Foden's noisy approach. PO Davies was at its controls, and by the look of him, enjoying himself. Stavely's certainty meanwhile ringing in one's ears and imagination: *Be there at finish. Bet your boots . . .*

Faith, Charlie thought. What *I* need.

Thinking then – returning Davies' cheery salute – write her a letter, for Tewksbury to post if we don't get back.

McLachlan had had a similar idea, it seemed. Early afternoon now: Charlie had left him and Tewksbury as soon as they'd finished lunch and gone over to the shed to supervise and help with the topping up of gas; came back to find Tewksbury departed and the Marine scratching away at a letter – metal inkpot on the table, bone-handled pen probably also borrowed from the orderly room. Charlie had stopped at their tent to collect his maps and navigational notebook, intending to use the time that was left in memorising courses, distances and ground-patterns which he might recognise if he saw them. He'd have the Aldis for illumination – map-reading, when or if he had to – the lamp in its bracket, down-pointed to contain its powerful beam within the cockpit, but having only two hands and at least a dozen things for them to be doing simultaneously at certain times it was essential to carry as much as possible in one's head.

McLachlan had his file of operational notes with him too, Charlie saw. Homework for him, then, as well as letters home. Names and addresses in Taisnières and such places, one might suppose. He'd need this map too, when they landed. Charlie told him, pulling a chair up to face him across the table, 'Your bike's back in its lashings in the cockpit, sir.'

'Ah. Good.' He'd wanted to be sure of not leaving *that* behind. He'd cycled all round Frévent this morning, and stopped to buy himself a beer in some pub.

'Writing to –' Charlie paused – 'forget the name of the place you mentioned – where the wild geese congregate?'

'Gullane. Pronounced "Gil'n" but spelt G-U-L-L-A-N-E. It's also where my son resides. He's three. Andrew. Hence the clear calligraphy, slow compilation and search for short and simple words. Actually he's just *over* three. If some Hun shoots me dead in Malplaquet or Taisnières-sur-Hon –' he tapped the letter – 'they'll give him the gist of this and keep it for him to read for himself when he's older. Wouldn't want not to have said goodbye – you know?'

'No. I'm sure one wouldn't.'

'I expect you wrote home before you left, did you?'

He shook his head. 'Don't write home much. Any case—'

'How about the Polegate or Eastbourne roots, then?'

He hesitated. 'Did think of it, but . . .'

'Don't you think you should? This kind of show, if we did come a cropper, it could be quite a while before news got out. And as she's presumably not your kin – oh, perhaps she'd hear from them?'

'Not a chance.'

'Never the twain shall meet, eh?'

'Oddly enough they did – years ago. Not in touch now, though.' He shrugged. 'Complications. Happens I did think of dropping her a line – and I appreciate the interest and good advice, but –' he smiled – 'fact is, sir, I'm counting on bringing us back safe and sound in any case.'

'I'm sure you will, too. Us plus the – er – freight. Cigarette?'

'Thanks but –' pulling out and laying on the table one pipe, tobacco-pouch, matches – 'if you'll put up with the stink?'

'Heavens, man!'

'Ask a personal question, may I?'

McLachlan looked at him, waited for it, having just picked up his pen.

Charlie asked him, 'Where your son is – at Gullane – you said *they'll* keep your letter for him. Is he not with his mother?'

'By "they" I mean my sister and my parents. My wife died giving birth to the boy.'

'Oh – hell, I'm *sorry*, I—'

'Perfectly all right. I tend not to talk about it much. Lot of water under the bridge since then, and – one doesn't much, that's all.'

'I'm more than sorry, sir.'

'No reason you should be. Don't think about it. I'll wind this up now, anyway.' Dipping the pen, but glancing across again. 'Wind holding steady, is it?'

'Except there's snow in it. I was going to say, but—'

'Actually snow falling?' Twisting round: the hut's only window was behind him. 'Oh. Well – very little. At the moment . . .' Left hand moving to touch wood. 'Do Handley-Pages operate in snow?'

'I doubt they would in heavy stuff. Stupidly, didn't think to ask. Shouldn't imagine that just a flake or two—'

'We'd be stumped, wouldn't we, if they were grounded? With the wind that's forecast for tomorrow.'

'Mean sitting here those two or three days before going in instead of after. Wouldn't *want* that, but if we had to . . .'

'You wouldn't want to go in without the Handleys, either?'

'No, I wouldn't. But this could be just a flurry, mightn't come to anything.'

He didn't think it would. Not from any Stavely-type faith but because there'd been no mention of snow in that forecast or warning of it during the conference at Ligescourt – which surely there would have been; if it was enough to interrupt their strategic bombing programme, they'd be very much alert to it. McLachlan was back at work on the letter to his son, Charlie unfolding the Bavay district map – McLachlan's actually, the one he'd need when he set off on his bike – to recheck distances and timings on that final stage. From south of Bavay – two miles south – where you'd get the Very-light signal and start down. These lakes on the approach to a place called la Longueville . . . There was quite a pattern of lakes there; if there was any moon showing through it might well be visible. Lakes, then a large-ish village. Port rudder there, to NNE, and – two and a half miles. At 45 mph – three minutes?

Checking that. Last three minutes in the air, and low enough maybe to be visible as well as audible. *Tense* three minutes therefore, and accuracy of navigation rather vital. Thinking about it – only out of the corners of his eyes seeing McLachlan, who'd folded the rather stiff paper he'd been writing on, surreptitiously touch it to his lips before sliding it into an official-looking brown envelope. Careful not to look at him at all now, in fact. And not actually needing to write to Amanda – this came into his mind ready-made as he reached for the other, larger map – because (a) at this stage he didn't know exactly what he'd say to her, (b) he *would* be back in a week or so, in any case, and (c) if one hadn't shown up within some reasonable period of time – fortnight, say – she'd only have to telephone old Peeling for news of him. Or get Sneem or bloody Caterham to find out for her.

16

Charlie looked back at Stavely, signalling one-handed and simultaneously shouting, 'Start her up!' SSP-7's bulk looming dramatically in the yellow light of flares set on a fifty-yard perimeter around her, the lights' reflections flickering luridly on her tight black skin. Those were portable braziers containing oil-soaked waste. He saw the AM on his feet, heard the clank of the starter handle as he shoved it in – and Tewksbury's last-second yell of 'Good luck!' – then Stavely's muscle-power had set the prop spinning and the big engine exploding into life, Charlie's left hand on the throttle opening her up a little, then both hands raised in a signal to PO Davies to let her go – handlers letting go of the guys by which they'd been holding her nine or ten feet off the ground, her nose into the wind. Lifting, moving, on her way, Charlie giving her more throttle. Six pm exactly – or no more than a minute past. Looking down on those flares now; as she lifted they seemed to be closing in to a tighter pattern, a contracting ring of fire. One hundred feet: and starboard rudder, having taken off into the northwesterly breeze, needing to get her round now to east-by-south, the course for Frévent and Doullens, distance from here less than three miles. Four hundred feet: and to the men on the field she was probably invisible already; they'd be dousing the flares in any case, before some Hun prowler happened along with bombs he wanted a lit-up target for – the shed, for instance, and/or tents. SSP-7 coming round nicely, 500 feet, the engine a smooth roar of power; black ship, black night, couldn't see any flares down there now but *should* get a letter 'Q' from the Doullens lighthouse any minute now. Settled on course for Doullens anyway, Charlie giving her some bow-up angle – a half-turn on the elevator control-wheel, then watching to see the effect of that – the aim being to increase dynamic lift, get her up there faster. All right – and more throttle now to match it. Making 40 now – mph – and wanting 45. No snow – with thanks for small mercies, that had been a false alarm. Compass course east, so easing the rudder. East-by-south, two degrees of bow-up angle and the needle in the airspeed indicator moving slowly but steadily towards the forty-five mark. Soft glow of the dials in the instrument panel, power supplied from the same accumulator the Aldis signal-lamp was wired to. If one was going to need the Aldis – it seemed unlikely but might in fact prove a Godsend in say an emergency landing back here, or for that matter on the ground at Malplaquet. Might need light for map reading anyway; but there again, much better to do without it. In any case, re-wiring had saved the weight of one accumulator.

Rate of climb increasing; Charlie remembering the Ligescourt SOO, Reynolds, airily telling the flight commanders: 'Within minutes he's over Doullens and at six thousand.' Actually, as amended, 6,500. Two thousand now, after five minutes. Reynolds might have been disappointed. A blimp surely *would* climb faster than a Handley-Page, but she wasn't a blooming rocket – and in any case there wasn't all that much hurry to get up to what would be her cruising height.

Reassessing . . . Wind abaft the beam to port, but not enough of it to take notice of at this stage. No moon, and no sight now of anything on the ground. The Canche, for instance, which he'd have thought he might have seen. Moon – the sliver that was left of it – would be up, all right, risen, but with total cloud-cover wasn't going to get much of a look in. So being in cloud oneself – as one would be at 6,500 – wasn't going to make any great odds either.

Stab of white light from the ground – and another. Now a dot – *short* stab – and another long one. Morse letter 'Q' – the Doullens' signature – right down there, pretty well under her round black nose. Which was fine, really *very* handy, and meant – well, it told him to bring her round just three degrees to port, on which course after twenty-two miles you'd be passing south of Arras, by that time having crossed the lines. Twenty minutes maybe to the actual crossing – one might say, to discovering whether or not the Huns' detection apparatus picked up blimps as well as bombers. Three thousand five hundred feet: six-ten now. Half an hour to the Handleys' take-off time. Visualising those big green kites lined up on the field; they'd take off, it had been explained – by Rudd, who'd also shown Charlie over his machine – in single file, one after the other, the squadron's take-off spread over five minutes, one machine leaving the ground about every half-minute. Front-runner (No.1 flight commander, Illingworth) leading on up to 6,000 and the others taking station astern of him at hundred-foot vertical intervals so that the tail-ender, Rudd, would be flying at about 5,000.

Until he passed under SSP-7 and spat out his green Very, at seven-twenty.

Climbing through cloud now. At 6,150. Freezing night air now also wet – goggles running with it. Wiping them to read 6,250. Looking astern now there'd be no sight of the Doullens flashes, no sight of anything at all in any direction whatever. This was how it would be all the way, he realised – unless one came down to about 6,000, which one had sworn one wouldn't – wouldn't be worth risking anyway. Might well not get even a glimpse of Arras, despite Hun-enforced blackouts not being a hundred per cent effective, according to Reynolds. In that case no sight of Valenciennes either, he supposed – blind, and dead-reckoning all the way. Definitely *had* better be in position to see that Very: to do so was absolutely crucial, the one way you'd know, in an hour and a quarter's time, exactly where you were. And Rudd – thinking of the crossing of the Lines, searchlights, ack-ack and flaming onions – at only 5,000 feet had better damn well watch himself.

No Rudd, no green Very.

Six thousand five hundred. Levelling her. Time – six-thirteen. Airspeed – 45 mph – 47. Adjusting throttle just a little – and watching that now, having given her more power to facilitate the climb. Throttling back a bit more . . . Meanwhile, of course, no panic, no sweat in the old Sidcot, only watching a trifle anxiously for any break in the cloud that might allow him a sight of Arras (the glow above it) on the bow, but neither expecting it nor really needing it. Blind, for sure, but on track and making the expected speed/progress, time ticking away unstoppably towards six-thirty and the crossing of the Lines – and *there* maybe a display of searchlights? If he did see them he'd take it as a navigational encouragement, not as any threat. Black dope and silenced engine, after all – the efficacy of both had been demonstrated, proven. What else had the trials been for? Don't question it, take it as read. No need to question one's own navigation by dead-reckoning either – although one had hoped to be scraping along under an uneven ceiling of cloud, not permanently shut into it but able at times to see major landmarks such as – well, large towns, or water. See Valenciennes, in any case. Maybe not Arras, which had been reduced to rubble in more than one period of bombardment, where the occupiers would be living like rats in cellars and other holes in the ground, or shelters amongst the ruins. South of there, anyway, at six-thirty, one would be altering to port by eight degrees. Over a place called Neuville, roughly – which obviously one didn't have a hope in hell of *seeing*, was only a Reynolds map reference, a label enabling one to pinpoint it on the map and refer to it in those discussions; from there, that alteration, you'd have thirty-five miles (forty-five minutes) to the point of passing south of Valenciennes, then another twelve and a half miles (sixteen minutes) to get past Bavay.

Six-thirty. Just a small touch of rudder to bring her round by those few degrees, smoothly and easily maintaining height and airspeed. Handleys as yet not even off the ground. Must have crossed the Lines oneself, though – maybe *now* leaving them astern. Although down there – *nothing*: no sight, no sound. Not a flicker of any light, let alone searchlights' strong reaching beams. Off to port, though – and close – Arras. Further over, Vimy Ridge, and Lens and Loos. Blood-soaked names, corpse-filled country. To starboard – well, Bapaume, Cambrai. And, he supposed, Flesquières, where Don Bishop had died setting up his Regimental Aid Posts. SSP-7 floating over all of that, ignoring it just as it was ignoring her. Huns down there in headphones tuned in to detect intruders and getting nothing. Inclinometer showing wind slightly closer to the beam than it had been only minutes ago: a swift check then telling him it was not a shift in wind direction, only that she was off-course by two degrees. *Only*, indeed: watch it, he told himself, watch everything – you *have* to see that green Very when it's fired and if you let her wander you bloody won't.

He wished he hadn't thought about Flesquières. He had a bad feeling about poor Bishop. It didn't belong here, but it had taken root; in due course he hoped to God it might be *up* rooted, but meanwhile – well, not *forget* it, just don't think about it.

Six-forty. The first Handley rolling forward, maybe, hitting about 80 mph before it lifted and banked round towards Doullens. Which would be sending out wireless 'Q's as well as visual ones, just as a number of other 'lighthouses' would be doing from other places, providing cross-bearings from which the bombers' navigators could get fixes via their own wireless set's direction-finding capability when they needed to. Lucky buggers in that respect – one man flying, one navigating and observing, and when the time came, bomb-aiming. He – the navigator – moved from his seat beside the pilot and crawled through a tunnel into the Handley's nose-cockpit to do that as they approached their target. The gunner was in the rear cockpit, and all the pilot had to do was bloody fly.

Not so lucky maybe when the searchlights and ack-ack

and the flaming onions came into it. They'd all have that in mind, he guessed – being off the ground by now, and by seven – a quarter of an hour, roughly – in the middle of all that and with their ceiling at 6,000, *not* having cloud to hide in.

Bloody cold.

He'd been looking for action astern in recent minutes and seen nothing, heard nothing. Had also had a weather eye out to port for any giveaway leakage of light or possibly searchlight activity in the direction of Valenciennes – could have been a thinning or even a break in cloud-cover – but no such luck. One's own fault for having so blithely offered to fly at this height: hindsight told him now that it might have been wiser to have proposed climbing to this level *after* Valenciennes. Or at say ten past seven. It was now five past. The Handley's would have seen their last flaming onion for a while, and please God may they have come through it unscathed. All nine or, at a pinch, ten – if a replacement for the one shot down the night before last had joined the squadron in time and had been considered operationally fit – plane and crew. Reynolds had doubted they'd be reinforced that soon, but it had been a possibility. Anyway, the nine or ten of them would now – again, please God – be racing up astern; SSP-7 with ten miles to go to the point where they'd overtake her near Bavay, and since at 45 mph she was covering five miles every six and a half minutes – and it was now coming up to seven minutes past the hour – well, the calculation wasn't exactly difficult and matched precisely what one might call 'Very-light time' of seven-twenty.

Six thousand five hundred feet. Airspeed – right, 45. Course – also spot-on, hadn't wavered from it or taken his eyes off the liquid-filled compass's soft glow for more than a few seconds at a time since – well, since passing Arras, anyway. Wind inclination similarly unchanged. She was trimmed – as Charlie had wanted her, had seen to in the shed before being walked out – slightly heavy, in readiness

217

for getting down over the Abbess's farm good and quick when the time came.

Seven-eighteen, say, start down. The DR *had* to be good enough; you'd know well enough where you were – where you *would* be – coming up for that little group of lakes and the big village, change of course to north-north-east and a steepish descent into the enclosed area of farmland two and a half miles ahead. Get down into it quick, into the shelter and visual cover of the trees, approaching as low as the trees permitted – a little over tree-top height, say – to be sure of seeing that comparatively narrow gap; and at at least half-throttle, having to take a chance on excessive engine-noise in the interests of not having to valve. Never mind the noise – the Handleys would be taking care of that. Seven-fifteen now: one could assume that in this and the next two minutes their front-runners would be streaming under – thundering under, down there – Illingworth's flight most likely past and gone by now – and making their twelve-and-a-half degree alteration to port; eighteen or twenty Rolls-Royce engines belting eastward only 1,000 feet below you, and not getting so much as a whisper of it, in one's own steady roar of engine-noise which extraordinarily enough was itself not audible on the ground.

Seven-*six*teen . . .

Start down?

As a preliminary, a gush of air via the scoop and the for'ard crabpot valve to expand that ballonet, drive gas aft and impart a bow-down angle. Matching this with the elevator control and getting the appropriate response: altimeter needle beginning its swing through 6,400 – 6,250 – 6,100 and—

Out of cloud. Back into it a second later, into its trailing lower edges, then out again. Air stinging like dry ice and through it – to port – an impression of up-thrown radiance. Wishful thinking, or Bavay's version of a blackout? Five thousand nine hundred – eight hundred: you were in what was technically the Handleys' air-space now but – please God, let there be no stragglers. One had to *assume* they'd bloody gone – including tail-ender Rudd, who wouldn't have been much higher than 5,000 anyway.

And *there* . . .

Definitely no wishful thinking – a green spark, lower and off to port. Floating star, small glowing splash of brilliant green with a softer aura spreading around it as it drifted earthward. Timing highly fortuitous: if he'd stayed up there until eighteen minutes past he'd have missed it; even if he hadn't wiped the wetness off his goggles the second time they'd come out of cloud, might have missed it. Rudd having in naval parlance warmed the bell, by about half a minute. Height now 5,700. It was tempting to come round to port immediately, cut the corner: holding on though, rather desperately wanting a sight of those lakes which he'd reckoned would be just off to starboard. Seven-twenty now and fairly certain that Rudd *had* pooped off prematurely. Height 5,250, descent quite fast but could be faster, one needed to see ground features as memorised, and could be sure there was now no danger of collision; in fact Rudd would have swung away at the same time as he'd fired that Very.

Four thousand eight hundred – on one's own now, one would be audible on the ground. Four thousand five hundred, and – glory be, could see his lakes down there. A couple of degrees to *port* of his present heading, in fact. Kicking on port rudder double quick, therefore. Had to be *some* filtration of moonlight through the cloud-cap for that shine of water to show up so well. One would be passing near enough over the top of them – lakes, large ponds, whatever – as she swung to her final course of NNE. Couldn't make out any village where he'd reckoned to, but – lucky enough to have seen the lakes, let alone a darkened village. Seven twenty-two now. Two and a half miles from this turn was how he'd had it measured, memorised and pictured – so the long southward reach of forest which he'd be crossing on his way to the gap and the farm shouldn't be more than a mile, mile and a half, on this course – NNE, steadied on that now, at 3,000 feet and getting down quite fast. No black mass of forest in sight *yet*. A large village close to starboard:

they'd be hearing her now, all right. No forest though, *definitely* no forest. Streaky silverish network of streams – like dark material with silvery threads in it – and another village there, not as large as the first one but . . .

Water to the right. Patches of it. Again, more ponds than lakes, but linked, a chain of them. And yet another village – or extension of this other—

Had gone wrong. Had gone bloody *wrong*. Made the turn too soon, perhaps mistaken one group of lakes for another. Otherwise, would have been over forest within about a mile of them. Sweating hard inside the Sidcot now. Thinking of turning back, turning again on to the previous easterly course at those lakes, then continuing to the ones he *should* have turned at. Might not find them, though – might *well* not – and in the process alerting the whole countryside, village after village, and throwing away the advantage derived from co-operating with the Handleys.

Sharply reducing chances of success, then. Hun patrols turning out, for instance.

Calm down, though. They'd still be hearing Rudd – maybe the rest of them too, more distantly . . . Taking some angle off her – at 1,800 feet – and seeing – dead ahead – at last, a dark mass of forest. Leaves or no leaves, forestry blacker than the surrounding darkness. Familiar too, in a way, in that at first sight it was similar in shape to the neck of woodland he should have crossed several minutes ago. An area of woodland with a name – some word McLachlan hadn't known, had searched for unsuccessfully in his dictionary. Hell with that anyway, this wasn't it, couldn't be within – oh, three, four miles . . . Throttling down though, in the approach to – God knew, but yet another pattern of streams and – waterways anyway – along the southeast edge of a squarish block of woodland. Coming up to overfly that black stain now – at 1,500 feet. One justification for holding to this course, not having turned back to search for what *should* have been one's track, was that this was the general direction in which Rudd would have made his diversion out to port of the rest of the squadron's new course – and back again, rejoining them – and one might reasonably hope that the Green's thunderous racket might still be taken as a part or remnant of all that. Straggler astern of the main body, chasing after them. Twelve hundred feet, and down to 30 mph. This woodland's south-eastern border with the water fringing it looked as straight as a ruler. Recent forestry work, tree-felling? Half or three-quarters of a mile of that, he guessed: could now see the top corner of it, virtually a right-angle – open ground beyond it as well as a north-easterly continuation of the water – but clear-edged forestry ruler-straight at this near end, curving away through west and northwards.

Shelter, anyway, in that recess. And no nearby farms or villages. So, for better or for worse . . .

Have to valve – to get down as steeply as he'd need to.

Nose into wind, and throttling back. The others would have their heads over the side, seeing what he was seeing, guessing at his intention – which was to drop over that edge of forest into the almost rectangular enclave obviously created by foresters' axes. Plenty of room, but one wanted – needed – to get in close to this corner, the wall of forest on one's left – with a view to getting her out again and still into a northerly wind in a few hours' time – drop in therefore as close as possible over the trees at this end. Have to get over and clear of them, obviously, before releasing the trail-rope. *Slightly* tricky, because one would need the trail-rope and its grapnel then to stop her. One hundred feet: into the wind and with only enough power on her to meet it and keep forward motion and steerage-way on her. Heading near enough north, but with no time for compass-watching: wind-direction and one's view of the wood and the cleared ground held what one might call one's full attention. The wind in fact might be lost altogether in the lee of that sheer wall of forest – large, probably centuries-old trees. Valve a little now. *No* . . . He'd been about to, but took his hand off the gas-release valve's line: asking himself what *had* the practices been for, for Pete's sake. At eighty feet, judging his moment to give her a bit more throttle, *drive* her down

221

into the – abyss. Black pit, down there. No water in it anyway, you'd have seen the shine, were *not* about to land in any lake. Seventy-five feet: touch-and-go whether that was high enough to virtually scrape over the last of the trees without the trailing guys getting caught in them. Holding his breath for that, not having thought of it until these last seconds – had thought of the trail-rope but not the guys. Anyway was now *over* the unclearly defined but fairly precipitous edge of treetops, craning over the side and looking aft to make sure of it, see the blackness rising astern as she powered down over it. *Now* valve. Thirty feet. All right, shut that off, release the trail-rope – which had the grapnel already on it – ringed on it – skimming down as the heavy rope itself unreeled. Twenty feet: trail-rope and grapnel gone, out astern and bar-taut.

McLachlan on his feet in the for'ard cockpit, preparing to release his rope ladder – port side one, the forest side. Stavely would be freeing his to thump down too. Air into both ballonets now to (a) weigh her down some more, and (b) make up for lowered envelope pressure due to that valving. Extra weight necessary anyway to compensate for the loss of two men's weight when they jumped. Fifteen feet. Crabpots shut. Ten. The trail-rope was holding her or trying to, jerking at her, grapnel ploughing through recently cleared forest floor. So windless down here in the shelter that it was easier even than it had been at either Slinfold or Jevington. McLachlan had climbed over, vanished; Stavely would be down there too, on the starboard side. Take that for granted. Charlie was ready for the upward lurch he knew he'd get as their weight left him, for which he'd compensate with another flood of air into the ballonets and maybe even a touch more throttle to hold her down – being bow-down, trimmed heavy enough now to pretty well *thump* down the last few feet if she didn't shed some weight. Disaster striking all in split seconds then, though, Charlie only seeing the tree-stump – actually stumps plural, stumps all over, surrounding them – about a second and a half before the car hit one. Jarring crash, wood splintering, car knocked rocking in its suspension, then the solid impact of its forepart – fore end of the port-side skid – ploughing into soil and/or undergrowth, or God only knew what.

First thought – *suspension gone?* Then – McLachlan, Stavely? On the ladders – catapulted off them? Car now at rest and leaning at an angle: suspension on that side he guessed very likely *had* carried away. In which case – Christ, you'd *had* it. He pushed the throttle shut and the Green was coughing itself into silence, deep night forest air pierced by McLachlan's furious or agonised, 'Oh, *bloody* hell . . .'

17

Stavely had jumped clear, and said he was all right, but McLachlan had been slammed against and over that tree-stump, seemed slightly concussed and thought at first he'd broken his knee, but actually – it seemed – had torn the ligaments at the back of it. In any case couldn't stand. To Charlie's huge relief the car's wire suspensions were intact, but several timber strakes on the port side for'ard had been stove in, and that skid and its supporting struts bent out of shape. Assessment of damage so far had been made by feel; further inspection by Aldis-light might be warranted at some later stage – before any attempt at taking off, for sure. Which didn't come into one's thinking at the present stage anyway, first essentials being damage-control and prevention of further, *total* disaster. Charlie and Stavely had manoeuvred her clear of the stump, had two handling guys and the trail-rope secured to scrulexes – Stavely having made all four guys fast to tree-stumps initially – a temporary measure, his own initiative pre-empting any Monk-type development and making it possible for Charlie then to remove his own weight from the damaged car. At that stage McLachlan had still been flat on his face wrestling with a scrulex, in fact having no kind of purchase on it, and that leg, the left one, obviously giving him a fair degree of hell when he tried to move it or his own efforts strained it. They were getting him back into his cockpit now, where his weight would serve some purpose. He'd muttered to Charlie, 'Let's *not* do a Monk, now,' and Charlie had assured him that there was now no danger of any such thing – while wondering what on earth they *could* do.

Only one answer to that, he realised.

Stavely went to see to his engine, shutting off fuel cocks and so forth, after helping to get McLachlan in, settling him down in the seat with that leg extended forward and supported/protected by wadded blankets. McLachlan growling for about the tenth time, '*What* a clumsy idiot I am!'

'If you'd lean that way, sir, so I can slide the bike out.'

A grunt, and shifting. Weight on one hand on the seat, other elbow on the cockpit's coaming. 'Right?'

'Further over – if you can?'

Easing the bike out from its stowage down beside his legs. Had it clear now. 'Stavely?'

'Here, sir.'

He was beside the car to receive the bike as Charlie heaved it over. Charlie realising only now that it would probably have been better to have kept McLachlan down there on the ground until they'd got the Sidcot and what he'd referred to as his 'French gent's natty suiting' off him, then the flying-suit back on before he froze; Charlie confessing, 'Done it again. Must have been brain-damaged. Should've got the bike out before we put you back on board. Would've been easier to get your gear off outside there, too. Think you could manage—'

'Think *you* can find the women and bring 'em out?'

Faceless in the dark. Scent of new-cut timber and resin and damp soil. He'd fetch the Aldis over from his own cockpit presently, for some essential map study. The Aldis lead would reach, all right. His answer to McLachlan's question was, 'I'll have to – won't I?'

'Despite the language problem.'

'Yes, that. I know. But I *can* ride a bike.'

'Good for you, Holt.'

'Nothing all that *good* about it, sir. Someone's got to, I've done *you* in, and Stavely's more useful here. Don't at all like leaving the ship, but . . .'

'One thing re the language problem – the mother's of English origin, so – well, long as she's *compos mentis* . . .'

'*That's* a thought!'

'Give me some room, I'll get this gear off.'

Unbelievable: have to be bloody dreaming. Continuing with preparations and precautions meanwhile – working with Stavely to secure the ship more thoroughly – two more scrulexes for the third and fourth handling guys, then shifting the trail-rope to a better position and fixing it with the still unpatented Charlie Holt Releasing Gear, and the head-rope to a stump thirty yards away. Working as in a dream – wasting no time, but as if it was real, happening, he – Charlie Holt – actually about to cycle into a French village and knock on the door of some old woman and her daughter: *Parly-voo Onglay?* But imagining the questions that would be fired at one in England if one didn't at least attempt it: *Having cocked up the navigation and the landing, Holt, you decided to call it a day? Knowing what was at stake – what you'd gone in there for?*

Charlie Holt – total failure, with tail between legs. Not a pretty picture to have in mind. Therefore, continue to defy reality.

Stavely said, 'See if I can get that skid straightened, while you're gone.'

'Yes. Good man.'

'Might have to get her back as she is. Mean landin' at Boobers could be awkward. What I *might* do though – where she's holed, make a tingle out of a cut-up blanket?'

'Damn good idea. Yes, best concentrate on that. Several thicknesses, eh?'

A tingle, in naval terminology, was a patch, usually of copper, shaped by bending and hammering and fixed externally over damage to a boat's hull, nailed or screwed in place with sea-pressure tending to improve the seal.

Charlie suggested, 'Use sticky tape, would you, inside and out?'

Might not hold, in the rush of air. In which case that

for'ard cockpit would be very, very cold, at 5–6,000 feet. It wasn't going to be exactly comfortable anyway for McLachlan, with his damaged leg and two women squeezed in beside him. *If* one got that far: found them and got back here with them – and then got off the ground . . .

McLachlan called, 'All right, Holt.'

Meaning he'd got his 'natty suiting' off and Charlie could now strip off and shift into it, semi-freezing in the process. He'd seen the major in that kit at Boobers – dog-robber's trousers, thick grey shirt, brown sweater, worn leather coat and beret. The coat, beret and shoes had been down by his feet in the cockpit. Shoes too small for him, he'd mentioned after his cycle trip, which meant they'd be much too small for Charlie, who had rather large feet. He'd keep his sheepskin-lined flying boots on, he thought.

Peeling his own Sidcot off, meanwhile. 'Shan't be a minute. Map work then, and – whatever you can tell me. Leg hurt much, sir?'

A grunt: McLachlan in the process of getting *his* Sidcot back on. Ignoring the silly question – leg surely agonising. Asking Charlie after a moment, 'When you've done my job for me, are you going to be able to take off – with the two of 'em on board?'

'Short answer, sir – hope so. Can't read the gas-pressure unfortunately, manometer's bust, glass broken and needle skew-whiff. I did have to valve a bit – in the course of dumping us on a lot of bloody tree-stumps.'

'You got us here, that's the main thing. Now, sooner you start, sooner you'll be back. Look here, take this Luger pistol – automatic, nine-millimetre—'

'Hang on to it, sir. I've a .45 revolver – simpler, I know how it works. You may need yours anyway.'

'Very much hope I will not. What you *will* find useful, though, is my pocket compass. Luminous, incidentally.'

'Well – *yes*. Thank you. I'll get the map in a jiffy, and move the Aldis over. Find out where we are's the first thing – then how to get to that village.'

'Taisnières-sur-Hon. The house is marked on the map.

You listening now? The girl's name is Hilde Martens. H-I-L-D-E, Martens. And her mother is Amy Martens. Actually Aimée, the French for it. In fact you'd call her *Madame* Martens, wouldn't you. Hilde's *Mademoiselle* – meaning "Miss". Not that you'll be standing on ceremony exactly, but if there were others present – well, just use your loaf. An airship in French, by the way – same word as our "dirigible", only pronounced *dirigeable*.'

'*Dee-ree-jarble.*'

'Christ. But – all right. Thing is, they'll need to be told about it, won't they.'

Charlie nodding in the dark, repeating, '*Dee-ree-jarble.* Hilde and Amy Martins.'

'Martens, with an "e".'

'Martens. All right. Ready now – I'll get the map. Have to edge in there with it – don't want the whole wood floodlit.'

'I'll stay to this side – keep my leg clear of you. Pass the Aldis over the top here, eh . . . Clothes all right?'

'Not overly warm, as yet.'

'When you get going . . .'

'Yes. I'm sure. Lucky we're about the same size, anyway.' He climbed into his own cockpit, dumped the Sidcot in a bundle and found the map, then passed the Aldis over to McLachlan. 'Pull in a few feet of the lead, sir, then I'll plug it in. Better not touch the trigger, time being.'

'There's another name you should remember . . . All right, got it.'

'Just a sec . . .'

Buckling on the six-shooter. Six bullets in it, and that was all. Could hardly envisage using it, in any case. He picked up the map again and climbed into the starboard side of the fore cockpit, which was actually quite roomy. He remembered having thought so when he'd first set eyes on this ship at Wormwood Scrubs, and taking the wireless out of it had made more room still. 'Here, now.' It was a biggish sheet of map but he'd folded it into an eighteen-inch square, which covered all one needed. Aldis now: his beret would have enclosed it, but – inside his leather coat was better. Alarmingly powerful light. So – beret *and* inside the coat, and inward-pointing, with the hand-grip and trigger *outside* the coat, having unbuttoned . . . McLachlan telling him, 'The name to remember is Elise de Semeillions. Married woman – husband's a POW in Germany – in her thirties, employs Hilde as housekeeper and used to help looking after the mother. She lives alone – except for some children – in a manor house –' squinting narrow-eyed at the map – '*here*. One kilometre northwest of this village – Hergies. That's how it's pronounced – try it?'

'*Air-jee*. Right, but—'

'The house – Elise de Semeillions' – is called the Manoir Hergies. *Manoir* meaning "manor". Biggish place, apparently. Any luck, you'll find the Martens at home in Taisnières, won't need to go anywhere near Hergies, but—'

'Help if needed. Elise Semlions. Now, sir – matter of finding out where we are, where I'm starting from . . .'

He saw it within a few seconds – at least, initially, how it *might* have happened. Tracing the line of flight south of Bavay, when he'd been aiming/searching for the lakes southwest of la Longueville. If he'd turned instead at this smaller group of lakes, to the east of a smaller village, Audignies . . . He'd seen no village: very likely wouldn't have, from 5,000 – whatever height he'd been at at that stage. Now – course from la Longueville was – *was to have been* – NNE. North twenty-two-and-a-half east. Which *would* have led to the farm of the wood of the Abbess. Parallel to that, therefore, but starting from – the *wrong* place, Audignies . . .

'Got it, sir. Here's where I went wrong. Should've turned here, turned *here* instead, mistook these little lakes for those. Got a bit worried when I didn't see this village under us – but did then see others. Here, and here. Hell, that was – what d'you call it – Taisnières? First knew I was wrong when we didn't find this stretch of forest – pushed on and found *this* lot instead, and – right *here* is where we are now!'

'Might be better than the other. No farm?'

'Just bloody tree-stumps.'

'*Bois de Blaregnies.*' McLachlan moved a finger. 'Realise we're in Belgium, here? Anyway – as you say, Taisnières is here. Two routes open to you, therefore. Across open ground here – down-slope to where I saw water lying, then on up to the road here, head south on that and fork right here, say. Eh? Or – alternative – through this bit of forest westward, and on to *this* road – taking you back into France, of course. Might be the easier way, dead straight to this inter-section?'

About the same distance, either way. Charlie agreed, though, that the west-about route was probably the best. He asked, 'Which end of Taisnières, then – if I'm pronouncing that right?'

'Near enough. Asking the way, they'd know what you wanted. Better *not* to, mind you; best play dumb as you can. Look there – see the red cross, my red ink? That's where their house is. On a street parallel to the main one. The way you'd be coming, d'you see – turn right here off the main road, then left here. Roads are built up on banks – watery terrain, must be. So you'd be bicycling along this fairly narrow road – a few houses but not many – and this turn would take you back up to the main road – shops, and many more houses, church on that corner. Got it?'

'The Martens' house is on the smaller road, though.'

'And coming the way you'll be, the fourth on your right. Small village house right on the road, with a passage down this side of it to the back door. Back door or side door – wasn't made clear, but you'd use that, eh? Better not to be seen banging on the front – on the street, in a place where everyone must know everyone else and a stranger must be an object of suspicion. The women in any case may be nervous of strangers knocking them up at night, so – softly-softly, eh?'

'They're not expecting anyone, you said.'

'Have not been given reason to expect, but the girl did ask for them to be brought out. No – no one's been told to expect anything or anyone. Not even the courier who brought the message out to Holland, from where it was passed to London; therefore not even Prince Réginald himself. It's his show, but – our people don't know how good his security is.'

'But a courier who can slip to and fro over an occupied country's frontiers, surely—'

'Can be caught and shall we say "questioned", so the less he knows the better. Anyway, that's not our business, Holt. Now look here – what's the name of the woman who *would* help us if she was able to?'

'Semlon?'

'De Semeillions. Madame Elise de Semeillions. And where did I tell you she lives?'

He peered more closely at the map.

'Here, somewhere. This place, pronounced – *Hairji?*'

'Look. Taisnières here – that's Taisnières-sur-Hon – and Hon-Hergies about a kilometre west of it. Then Hergies – here. Pronounced *Air-ji* – the "H" is silent. And another – oh, about two kilometres northwest of that, close to the intersection with this road coming up from Bavay – a big old manor-house, Manoir Hergies. Home of Madame de Semeillions. Educated person, incidentally, probably speaks English. All right?'

'But if Taisnières's where the women are . . .'

Studying the map all the same, getting the route into his head while McLachlan told him, 'She's an ally, that's the point. Friend of Prince Réginald and his sister Princess Marie du Croy – the one they gaoled, lived at the Bellignies château and was a friend of Edith Cavell. A *real* ally, therefore. It was in the de Semeillions house that the courier met Hilde Martens and all this started. Hilde having told Elise de Semeillions that certain vital intelligence had come her way, and Elise de S. then arranging – somehow – for the courier's visit.'

'Right.' Charlie changed the subject slightly. 'Do we know whether the Huns have patrols out in the countryside or the villages at night?'

'No . . . Don't *know*, but – might have in some localities, I suppose. Around that château, for instance, one might imagine. I'd guess that in the villages there'd be ordinary French police. But – you've just one village to enter, one house to call at. Obviously go cautiously, but . . .'

'What I foresee is knocking on the door and getting a stream of French – wouldn't understand a word.'

'You know their names – you can tell them yours and what you are – *lieutenant* – same word, eh? Royal Navy – *Marin Royal*, that is – *Marin* as in "Mariner" – and "British" is *Britannique* . . . As I said, the girl did ask for them to be brought out. She'll surely have been *hoping* something might come of it – can't be a complete idiot if she hears someone talking pigeon-French at her – and mama probably quite at home in English – that'd be the saving grace, uh?'

'Airship's *dee-ree-jarble*.'

'As near as makes no matter, yes. You'd better be off, Holt.'

'Yes.' The map again: his route due west – through and out of the trees, about a kilometre to that road. 'Pocket compass?'

'Of course. Here.'

The size of a pocket watch, with a streak of luminosity on the north-seeking needle and a blob of it at the 'N' on the outer ring. As much as he'd need, and with no stars in sight, invaluable. Checking the map once more, because from here on he'd be in the dark – at least until the women let him into their house. From the road when he got to it, to the intersection where he'd go left for Taisnières, would be roughly four kilometres. Two and a half miles, say. Then no more than a kilometre – or allowing for the turn-off to the right, the minor road circling round south of the village, say one mile. Total distance less than four miles, and if the women were ready to come right away – return journey on foot, he supposed, probably with the old one on his back . . .

Show them the map before starting back: they might know a short-cut or two.

'Mind if I cut this square out, sir?'

'I've no further use for it.'

Using his seaman's knife. Then folding the eighteen-inch square of it small enough to go in an inner pocket. He took a breath. 'Right. Be back as soon as I can.'

'If not sooner. Best of luck, Holt.'

'You there, Stavely?'

'Sir.'

Dark, squat figure offering him a hand as he climbed out. Hardly any wind. You heard it in the treetops but felt none of it down here. Really not a bad spot at all they'd blundered into. He told Stavely, 'I had a thought – the plywood of that so-called voicepipe – it's held together with small screws. Might patch the bow of the car with that, rather than with blanket?'

'Might *that* an' all . . .'

'Major could supply you with light from inside. I've left the Aldis with him. Be very careful with it, mind.' He was tightening his gunbelt. The leather coat covered the holstered revolver all right; in the dark, at least.

Knee-deep in fallen leaves, and pushing the bike, pausing every twenty-five yards or so to check his direction with the compass. Getting towards nine-thirty, which was about two hours later than McLachlan had envisaged setting off – from the other place at that, only half the distance to/from Taisnières. As well to push it along a bit, therefore. Be at the house in Taisnières by ten, say, allow half an hour for the girl and her mother to be ready, then perhaps as much as an hour getting back to the ship. Or more – eleven-thirty, say. Midnight, even – since one might well be carrying the old woman, have to take a breather from time to time. So – take off by twelve-thirty – touch wood – set course for Doullens at about 48 mph, flying at 6,000 feet – under cloud, but not far under: have it in easy reach to hide in it if Hun fighters were about.

No reason they should be. Except maybe for dawn patrols, and you'd be back on the ground at Boobers long before the dawn.

Edge of the trees. They hadn't thinned before they stopped: you were in forest one minute and out of it the next. Forgetting Doullens and all that – mind on nothing but *this*, now. A degree of satisfaction in having emerged very close to a corner of this section of the forest, thus – as shown on the map – with only about 200 yards of open ground to cross to reach the road.

Owls were screeching. No other sound; no movement and no light. Hard ground – forest litter carpeting it at first but then just bare and humpy. Carrying the bike over this stuff, not pushing it, and heading northwest, not due west as in the forest, and – surely *less* than 200 yards to the road.

Unpaved road, though. Hard, ridged mud. Not at all the surface he'd envisaged. Nothing to be seen: north-eastward the road disappeared into forest; southwestward only its ruler-straight edges as far as one could see them pointing into empty night. In fact, two and a half miles southwestward he knew it cut at right angles across the roads linking Taisnières and Hon-Hergies. Having the map in mind and being set on *keeping* it in mind. There'd be several other crossings and forkings-off, but most of them would be much closer; then a few hundred yards before the left turn to Taisnières you'd pass a village with no build-ings on the left-hand side, only the start of a minor road leading due east.

So – all right. Might as well make the most of what promised to be the fastest section of this trip – and looked and felt even better when after only a few minutes one was off the washboard mud surface and on smooth, tarred road.

French road now, he guessed, as distinct from Belgian.

Then – ahead, but couldn't really see how far – a flicker of moving light . . .

Free-wheeling – still covering ground quite fast but wary of that shifting, yellowish flicker. Not wanting to come up with it so fast he wouldn't have had time to put any thoughts together, consequently when stopped and ques-tioned could only – well – play dumb, as instructed. Point

234

at one's mouth, make sounds as if trying to speak but not able to. Unless of course that had been tried before so often that it wouldn't wash. Pedalling again now anyway, the light having vanished. Might have been a lantern, carried across the road from one house to another, or from house to farmyard. There *were* a few small houses and farm buildings here and there. And one should be passing the other place fairly soon, the one that was all on the right-hand side, with a turn-off on *this* side. Getting back over – he'd been riding on the left, the *wrong* side. But – this might be it, coming up now . . .

A large farmstead and a single cottage was all there was of it. The turning was there all right, though – that *had* been it – so next would come one's left-hand turn to Taisnières. In about half a mile. If one missed it and rode on, after a couple of hundred yards you'd be at the right turn for Hon-Hergies. And between those two intersections was a bridge over the river Vanne. Memory needing to be given exercise more or less constantly, circumstances being as they were. But – lights, ahead there: car head-lights, he thought—

Jolting memory then: wouldn't there be a curfew? Wasn't there always a bloody curfew?

McLachlan hadn't mentioned it. Not even when asked about Hun patrols. But assuming they did have a curfew, wouldn't there be patrols out to enforce it? Time now being – by his watch's green glow held up close to his nose – twenty-one minutes to ten. Curfew might start at – hell, any time after dark. Could be in force now, might not be until midnight. Worth bearing in mind – in relation to getting back to the ship, or at any rate into the forest – well before that. As one *would* though, surely. Ask Hilde or her mother what time . . .

It did look like some sort of road-block, ahead there. Vehicles with lights. There were cottages on both sides of the road just here. Had to be comparatively high ground, there-fore, not boggy as a lot of it that he'd passed earlier had looked and smelled. And those two motor vehicles which he could see now more clearly, one illuminated by the other, were at the second intersection, the turning to Hon Hergies. Therefore – the point about the ground down there as likely as not being firm – one might either skim around this next corner, taking a chance on not being spotted or otherwise caught up in whatever was happening along there; or climb over the wall here, carry the bike across to the Taisnières road thirty or forty yards along from the corner, say.

Time was a factor, though. Also the chance of being seen from the nearer of the cottages on this side. Not every Frenchman was anti-German, McLachlan had observed at some stage. Best thing, Charlie decided – certainly the easiest – and if it came off, by far the quickest – would be to take one's chances with the road-block, or whatever it was. One vehicle – from closer range now, looked like a truck or lorry – was in this road but at an angle, slewed across it; the other, which had its headlights shining on that one, had come out into the intersection on the road leading from Hon-Hergies. Long bonnet and rather high wind-screen visible, vaguely illuminated, and men moving around, casting long shadows. Charlie's corner coming up now though: Charlie free-wheeling into it as it were diagonally – i.e. on the wrong side of the road again for a little while – half expecting shouts or shots or the cars' doors slamming, engines starting . . .

No such thing. Charlie pedalling southeast now, was all, with about 500 yards to go to the edge of Taisnières where he'd turn right. As now, just minutes later, or even *a* minute, having not seen the turn, pedalling hell for leather until he was just about right on it – swinging at what felt like exces-sively high speed into this sharpish curve of built-up road, embankment raising it above flood-level. Slowing: not braking but free-wheeling, having a hundred yards, roughly, to the left turn on to the Martens' road. Time – one minute to ten. This end of the Martens' road was also banked up, but the fields though low to start with rose steadily as he plugged eastward – pedalling again – with most of the village over to his left, this road and that main street virtually parallel and only about fifty yards apart. Level ground now too, and no embankment. Cottages and what looked like stabling on the left, more small dwellings ahead there on the right.

Also a vehicle – van, actually – parked with its weak, masked headlights burning – and men's voices. He saw a French gendarme's *képi* and three or four Hun soldiers in those distinctively-shaped helmets.

At the fourth house, or beyond it?

Keep going, anyway. Important not to dither. Not to appear to dither anyway. Especially as one had no business here, couldn't have explained one's presence in any way. *Shouldn't drop airships on tree-stumps, then* . . . But – mind on *this* job now – liking it or lumping it. Scared to jelly was the answer to that: but having to get into the Martens house, and no other way to it that he knew of. The answer to enquirers, if any, would be – well, visiting old friends. Thought the curfew in these parts started at ten pm and that he'd make it to their house by that time, with Madame Martens' kind permission spend the night there – sleep on the floor if necessary. Actually, sneak out – back way out – *with them.* Although how to put the other stuff over either to Hun soldiers or Frog rozzers . . .

Wouldn't. Being inarticulate, even perhaps simple. Grunt, shrug, point, mumble, 'Amy Martens?'

The van with the men around it was parked *beyond* the fourth house on the right. Voices ceasing as someone – people, elderly couple – tall man, woman shorter and thicker – and the tapping of a stick on the cobbles or the bottom of the house's wall – appearing from out of what had to be the alleyway that led down to the Martens' back door, according to McLachlan. Elderly visitors departing: well timed, also one might assume curfew *not* yet in force. Or it might start at ten and those people live only a few doors away, be practically home already. They were passing through the light from the van now – close together, arms around each other. It was the husband who had the stick, was tapping his – their – way across the road, growling now without looking at them, '*Bon nuit, messieurs.*'

'*Nuit, m'sieur.*' The gendarme – replying to that. Charlie thinking, *All right, they're out, I'm in.* And the Martens women must presumably be at home. Even though one was going to have to pass through that outfall of half-light – and if challenged had no idea even at this last moment how he'd react.

But he couldn't have not agreed to take McLachlan's place. Well – *could* have, but . . .

Truthfully, could *not* have.

Dismounting. Conversation had resumed, in German. Harsh, unpleasant-sounding lingo. A match flared between cupped hands over the bowl of a pipe and under the rim of a helmet, and a voice – not that one's – called, '*Eh – qui va la?*'

Addressed to him, as he came along close to the house fronts looking for the Martens' alleyway. He glanced that way briefly, raised a pointing arm, enquired brusquely, '*Madame Martens?*'

The pronunciation at which McLachlan had winced didn't seem to upset the gendarme, mercifully. He waved some kind of stick towards the passageway, grunted what sounded like an affirmative, and Charlie by that time was *in* the passage, left hand feeling for a doorway.

Wouldn't get away with *that* more than once, he thought, sweating slightly. But maybe they'd piss off soon. The Martens women might know what they were there for and how long they might be expected to hang around.

Door, recessed in the brickwork. And light inside, lamplight visible around its edges. He leant the bike against the wall beyond it, then came back and knocked.

No response after fifteen or twenty seconds. But they had to be at home – no-one who lived in a hovel such as this would go out and leave oil or candles wasting.

In there but too scared to answer a knock on the door at night?

After a second knock went unanswered, he pushed at the door and it creaked open. Warmth, light, strong odour of candle-wax and dust, old clothes – other elements as well – human smells. A woman's murmur of surprise or alarm – in

238

French of course: he had only the tone of it to go by. Hearing himself slurr, '*Excuse . . . Madame Martens?*' As before, the echo in his own ears was something like *Mum Mutt'ns.* He was inside by this time and pushing the door shut to keep the cold out, meeting the eyes of several women, all of them old and shawled. Two of them were seated on a *chaise longue*; in front of them on a pair of trestles was a smallish, rough-looking coffin with a body in it, body covered up to the neck but the face uncovered – small, narrow old woman's face white as chalk under a sort of nightcap with lace around its edges. Eyes shut, wisps of grey hair visible under the cap, sharp little nose pointed at the ceiling like a dog's snout upturned to howl at the moon. The women all staring at him, doubtless wanting to know who the hell he was. The two on *this* side of the coffin were on their knees – actually on cushions – straining their shawled heads back to look up at him. He'd removed his beret, now bowed his head and shut his eyes: classic behaviour for an ostrich, while thinking that this must surely be Hilde's mother and that by and large it should make things easier, if he could now (a) find Hilde, and (b) have her to himself for long enough to identify himself – *without* the aid of an interpreter . . .

Clumping footsteps on the boards above. First reaction: *Hilde?* Then – *no* – not unless she was an Amazon and wore hobnailed boots. Those were a man's movements, surely. Charlie crossed himself: had seen it done, *hoped* he'd done it the right way round. Must have done – the nearer of the women on this side was shifting up against the one on her left, making way for him. So – when in Rome . . . But whoever this was, was coming clumsily down the stairs and dragging some burden with him. Charlie on his knees but watching with near-shut eyes: some minutes ago he'd seen the foot of the stairs on the far side of the big iron stove, so knew where to look now while ostensibly still praying. Prayer being a deterrent to conversation – in present circumstances indispensable. He was focusing now on an elderly, shortish, stocky man in a grey overcoat who'd turned back to pick up the object he'd been dragging –

laundry basket full of clothes or linen – and lump it down off the stairs. Straightening then, massaging the small of his back while glaring at Charlie in a suspicious, challenging way. No one challenging *him*, so presumably he had some right to be clearing the place out – mother being dead and Hilde absent. Absent *where* – and how to find out? Wasn't upstairs, not a sound from up there now. He shut his eyes properly again, inclined his head, hearing a muttered exchange – questions and answers, by the sound of it, between the man and one of those on the couch. Could have been something like, 'Who the hell's *that?*', and the woman's answer, 'God knows. You off, now?' A grunt: seemed he *was* off, anyway, lugging the basket to the door and out, door thumping shut a moment later.

Charlie telling himself, Got to find Hilde . . .

Raising his head, he found that the woman to whom the old man had spoken, the fat one on this end of the *chaise longue*, had her eyes fixed on him: tear-stained brown eyes, not hostile as the man's had been, only curious. Charlie moved his hands in a gesture indicative of shared grief, then asked her in a whisper, leaning closer – 'Hilde?'

'*Les sals Boches l'ont saissi, monsieur!*'

He knew what '*sals Boches*' meant. Somehow. From cartoons and suchlike. Filthy Huns. And the tone in which she'd spoken suggested they'd done the dirty on Hilde in some way – but how, what, where? Above all, where might she be *now* . . .?

Not here, anyway. And no way of asking where. Or of understanding any answer he might get even if he *had* known how. Even if they were well disposed – as they *might* be, if the reference to filthy Huns was any more than a habit of speech – which you couldn't count on anyway. McLachlan certainly wouldn't have. When it would only take one of these four to start screaming blue murder – with soldiers and gendarmes well inside screaming range, at that. The thought of McLachlan, though – what *he'd* do, or advise – hell, what about that other woman? Mind gone blank on it – but it would come, bloody *had* to . . .

18

He'd remembered the name – Semlions – and that she lived in a manor house beyond Hergies – pronounced '*Airjee*' – name of house, Manoir Hergies. Recalling this in one fell swoop while getting to his feet, throwing a last sad look at the old bird in the coffin and gesturing goodbye to the rest of them. Then he was out, leaving a murmur like pigeons cooing behind him, pulling the door shut and seeing his bike was still there, thank heavens. Reversing it, wheeling it up the narrow passageway – and a new sound now, commotion in the street, men's voices – French – one hectoring and one defensive. Couldn't afford to wait, anyway; with luck, while that was going on, might slip away unnoticed – duck away to the left, mount, and away like greased lightning. Ten-thirty now: four miles roughly to the manor – with some twists and turns, as he remembered it – McLachlan's forefinger tracing the road through Hon-Hergies then Hergies. Make that distance in twenty or thirty minutes, say, hope to God to find the Semlion woman there and that she'd have Hilde with her.

Going by what McLachlan had said about her, very likely *would* have her there: mama having pegged out, Hilde in need of company and comforting.

Clatter of a horse's hooves – within yards of him. Horse not on the move, just fidgeting, and squarely across the end of this passageway, in the shafts of some cart. Or trap – pony-trap – and the old boy who'd been in the house had just

241

slung that basket up into it, turning towards those others in the spill of light, spreading his arms in what looked like exasperation, shouting – astonishingly – 'Manoir Air*jee*! Madame de Semeillions – *hunh*?'

Addressing the gendarme?

Charlie had stopped. Wouldn't be visible to the old man here, even if he had reason to look down this way. Which he hadn't: was hauling himself up into the trap and picking up the reins, while the gendarme called back to him in a mocking tone that made a German laugh – still laughing as he translated it to his friends. The old man flipped the reins, grunted to the pony, was moving off. Charlie waiting, still. That bunch would be looking this way, past the end of this passage, watching the trap go. Charlie's initial surprise at the old fellow shouting out those names blossoming into certainty that Hilde would be there, at the manor, Madame de Semlion having sent the trap here to collect her things. *Sals Boches* or no *sals Boches*, it made perfectly good sense, he thought – and *sals Boches* did come into it: here they were, with the gendarme assisting for linguistic purposes and/or local knowledge. Whatever the detail of that, it would fit in, all right. So – back to the timing: if one got to the manor by about eleven, left with Hilde by eleven-thirty, say – get her to the ship by midnight?

Manage that, wouldn't have done badly, all things considered.

Clip-clopping of hooves plus iron-shod wheels on cobbles gradually fading. Quiet exchanges resuming, mainly in German, up to the right. If they'd parked themselves there after following the old man in the trap – which was conceivable, might explain their having been here in the first place – now that he'd gone mightn't they shove off too?

On the other hand, the gendarme might come down here to the back door before leaving. *Might*. To check on who was here and who wasn't – and who he, Charlie, might be. Which would be distinctly awkward. Chance it, therefore, sneak off now. As quietly as possible, up to the end of this passage: pausing, craning head round to the right. Couldn't in fact see much, but he *thought* they were clustered at the rear end of the van. Might even be inside it, some of them. The going might be as good as it would ever be.

Out and to the left, staying close to the dark house fronts, on this narrow pavement with the bike's wheels in the gutter, smoother and quieter than on cobbles. New bike anyway, well oiled by Stavely and having as yet no squeaks or rattles. Pausing now and mounting – one shove on the pedals, then free-wheeling. Not so bad – a feeling of having got away with it. *This far*, got away with it. With what, precisely, wasn't clear, having no idea what that team with the van might have been there for anyway; whatever, if one had *not* got away with it one might by now have been inside the van oneself, being interrogated – and they'd have found a loaded pistol, which wouldn't have helped, exactly.

He was on the banked-up part of the road now, swinging right: 200 yards to the next corner, where he'd go left. Aware that he might run into a problem when in a few minutes' time he reached the long road he'd come down to start with, where there was a bridge over the Vanne before the turn to Hon-Hergies, where there'd been that motor blocking a truck and he'd turned short of it and felt pleased with himself getting away with *that*. The blockage might still be there, might not. If it *was* – well, turn right instead of left and then take any of the turn-offs leading north or northwestward. If they continued as they started, didn't turn back on themselves as country lanes so often did, you'd be heading parallel to the Hon-Hergies road; might even be better, by-passing the village.

But whatever had been going on there would probably have packed up by now. Hun motorcar having waylaid a lorry – as well as he'd been able to see it – and unless they were spending the night there, stopping everything . . .

They weren't. Seemed to have gone. No lights showing, anyway, from this other intersection, the Taisnières turn. He swung left, rode over the hump of bridge and then right, and – all clear. Hon-Hergies maybe 300 yards ahead, with this major road passing through the village and circling left.

Picturing this as it was in McLachlan's map, main thoroughfares shown with double lines, smaller roads with single ones: as one followed that curve round to the left, either of two offshoots to the right would take one in the right direction. All right, with a few twists and turns, but still be the most direct route to Hergies, whereas staying on *this* road you'd be making a wide sweep west before turning north – adding at least a mile or two and surely taking longer.

In Hon-Hergies now at – ten-forty. Smaller place than Taisnières. Nothing moving, not a sound other than one's own hard breathing and the hum of the bike's tyres – not a glimmer of light anywhere. If there was any ambush, road-block, admittedly you'd be riding straight into it, there'd be no warning that you'd see; the same would apply anywhere along this route though, and time *mattered* – one couldn't bloody dawdle. Ten-forty meant one had left the others at the ship an hour and ten minutes ago, which admittedly wasn't bad, although it felt like much longer – but one hadn't got to her yet, hadn't found her, couldn't guess how long it might take. Hold-ups *could* occur – like the waste of time on one's knees on a stone floor . . . All right, if she *was* at the manor and this rate of progress could be maintained, i.e. no real setbacks – and a bonus would be if she had a bike of her own there – that would be really capital . . .

Into the long bend to the left now. One turn-off at the top of the curve – he'd missed that, somehow. Slowing, looking more carefully for the next.

Here – almost at once, and easy, less turn than fork. On to what felt like a hard dirt or dirt-and-gravel surface. Maybe should have gone for the longer way round, although that way you'd have been missing out Hergies altogether, whereas on this route – map in visual memory again – when you came to it you'd know you had about two kilometres to go, after a right turn into Hergies' main street, and then a ninety-degree turn left.

Seemed to be taking him on a never-ending circle, this

track. When at last it did end, at a 'T', giving him the choice of right or left, he had to pull up and check by compass. The answer was *left*, and 500 yards from there, *right*. Slowing down, not wanting to miss any of these small turns – especially as this was an embanked route – shine of water back there on both sides.

Now a guess – *left?* Good guess – he was back on tar and picking up speed again. Yet another feat of memory or divination telling him that within a couple of hundred yards a right turn would take him into Hergies. A T-junction again, as he pictured it.

Correctly, as it happened. A jumble of houses crowding around the junction where he turned right and found he was already in the village – in as much of it as there was. Houses thinning out after only about 50 yards from the turn, then none for 100, 200 yards. Pasture-land or bog, whatever, on both sides, although after the turn to the left which he'd be taking very shortly there'd be more houses – or farmsteads, whatever – black shadings on the map. Meanwhile a dead-straight stretch of smooth-surfaced road. Pedalling hard again now, bike fairly flying.

Car coming, though – very audibly. Seeing it then – lights coming up to the turn he was making for. No cover here, no turn-off or even gateway, only the open, empty roadway he'd been – was – pelting down. He swung sharply to the right, hurtling over the grass verge and into hedgerow. Bike over on its side in long-ish coarse grass: he'd simply let it go and flung himself flat – no ditch, it seemed, but a hump, hedge trailing all over it, black thorny mass of it above him and the hump forming – leaving – a ditch of sorts, a depression into which he'd now rolled. Hearing the car coming as if its driver had already spotted him and was putting his foot down to get here fast – thinking anyway of the bike's metallic shine showing up even in the weakly diffuse beams of masked headlights – too late to do anything about it now. Or anything *much*. Flat on his face, hands under him unbuckling the revolver belt, *knowing* they'd see the bike – if they hadn't already seen *him*.

Second thought then: if there weren't many of them – just one or two, say – take them on, make a fight of it?

Now – judging by the sound – they'd see the bike. He had the pistol in his hand. Car still coming on though, as if passing . . .

Had *not* seen anything. Noise had peaked, passing close, was falling as it rushed on by. Not particularly looking for anything or anyone, perhaps, only travelling from A to B. And gone. Charlie half up, in brambles as well as grass, in time to see it turn left, as for Hon-Hergies. He put the pistol down while refastening the belt, then reholstered it and went to recover the bike – which seemed not to have suffered.

Humiliating, rather. Feeling of having panicked – instinctively trying to get rid of one's only weapon. Why carry the bloody thing, then? But if he *hadn't* thrown himself off – had been caught – which undoubtedly he would have been, and *with* the gun – while trying to explain himself, in English?

Now – two kilometres. Might be slightly less. Thinking back to McLachlan's directions, remembering that this road would bring one eventually to the highway that came all the way up from Bavay and continued over the Belgian frontier to – oh, wherever – and that the manor was some distance off to the east – *this* side – of that road. Before one got to it, therefore, there had to be a fork or turning to the right, with the manor set back to the left of that minor *minor* road; and when looking at the map while listening to McLachlan he'd thought the distance from Hergies might be nearer a kilometre and a half than two.

Turning coming up *now*. Sort of an apex at the top of a bend in this untarred roadway, a narrower one leading out of that. So – slowly now, although a very large manor in fairly empty countryside shouldn't be difficult to find. As indeed it wasn't. At least its surrounding wall wasn't. And he found the entrance gates before he saw anything of the house, having followed this stone wall from a junction of two lanes half a mile back, and coming now to stone pillars

246

flanking tall iron gates, drive curving away left and right inside, and an edging of rough grass beyond it. Some sort of heraldic figure on top of this nearer pillar – probably on the other, too. Gates were bolted and – feeling for it, on the inside of the bars – locked. Also taller in the middle here, with curved, spiked tops. If one was going to climb them it would be easiest at one side or the other, using the hinges as footholds.

Distant-looking smear of light. A curtain not fully closed, maybe. Distant-looking but could be at any range from fifty to a few hundred yards. Might also, though, be another entrance – stable entrance, where that old man would have driven the trap in about a quarter of an hour ago, he guessed. Unless he'd used this entrance. Take a quick look along there anyway: could be another gateway standing open. Otherwise, come back and climb over here. Wouldn't be difficult – unlike the wall, which was smooth to the touch and seamless, with no foot- or hand-holds. Prospect a bit further round in any case; if the house was where that light was showing, one would imagine that the stable-yard would be behind it, so any stable entrance would be along there somewhere. He started off again – walking, pushing the bike, following the wall which curved away to surround the house fairly closely on this side, the main acreage of walled demesne being on its western side – the way one had come, following that considerable length of wall.

Here, now. *Timber* gateway, this one. As wide as the main entrance, and – groping around, exploring by feel – with a keyhole, but no key. No handle either, just a keyhole big enough to stick your thumb in. Splintery timber – but surmountable all right, and easier than the main entrance gates.

Leave the bike here – other side of the lane, pushed well into the hedge. He'd crossed over, found there was a ditch and that the hedge was penetrable enough to hide the machine in, when he heard the trap coming – trotting hooves on hard mud and the rumbling of wheels. *A* trap anyway, and odds-on that it was *the* trap – if the old man had taken the long way round, as he might well have done.

Prone again, in the ditch. Bike in the hedge, well hidden. Trap's approach slowing, trot changing to a walk, pony snorting and chomping at its bit, gruff old voice intoning, '*Heh, Hercule . . . Heh, Hercule . . .*'

He'd get out and open the gate now, then lead the pony through. Charlie getting himself into position to move quickly when the moment came. Slip in and get out of sight – in whatever cover there might be on that side of the wall – or leg it for the front of the house. The trap had stopped and the old boy was climbing down, grunting to himself. He had to be a Semlion employee, but as he'd seemed not to like the cut of one's jib when one had been on one's knees beside the coffin, best avoid further confrontation here. Even for *his* sake – in case it brought on a heart-attack. Crouching at the roadside, hearing the pony's hard, puffing breaths, old man at the timber doors, clink of heavy keys, big old lock scraping over.

Pushing the doors open, then he was back at the pony's head.

'*Viens, Hercule . . .*'

Scrape of hooves, the trap's forward lurch and absorption in the blackness between the pillars. Charlie at the right-hand pillar, then inside, around the open timber door and back to the inside of the wall, crouching there as the old man came plodding back to swing the doors shut and lock them. A moment later he was on board again, the trap grinding forward. Driveway angling to the right, Charlie moving left, over grass – looking for the leak of light he'd seen, but from this changed perspective only heading for where he guessed it *might* have been. Keeping the wall on his left though, couldn't go far wrong. This was parkland: occasional tall trees, and the scent of pines. Distantly, a dog barking its head off. He saw the light then, the badly drawn ground-floor curtain, altered course towards it and a minute later stumbled into a curve of driveway which he then followed to the right – the front of the house. There was a wide flight of steps; the light was to the left of them, front door obviously central. Climbing – getting words straight in his mind – *Madame Semlions, dee-ree-jarble* . . . At the top then, feeling around the door – carved timber with iron studs in it – he found a bell-chain and tugged at it, expecting to hear a bell clang in the depths of the house, but – no such sound, no sound at all. *Considerable* depth of house, of course. Eleven now? At least that. Focusing on the luminous glow – for the moment resisting an urge to pull at the bell again – he saw it was twelve minutes past the hour. Thinking of McLachlan and Stavely again, the midnight deadline he still had in his own mind and they'd as likely as not have in theirs – at least would take lugubrious note of when it passed. Not that he'd promised anything – obviously could not have. Any more than McLachlan could have – remembering his response when asked at Boobers about his own hopes or expectations, his snapping in that peremptory tone of his, 'Absolutely no way of guessing . . .'

A sound, at last. Withdrawal of a bolt. And another. Key rasping over. Not much less than the raising of a portcullis. Antique, no doubt, and all fairly massive. But – finally – door opening . . .

About two inches: had come up solidly against a chain. Long slot of yellow lamplight matching the stain of it on a stone window-sill along there to the left, and a voice then – female, strident, shrieking something like, 'Who's there and what d'you want, this time of bloody night?'

Charlie tried, 'Madame Semlion, please?' Then – with further squawking in there, a cry of what sounded like alarm and then a whole stream of it, much as he'd postulated to McLachlan – he tried again with, 'Madame Semlions? My name, Holt. *Lieutenant – Onglais – Marin Royal* – no speak French unfortunately, but—'

'Madeleine?'

New voice – female and French again, and expressing surprise but a lot more composed. Madame Semlion – he guessed and hoped – asking the first one what was going on, and getting a high jabber of, '*Dit qu'il est Anglais, mais—*'

'Madame? My name Holt – *lieutenant, Marin Royal Britannique* – I've come for Hilde Martens, Madame!'

Continuing murmur in there now, and – thank God – she was taking the chain off. Charlie pulling his coat straight, making sure the revolver was out of sight.

Elise de Semeillions was tall, and quite a looker: dark-red hair, blue eyes, sharply intelligent-looking. Quite young, too – noticeably attractive figure in a pale green jersey smock affair that overhung a satiny off-white skirt. She spoke practically flawless English, too – which put *him* in the shade. She'd told the cook – an exceptionally large woman with greying hair in a bun – that she could go to bed, then changed that, asked her to make a jug of coffee first. 'In the morning room, Madeleine.'

'Because –' switching into English – 'there is a fire in here. The drawing-room is less cosy when one is on one's own.'

It wasn't all that small a room, though. Not all that comfortably furnished either, by English standards. But warm, all right. They sat on hard chairs at a round table; he told her his name and rank again and repeated that he'd come for Hilde, would like to take her with him as soon as she might find convenient. There'd been a message received in London—

'I don't wish to seem rude, Lieutenant, but – I'm to believe they'd send a man who speaks no French?'

Charlie explained: 'I pilot an airship. *Dee-ree-jarble*? I said lieutenant, but actually *flight* lieutenant – Royal Naval Air Service. My ship's in the woods a few miles away. I brought in a major of the Royal Marines who does speak French, but we had trouble landing and he's done his leg in – can't walk, can't even stand.'

'So you came in his place.'

Charlie nodded. 'Is Hilde here?'

'I'm afraid not. Why did you think she might be?'

He hesitated, seeing no reason she wouldn't speak the truth, but – facing disappointment of a major kind, telling her in a tone that probably reflected this, 'I went to her mother's house in Taisnières – to collect her and her mother. That was what she'd asked for—'

'I know. It was in this house that she made such a proposal. I was present – as was a person named Michel who I'm glad to know did after all get back to – to where he is based . . . But if you went to Hilde's house, you must know her mother has died?'

'Yes. There were Hun soldiers and a gendarme in the street outside, and—'

'My groom with a pony-trap?'

'Yes. Collecting stuff. I think they may have searched the basket he brought out – clothes, I think.'

'Hilde's things. Yes, probably they would have. I didn't know they were watching the house – but that too . . .'

The cook then, bringing coffee.

'Thank you, Madeleine. Sleep well, now, I've kept you up too long. Goodnight.' Leaning over, pouring into outsize breakfast cups decorated with hunting scenes. Looking over at Charlie again then: 'My groom, you say . . .'

'He's back. I was going to climb your gate when he drove up, and I nipped in while it was open. He didn't see me – not here – did see me in Taisnières, inside the house. I made it faster on my bike than he did with the trap. But those Huns and the gendarme – when I arrived the gendarme called out and I asked did Amy Martens live there, but they didn't stop me, weren't taking any notice when I left, either.'

'Aimée being dead, and the funeral taking place tomorrow, friends *would* visit, so . . .'

'Why'd there be Huns there, though?'

'I'll tell you – as well as I can. The Boches have got Hilde at the château – Bellignies – where there is a new so-called security officer who is – what's the word – persecuting her. He thinks she's a spy, so he's arrested her and they're taking her to Brussels. They've found some person who'll give evidence against her, apparently. But he believes – this man Koch – not only that she's a spy, but that she must have

251

some way to pass out such information as she has received – eh?'

'He's right, isn't he? She does have – certain intelligence, which is why we've come for her.'

'She never spied. And has no such contact. Except myself – and *I* have, certainly. But that's what Koch would be looking for – an attempt by someone else to contact *her*. As it happens, a young German officer gave her information she never asked for, and wanting to get out – especially to get her mother out – well, she thought she'd – as you might say, *use* it. In fact it was quite largely *my* idea.'

'Was it. Was it . . . But gone up in smoke now, eh?' For Charlie, this was really only just sinking in. The whole effort having been for nothing. Rotten for the girl too, of course, but – shaking his head – 'We've come too late.'

'It would seem so, but . . .'

'Only *seem* so? You mean there's some chance still?'

'There might be – as it happens – a very *small* one. Since you've come tonight and not tomorrow night. I'll have to think this out – rack my brains. I can't say there *is* a way, but . . .'

'In any case, we have to take off before dawn. Sooner if possible, but for the ship to be still there in daylight would be – well, not *on*. Two reasons – three – bad weather coming, winds we couldn't cope with – that on its own means we can't hang around – second, if we were still here after sunrise and were spotted – well, that'd be *that*; and if we took off in daylight we'd be seen and they'd send fighters after us. We have no gun, no defences—'

'*Tomorrow* night, then?'

'You mean the ship sitting there all day?' He shook his head. 'Big thing, an airship. This one's a hundred and forty feet long and more than thirty in diameter – the car we sit in hangs under that. She's not *in* the forest – you can't land or take off amongst trees – she's out on the edge, in good shelter as things are now, but with the weather going the way it's forecast—'

'You are saying in effect that in order to ensure your own

'safety you will have to go without poor Hilde.'

He didn't like that much. Realised she hadn't intended him to like it. He paused, holding her hard stare, then changed the line of the discussion slightly.

'You say they've got her in this château . . .'

A nod. 'Some stabling has been made into cells. On the perimeter of the demesne, actually the outer wall – but metres thick, those walls, very – how d'you say – *massif* . . . It's been done just recently; before this, Hilde was under what you might call house arrest. Then Koch or his colleagues got hold of some other witness – in Brussels – this is in connection with things she's supposed to have done two years ago – and at the same time the young *leutnant*, who for some reason – well, he'd had too much to drink and was trying to impress her – blurted military secrets to her – now apparently he's confessed it. He's a weakling. I thought so when I met him, when he and others were billeted here. That was when—'

She checked the flow, shook her dark-red head. 'It makes no difference, does it? Telling you all this.'

'Would you explain what you meant when you said there might still be a chance? Get her out of the château somehow?'

'Oh, no. The château's full of Boches, and Koch's a fanatic – *he*'ll take no chances. I should explain, perhaps – my information comes, one might say *guardedly*, from Ulrich von Bodenschatz, the commandant at Bellignies, with whom you may be surprised to hear I am on good terms. He's a sick man – can hardly breathe for asthma – but he was a cavalryman – as incidentally my husband is also – and horses are an interest we have in common. It's through him, in fact, that I've been able to arrange for Hilde to attend the funeral of her mother. I went down on my knees, almost – purely and innocently for poor Hilde's peace of mind – she's so utterly *devoted*, it would be absolutely *cruel*—'

'Funeral tomorrow . . .'

A nod. 'And von Bodenschatz has insisted to Koch that

Hilde must be allowed to attend it. Funeral mass at Taisnières – ten am, before the usual mass at eleven – then the interment at Entre Deux cemetery. As soon as it's over Koch intends taking her straight to Brussels. Where one may assume she'll get about as fair a trial as her beloved Nurse Edith Cavell was given. I imagine you know about Edith Cavell?' Charlie nodded. Elise shrugged, finished with, 'But, in any event, since you have to make your departure before dawn—'

Charlie cut into that with a recollection of the Edith Cavell business. 'On the day the news came that the Huns had so-called "executed" Nurse Cavell, ten thousand of our men flocked to the recruiting offices. There was no conscription at that time, you see, joining up was voluntary. But that was the effect it had – ten thousand, in one day. She was a marvellous woman, wasn't she?'

'An extraordinary woman. Very small, very quiet, and the heart of a lioness. Hilde worshipped her, worships her memory.'

'And they're saying now that she worked with her, getting chaps out?'

'That she had something to do with it – yes. I don't believe she did. And she denies it. But they have all this new evidence, so they *say* . . .'

'*You're* saying – are you – that there might be some way of – what, spiriting her away from the funeral?'

'There's certainly no *other* hope for her. Or for you, therefore – what *you* want.'

The saving of a million lives. Against that, the risk to his own, Stavely's and McLachlan's, and possible loss of a blimp that cost about five thousand pounds to build and equip. Not such an *enormous* price.

'If there *was* some way, and we – look, if the man I told you about agreed—'

'The one with the broken leg?'

'Damaged leg.' Charlie nodded. 'He's – well, my commanding officer. If he agreed to chance it – if there *was* some way . . .'

'There may be. As I said, I'd have to –' tapping her forehead – 'put my mind to it. If your people had thought to let us know you were coming . . . Well, they didn't, so here we are with only a few hours. And Koch will be at the funeral – also guards at the church, you can be sure of that. But Lieutenant – you are hardly in a position to consult now with your injured colleague?'

'My bicycle's in the hedge outside your stable-yard entrance. I imagine I'd head about due east from here – half an hour each way, say. Anyway, I have a map, and—'

'That would be very dangerous, very rash. You're talking about cycling back to where your airship is hidden, consulting with this person then returning here?'

'Surely not all that dangerous. I've been riding around all evening.'

'Then you've been very lucky and I'd advise against counting on such luck again. Koch has patrols out – they may not know what they're supposed to be looking for – maybe *he* doesn't – he's just throwing his weight around, making a show of it and I dare say hoping something might turn up – something like *you*, perhaps. If they caught you pedalling away into the woods, or coming back – that's two chances you'd be giving them – *wouldn't* that make his day! But think of this, now – it would also finish *us*, and put Hilde in front of a firing-squad, as a spy who they could then *prove* had contact with their enemy!'

Gazing at her. Nodding, then. 'I admit I hadn't thought of that. But – look, I don't have to get caught, if I go carefully. At Taisnières, for instance—'

'You were paying your last respects to a dead person. And when challenged, telling them her name. If you'd enquired for *Hilde* Martens – different, huh?'

He shrugged. 'Perhaps.'

There was also, come to think of it, that near-squeak experience at Hergies. His own recognition then that he wouldn't have had a hope in hell. In fact that embarking on this at all – *his* doing so, with his own personal limitations, linguistic especially – had been – well, at the *least* rash. Some might say practically lunatic.

Elise asked him quietly, 'The information Hilde has offered you is of great significance, I would guess?'

'Enormous.' He leant forward, forearms on the table. 'It could save us and you from losing the war before the Americans get their thousands of fresh young troops into the line.'

'Is that actually in prospect?'

'A possibility, I'm told. Then the Huns would have only the Americans to take on. What Ludendorff will be aiming for – with huge reinforcements from what was the Russian front.'

'Can you spare one hour now, Lieutenant?'

'An hour . . .'

Eleven-forty now.

'Then either you go back to your airship and take off, or if by that time I've seen a way that looks good and you agree it does—'

'Leave the ship there the rest of the night and all day tomorrow . . .'

'Only if I can think of some way. And I would hope not *all* day. Oh, but you said you would not take off until dark in any case, so – yes, I beg your pardon, all day it would be.' She spread her hands: 'One hour – please? Then *your* decision?'

19

Charlie woke out of a nightmare in which it had been Amanda in that coffin; those four old women had been hammering the lid down over her while she'd screamed and he'd watched in impotence, unable to speak or move a muscle. It hadn't been the old witches' hammering that had woken him – he already knew he'd dreamt *that* part – but Amanda's frantic knocking from inside.

Bollocks. He was lying bewildered and still shaken in the dark, between sheets and under blankets, dismissing all of that while facing up to an entirely different nightmare, which though real was almost more difficult to believe in: the fact he'd agreed to take part in this – Christ, this . . .

Charade.

Bloody dangerous. And leaving the others out on a limb, in that wood, knowing not a damn thing of what was going on. What was more – one's own personal decision, all this.

Needing the French for 'Come in', he'd managed a loud 'Huh?', and the big woman – Madeleine, officially the cook, but seemed to do everything except drive the trap – and really *was* big, from the waist down gargantuan – was setting a candle on the chest of drawers and telling him it was five am. That had to be what she was saying, because (a) it did happen to be five, and (b) it was what had been agreed – or at any rate stipulated by Elise de Semeillions. Early start because of certain essential preparations for the funeral operation: a funeral which Charlie himself would not be attending, instead would be hiding-out in some farmstead in which he was to install himself before daylight – and staying out of sight until it worked or – more than likely – blew up in their faces. Especially, he thought, in Elise's face. The part *he* was to play was hardly even a walk-on, was in fact the only part that had an escape mechanism more or less built into it.

It had been getting on for one am when they'd finished ironing out the detail and Elise had shown him to this bedroom, and to where there was a WC with a hand-basin in it, just along the passage, then gone on up to the top floor to wake Madeleine, give her these orders for the morning: all up at five, breakfast at a quarter past, the groom Jeannot to have Hercule and the trap ready for the road by six. Jeannot lived over the stables, apparently. He'd be dropping Charlie off at this farmstead about a kilometre north of the cemetery, then turning back into Hon-Hergies to pick up a young woman by name of Marie something-or-other and bringing her back to the manor.

Out of bed now: in vest and long-johns, picking up a towel and the candle on its enamel saucer. Madeleine had lit it from her own candle while ensuring by means of continuous loud French chatter that he'd stay awake, not drop off again when she left him. He was heading for the WC now, in vest and pants: cold, but decent enough. Anyway, Elise's room was in another wing, probably about a hundred yards away. It was an enormous house. And she was a truly remarkable woman, he thought. Remembering her long, silent perusals of the maps, and the way she'd gazed at him for minutes on end across the table – not seeing him, only using him as a point of focus for those *very* wide-awake blue eyes. Breaking off at one stage to ask, 'Tell me where exactly is your *ballon*?'

'You mean airship.'

'Ah, yes – air*ship*.'

Like air*sheep* . . . He'd shown her, on McLachlan's map. 'Here.' Turning the map her way.

She'd studied it, murmured, 'Trieu du Bois. Blaregnies.

Well, that's convenient enough.' Glancing up at him: 'They are felling some thousands of trees there, uh?'

'Have been, yes.' A disturbing thought then: 'Might be at it again tomorrow?'

'Sunday? No – not on Sundays. And this time of year, no picnics or mushroom-hunting, either. Especially with snow expected.'

'Is it?'

'So one is told.' A shrug. 'The village weather experts, you know.'

'What are they saying about gale-force winds?'

'Nothing that I've heard.' A shake of the head, and concentrating again. The focus of her attention seemed to be on the area northwest of Hon-Hergies marked Entre Deux, where the cemetery was shown. He'd passed through that tangle of lanes on his way here, he realised: not on the erratically looping bit that gave access to the cemetery, but via the lower one – where he'd forked, *would* have turned off on the other but had missed it.

She'd told him eventually – after rather more than the agreed hour – 'There is a way it might be done.'

'Just *might*, or—'

'A lot will depend on Ulrich von Bodenschatz. But I *believe* I will prevail. Prevail, that is, over the disgusting Koch. I'll be begging, absolutely *begging* von Bodenschatz to allow me to bring Hilde with me in the trap from Taisnières to Entre Deux. *Here.*'

'To the cemetery.'

'On the face of it, yes. Not quite that far, in fact, but – anyway, *you*, Lieutenant, will be here – at this farm.' Pencil-tip touching it. 'Jeannot will bring you here in the trap, before sunrise.'

'Could go on my bike, if—'

'Take it with you in the trap. You may need it later. I hope you will not, but – may. If it goes well with Hilde, I think better on foot, the pair of you.'

'Hilde makes a run for it at some point, joins me at this farm?'

She nodded approvingly. 'First things first, though.'

'Only it sounds – well, rather *simple*. Place alive with Huns, and she just jumps out and runs for it?'

'It is simple, yes. Simple I think is best, Lieutenant. Affairs of this type that become *compliqués* – complicated – can so easily go wrong. See here – she runs, yes – supposedly in one direction, actually in another, and with these – would the word for them be "dykes"?'

'You mean the embanked roads?'

'Very well. Embanked roads. Using them as I'll explain to her, she is never in sight from – from anywhere – not from this side where they're coming from Taisnières, nor from the cemetery itself. Not even from these embanked roads here – as you might imagine if you are going only by the map. Since the map does not show the ups and downs, uh? I happen to know the district very well – Hilde also, having travelled between this house and her mother's every single day. And the embanked roads there are higher, you see. What's more – much more – the Boches and whoever else is in the cortège behind us – we'll be following the coffin, Hilde being the chief mourner, naturally – all will be looking – searching – *this* way. Huh?'

'When they find she *didn't* go that way, won't you be held responsible?'

'I think not. I and the girl who'll be with me – whom I want with me partly for a witness – as well as Madeleine and Jeannot, of course – we'll all four have seen her go that way, then somehow vanish. We don't have the least idea how – except there are a lot of the embanked roads around here, and she knows her way around so well – then for heaven's sake she's in Hergies almost, although it's anyone's guess which way she went! All right, they'll have to search the village – every house, eh, how long will *that* take? Please God, she's with *you* long before it's over. Nobody in either Hergies or Hon-Hergies knowing anything of what's happened, incidentally – it's the plain truth – they don't and they won't!'

'Yes, that's good. The fewer who know anything, the

better.' Charlie nodded. 'But again – if *you've* persuaded von Bodenschatz to let her ride with you, surely against the advice of his security officer—'

'He – von Bodenschatz – will be held responsible. I'm sorry for it, but I can't help that. She would not escape if she remained in Koch's hands, so it's poor old Ulrich who's taken the risk and lost her. *If* he does, mind you – everything depends on that. He might not want to have a real showdown with Koch, for instance. Rank isn't everything, is it, especially in matters of security, so forth? Against that, I do have – well, some persuasive powers, and the best of motives for wanting her with me up to the last moment: she's been like a foster daughter to me, I'm terrified by what's going to happen to her – I *am*, that's true – and she's also a close friend of the young girl who'll be with us, who'll be in tears, absolute desperation!'

'Do you really need the girl, though? Seeing as you have Madeleine and the groom anyway?'

'Yes. I think her participation will help us a lot.'

'Only thinking of what we just said – the fewer in the know the better?'

A shake of the glossy head. 'Never mind . . .'

'But you're terrified, you say – for Hilde's chances.'

She'd shrugged. 'I exaggerated. A little nervous – yes.'

'You do realise, then, it's a very risky business.'

'A small piece of bad luck could wreck it, certainly. But, Lieutenant, nothing of this kind can be certain or risk-free, I admit. If for instance she was seen as she crossed this piece of road between the embanked sections here and here – just in those few seconds some Boche turning his head . . . No reason it *should* turn out that way, however, and recognising that it *could* would not justify screaming, Oh no, it's too dangerous, I dare not! Eh?'

He let that go. Wondering whether she understood that the risk was going to be mainly hers. But McLachlan's and Stavely's too, stuck out there . . . He was peering more closely at the map: 'At that point she'd be only about five hundred metres from the farm where I'm waiting for her. She's going to have to run like a hare, isn't she? Quite short distances, but—'

'She quite likely could out-run a hare. But no reason any of them should be taking any interest – at that time, in that direction. Maybe you cannot see it, Lieutenant, but I can. And see here, now. You are in the farmstead, and all this will take place between let's say eleven and eleven-thirty. By that time – eleven-thirty at the latest – she should be with you, and it's then up to you whether to clear out immediately, or wait some little while.'

'Depending on how things look. If there's a great hue and cry—'

'Might be best to wait for darkness. But what I'm saying – if we have not succeeded, if Hilde does *not* join you – well, you have your bicycle. You *would* wait for dark I suppose, and then – *adieu, mon lieutenant.*'

'Leaving you to face the music.'

'If there were to be such music – Wagnerian, eh? – your continued presence would be no help to any of us. In fact far from it.' She reached over, patted his hand. 'Don't even think about it.'

Breakfast was porridge and coffee, served in an annexe to the kitchen. It was quicker, warmer and more convenient, Elise explained. She and Madeleine were already draped in black; and while drinking her coffee she wrote two notes – one for Charlie to give the farmer to whom Jeannot would be introducing him, and the other for the girl – Marie – in Hon-Hergies.

'The farmer's name is Emile Voreaux. He is one of us, he will help all he can. The only thing is, to take no chances that might compromise him. Don't risk allowing yourself to be seen – not only by Boches but by *anyone*, huh?'

'One of us' didn't need to be elucidated – the implication was clear enough. She gave him the note, he pocketed it and she called to Madeleine, 'Has Jeannot been in for breakfast yet?' He had, apparently, was now seeing to Hercule and the trap. Elise told her, 'Ask him to come in for a word with me.' In the cook's absence then she told Charlie while still scribbling her second note, 'He's a grumpy little man but his heart's in the right place. He was a trooper in my husband's regiment of *chasseurs*, retired through some injury to his back a long time ago and has been with us – oh, an age.' A movement of the head: 'Here he is.'

Madeleine came through. 'Jeannot to see you, Madame.'

'Ask him to come in.'

The man himself – cap in hand. Focusing on Charlie then, and mouth dropping open: it didn't have many teeth in it. Elise told Charlie, 'This is Jeannot Brefort, Lieutenant.' Then a longish burst of French to Jeannot: Charlie heard his own name and rank, the word *Britannique*, and what he guessed might have been something along the lines of: 'You've seen each other before – he's told me. He's here with a way of getting Hilde Martens away to England – in which we'll help all we can, uh?'

Jeannot nodding, muttering, '*Bien sûr. Bien sûr.*' Still looking at Charlie as if he thought he might not be real.

Charlie suggested, 'Best not to tell him I sneaked in behind the trap. Might have left the bike in the hedge and climbed that gate.' Getting up from the table as he spoke, he went around it and offered the old man his hand: 'Jeannot.'

'*Grand honneur, mon lieutenant!*'

Elise looked pleased. 'Jeannot, sit down for a moment. Madeleine, bring another cup. Now listen, Jeannot . . .'

She was really something special, Charlie thought. If one had been – well, ten years older, and with origins of a somewhat different kind . . . Anyway, she had a husband – and children, two girls apparently, at some convent but coming home this next week for holidays. Hardly the best of times to be risking all she *was* risking, he thought. She might have made a perfect wife for McLachlan, though: you could imagine the two of them ordering each other around, McLachlan being at home in French – and almost certainly a horseman.

Feeling fairly desperate too, by this time, one might guess. Watching for the first streaks of dawn to lighten the clouded sky, knowing that unless he, Charlie, turned up with or without Hilde in the course of the next hour, they'd have a whole day to see through – with the wind getting up. Force 5 by noon, for God's sake. They'd be guessing at a more drastic scenario than that, too, he imagined: at his having been shot to death somewhere – as McLachlan had half-jokingly envisaged for himself – but shot, or caught, the question then being what should he and Stavely do?

If they weren't somehow discovered, didn't find themselves surrounded suddenly by Huns . . .

Start walking?

Forget them, though. Stop worrying about the wind, too. How it would be at dusk, *that* mattered – and touch wood, you'd be with them by that time. Which was a *good* thought, finally, better than all those others.

He'd been about his own business, now arrived back in the kitchen where they were waiting for him.

'Sorry . . .'

'Hercule and the trap await you, Lieutenant. I have explained to Jeannot that there is a bicycle to pick up outside the gates, and suggested that you should sit on the floor of the trap, try not to be seen. A rug over your head, even. Although it's dark, if you were to meet a patrol . . .'

'Yes – all right. And – Madame, thank you so *very* much—'

'For nothing. Listen – if it goes as it should, you'll be leaving the bicycle, won't you? Tell Voreux it's his, but if there's speculation or rumour going around he should keep it out of sight for the time being.'

'Good thinking.'

A smile: 'Good luck.'

'Good luck to *you*.' He was holding both her hands by this time, and on a sudden impulse kissed her cheek – lightly, since he hadn't shaved. 'I think you're stupendous.'

'That's very nice. Thank you. When the war's finished,

come back and see us. My husband would be very happy and our daughters would be thrilled to bits.'

Jeannot unlocked the timber gateway; Charlie went through, found his bike and extracted it from the hedge, loaded it into the trap while the gates were being shut and locked again. He climbed in after it and sat on the floor while the old boy threw a carriage rug over him. All of that took about a minute, and the trap was already rolling – still a few minues short of six am. One and three-quarter kilometres to Hergies, to the right turn where that car had damn near stopped this business in its tracks. That near-disaster stuck rather in his mind: it was unquestionable that if he had *not* flung himself off as he had, (a) he'd have been in some lock-up since then, and (b) after the funeral this morning Hilde would have been on her way to Brussels.

As she might still be. It was still hellish chancy. And he thought Elise might be under-estimating the danger to herself. If it came off, the Germans would no doubt hold von Bodenschatz responsible – but only for agreeing to what *she'd* have proposed, begged for. Koch, whom she'd described as a fanatic, wasn't likely to let that go.

At Voreux's farm – six-twenty, and still dark – Jeannot turned into a cobbled yard and leaned over to pull the rug off his passenger. Elise had been insistent that he should waste no time in getting back on to the road into Hon-Hergies; his visit to the girl Marie was perfectly legitimate and explainable, but it was important that no Hun interest should be directed *this* way, either now or retrospectively. If stopped and asked to explain his visit here the old man would say he'd come to ask Voreux whether he had a dozen bales of straw to spare, could maybe deliver them to the manor in the next few days. All right, it wasn't a matter of such urgency that you'd normally set out about it before dawn, just happened he'd this other business to see to in the village – Madame de Semeillions' need of a replacement for Hilde in her household, which *was* of a certain urgency, Madeleine Vicot having heard that the girl – Marie Fonquereuil – was thinking of moving to other employment in Bavay. Elise had laughed, told him, 'It's an art – not just of telling lies: you can bore them to tears with such explanations, they lose all interest. You should bear it in mind, Lieutenant: when you find that some young lady is going out of her way apparently to bore *you* . . .'

He'd thought – Amanda?

Well. *Might* bear it in mind. If and when . . .

At least one oil-lamp was burning in the farmhouse, and at the sound of Hercule's hooves and the trap's wheels on cobbles, a man came out of an outhouse and advanced slowly towards the trap as Jeannot reined-in. '*Eh, Hercule . . .*'

'What's up, Brefort?'

'Anyone wants to know, called by to ask d'you have any straw you'd sell us. Truth, though, brought you a visitor. You'll see, he has a letter for you.' The old soldier got down, Charlie passed the bike down to him and then followed. Jeannot adding to the farmer, 'Letter from Madame de Semeillions. Private business. A dozen bales, if you could spare 'em?'

Charlie said, shaking Voreux's thick hand, 'Holt. *Onglais. Je ne parle pas Fronsy.*' Elise had taught him that. He gave Voreux her note, and the man went back into the half-lit shed to read it.

Jeannot, already back in the trap, called down to Charlie, '*Bien, alors?*'

Going by his tone, something like, 'All right, then?' Searching his brain, Charlie came up with, '*Merci, Jeannot!*'

'*Adieu. Bonne chance.*' Flip of the reins. '*Eh, Hercule . . .*'

Elise de Semeillions asked Marie Fonquereuil, in the morning-room at about eight o'clock, 'Is that satisfactory, Marie?'

'Oh, yes.' Rapid blinking. A well-built girl – brown-haired, brown-eyed, blob of a nose. 'Entirely, Madame!'

'It's not as much as I was paying Hilde, but when we've got to know each other and you've proved your worth, we'll think again. To be frank with you, Hilde's a smart, clever girl and a very hard worker – that's what you have to try to measure up to. She told me, incidentally, that you'd have liked to work here: you could say it's on her recommendation that I'm making you this offer.'

'Well. We're like sisters.' Face crumpling: 'It's *terrible*, what—'

'I do know that you and she were friends in your schooldays – and you helped her with her mother at one time?'

'When she herself was unwell. And you were away, looking after some relative near Lille.'

'And you wouldn't take payment for it.'

'From *Hilde*, or that dear old lady?'

Elise smiled. 'Change of subject now. Tell me – how do you feel about the *Boches*, Marie?'

'*Sacrés Boches* . . .'

'Exactly. Primarily it's Hilde I'm thinking of when I ask that question. What they're doing to her, and what they did to Madame Cavell. Tell me, though – this is a personal question, forgive me, but I'd like to know – do you have any friends amongst them?'

'Amongst the *Boches*, Madame?'

'Don't feel insulted. Hilde as it happens did get to know one of them quite well – as I'm sure you must know. Also, it's important to me that you don't have any false impressions – I myself am on quite friendly terms with the commandant at Bellignies, Major von Bodenschatz. The background to this is a common interest in horses – hunting, and so forth, equestrian matters generally. Wait a minute, I'm about to explain why you have to hear all this. You're coming with us to the funeral this morning?'

'I'm so grateful – Jeannot did mention it. I have my black coat, and—'

'The point is, Marie, Major von Bodenschatz will be there, and you'll see me in conversation with him. He's – quite old, and he has breathing difficulties – asthma. He was a cavalryman, but is unfit for active service now – it's why he has that job. But at the church, as I say, you'll see me talking with him. I intend – *must* – persuade him to allow Hilde to come with us in the trap from Taisnières to Entre Deux. We may never see her again – you realise? And if ever a young girl needed to be with friends – loses her mother, then the arrest . . . There's a real *pig* of a German by name of Koch, a captain, actually some kind of policeman—'

'We've all heard of him, Madame.'

'He's the one behind this. Major von Bodenschatz is of course his superior officer, but may still find it difficult to over-rule him – which he already has done, in fact, in allowing Hilde to attend her own mother's funeral.'

'I know.'

'You understand, then. And the more – moral force, persuasion, the better chance we'll have. You, as a lifelong friend of Hilde's and of her mother – of *course* you'll be overwrought – wanting Hilde with us. If necessary you'll beg, and cry . . .'

'I *will*. I *will*. Poor darling Hilde . . .'

'But there's more to it than that, Marie. In telling you this now – and asking for your help in it – I'm asking a lot, but also placing a great deal of trust in you – even my life – Hilde's too – in your hands. It's quite a *lot* of help we need from you. Listen, now . . .'

She asked Madeleine – in the kitchen, while Marie was in her room on the top floor, unpacking her trunk and changing her clothes, Jeannot grooming Hercule and washing down the trap – 'You see the point, do you?'

'Of having her with us?'

'You might have questioned the wisdom of bringing her into it. An outsider, as she is.'

'I'd say that *is* the point. I and Jeannot being – if I may presume as to say so – almost family—'

'You *are* family. There's no presumption in it. And people would say, "Oh, they *would* support her, swear to whatever she wanted to put across" – huh?'

'Of course. And we would, too. But also to have more of a crowd in the trap might – confuse them?'

'Let's hope so. But primarily the business of chasing after her. Not quite *your* style, Madeleine?'

'Chasing across those fields?' Slapping one enormous hip. 'Me? Who'd believe *that*?' A shake of the head, then, '*Would* she chase after her, though? Hilde being her dear friend?'

'Yes – and she's happy with it. Not to catch Hilde, obviously, but – as it were – lead the hunt. In fact of course *mis*lead it. She'll be in panic – scared for *Hilde* – don't you see?'

There'd been no noticeable increase in wind force yet, but it *had* veered to northeast, which regrettably tallied with the forecast. His view from the hatch in the end of Voreux's hayloft was southward, and chimney-smoke rising from Hon-Hergies clearly had a left-to-right component in it. Blue-ish, rising and drifting, and even against the wind and from this distance – mile and a half maybe – identifiable by scent as woodsmoke.

Eight thirty-five. Plenty of time for the wind to come up to force 5 by noon. It *might* not – the forecast might turn out to be wrong, even by just a few hours. Not much to ask for – except that one was praying for a few other long-shot mercies as well as that one. For Elise's slapdash scheme to work, for instance. For von Bodenschatz to allow Hilde to travel with her in the trap, to start with; then for the deception ploy at Entre Deux not to be the disaster it might be. Please, God, let Hilde get away and let Elise get away with *getting* her away. Hell of a lot to ask for, he thought, reaching for the heavy old telescope Voreux had been so kind as to leave with him. It worked well enough, although its prisms could have done with some spit and polish. Focusing again now – line of sight straight down the mostly embanked road to the junction at Entre Deux, cemetery slightly to the left of that. What he could see of the cemetery was its end wall, this northern end, and over it the upper parts of memorials, one especially tall marble angel standing out clearly in its whiteness. Nothing moving: grave-diggers either working nearer the other end, or had done their stuff already. The entrance, at that southern end, could be approached from either direction, depending on which road one took out of Hon-Hergies – the one he'd missed last night or the one he'd taken, which as it happened was the one the trap would be coming on in about two and a half hours' time.

20

A single bell was tolling. Hilde glancing up at the church tower, after the corporal who'd ridden inside the van with her had given her a hand down. In leg-irons and handcuffs she'd hardly have managed without that help, but Gustav Koch hadn't been thinking of providing any, was just standing there, watching her. There was a German army truck parked on the corner of the side road that led down to the Martens house, and this side of it a staff car, and the small green van in which Hilde remembered having been fetched from the manor for that second interview with Koch. Closer still, right outside the church, was a flat-topped cart, property of Jules Quillot, a market gardener who did this sort of thing as a sideline, and a motorcycle combination parked right on the pavement.

People were waving to her, and some women blew kisses. Dr Fressin, from Bavay, raised his black Homberg and gave her a little bow before resuming his conversation with Leroy the village gendarme. Just about all Taisnières was here, filling the street and pavements and thronging the courtyard entrance to the church – a paved yard behind railings which a long time ago had had silver paint on them and still showed traces of it – but leaving a clear space around a squad of helmeted Hun soldiers.

The corporal muttered and gestured to her, indicating that she should get moving – into the church, presumably. She began to – then stopped, shaking her head and holding up her manacled arms, looking down disgustedly at the leg-irons. A murmuring from the crowd grew louder and more positive: pointing, gesturing, their expressions and tones varying from mildly indignant to furious. Koch shouted to the corporal, 'Get her inside!'

'*Jawohl*—'

'Hauptmann Koch!'

Von Bodenschatz: he must have been sitting waiting in the staff car – she'd heard a car door slam, hadn't looked that way until now. The Bellignies commandant's seamed grey face was taut with disapproval. Pointing with his swagger-cane: 'Remove the iron-mongery, Koch. She's attending her own mother's funeral, man!'

'If those are your orders, sir . . .'

'Are you deaf, then?'

Koch beckoned to the corporal. 'Here.' A bunch of keys. 'Remove the irons, lock them in the van, put them on her again when we continue to the cemetery.'

'Sir.'

As he unlocked the cuffs, some of the villagers applauded. Hilde, massaging her wrists, looked down expressionlessly at the German as he took the leg-irons off. She wasn't conventionally attired for church-going: a rather dreadful old brown leather coat, an oatmeal-coloured skirt showing under it and a vividly green silk scarf as head-covering.

Five or six minutes to ten, and the bell still tolling. She'd nodded her thanks to von Bodenschatz, but he'd turned away, ignoring it, and hearing – also seeing, now – the approach of the Manoir Hergies pony-trap. Hilde had also heard and seen it, faced it now with longing in her expression. The crowd was dividing left and right to let it through. Old Jeannot at the reins, in a black cap and overcoat, Elise de Semeillions elegant in black, Madeleine Vicot elephantine in hers; and – clearly to Hilde's delight – Marie Fonquereuil, waving happily but discreetly to her. Jeannot was having to pull up abreast the hearse on account of the black van and other vehicles filling the kerb-space beyond it.

272

Elise reached Hilde first: both were in tears as they embraced, Hilde gasping, 'How sweet of you to bring Marie!' and Elise then, 'I have a lot to tell you, but first I *have* to speak to von Bodenschatz. I'll be right back. Meanwhile . . .'

Meanwhile Hilde was embracing Marie and Madeleine. Jeannot raised his hat: he was at Hercule's head, turning the trap in the narrow and congested roadway.

Elise, dabbing at her eyes, asked von Bodenschatz, 'Might I have a word, *mon commandant?*'

'But of course, Madame.'

Koch was watching, and no doubt straining his ears. Elise turned her back on him. '*Mon commandant* – you can imagine how I and my household feel about poor Hilde?'

'I can indeed, Madame. And I regret – can only hope that the investigation will prove her innocence.'

'I'm sure it *must*. And may I ask you – *beg* you – because this is so short a time for us to – oh, to share her grief and be *with* her, perhaps comfort her a little – you see, for me especially, she could be my daughter, the way I feel for her. And that young girl there – Marie Fonquereuil – they grew up together . . .'

'Yes. Yes. I'm sure. Unfortunately it's not in my own field of responsibility – as I hope you understand, Madame.'

'I want only to ask – especially as you've been so kind in other matters – after this mass, let her come in the trap with us to Entre Deux?'

He was thinking about it. Frowning. A shrug, then. 'I don't see why not. No – I don't. On your own responsibility, of course.'

'Oh, *thank you* so very—'

'Hauptmann Koch!'

The bell still tolling. And snow falling: not much, but enough for mourners to be turning their collars up. In fact most of them had gone inside by now. Marie and Madeleine surrendering Hilde to Elise but staying with them, the young girl and the huge woman close enough to ensure some degree of privacy from the villagers crowding round. Elise told her group quietly but triumphantly, 'Hilde is being permitted to drive with us in the trap to Entre Deux.'

Madeleine crossed herself. 'Thank God.'

Marie murmured, 'That's *wonderful*!'

Hilde began, 'He's more or less a human being, that one. I tell you, just before you arrived—'

'Hilde, tell us later. Don't show excitement at what I'm about to tell you now, don't show *anything*. We'll go into detail during the drive – it's all planned. Hilde, your message did reach London. There's an Englishman waiting for you at Voreux's farm. Yes, it's true, believe me, but show nothing – only grief for your dear mother. Whom in fact you will not see buried. Just think how happy she'd be for you if she could know this. Perhaps she *does* . . .' The priest, a robust, bald man, had emerged from the church and was beckoning to them. Elise, with an arm around Hilde's shoulders in that terrible old coat, assuring him, 'Yes, Father, we're coming . . .'

Ten o'clock, and the bell had fallen silent.

Ten twenty-eight: half an hour since that mournfully tolling bell had ceased. They'd be about coming out of church, Charlie guessed. And if the hearse travelled at say five kilometres per hour – Elise had told him it would be a horse and cart – well, they had to bring the coffin out and load it on, to start with, and pall-bearers usually didn't exactly race about, so with two kilometres to cover it would take about half an hour.

The snow hadn't amounted to much, as yet, but this was the second shower and it was heavier than the first had been; and Elise had said it was expected. Quite likely therefore *would* set in, and snow plus high winds equalled blizzard. Best not even think of that: the possible inevitability of spending another whole night and day on the ground – with Hilde, if this business had come off, in which case you'd have troops all over the place, even maybe reconnaissance aircraft over. You'd be starving, too, and in that length of time the leakage of gas might well become significant.

Don't think about it. Take it as it comes. May not be *that* disastrous . . .

Ten thirty-five.

Vehicle of some kind approaching the cemetery. He slid forward – off the hay-bale he'd been sitting on – on to his knees, rested his elbows on the bale between himself and the hatch, focusing Voreux's telescope first on the marble angel and then on the junction of those lanes. It was a truck, coming from the direction of the Manoir Hergies, or of Bellignies, perhaps. German army truck, that drab greenish-brown. It would be coming to the cemetery, he guessed, bringing a load of Huns. All right if they took up positions around the cemetery – for what purpose, God only knew – but very much less all right if they were used to patrol those lanes. Quick shift southward, to where the hearse and cortège might show up in about – ten-forty now, so probably not in the next ten minutes, more likely fifteen or twenty; and where the trap with Elise and company in it definitely *would* appear. It was the way they had to come – Elise's plan hung on it absolutely, no matter what the rest of them did. Nothing was moving on that side now, anyway. Back to the truck, then – as it reached the intersection, might even have turned up *this* way.

Hadn't. Was going straight over, heading for that end of the cemetery and passing out of one's range of vision. If it wasn't stopping there it would shortly reappear on the loop of lane running up the cemetery's eastern side.

And had not. Therefore had stopped, and ten to one on, would be disembarking troops. Brought here from Bellignies, he guessed – wouldn't have come from that direction if they'd been transferees from Taisnières. But they – meaning Koch – almost certainly would have troops deployed at Taisnières, and one might guess they'd come on here with the funeral cortège. Which would mean this place being fairly lousy with them by the time the action started.

The coffin was on the hearse with a few wreaths on it, and

Quillot was up on the driver's seat with two pall-bearers beside him. The horse, a grey, was looking round at Hercule as Jeannot led him and the trap up to the position it had occupied before – abreast the hearse, but leaving Quillot room to pull out when he was ready to. Quillot pointing with his whip, telling Jeannot, 'We'll go this way – down there and to the right, right again at the bottom.'

'Didn't *think* you'd be going through Bavay.'

Sarcasm. All Quillot had meant was that he wasn't thinking of trying to turn in order to leave by way of the main street. Which was thronged again as the church emptied. Jeannot removing his cap briefly as Elise arrived with an arm round Hilde: both were composed now but pale and tear-stained. Madeleine and Marie were close behind them. Snow was falling again, and Jeannot had been quick to cover his bald head; he told Elise as he gave her a hand up, 'Hercule's playing up. Likes the looks of that nag of Quillot's, the old devil.'

'Too much oats, Jeannot. You spoil that animal.' She pulled Hilde down on her right where the seat curved around and up that side, and Marie on her left; Madeleine crammed herself in then, and Jeannot clambered up. Elise said, 'It was a simple but very moving service, I thought.' Raising a gloved hand in response to von Bodenschatz's inclination of the head: he was at his car then, his sergeant-driver opening the rear right-hand door for him. Elise saw Koch climbing into the front of the black van.

'Jeannot. When Quillot gets going, follow close behind him and stop level with the van so it's shut in and Major von Bodenschatz's car will be the next behind us. Understand me?'

'Understood, Madame.'

'I'll explain this as we go along, Hilde. The others know what they have to do, but – please, everyone, listen carefully and raise any questions you like – let's make absolutely sure of it.'

Hearse pulling out now: Jeannot flipped his reins, got Hercule moving. At the corner, soldiers were embarking in the truck. Hilde asked Elise, 'Tell me about the Englishman?'

'Well. The first thing is he doesn't understand a word of French.'

'*Doesn't?* But that's—'

'Crazy – yes, that's what I thought. But he's a pilot, flies a dirigible – they call it an air*ship* – and at present it's on the edge of the forest at Blaregnies. Trieu du Bois, know where I mean?'

'Of course!'

'He brought with him another person who *does* speak French but broke his leg or something when they landed, so this pilot – naval pilot, a lieutenant – took the injured one's place. He went to your house, where he learnt of your mother's death, and came to me then at the manor. On a bicycle, would you believe it. We sat up until the small hours devising this scheme – which I admit is not without its risks and dangers, Hilde dear.'

'I'm up to the neck in those already – but what about *you*, Madame?'

'Don't worry about *me*.' She looked back. 'Jeannot, the major's driver is wanting to pull out. Go on, but not too fast, eh?'

'*Eh – Hercule . . .*'

They'd been blocking the black van in. Now its driver could hardly force his way out ahead of von Bodenschatz's staff car, had to display good manners and respect for a senior officer, let them precede him. Elise was glad to see that the van's wind-screen was misted up: wipers hard at it and the rest of it snow-streaked. The snow seemed to have settled in for a long stay this time. She told Jeannot, 'You did that very well.'

'Catch up on Quillot, shall I?'

'No. Let's stay as we are. Then von Bodenschatz may keep *his* distance. It leaves the danger of Koch pushing up between us – I guess he may be quite angry now – but the only way to prevent that – well, there's *no* way – any gap at all, he *could* do that. And it would be very bad for us.' She spread her hands. '*Many* dangers, Hilde. But now listen—'

Hilde tried again: 'If I get away, what happens to *you*?'

'I shall be utterly *distraite*. I would never have dreamt you'd so take advantage of my affection for you. I'll be stunned with surprise and chagrin.'

'You really think Koch won't realise . . .'

'Won't be able to *prove* it. And I have von Bodenschatz on my side. Now just listen . . .

Snowing quite steadily; beginning to settle, too. Slanting down from the northwest, which meant the ship wouldn't be as well sheltered as she had been. He'd realised this earlier – *much* earlier – when he'd made his messy landing and he and Stavely had secured her there, having that forecast very much in mind but no way to do anything much about it except secure her with all four handling guys plus the trail-rope and head-rope. She'd still be in *partial* shelter, from that top right-hand (i.e. northeastern) corner of the Trieu du Bois. Whatever Trieu du Bois might mean. Thinking of them there, though, and of their likely state of mind: acute anxiety, obviously, but wouldn't be giving up hope quite *yet* – would certainly hang on until dark. Until the pre-dawn hours of Monday, probably: they'd be telling themselves, 'Hang on, hang on . . .' And even *then* . . .

They'd have two options. No, they wouldn't. With McLachlan's leg out of action the only chance they'd have would be for Stavely to try to get the ship up on his own. Which he *might* manage, if he had luck. He'd know the odds were against him, in various ways – especially of course when the wind got up, which it was pretty well bound to do some time this evening or tonight. Nicer to tell oneself it might *not*, but – forget it anyway. Sufficient unto the day . . . Stavely's chances, though – McLachlan's preference would be to wait, continue hoping against hope, although there'd be nothing to eat or drink – they'd have eaten all the sandwiches and drunk the coffee by this time – and they'd be very, very cold.

And that leg of his . . .

He'd be glad he'd written that letter to his son, Charlie thought.

Get to them this evening, anyway. With Hilde or without her. Preferably *with* – obviously – but otherwise cut one's losses, save their lives and one's own and get the ship away.

The Hun soldiers who'd come in that truck were inside the cemetery, their helmets and shouldered rifles occasionally visible above the end wall. The good side of it was that they were keeping the angels company, *not* disporting themselves on the approach roads. At least he'd seen nothing moving on any of those lanes or in the stretches of them that he could see. The intersections especially one would have thought they might have picketed – three intersections at this top end, as well as his own particular interest now – at ten fifty-five – the lower, circular road which started in Hon-Hergies at the right fork he'd taken last night, then circled right-handed to the point where he'd rather lost his bearings.

Forget the cemetery now, in fact. Concentrate on that lower road. Or on as much as one could see through the falling snow.

Which, come to think of it, might improve Hilde's chances.

If she'd been allowed to ride with them in the trap. That was the crucial thing; for all he knew she might *not* have been, in which case this whole business was a washout.

Less than a fortnight: only that long since McLachlan, then a total stranger, had told him in old Peeling's office: 'Need someone to fly an airship on a special mission. What d'you say, Holt?'

Checking the time again – close on eleven. Should have remembered the old training-ship principle, never volunteer for *anything*. He'd been rather floating on air though, at that time – on the excitement of Amanda. Distraction more than excitement *now*. He put the telescope up again . . .

Hercule going strong and steady, hauling them through

Hon-Hergies. Church-goers in Sunday best pausing here and there to watch them pass. An encouraging factor only minutes ago had been that the last vehicle in the cortège, the truckload of soldiers, was no longer with them, had gone straight on – towards Bavay – at the last turning; Bavay was most likely where they'd come from. Cortège consisting now therefore of the hearse, this trap, von Bodenschatz's staff-car, the black van with Koch in it, the smaller, green van and the motorbike – which was the priest's. Elise and Hilde had known this and had been surprised the others hadn't.

'See –' Elise with her map, showing Marie – 'if she'd gone this way, between the lakes there, then over to the Hergies side of this embanked roadway, and gone either right or left, you wouldn't know which way or where the devil – and see, all these farms and cottages she *could* be in?'

'Should I chase that far, then?'

'Wouldn't you? Once you'd started?'

Madeleine warned, twisting her large frame half round, 'The motorcycle is trying to pass the black van. It's good we've lost the soldiers, eh?'

'It's excellent.' Elise persisted, 'Marie, look. My bet is that if this works as I'm convinced it will, when Koch finds himself stopped and sees you marking Hilde's trail for him, he'll try to cut her off by getting back on to the main road – this way, Pont des Bergers and to the right here. You'd better be ready for that – it's *you* he'll catch up with – don't let him think you're scared of him, only be frantic for *her*, saying how she must have panicked, simply not known what she was doing, and your aim in trying to catch her is to persude her to come back. All right?'

'I'll do my best.'

'Just convince yourself that you're chasing after her for her own sake and that she's vanished – you want him to understand she's not ill-intentioned, only under terrific strain – that kind of thing. And good luck, my dear.'

'You too, Madame.'

'Hilde, I don't have to say it, but *one* day . . .'

'I'll pray for that day, Madame.'

Madeleine said, 'Here he comes, your *curé*!'

The motorcycle combination: the priest with his head down, eyes slitted and teeth gritted against the snow, soutane flying in the wind; that was probably one of his altar-boys in the side-car, along for the ride. He wasn't overtaking the trap though, was veering away to the right, on to the narrower but – despite the way it looped around – shorter route to the cemetery. Wanting to get there before the hearse did, one supposed, be there to meet it. Elise chuckling, 'Fine fellow, Father Deschamps. They're lucky to have him in Taisnières. I'd like to steal him for Hergies. Bat out of hell, eh?' The bike's high-pitched racket fading as Hercule hauled them at a gentle trot past that first turning. Jeannot had had a word with Quillot and they'd agreed to come this way; Jeannot would have anyway, but it was helpful to have the hearse to follow, rather than diverting from it in a way that might arouse suspicion and would certainly have called for later explanation – Jeannot's eccentricity, the explanation would have been. He was steering Hercule into the right fork now, with about 300 metres to go to the intersection on the north side of the small round *étang*, only a few seconds after which . . .

Well – action stations. Proof of the pudding. Actually, terrifying. Elise was holding hands with both the girls. Nothing more needing to be said – except silently, in prayer – but Madeleine reported, 'The commandant and the black van are still with us. I think the small van went by the other road. Can't see it, anyway.' Nobody was seeing any *great* distance through the steadily falling snow; even the hearse was barely visible as it approached the continuing curve of road ahead of them. Jeannot had his eyes on some barns just along there on the right; he growled now without looking round, 'God be with you, mam'selle.' He didn't know Marie very well. But it might have been Hilde he'd addressed, although he and she had never got on like a house on fire.

Elise called sharply, '*Now*, Jeannot!' Hercule checking in

mid-stride, tossing his head in reaction to a cruel snatching and sawing at his mouth, and swerving to the left side of the lane. Madeleine on her feet, vast and swaying dangerously while screaming at whatever she was looking at out to the left. Marie going out that way in a flying leap, hitting the roadside running – pointing, waving, yelling at someone to stop, come *back*! Madeleine by now hysterical, Elise half up off the seat but collapsing and grabbing hold again as the trap slewed diagonally across the lane, rocking violently on its springs. Hilde was crouching on the floor, Hercule obviously panicked out of his wits doing his little dance as Jeannot struggled to get him straightened out, further illtreating him in the process and the dance carrying him and the trap over to the right-hand side now, up close to the huddle of barns, trap's *left* side now presented to von Bodenschatz – and to Koch and von Bodenschatz's sergeant-driver too. From its blind side Hilde slipped out and into cover. Madeleine still howling, 'Marie, *Marie*!', Marie being still in everyone's sight, approaching higher ground where a farm track passed between two lakes. She'd stopped now, though, arms spread helplessly, pivoting to gaze in all directions.

Elise was out of the trap – unsteady, and calling to von Bodenschatz, 'It's not possible! Not *possible*! She simply *wouldn't*!' Von Bodenschatz perhaps not yet quite grasping what had happened, looking round at Koch, who'd shouted something in German and was doubling back to the van, yelling orders at its driver – to back up, of course, get down to the main road to cut Hilde off.

Charlie had seen a motorbike and side-car come racketing up the straight from Hon-Hergies and into the loop of road east of the cemetery. Losing sight of it there and shifting back to where it had come from – a car, now. No – a small van. Would not, surely, be preceding the hearse? Had guessed correctly – bike and van taking a short-cut; hearse now on the lower road, hearse being a dray with a coffin on it and several men on its high driving-seat – one in a top hat, for God's sake – and one powerful-looking dray-horse – a grey, he thought, but the snow and the range of it from here made it seem rather like looking through a tattered bed-sheet. What about tracks, he wondered, when Hilde makes her break for it? Probably not deep enough yet to hold them – especially on the steepish sides of the embankments, which was how she'd go. He had the trap in his telescope's single and slightly murky eye: forty yards maybe behind the hearse, and a car now about the same distance astern of the trap, which was approaching that rather hairpin turn-off – sharp turn back to the left – where he knew there was a small lake but couldn't see it from this angle. The trap looked overcrowded: he guessed Hilde *was* in it. It had passed that turning, with the car – von Whatnot's, he supposed – maintaining its distance, and some way astern of that now a van. Prison van, probably – Hilde's, but touch wood Hilde not in it now. Trap coming up towards those barns – moment of life or death for Hilde coming up; maybe for others, too. For Elise especially. Out of his sight now, though – the barns in his line of sight, he could only *imagine* it as it would be happening beyond them. *Was*, too – *had* to be – van and staff-car crowding up together, maybe skidding, the car having braked first and the van slewed up behind it. Hilde would – please God – be in one of those sheds by now, but he couldn't see Marie on her cross-country sprint either, on account of the top end of that half-circle of lane being banked higher than the rest, so that farther along it was dead ground, from this perspective. He'd see her – probably – when she got to the region of the lakes – snowfall permitting, at that range. The trap was in sight again now anyway – between some of those structures – Hercule seemingly back under control but the Germans apparently confused: one of them had turned and was running back . . .

Envisaging Hilde crouching in that barn. Moving from one of them to another when she could see the coast was clear. Elise had made some remark about her out-running a hare, so she had to be reasonably athletic . . . The van was reversing at high speed now to where the embanked side road led down to the main road and to where a right turn would take it towards Hergies. Van-driver's aim being to cut off Hilde's supposed line of escape to the village, where no doubt she'd have friends who'd hide her. One of Elise's great hopes, this had been – that it would take the pursuit and direct all the Huns' thinking in that direction. Possible snag – duly foreseen by Elise – was that having got there and not seen hair or hide of her they might conclude – well, might smell a rat. But Marie would be there, to swear blind she *had* gone that way; and it wasn't all open ground – there were not only embanked roadways, there were buildings of various kinds: a marble quarry, with dwellings and workshops around it, for one thing . . . Back to the trap though, and those barns. Trap still there, and the two Germans from the staff-car, doubtless questioning Elise, Madeleine and Jeannot, maybe waiting for the van to return with Hilde inside it. Whereas she just *might*, Charlie guessed, be moving – by stages, cautiously and as far as was possible under cover – from barn to shed to barn, then when the coast was *really* clear, along the bottom of the embankment.

But not while anyone might be watching from the south end of the cemetery. She'd be wise to that danger, he hoped. Couldn't see that end of the cemetery from here, but the troops in there surely would have been alerted by this time. Thinking of Hilde's view of it though, since it was one thing to make plans on a map, quite another actually to—

Now what's *this* . . .

Motorbike on the road again. He'd refocused the 'scope on the marble angel and then shifted to the right, to the intersection where eventually Hilde would have to cross, and it had shot suddenly into view. Dark figure crouching over its handlebars, careering into the crossing and then off to the left – someone in some sort of robe or vestments – padre, therefore? – on his way to find out what was holding them all up. And then – *unbelievably* – a figure running crouched, baboon-like, tearing across the lane

284

only yards behind the bike. Charlie still hardly believing he'd seen it, but realising that in a brilliant way she'd actually used the bike, its movement and noise, for cover, and was now *in* cover again down on the northwest side of that embankment, which was steep and high. She could now crawl along the base of it to the west side of the intersection and pick her moment to take an even more wildly dangerous chance, after which – as he'd observed to Elise at some stage – she'd have only about another 500 metres to – he'd crossed his fingers – to crawl, run on all fours, or whatever, to get *here*.

The two Germans were returning to the staff-car and the trap was coming out from behind the screen of barns. Motorbike swerving dangerously around the trap, Jeannot having to rein-in just as he was getting started. Some padre, that . . . But all heading for the cemetery now – where one might guess that despite Hilde's and Marie's absence they'd get on with the interment.

If you're at that crossing, Hilde – stay there.

Priest would want to be getting on with it. Very likely had other masses to attend. Sunday, after all . . . Charlie, watching the intersection, saw the bike hurtle into it and to the right, and then the trap, much more sedately. Only three people in it now instead of five. Madeleine's figure twice the thickness of Elise's.

Stay put, Hilde. Motor coming now . . .

Motor with noticeably large headlights, fine sweep of mudguard and unusually high wind-screen. Clear sight of it now as the trap swung right and out of sight. He'd seen that car before, he thought – the one that had stopped the lorry last night at the Hon-Hergies intersection. Making its turn now, and gone. Good riddance, too. He was holding the 'scope steady on the top of that high embankment, thinking that with the priest, trap and now that Hun car arriving at the cemetery, nobody'd have reason to pay attention to what was or might be happening – well, admittedly only about a hundred yards from them—

He caught his breath. Having made his second sighting of her. *Something*, anyway. Then – yes, *her*. In the next second or maybe second and a half, that same crouched figure launching itself up out of nowhere, streaking over . . .

Eleven-forty now. A few minutes ago troops from the cemetery had moved at the double up that road – via the intersection where Hilde had crossed about a minute earlier – to be deployed, Charlie guessed, in the direction Marie had taken. Ten or twelve of them, was all. Sent by von Bodenschatz, probably. Should from the Huns' point of view have been moved out earlier, only thank God had not been. He'd put the telescope down, didn't need it to watch *this* road. She'd get herself up close to the farm's entrance before nipping over, obviously. From the cover of the embankment – and trees, on that side – straight over and into this place. There was an acre or so of trees – leafless, might be young oak, certainly didn't look like beech – and a farm road encircling them and leading to Hergies.

Motorcar engine. *Approaching* . . .

Hilde heard it too. She'd been stopped, lying flat, face down, having an impression that the running soldiers hadn't turned left but had gone straight on, in which case from that high road they'd have her directly in their field of sight – sights plural, rifle sights. And now the car she was hearing definitely *was* coming up this road. Soldiers watching from back there, motor doubtless with more Huns in it passing – about to pass – virtually within spitting distance. The farmstead entrance – Emile Voreux's – was further along there, where the trees ended at a by-road known as La Queue du Chien, but she had some way to go before she'd be in *their* cover.

Car passing *now*. She began to squirm around, for a cautious look back to where the Germans *might* be. The car meanwhile braking, slowing right down. In order to turn into Voreux's farm? If the English flyer person had shown himself, maybe . . .

No. Turning left. Into La Queue du Chien, which would

take it either into Hergies or to the area of lakes south of Hergies, which Marie would have been making for. Pincer movement designed at trapping *her*, maybe. And – thank God – there were no soldiers in sight back there, must have gone the other way after all. So – move . . . Hearing men's voices shouting in the distance. Soldiers having spotted Marie, maybe. What might happen to *her* now, poor kid? Maybe not much – they wouldn't see her as important; a lot closer to the bone was what might happen to Elise de Semeillions. For all her *insouciance* – which she'd maintained even though her daughters were coming home this week . . .

Scaling the embankment slowly, carefully. The last metre or so even *more* slowly.

Nothing on the road – except a few centimetres of the white stuff, which one was going to have to look out for, in terms of leaving tracks. At least she guessed they would. And even now, just crossing it . . . She got up, sighted on the farm entrance and scuttled over.

Charlie had watched the green van slowly pass the farmstead and turn left beyond the trees. He'd moved back closer to his position beside the trap then to watch for the girl, and about half a minute later, sure enough, she'd come scooting over. He waited, not knowing whether she'd have been told to come up to the hayloft, but as it turned out she'd trotted across the yard and into the Voreuxs' kitchen. She knew them, of course – probably even better than Elise did.

He climbed down the rough, splintery ladder, and to his surprise they met him at its foot: Voreux with his hand on the shoulder of this tall, quite attractive but scrawny, wild-looking girl: black hair, dark eyes, wide mouth, bruised cheekbone.

He put both his hands out to take hers: 'Hilde?'

'*Si*.' A nod, and hard, fast pumping breaths. 'Hilde Martens. Sank you zat you are coming.'

Voreux asked bluntly, 'What time *going*?'

21

The best of all moments to look back on, despite anxiety about the weather, was when he and Hilde reached the edge of the tree-felling area at Trieu du Bois, in pitch darkness not long after six, and he heard McLachlan's sharp, 'Who's there?' and then much closer, actually in the trees where he and the girl were coming out of them, Stavely's, 'Flight Lieutenant Holt sir, is it?'

According to Charlie, his reply was, 'Well, since you ask—', and then, 'I've got Hilde Martens with me. Her mother's dead. Huns had Hilde in a cell in that château, that's why I've been so long.'

They'd started out from the Voreux place at four-thirty, by which time it had been dark enough and still snowing – which was good, in that it should fill their tracks which might otherwise have been picked up and traced back to the farm. Rising wind *less* good. Anyway – if he'd been on his own he'd have found his way to the Blaregnies wood all right, having both map and compass and a box of the Voreuxs' matches, but Hilde knew every lane and track, and cut some corners, at one time leading him by the hand. On reaching the ship though, he'd led *her* by the hand, as with Stavely in close company he'd picked his way between the beech stumps to SSP-7's car, where he'd picked her up and placed her in the for'ard cockpit beside McLachlan. She'd squawked a bit, and McLachlan, as pleased as punch, had erupted into French.

Charlie cut in, 'If you're saying sorry about her mum, sir, say it for me too? I tried, but I don't think she got it. The old girl had keeled over before we got here, they buried her this afternoon. How's the leg, sir?'

'Bloody awful. But yes, all right.' Back into French again – soothing tone, punctuated by soft acknowledgements.

Stavely then admitting, in reply to a question about how things had been, 'Not what you'd call a laugh a minute, sir. Ate an' drunk all there was. Couldn't do nowt with that skid or the struts . . .'

He'd fixed the damage to the car, though, and hadn't found any other problems. They'd been expecting the wind to rise, had *really* begun to worry about it during the past hour, had also of course been deeply concerned as to what might have happened to Charlie and what they'd do if he simply didn't come back. There'd also been the possibility of being spotted, especially by overflying aircraft. Fortunately there hadn't been any. Stavely had cut a strip of blanket and used it to bind McLachlan's leg tightly with a spunyarn lashing on it: McLachlan's own idea, that it should be held straight and as near immobile as possible. While listening to this report from the AM, Charlie had got his Sidcot out of the car and was throwing off outer garments. Pistol and belt back into the cockpit, then pulling on the suit, and the boots again, and helmet. He thought the snow was falling more thinly than it had been earlier, but even in a fair degree of shelter here what there was of it was travelling almost horizontally. There was no way to clear the stuff off the ship's horizontal fins unfortunately, except to get her up into the sky and hope to have as much as possible shake off or blow off before at 5–6,000 feet however much was left froze solid.

Dressed and ready, he checked the Charlie Holt Releasing Gear by feel, found no snow on it – which there might have been, and which might have turned to ice, in which case the gear would *not* have released; Stavely confirmed that he'd seen to that, periodically checked all the moorings. He asked, 'Want the guys cast off, sir? I shifted your head-rope, see – when the wind shifted like.'

'Well done you. And yes, let's get on with it. As you say – guys off first. You for'ard and port, me aft and starboard. Leaving sculexes in the ground, OK?'

'Aye, sir . . .'

'And then – well, look here.' He explained, 'Need to float her up vertically, so she'll clear the stumps. Trim may be a problem – weight of snow aft, so we'll shift all exernal ballast to where I can get at it amidships and ditch as much as necessary. Trail-rope'll have her then – we'll start up and when she's clear I'll put her ahead. May sling some ballast to you if she gets lighter aft once we're airborne, OK?'

He cast his pair of guys off, then joined Stavely in moving the sand-ballast – in bags suspended from a rail that ran around the outside of the car – to within his own reach from the centre cockpit. Climbed aboard then and felt around for this, that and the other. The Aldis was back in its stowage, he noted, and its lead coiled out of the way. Stavely had certainly kept himself as busy as he could. Very pistol then, and cartridges. Needing a red, he remembered, and finding one, the base of a red Very cartridge being gnarled all round, as distinct from only a half or quarter of its circumference, as was the case respectively with greens and whites. He loaded the pistol and it put back where it belonged. Calling to McLachlan then – interrupting a continuing exchange in French – 'Ready to take off, sir?'

'Sooner the better. In good order, are we?'

'Far as I can tell. Hilde well wrapped up in blankets, is she?'

'Of course she is!'

'Right. Six-forty now, so—'

'Tell you another thing, Holt – this girl's a winner!'

'Certainly is. I've quite a story to tell you, when we're—'

'What *she's* telling me, I'm talking about. Every detail memorised and absolutely the real McCoy!'

'Well, that's – terrific.'

Was, too. Hadn't all been for nothing – as it *might* have been. That possibility had occurred to him – must have to McLachlan and his people in London, too – that she might have been tricking them, concerned only to get herself and her mother out. He thought that having Elise de Semeillions' backing would have provided the guarantee, as far as London was concerned. He turned back to Stavely: 'Right, start up!'

The thrill of it – pleasure, anyway, satisfaction – was to be back doing what one knew about, had been trained for and was practised in, good enough at actually to enjoy. In contrast to more recent antics. But there was also a high degree of urgency – to get her up out of here, and away, and down again, before this rising wind reached or even approached gale-force. Force 5 now, he reckoned. Since casting off the handling guys the ship was acting up, too, tugging and lurching both trail-rope and head-rope. It wasn't a comfortable or even a *safe* situation; he was relieved to hear Stavely fit the crank handle, then the clatter of it – Charlie's hand hovering above the throttle – and the big engine barking and hammering into action. Elevators level, rudder amidships. Car being level now of course, off the ground and the bent skid, six or eight feet up – above tree-stump level too, therefore – but the wind was still a menace, *could* catch her wrong and slam her down – and even Monk hadn't had tree-stumps under him. Adjusting the elevator-control so that when he put her ahead and released the head-rope she'd acquire some bow-up angle, for dynamic lift. Gas-pressure might be on the low side and he didn't want to scoop air into the ballonets just to maintain pressure in the envelope, in the process making her heavier than she had to be. Thank *God* for this wind being – oh, no more than force 5. Ditching the contents of one sand-bag from each side now. Items already dumped included the two spare scrulexes, two heavy hammers and one axe. She was head to wind all right, thanks to the head-rope, which was truly earning its keep this evening. Another ditching of sand-ballast – and give her some thrust *now* –

throttle – and let go the head-rope. Ten feet: so all right, cast off the trail-rope – by CHRG, a good hard tug on the hemp line. Which did the trick, and she was on her own, the last of the head-rope thrashing out and away through its D-ring – a present for some forester, plus axe, assorted clothing, 14-pound hammers. Bow-up by two or three degrees, and – he bellowed, 'No you bloody *don't*!', sure that she'd been just as it were *contemplating* coming off the wind now the head-rope wasn't there to restrain her, and with revs still too low. He'd jammed on rudder and backed it with full throttle – needing that, to meet the wind's force as she lifted into it. If he'd been two seconds late on it, she'd have been in the trees. Thirty feet – forty. Feeling the wind like a boat butting into a rough sea. At 500 he'd bring her round on to course for Boobers, and carry on up to 6,000 or wherever the cloud-base was.

The snow made things slightly uncomfortable – the usual plastering on goggles for instance, and the deep-freeze effect – but otherwise the hard work and concentration was to hold her on course with the wind abaft the beam doing its best to push her off it. Force 5 rising 6, he guessed. More than you'd choose to fly in normally, but with only seventy miles from Bavay to Boobers – well, get her back on the ground, touch wood, before it got out of hand. Staying below cloud all the way, most of the time at about 5,500, he did see a haze of diffuse radiance over Valenciennes, and south of Arras first German and then British searchlights sweeping and probing around. Charlie sparing only a second or two at a time for such observations, eyes fixed pretty well continuously on the compass, adjusting helm constantly to hold her on course or close to it; and SSP-7 in any case darkly aloof to all that – whatever anyone was playing at down there, she herself was invisible and inaudible, and with the wind well back on her quarter making the best part of fifty miles an hour. Actually she'd done them proud, he thought.

He had her over Doullens just after eight – having spotted

its Morse 'Q' and needing to alter by only a few degrees to fire the red Very from about 1,000 feet right over them, then an immediate ten-degree alteration to starboard and continuing down to 500 in search of Boobers – which was easy as pie since they were in the course of lighting their flares around the field, having been alerted by the Doullens night-sky spotters. Charlie circling twice then while nosing down – once to give them an extra few minutes to get the red carpet out, so to speak, and a second circuit at fifty feet to come in on a course of northeast-by-north, directly into the wind and with the twin luxuries of a handling party down there waiting for him and large reserves of bottled gas so he could valve as much as he needed to. Just as well, as it was all of force 6 by this time. He got her down to them all right – trail-rope in their hands first, a bunch of them running with it so as to hold her bow into the rising near gale while he valved her down into the reach of the others' hands, the drag of thirty or forty men's weight. At that, they still had their work cut out, getting her into the canvas shed.

Things happened quickly then: McLachlan was moved on a stretcher into the shared tent, and an Army doctor arrived only minutes later in a Crossley tender from – Charlie thought – Frévent. Hilde was meanwhile escorted to what had been the officers' mess hut; food was being laid on, and meanwhile she was provided with ablutionary facilities while Tewksbury stood guard outside. Charlie was in the tent shifting out of his Sidcot while the doctor examined McLachlan, rewrapping his leg in bandage instead of blanket and telling him it should be in plaster as soon as possible and that he'd then be able to get around on crutches, but meanwhile—

McLachlan cut in with, 'Where and when, this plaster?'

'Well – we have full hospital facilities at Abbeville – that's the nearest.'

'It's also in the wrong direction! I want to get to London! In fact it's imperative that I do so – *and* that the girl comes with me!'

The doctor hadn't heard about any girl. As for getting to London, though – via Calais – he suggested that the best thing might be road transport to Hesdin, which was the rail-head for these parts *and* had a hospital.

'Distance from here?'

'Twenty kilometres. We could send you there tonight, in the tender. I'd telephone, of course, make sure they had a bed for you.'

'Beds plural – for me *and* for the girl. A hospital's ideal – she needs some kit and they'll have nurses' stuff. She *is* a nurse – or was. Listen – I have absolute authority for this. I can give you a name and a telegraphic address in London that'd put the fear of God into anyone below the rank of field marshal who doesn't bloody jump to it. Eh?'

The doctor said tiredly, 'I'll call the hospital. When you're there, *you* can call the RTO about onward transport via Calais.'

McLachlan said, both of them puffing at cigarettes, 'I suppose they're right and it'll be a day or two before this gale blows itself out. When it does, you'll get yourselves over to Polegate, of course. By about mid-week, d'you think?'

'Well – whenever . . .'

He was having difficulty in accepting that it was over. That they'd done it. Linked with this was recognition of the fact that without Elise de Semeillions' very consider-able help, they could not have brought the girl out. And there was a less-than-happy awareness of what might be facing Elise now. Now, or tomorrow, or next week . . . McLachlan telling him, 'My people – the birds who set this up – I've said this before, I know – will certainly want to see you, hear your own account of it. I need hardly tell you I'll be recommending you in the strongest possible terms for promotion, a medal—'

'May I suggest, sir, not to forget Stavely? He did damn well for us, you know.'

'Yes – I agree. Absolutely.'

'If it was up to me I'd say a DSM and advancement to petty officer. But – er – would you think there's any real chance of – as we discussed earlier – for *me*, this is – getting in on the rigids development programme at Barrow?'

'A very good chance, I'd say. You've earned whatever you damn well want, Holt, within reason. And you could hardly be better qualified. I'll tell 'em you're mad keen, and you can take it up with 'em yourself then.' He paused. 'You'd find it plain sailing, would you, leaving Polegate?'

'Plain sailing . . .'

'The roots, man! Uproot her too, would you?'

'I – doubt it. There are – uncertainties, in that area.'

'So you're a free agent? Good. He travels fastest who travels alone – what? But I say –' lowering his tone – 'speaking of young women, isn't this one an absolute knockout?'

'Hilde? Well – yes, I suppose . . .'

'*Suppose*, be damned! And – great heavens, man, considering what she's been through . . .'

The Crossley tender, driven by an RAMC lance-corporal and with McLachlan and Hilde in the back of it under a tent-like roofing, set off for Hesdin soon after ten pm. Hilde had kissed Charlie on one still unshaven cheek, squeezing his hand and murmuring, 'Sank you, *sank* you, *mon lieutenant*,' and McLachlan, watching from his stretcher as they were loading him into the vehicle, had looked – well, surprised, but something more than that, too. Charlie wondered, on reflection, after the increasingly stormy night had swallowed them, whether the major might not be seeing himself as on to rather a good thing.

The wind was gusting gale-force by midnight and, as was now forecast, went on doing so through Monday and Tuesday. There wasn't a lot to do at Boobers itself, but on the Monday Charlie went into Frévent with Tewksbury and had a meal and a bottle of wine in an estaminet that he – Tewksbury – knew well. He spoke some French, and negotiated the purchase of a bottle of champagne for Charlie, who'd remembered having promised Amanda that he'd bring her some. Then on the Tuesday he had a visit at Boobers from Rudd, the RFC flight commander from Ligescourt; the Handley-Pages were grounded too in these weather conditions, and Rudd had come to find out how SSP-7 had got on. Charlie told him, 'Turned out all right in the end, but I landed in the wrong place and darned near smashed us up.' He showed him the ship and Stavely's temporary repair to the car, explained the controls and general principles, after which they went into Frévent, Charlie on the pillion of Rudd's motorbike, to pass another hour or two in that same pub.

The forecast for Wednesday the 19th was good, and sure enough it dawned calm and clear; he and Stavely took off at nine and were on the field at Polegate in mid-forenoon. Bob Bayley, flight lieutenant-commander, asked him after seeing the ship walked into her shed, 'Lost your leatherneck major, then?'

'Mislaid, say.' Charlie added, 'Never mind, plenty more where he came from.' Then, 'Oh, here.' The Webley-Scott, which he'd had loose on the cockpit floor. 'Many thanks for the loan of this. Didn't have to use it, but came near to it once or twice.'

'Did you succeed in whatever you were supposed to be doing?'

'Yes, we did. Sheer luck, but – yes. Actually the major's intact – more or less – came back by train and steamer – and not alone, I may say.'

Which brought *her* to mind . . .

But no. No telephoning in advance. Get on the old bike this evening and – see how it goes.

His DSC for sinking the U-boat had come through, Bayley said, and old Peeling wanted to see him about it – wanted to see him anyway. But the first thing was to clean up and get out of flying gear, and check the Douglas to make sure it would start – or better still get an AM to check it over. Better see the Old Man before lunch anyway, he thought:

otherwise might meet him in the wardroom and incur the old boy's displeasure.

Six o'clock. Get to her by about half-past, he decided. The Douglas was in fine fettle – hadn't needed any attention, according to the AM who'd given it the once-over and reported that she'd started like a bird. Which almost certainly meant it had been used by some other bugger during his absence. Anyway, no harm done. No harm *anywhere*, this far; in fact the ambience was distinctly jolly. Peeling's congratulations and complimentary remarks still rang in his ears; he had the champagne bulging his great-coat pocket and in another the ribbon of the DSC – which he'd get sewn on at Hudson's in Terminus Road maybe tomorrow. Peeling had said it was capital to have Charlie and his 'pusher' back and on the station's strength; in a day or so no doubt he'd be keen to resume oversea patrols? Charlie had said yes indeed, but (a) he'd be grateful to be allowed a few days off – during which time the port-side skid and struts could be refitted and the car's forepart repaired, and while she was in dock her envelope might be re-doped in the normal aluminium-grey – and (b) he was supposed to be on stand-by for a call to London. The Old Man had known about that, had had a call yesterday from McLachlan. Finally, concluding the interview, Charlie had asked him, 'May I take all-night leave –' and seeing the nodding start had added – 'these next few days sir?'

At six thirty-five he free-wheeled into the yard behind the cottage. No snow here now: no other vehicle, either. She might of course not be back from work yet. He went round to the front and hammered twice with the iron knocker.

No reaction. The green glow of his watch told him it was six thirty-seven.

Then – sound of key in lock. In him, that old thrill . . . Key in lock not turning, though; instead, her voice through the letterbox flap: 'Who's there?' He took a breath and announced himself: 'Charlie Holt.' With the thought springing to mind – as she began to go berserk, and the lock clicked over, door wrenched open – *Who did you think it might have been?* But with the lamplight glowing behind her and her arms round his neck – and all that, while sort of waltzing her inside – what had become the general drift of his thinking in recent days crystalised into the fact that there was an answer of some kind somewhere, and sooner or later he'd get to know it, but meanwhile who gave all that much of a damn?